An Adventure Calls Mystery,
Book Two

MURDER, COTTONWOOD STYLE

KATHY MCINTOSH

This is a work of fiction. All of the characters, organizations and events portrayed in this novel are either products of the author's imagination or are used fictitiously.

Published by Dogged Kat Press
Cover by Steven Novak

ISBN: 978-0-9992930-5-8
www.KathyMcIntosh.com

Dedication

To Mark, who's kind when I'm cranky, and enjoys my singing old songs.

Also by Kathy McIntosh

HAVOC IN HANCOCK SERIES:

Mustard's Last Stand
Foul Wind

ADVENTURE CALLS SERIES:

Murder, Sonoran Style

Acknowledgments

Little is accomplished alone—chewing and other bodily functions excepted. I am hugely grateful to my beta readers: Adele Chong, Judith Horner, Elise Moore, Mary Jo Pollack, D.R. Ransdell, and Jesseka Zeileke; to my Writers' Workshop team: Victor Chacon, Hun-Seng Chao, Peggy Forbes, Eleanor Nelson, and our founder and member emeritus, Maryl Barnes, for their sage inputs; to the Tucson Writers' Table gang, who joined me "at table, whether real or virtual," every Monday; and to my magnificent critique partner, Conda Douglas, who knows the written word and words of encouragement. My book is better because of each of you.

Sergeant Monica Kuhlt of the Cottonwood Police Department, and Marie Carpenter, Communications Center Manager for the Cottonwood Police Department, provided generously of their time and information. I then proceeded to transform facts into fiction, with little regard to reality. They inspired me, but the book and characters sprang from my mind. I'm grateful to both and take all blame for misinformation.

Thank you, Mark, for reading every word of this manuscript in record time.

Thanks to the Desert Sleuths Chapter of Sisters in Crime, amazing and kind editor Jessica Morrell read and edited my first chapter. That chapter is long gone, but her advice improved the book.

I'm also, as always, grateful to each person who reads my books.

My gratitude to all of you has no bounds.

1

Not My Problem

Cottonwood, Arizona, boasted a number of hotels. Why did the one I sought have to look as if its inhabitants were either ghosts or derelicts?

I brushed off my khakis, ran my fingers through my hair, took a deep breath and entered the gloomy old hotel. I looked up, expecting cobwebs, but instead saw a gleaming antique brass chandelier. At the front desk, a bored young woman looked up from her cell phone and told me Ven and Wes Sturgess were in the bar. She nodded to her left.

Reminding myself to breathe, I turned and walked through the wide entryway to the bar. I did not count my steps.

The bar's stained-glass front windows scattered light throughout the large room, reflecting on large, ornately framed mirrors. The elegant furnishings took customers back to Cottonwood's mining heyday, when wealth was flaunted by the nouveau riche. A Silicon Valley of yesteryear?

A man in his forties or fifties stood behind the bar, washing glasses, getting ready for the happy hour crowd. He had a crewcut on the longish side, with dark brown hair streaked with gray and a beard stubble, obviously well-nurtured. A woman holding a tray filled with salt and pepper shakers walked around the room, placing a set on each table. She glanced over at me, then proceeded to a couple in a booth in a far corner, asking, I guessed, if they needed a refill. She had long brown braids that pulled back from her forehead and trailed down her back. Her approach to grooming seemed more my style, simple, fast and neat.

I walked to the bar. "Wes Sturgess?"

The bartender held up a hand. "Guilty."

"I'm Madrone Hunter. If you have a few moments, I'd like to speak with you and your wife."

The woman waiting tables heard me, because she walked to the bar, a question on her face. She tilted her head my way. "I'm Lavender Sturgess. Call me Ven."

I gave her my most professional smile, which I hoped didn't look like I was sucking a lime. "As I told your husband, my name is Madrone Hunter. I work for Adventure Calls Touring and led the tour to Indian Country your mother recently returned from. I . . . a few things happened during the trip I think we should chat about." Chat about? Had I ever used that pompous phrase in my entire life? I straightened my shoulders. This was something these people needed to hear and I was the unfortunate messenger.

Ven's expression tightened. "What did Mom do? Is she in trouble?"

Interesting she'd jump to that conclusion.

"Trouble? Not at all," I lied. "I thought you should know a couple of things."

Eco-tour guides see people at their best and their worst. I revel in the wonder on the faces of my guests when they first see the beauty of Monument Valley, Oak Creek Canyon, and Sedona. Suffer with those who dismount their horses after a two-hour ride—their first in years. Hide my amusement at a guest's early morning entrance to the dining room of a B & B, groggy, with bed-hair, and jonesing for that first cup of coffee. Worry about the safety of those who took on more than their bodies were ready for.

Violet Brock, Lavender Sturgess's mother, did that—took on too much. In her seventies, slender but sturdy, she was excited and vigorous when the tour began. She wanted to do it all, see it all. And I wanted her to do that, as well. However, some of the hikes were tough on our fit-forties guests. When others turned back, Violet persisted. I admired her persistence, but it took a toll. She grew wearier as the tour progressed, and her exhaustion turned to frustration, which she took out on me and my driver, Roadkill.

Should I tell Lavender Sturgess I was afraid her mother might be starkers? Lots of guests overdid and recovered once they got home. So no big deal, right? But I couldn't shrug it off. I thought there was a chance more was wrong than weariness with my client.

Lavender Sturgess sighed, then waved toward a barstool. "Please, take a stool. Wes may have to take care of our few customers. The waitress comes in later."

I scooted onto a stool, and Ven did the same. Her husband gave the ceiling a long, slow examination, then sighed. "We should never have let the old woman join that tour. She's out of control." Rugged and burly, with strong features, his nose had been broken more than once and reddened cheeks spoke of outdoor work or too many stiff drinks. If forced, I'd have chosen the latter. But boy howdy, the man hit the target about his mother-in-law. Did I have at least one ally? My chest relaxed the tiniest bit.

Ven laughed, her face flushed. "And who was gonna tell Mom? Nobody tells Violet Brock what she can or can't do." She touched her husband's hand across the bar. "Wes, honey, offer our guest a drink."

I accepted a glass of prosecco. Wes pulled a draft beer for his wife and a shot of Bourbon from the top shelf for himself.

With both of them staring at me expectantly, I tensed. What to say that wouldn't sound defensive or critical of Violet Brock? I swigged back too much of my sparkly wine, almost snorting it out my nose. I clamped my hand over my mouth. No slurping, no burping in front of clients was one of the little slogans Tripp Chasen hauled out during new guide training. I was glad neither of the two partners in Adventure Calls was here.

"You're right that Violet is strong-willed," I said. "I think that's what kept her going on this tour, which was a little too vigorous for someone her age. She insisted on doing everything and tried hard to keep up." I paused. "It may have worn her out, but I'm sure she'll be fine, physically, with a few days' rest."

"Sounds like Mom," Ven murmured at the same time her husband said, "Just like the stubborn old bat."

"I enjoyed meeting your mother. We had some enjoyable conversations, particularly at the beginning of the tour," I said. "However, as time progressed, she grew upset and seems to have issues with Adventure Calls."

"Did something go wrong? Was she hurt?" Ven leaned toward me. "I spoke with her right after she got home. She said she was tired but fine."

Wishing for instant courage, I again gulped too much bubbly. "She suffered a very minor fall at Canyon de Chelly but wouldn't let me phone you about it. We took her immediately to the medical center at Chinle where they checked her thoroughly and were satisfied she had only a few minor scrapes and scratches. Our driver saw her stumble and caught her before the fall was serious. However," I swept on before either of the Sturgesses could interrupt, "Violet later decided that the driver had tripped her. I assure you, he did not."

Ven's face paled when I reported Violet's fall. She fiddled with her braid. "You should have called me. I would have come, brought her home."

"I wanted to, suggested it strongly, but Violet was adamant that she was fine, that she wanted to finish the tour. She seemed completely fine."

Wes rubbed his chin, almost as if he'd once boasted a long beard, and gave me a steady look. "Nothing more you coulda done. No one argues with Violet and wins. Plus, once you're on her wrong side, that's where you stay. Take it from me."

Yes indeed, I had an ally.

His wife gave him a long look. "Mom's a pretty good judge of character."

Wes ducked his wife's look. My ally obviously had clay feet. Drat.

Ven looked at me, her clear blue eyes serious. She crossed her arms. "As long as you're sure she's fine now. I'll take her to her local doctor."

I wished I could assure this woman her mother was perfectly fine and our conversation could end with that. I looked down at my now empty wine glass and yearned for more, maybe a full bottle. Possibly a huge party crowd could walk in and keep the couple occupied.

Nothing that fortunate happened. I remained on my stool, with both the Sturgesses focused on me. Why not thank them and leave? Right. And say adios to the job I loved? Guiding tours was a twenty-four seven job, dealing with schedule changes, special diets, questions and grumbles. But I loved it all—the places we saw, people I met, challenges I overcame—I didn't want to lose it. Couldn't lose it.

I licked my lips before I spoke, another stall. "Umm. As our tour progressed, some of your mother's behaviors concerned me. She became forgetful, misplaced her camera and her purse, repeated questions to our local tour guides. At one point, she began weeping and muttering about regrets, but wouldn't clarify."

They nodded as I spoke, and then Wes said, "Sounds par for the course for her." His wife shot him an irked look and drank deeply of her beer.

It seemed important to establish a few facts about Violet, facts that proved her behavior had changed from her normal stubbornness. "Perhaps it's because she was in a different environment, but some of the things she said and did made me wonder if she was suffering from the onset of dementia. She called me Rosie at times."

Their expressions tightened, both of them focused on me. Ven scowled. "Mom? Crazy? She's as sharp as a tack." She didn't explain who Rosie was.

Wes chuckled. "The old woman stays on top of things at her shop. Wouldn't let us help her, or even offer advice. Kirsten, our daughter, manages for her these days, but she doesn't give her much leeway, even though our girl has some terrific ideas. Yeah, Violet is outspoken. But loony?" He spun his index finger near his ear and shook his head. "No way."

I didn't know what to say against their assurance. "Violet became convinced that my cooking was making her ill and that our driver, a commercially licensed, cautious driver, was trying to harm her. Neither of those accusations is true and every other guest expressed satisfaction with the tour."

"The old bird can be pretty picky about getting her own way. But she's sharp. Must be a kernel of truth in what she claimed," Wes said. He pulled at that imaginary beard, then cocked an eyebrow at his wife.

"There you are!" a familiar voice sang out from near the entrance. Violet Brock strode into the bar, looking more spry than she had hours earlier. Her white hair shone and I'd swear her curls were perkier. She was shorter than her statuesque daughter, but her prominent cheekbones and wide-set eyes spoke of their relationship. Her lips were rosy and smiling until she caught sight of me.

Her steps slowed and she approached with an angry glower for me. Before she uttered another word, she hugged Ven. Then she turned to me. "Trying to hide the truth about the way you treated me?" she said, spitting out each word.

"I . . . was . . .am concerned about your health," I stammered.

"And you wanted to poison the well before I had a chance to speak to my daughter. I came here for some happy catching up and you're ruining it." She didn't even acknowledge her son-in-law's presence behind the bar. "Don't believe what she's told you. I'm perfectly fine," she said to Ven.

"Violet, yelling 'We're all gonna die' while driving through Oak Creek Canyon is a little over the top," I said. I no sooner spoke the words than I wished I hadn't. If I'd learned anything in the past days, it was that it was futile to argue with Violet Brock. Besides, it made me look petty.

"I only spoke the truth. That pea-brained excuse for a driver, Rodentbreath or whatever he called himself, practically killed all of us. And me, he decided to trip at Canyon de Chelly. Even if no one will believe an old woman."

I glanced at Ven and Wes. She stood perfectly still but her hands gripped her beer glass as if it might escape. Wes lifted one eyebrow, gave a wry smile, hoisted his shot glass to his lips and downed it. Ven said, "We believe you, Mom."

I wanted to wipe off the sweat on my forehead but didn't dare reveal how upset I was. "His name is Cliff, or Roadkill as he was known when an activist, and he has excellent driving skills." I looked at Ven. "I'd like you to understand that I came here today out of concern for your mother."

"You came here to save your skinny ass," Violet said, as calm and sane as I'd seen her since the start of the tour. "But I have a right to tell the truth, about your stupid tour and about whatever I choose to talk about. Believe you me, that so-called vacation will be part of the memoir I'm writing. Now leave. You're not wanted here. Why don't you head on over to Sedona and hang out with those rich, snooty tourists who probably gave you humongous tips you didn't deserve. Hmmph. Normal people live here in Cottonwood, not woo-woos and idiots in hiking boots like Sedona."

Ven peered at her mother, her anxiety apparent. Then she turned her gaze on me for a long, steady moment. Finally she said, "Mom will settle down now she's home. I appreciate your concern, but I seriously doubt it's anything more than weariness. However, if she's registered a complaint, I'm not sure it's appropriate for you to be coming to me with accusations that she's losing her grip." Then she smiled, but it wasn't warm. "I'm sure you meant well."

And I was sure she didn't mean that.

"And now it's time for you to hit the road, make tracks, say 'Hasta la vista, baby,'" Violet said to me. "I have important things to discuss with my daughter. Like her daughter and her smart-aleck boyfriend." She sent me a sly grin. "Who happens to share your last name. Didn't I mention that on our trip to hell and back?"

I had already slid from my stool, and now I fell back a few paces. "Mateo? Your granddaughter? Your daughter?"

Ven gave me another of those half-hearted smiles. "I assumed you knew that. Mateo speaks highly of you."

"No, I haven't spoken to him except to arrange to meet for dinner tonight. That's . . . interesting." Interesting? Was that the best I could offer?

"And Kirsten's not paying enough attention to my shop, what with her infatuation with your brother," Violet said. "She won't listen to me. He's a bad influence like you're a bad cook and a worse guide."

Ven paled. "Mother, really. You go too far. Why don't you sit down and you can tell me all about that tour? I'm sure you have some good stories to share."

"You can bet I do," Violet said to her daughter.

Ven turned to me. "Thank you for stopping by. I'm glad we met." Her expression belied her words. She hadn't believed a word I said.

I clung to my wine glass like a life preserver. I stretched to place it on the bar and noticed the silent Wes's expression. Did I catch a bit of sympathy in it? Or was it annoyance with me or with his mother-in-law?

I'd made a huge mistake coming here. Had I made things worse for Roadkill and me? And what, oh what, was my little brother up to?

2

SURPRISE ON THE MENU

I swiped my hair back from my face and jogged into The Tavern Grille where Mateo had told me to meet him. The hostess led me past a U-shaped bar backed by a ceiling-high mirror to one of the booths that lined each side of the restaurant. Of bare concrete, with a few rebars still showing, the walls were sprinkled with some amazing art.

Mateo sat beside a slim young woman with long blonde hair held back in a ponytail. Both were laughing as I approached.

He jumped up and gave me a hug. "You wore a skirt," he said, eyeing my sedate calf-length wrap skirt. "I'm honored," he added with a wink. My little brother knew I rarely dressed up. "Sis, let me introduce Kirsten Sturgess."

Kirsten slid out of the booth and hugged me as soon as Mateo released me. "I'm so glad to meet you. You're Mateo's favorite sister."

I chuckled. "I'm his only sister." Kirsten seemed a delightful young woman, very close in age to Mateo's twenty-one years. She'd soon find out I wasn't on her parents' list of favs. Or her grandmother's.

I slid into the booth opposite the lovebirds, and smiled at Kirsten. "Mateo kept you a complete surprise, but it's a good one. I'm looking forward to getting to know you."

She grinned at me. "I'm sure you already know a lot about me, since Violet Brock's my grandmother."

I leaned back against the cushion. "You manage her shop. She always smiles when she talks about you." Except for earlier this afternoon, and I saw no need to mention that outburst.

"That's me. Some of what you've heard about me might even be the truth. And I'll bet, if you spent twelve days with Nana Vi, you need a drink."

A quick glance at the table told me they were both drinking coffee. I'd already decided to abstain when I was with my brother. "Ice water works for me."

"It's okay to have a beer. I'm learning how to cope when others are drinking," Mateo said.

"I'd prefer a V-8," I said.

Kirsten laughed, a hearty laugh with no self-conscious mouth covering. "Mateo told me you were strong. You must be, to have survived Nana Vi intact."

Not sure of my ground, I smiled and raised an eyebrow. "I'm not positive I am intact. Violet is definitely a strong personality. Let's you know what's on her mind." I rubbed my neck. Maybe Violet's just outspoken. Figures she's old enough to know her own mind. Maybe not sick, but stubborn. Still . . .accusing Roadkill of tripping her, me of poisoning her?

"She's a witch," Mateo said. "Or better put, a nasty, demanding rich old—"

I threw up my hand in a "halt" gesture. "She's our elder, and Kirsten's grandmother," I said. "She deserves respect."

Kirsten shook her head, smiling. "She's my grandmother, and I used to respect her, idolize her, even." She twirled a strand of longish bang around her finger. "Now . . . she seems to be more outspoken, less conscious of, or at least less concerned about, the impact of her words and actions."

Wow. The granddaughter was more clued in than the daughter. But I didn't want to put Kirsten between me and her mother, so I didn't tell her that her parents didn't share her opinion. I smiled but said nothing. Instead I spoke to Mateo. "Will others be joining us?"

He chuckled. "Nah. I wanted to have you all to myself when you met Kirsten." He pulled Kirsten's hand to his lips and kissed it. "You're both important to me."

I'd been reading up on addiction since Mateo's problems began and I knew people could transform their addiction to drugs into an addiction to a person. But Kirsten seemed like a funny, caring person, and Mateo was an adult, responsible for his own actions. Who my brother dated was not my business.

I needed something inconsequential to talk about. I gazed around the café and my eye was again caught by the colorful acrylic paintings on the walls, many with small price labels beneath them. Some were landscapes, a few were abstract. "Nice place. I like the art. Is it by someone local?"

Mateo laughed and Kirsten threw up her hand in triumph so he could high five it. "Pie's on you," she said.

"Some of the landscapes are Kirsten's. She's good."

"Very impressive," I said, nodding.

Mateo leaned over the table toward me. "The question here is, what have you done with my protective older sister? I told Kir you'd want to know where, when and how we met, and that would be for starters."

My face heated. "I'm that bad?"

He smiled. "You love me and care about me. Not a bad thing, but sometimes . . ."

Sometimes what? Was I that annoying? Too much like our doting but occasionally exasperating mother? And, yes, I did want to know how his program was going, but I would definitely not ask. At least not tonight.

"Mom will want a report," I said, winking at him.

"We should order," Kirsten said. "This place makes great salads. My favorite is the root vegetable."

I put my menu aside. "Sounds good to me." Suck up much, Madrone?

We ordered, and I opted for a prickly pear iced tea with my salad.

"Do you remember Leah McCall?" I asked Mateo. "I went to high school with her. She's an interior designer and is letting me stay in her home for a few days. I'm hoping she'll get back before I have to leave, so we can visit, but for now, I'm spending time in her cottage. It's peaceful, beautiful and quiet."

"You must appreciate the peace after spending time with Nana Vi," Kirsten said.

"It's nice not to be responsible for anyone but myself, I confess," again skirting answering her comment. What would Kirsten think when she heard what I'd said to her parents about her Nana Vi? I chugged some iced tea. "Now what about you? Really, I am interested in how you know each other, although I'm beginning to realize this isn't a huge town. Not like Tucson. Do you like it here?" I aimed that last question at my brother. He'd come here after rehab in Tucson, avoiding a prison term for possession and use of opioids by the grace of a county program that favored treatment over incarceration.

"I definitely like it. At first I felt as if I'd been exiled to some boring, tiny burg. But it's a good place, with good people." He gazed into Kirsten's blue eyes. Even that was too much intimacy for me, but I kept my eye roll internal. "You can meet my boss tomorrow. He's dope."

Was I approaching senility at twenty-nine? For an instant, I thought about drugs instead of realizing Mateo liked his new boss. Ha! Talk about a brief glimpse into the future. Could thoughts become reality, like the woo-woos in Sedona preached?

I wanted to ask Mateo if he still went to meetings. If he saw a counselor. All those things Mom insisted I find out. But I didn't want to get into it around his new girlfriend.

Addiction was tough. Staying away from your old friends was often advised. The people in Mateo's rehab center had suggested the move, helped him find housing and a job up here, where he'd have a better chance of staying clean.

I hoped it was working.

Silence settled over the table, but not a welcome, comfortable stillness. I fidgeted, unfolding and refolding my napkin. I am not generally a fidgeter.

Mateo chuckled. "Okay, big sister. I know you want to know if I'm staying clean, attending meetings, being a good boy." He paused, again glancing at Kirsten. "I am. I go to meetings at least once a week, see my sponsor, plus a counselor. I'm clean and I intend to stay that way." He took a breath. "The fact is, I met Kirsten through my Narcotics Anonymous group and she's helping me with my program."

Oh, great. He came all the way up here to avoid other addicts and now he's dating one. "Thing is," I said, "Mateo moved here to get away from the people he knew when . . . " I was falling into a pit and snapped my mouth shut, pressing my lips together to keep the words inside.

Kirsten smiled. "I understand. He's your brother and you love him and want to keep him safe. I've been clean and sober for two years plus. It's generally acceptable to date after you've been in the program for a while. We're cheating a teensy bit because Mateo's new, but the attraction was pretty strong. And he meets with his sponsor, maybe more often than he sees me." She brushed her bangs back.

I appreciated her honesty. Still. . . If Kirsten was from Cottonwood, she no doubt knew many from her "former" life. It was petty, a form of prejudice, to want my brother to associate only with so-called "clean" people, but he was my baby brother.

Relationships come and go, siblings are forever. Unless you alienate them. But this was my only living brother. "He was right. I'm the big sister. I worry."

Mateo toyed with his coffee cup. "What I worry about is my sister poking her nose where it isn't needed. Or wanted."

Kirsten punched his arm. "Chill! She loves you. Caring's important, I understand." She sipped from her water glass. "I got into trouble when I worked in Phoenix, went to school part-time, and got hooked on cocaine. I needed to escape that crowd, that lifestyle, and Nana Vi offered me a job in her gift shop. Pissed off my parents because she'd never allowed either of them to help her out. But it was a lifesaver for me, even if she can be grumpy."

Mateo slammed his coffee mug on the table so hard the dregs in the bottom splashed onto the table. Was he angry at my concern or at what his girlfriend was saying? "Grumpy? Ha! She runs Kirsten ragged and never lets her forget how much she owes her. I keep telling Kir she should find another job. Relatives can be a pain in the ass," he concluded, with a snarky look in my direction.

Okay. Maybe he's irked at both of us.

Kirsten rubbed his forearm. "You forget that I love the shop. Love the customers, love being my own boss. For that, I deal with Nana Vi."

Thankfully, our meals were served and we all seemed to tacitly agree to chat about less volatile things—local events, family news. Afterward, I had scrumptious pear pie, and Kirsten and Mateo both had apple pecan. Even though I offered to pay for everything, Kirsten made sure Mateo coughed up payment for the pie.

As I gathered my things to leave, I said, "One of my old friends is meeting me for breakfast tomorrow. Nine o'clock at Crema. I'd love for you both to join us. I know I've mentioned Roadkill to you, Mateo. From Idaho? Well, now he's a driver for Adventure Calls."

The two slid out of the booth and Kirsten said, "I'm afraid I'll be busy at the shop. My grandmother wants to find out how much I've destroyed since she's been on holiday."

Mateo stepped close to his girlfriend. "If only she weren't deadly serious. That old harridan. Ross—my boss—is at The Whistle Stop to open most mornings, so I should be free to join you. After all you've told me about Roadkill, I definitely want to meet him."

I smiled at Kirsten. "I'm sure there will be other opportunities. Poor Roadkill's in love, or at least, 'like,' and wants my advice. Not that I'm one to give it."

"Oh, I don't know about that," Mateo said, with an annoying smirk.

I turned to swat him on the butt. And ran into someone's chest. First thing I noticed as I staggered back, was that he smelled good, kind of woodsy. Second, that he had a few inches to my five foot eight. Maybe six feet? He grabbed my shoulders to steady me.

"Forgive me," I said.

"No worries," he said. "Beautiful women don't often hit on me."

"I wasn't—" I stopped, stunned by his brilliant white smile against dark tan skin. He wore his dishwater blond hair too long and he had a heavy beard shadow.

"Ash," Kirsten screamed. She threw her arms around the newcomer, who was obviously a good friend.

Mateo joined us, smiling, hand extended. "Hey, amigo."

"*¿Qué ondas?*" the newcomer said, a Spanish greeting among friends.

They obviously knew each other well, and my anxious mind immediately concluded that he knew them from Narcotics Anonymous.

"Madrone, this is Ash Coretti, someone you should steer clear of," Mateo said. "This is my sister, Madrone. I warn you, she's tougher than I am."

I shook hands with Coretti, as he flashed that smile on me again. I smiled back, unable to stop myself. My gut told me this one could be dangerous, even though his smile on the surface seemed innocent enough.

He explained he was meeting friends for coffee and expressed hope that we'd see each other again. I told him I wasn't in town for long, a quick visit to see my baby brother.

"My loss," he said.

"I warned you," Mateo said, "This one's too slick by far, Sis."

We all chuckled, but I wondered if there was a kernel of truth in my brother's warning.

I assumed we'd part on the sidewalk outside the bistro, but Mateo and Kirsten insisted on walking me the few short blocks to Leah's home, despite my protests that I'd be fine. Their consideration made me feel as old as Violet, but also well cared for. I tried to appreciate that part.

Before bed, I told myself I was glad Mateo had a new friend. That I wasn't worried she'd break his heart and send him back into addiction.

3

Does Someone Need Coffee?

Morning found me strolling down the main street in Old Town Cottonwood, appropriately named Main Street. I'd slept little the night before, jolting awake from bizarre dreams that mixed together our most recent tour with earlier ones. I awoke around five and meandered out to Leah's back patio overlooking her swimming pool and watched the sky lighten and clouds redden from the rising sun. Early birds greeted the day, their warbles, chirps and coos soothing. I sat and observed my breaths, in, out, in, out. The problem with Violet was more than likely minor, all part of running a business. "All will be well," I whispered.

Cottonwood, particularly Old Town Cottonwood, had a very different vibe than Sedona. Both towns catered to tourists, but Cottonwood traipsed the tourist trail years after Sedona. Sedona was considered one of the world's top spiritual places, with possibly more crystals per capita than any city in the U.S. If you have a yen for yoga on the rocks, it was perfect. The red rock canyons surrounding Sedona were more spectacular and offered excellent, varied hiking, but Cottonwood, with its recent revitalization of historic Old Town, maintained a cozier feel. It was also less expensive to live here, making it home to many Sedona tourist trade workers.

Running a gift shop in the smaller town couldn't be easy. People expected better deals here than they'd get in Sedona. Kirsten no doubt worked hard to keep her grandmother's shop thriving, and the poor thing didn't need her suspicious relative constantly judging her. Mateo had a point. It tickled me that he stood up for his new girlfriend, but he'd better tone down the criticism of her grandmother. Blood relations generally take precedence over new loves. He might sound off one day and find himself without a girlfriend.

A flash of movement caught my attention and I paused to look around for the source. On a sycamore tree branch, a male Vermillion Flycatcher perched and preened. His less showy mate was likely off doing the hard work of catching insects. That reminded me of the Sturgesses. It was an easy bet that Ven did the hard work managing the hotel while Wes stood behind the bar and schmoozed. Males were the same, feathered, furred, or hairless. But it seemed to me in our brief encounter that the two were comfortable with each other. My suspicion that Wes might have an issue with alcohol was just that, a suspicion based on appearances. Not my business.

My stomach let out a rumble that passersby could have heard. I'd been told Crema was popular, and I wanted to grab a table for three before Roadkill arrived. He wasn't expecting Mateo to join us. Roadkill might not want to spill his heartache in front of my brother, another good reason for having him join us. I was a chef, not an advice columnist, or "agony aunt" as some called them. My stomach gurgled again. A hungry chef, one who looked forward to a meal somebody else made. Not only did I enjoy being served by others, other cooks' creations often inspired me.

Loud voices broke the morning's quiet. My stomach shifted from growl to clench. I knew my brother's voice, from whisper to holler. Who was Mateo having a shouting match with? My head swiveled like a quail looking for its babies. There. Oh, jeez.

Violet Brock and Mateo stood on the sidewalk beneath a sign announcing the shop as It's All Goods.

Violet's chin jutted out as she glared up at Mateo, who stood at least a head taller. "I'm not going to tell you again. Stay away from my granddaughter. You're a bad influence."

"I'm a bad influence? As if you're a great role model. Squeezing every nickel, cheating gullible tourists, treating Kirsten more like a slave than an employee."

"If I find out she told you that, I'll fire her."

"She never complains. Any fool can see you treat her like dirt. If only she'd walk out on you, you hateful old witch. You're awful to her and yet she still loves you."

"Because she knows the value of family."

Determined to stop the spectacle, I jogged across the street. Yes, after looking both ways.

Violet saw me nearing them. "Here she is, your big sister," she said with a sneer. She turned on me. "You keep your smart-mouthed little brother away from my granddaughter. He's turning her against me."

Several shopkeepers had come out onto the street, along with some tourists, to catch a glimpse of the fracas. I laid my hand on Mateo's shoulder. He shook himself loose and glared at Violet. "You can boss Kirsten around in your store, but not in her life."

"Wait and see. If she's hoping to inherit—"

Mateo surged closer to the old woman, close enough to fog her glasses. "Enough with the threats. One of these days someone will shut your nasty old trap for good and I'll be cheering."

I gasped. "'Teo, you don't mean that." I tried to squeeze between them but Violet shoved me aside with surprising strength. Mateo glared at me, then returned Violet's hateful look. Her face pale, she muttered, "You, you . . . " A hand on her chest, she panted, then took a deep breath. She spat on his face.

He narrowed his eyes and wiped his face with the back of one hand. "You go too far, old woman."

In my opinion, this whole thing had gone way too far. I again thrust my body between them, expecting to feel Violet spit on my neck at any moment.

I shoved Mateo, forcing him to back up a few steps.

I caught sight of Roadkill across the street. He lifted an eyebrow and tilted his head in my direction, as if to ask if I needed his help. I shook my head, shoved again at my angry brother. "Cool it," I said in a low voice. "What the hell are you doing?"

Ven Sturgess stomped up the sidewalk to us. She grabbed Violet's shoulders in a none-too-gentle grasp. "Mother, you're making a spectacle of yourself. You need to go into your shop or go home. Do I have to walk you there?" She shook her head. "For pity's sake." She turned to Mateo. "And you, young man. Walk away. Do not say One. Word. More." She sighed and dropped her shoulders. "I am ashamed of both of you. You both should know by now how to control your tempers."

Mateo hung his head and said nothing, and I believed he honestly felt contrite at his outburst. Violet darted venomous glares at her daughter, at Mateo, and at me, and then turned and stalked into her shop. No contrition there. It seemed obvious that she was unaccustomed to anyone talking back to her.

At that moment, the cops chose to enter the scene. Well, a citizen volunteer, as his identification badge read. Someone had decided it was time to call the law in.

Ven Sturgess shook her head, gave me an exasperated look, and stalked off, ignoring the new arrival.

I opened my mouth to put up an argument for my brother but he laid his hand on my mouth. "My problem, Sis. I'll handle it. I'll come to breakfast as soon as I can." He turned me toward the street and gave me a light shove. I fell against a nearby bike rack and would have tumbled off the curb had he not caught me and gently held me for a second. "It will be fine. Go."

I stumbled across to join Roadkill, tasting blood from my bitten lip, picturing all kinds of horrible scenarios for my brother. Who knew what this would mean for his parole?

4

An Empty Seat

Mateo was right to stop me from talking to the pseudo-cop. I'd wanted to help him, to explain about Violet, but this was something my brother had to do on his own. I'd come to Cottonwood to visit my brother, not to save him.

That was beginning to sound like a good mantra.

Dang that Violet. First she gets me in trouble, and now my brother. Not that Mateo wasn't as much at fault. More. Violet was an elderly, fragile woman. Mateo should not have gotten into it with her.

When I entered the café, I was sweating as if I'd run three miles. Roadkill stood near a booth and I hurried to join him. I gave him a fierce hug. "I'm glad to see someone normal."

One eyebrow rose and he shot back his signature saucy grin. He looked down at his vest, stitched into patchwork from the skins of dead animals he'd found on roadsides. He'd tanned and joined the hides together, then sewn the vest himself. "Normal's not a term generally used to describe me," he said. "But I *am* peaceful and come only in search of love."

We slid into the booth, Roadkill facing the entrance, as he always did. "If I guessed the young guy Violet was reaming was your brother, would I be right?"

"You would." I grabbed a napkin and wiped my face. "The fates are kicking up a fuss. He's dating Violet's granddaughter."

"Whoa. Some coincidence. Hope she's nicer than her grandmother. Who was the woman who grabbed Violet? His sweetheart?"

"Oh, please. That was his sweetheart's mother. Violet's sainted daughter, Lavender." I picked up the menu. "I'm famished."

We'd placed our orders and were sipping our first cup of excellent coffee when my brother entered the café and waved our way. He rubbed his hands together and headed for the restroom.

My stiff shoulders softened. I closed my eyes and thanked the universe my brother wasn't back in jail.

Roadkill frowned, maybe not as pleased as I was to see Mateo. "Erin's heading back to Colorado in two days. I need advice, Madrone. Do I detect some deflection?"

My face heated. Were my motives that transparent? "Nah. I want you to meet my brother, and him, you. You're both important to me."

"Right. We've been friends too long for you to expect me to swallow that one. You owe me, friend." His frown transformed into a smile when Mateo joined us. He stood and put out his hand. "Slide in, buddy. You're almost as good-looking as your sister."

Mateo grinned. "I've always been the best-looking one in the family. But she ain't bad. Good to meet you at last, Roadkill."

"Likewise. Of course, she never talks about you."

The grin slid sideways. "Right. I imagine you know every dirty secret."

I thought about crawling under the table to hide my embarrassment. Why hadn't I expected this?

Roadkill smiled. "Mostly, she brags on you."

Another reason to like this man. I'd confided all my worries about Mateo to him, but he lied for me. Maybe I wouldn't have to search for gum under the table.

"Sorry about all that." Mateo waved toward the street. "Once again, the old woman got on my case for seeing her precious granddaughter. I know she did Kirsten a favor, and I know she's done a lot of good things for this town. She's got a great sense of humor and sometimes I really admire her. But I'm getting pretty sick of the crappy way she treats her granddaughter. If she was only harping on me, I could take it, but she harangues Kirsten all day—the shop's not making enough money, she needs to work more hours, work smarter not harder, the store's messy, *and* she has bad taste in men. It isn't right."

"That doesn't excuse you fighting with her. She's your elder."

"Precisely what my conscience said. And the police volunteer."

I gasped and grabbed his arm. "But he didn't call the real cops to arrest you or you wouldn't be here. Tell us what happened."

"Fortunately, Violet's well known in Cottonwood. He reminded me she was an old woman, even if she was a crank and suggested we keep our little tiffs inside."

"He really called her a crank?" Roadkill let out a laugh. "A cop with a sense of humor. Thought I'd lost them in Idaho."

Unlike many activists, who'd turned to the dark side, abandoned their forest names and found legitimate jobs, often for activist causes, Roadkill had remained a vigilant and vocal forest advocate. When his funds ran too low, he took temporary jobs like the current one driving for Adventure Calls. This time, however, I hoped he'd stick around. He was a good driver and the guests liked him. Except Violet Brock.

In honor of the excellent food, we kept conversation over breakfast innocuous. I liked that my brother and my good friend seemed to enjoy each other.

Roadkill got a refill for his coffee. "Now to the topic at hand."

Mateo ran his hands through his hair. "Kirsten's mother is pissed at me, too. I was hoping she was on my side."

Roadkill slapped his hands on the table. "No, no, no. I'm the center of attention today. With your luck finding a girlfriend after only being here a couple of months, you can be my Carolyn Hax, too."

"Who?"

"She has an advice column, and I'm thinking she's much better than me," I said. "Why not email her?"

He winked. "Hey, Gabe can't take his eyes off you. You must know the game."

Warmth crept over my face and I had to force myself not to touch my cheek, where Gabe had kissed me when we last parted. Did our boss really like me? The fact that he was my boss meant the attraction had to go no farther. I shoved my rotten romantic track record out of my mind and focused on Roadkill with a stern expression. "Number one, it's not a game. Erin's a person, interesting to talk to, be around. So are you. Be natural."

Erin, one of our boss Gabe's three sisters, had joined our recent tour as a guest—paying—to "see what my brother's up to these days." She worked in Durango, Colorado, at their father's construction firm. Gabe and Erin grew up apart, the girls with their mother in France, and the boys in Colorado with Dad. Thus they didn't know each other well. So far I found Erin smart and endearing and kind. Raised in Paris, she dressed, even for hiking, with more flair than most tourists. She spent more time with Violet than our other guests, ignoring the older woman's sharp tongue and judgmental tendencies. That made her a gem in my mind, a beautiful gem at that. Maybe Europeans had more respect for their elders. Whatever, I appreciated Erin.

At first I'd wondered at the growing fondness between Roadkill and Erin. How could two people be more different, have less in common than an Idaho-born activist and a France-raised sophisticate? But they shared a passion for nature, a deep-seated love of humanity, and a quirky sense of humor that drew them close.

Mateo chuckled. "Sharing food is always good, and shower her with compliments, man. Women like that stuff. And the real question...is she hot?"

I slapped my hand over Mateo's mouth. "I hope you're kidding, because that sounds suspiciously like you are clueless as well as sexist." I shot Roadkill a look. "Seriously, Erin will be going home soon. Are you planning to follow her to Colorado? Otherwise, much as I like her, she might be an experience, a fortnight's fancy. Practice for the real thing. You don't know her well." A fortnight's fancy? When did I become a poet? One who didn't know when to shut up.

As if I had not spoken, Roadkill said, "I'm thinking of changing my name back to Cliff, not that it's much of an improvement. What were my parents thinking?" He put his head in his hands.

"Cliff? Clifford? Seriously, like the big red dog?" Mateo snickered. He pondered for a few moments. "I'm liking RK. And never revealing what it stands for."

"Your name is not important," I said. "Neither are your looks, as long as you shower often and smell good. You are witty and smart and know about important stuff. You're generous and kind and a good friend."

"So is a dog."

Mateo snickered again and I shot him the stink-eye.

Roadkill looked up at me, so much like a puppy dog I smiled. "I was thinking you might put in a good word with her," he said.

"I don't know her very well, even though I liked what little I saw on our tour. Plus I'm in Cottonwood, she's in Sedona."

He stirred the scant remains of his breakfast with his fork. "Umm. I may have invited her to go to Jerome with us tonight," he said.

I feinted a punch at him. "What happened to an evening without guests?" I shook my head. "No promises. I'll see you both tonight. I'll observe. If, and only if, the time seems right, I'll chat with her. Or maybe I'll check out your moves and give you feedback. Pass little notes?"

Mateo took a turn with the puppy eyes. "What about me? Am I invited? With a plus one?"

"You are. Maybe you can invite Violet, and patch things up."

"Brilliant idea, sis. But maybe not." He grimaced. "I'd better get to work. Text me the details about tonight. Looking forward to meeting Erin, RK."

Roadkill smiled, looking thoughtful. "Yeah. RK. I like it."

I waved my brother off. Watched him go. I couldn't stop worrying about his encounter with Violet, his anger at the elderly woman.

"I'm going hiking with Erin later," the man previously known as Roadkill said. "Then we'll come by and drive together to Jerome?"

I nodded, then dragged myself back to the present. "Fine. About 5? And, listen, one piece of advice. You know a lot about a lot of things, especially in the natural world. Don't pontificate. Be yourself."

We both left cash on the table to cover our meals and the tip and walked together toward the exit. Before we parted, RK spoke.

"Thanks for your help. I've got the picture now. Don't talk too much, but don't be a statue. Let her know I care, but don't come on too strong. Compliment her, but only when I mean it. Total piece of cake."

5

A Surprise at The Whistle Stop

After breakfast, I found myself alone and on edge. I'd done what I could to alert Violet's family about her possible illness—and maybe there was no problem, her behavior was typical Violet. As to Mateo and his animosity toward his girlfriend's grandmother, I couldn't control anyone besides myself. I would not be a helicopter sister. As for RK? My sweet friend would either succeed or fail in his romance with Erin, but I hoped he'd not fallen for her so deeply that he would be hurt if things didn't work out.

Still, I'd known him quite a while, and never known him to be this taken with a woman. Why did she have to be related to our boss?

RK was spending the day with Erin, which meant I was on my own until we left for Jerome. I packed a lunch in my daypack and headed to Tuzigoot National Monument. It lay a brief fifteen-minute drive from town. I parked and left a note on the dash about my plans—even though it wasn't as if I were venturing into the wild, it was an ingrained habit. After some time exploring the museum, I'd head to the old pueblo and explore it, then tramp a bit around the marsh.

I took a leisurely tour around the ancient pueblo. As I walked, I tried to imagine the Sinagua people who founded the pueblo. Did they have crazy old women who caused trouble for others? Did they worry about their families? Dumb question. As long as there have been people who gathered in clans, there have been interpersonal issues. The drugs were different now, but the emotions were the same.

Reflecting that humans had been experiencing similar clashes, similar crises, feuds, what have you, comforted me. I finished the afternoon feeling more relaxed and upbeat than I had since the recent tour began, and looked forward to dinner in Jerome with friends and family.

Back at the casita, I showered and dressed and walked to The Whistle Stop to visit with Mateo before Roadkill and Erin picked us up for the drive to Jerome. I'd texted him to come to The Whistle Stop by 4:00 so we'd have time to investigate Jerome before dinner. Dusk comes pretty early in Arizona.

I was eager to meet Mateo's boss. I wanted to get to know everyone Mateo associated with, in case problems, even illness, arose. Ack! Helicopter sister, begone.

My entry to The Whistle Stop was announced by the melodic ringing of the brass bell beside the door. Inside, I stopped and gaped at the mural on the facing wall. Entranced, I walked forward. As I drew closer, I had an urge to genuflect. There were the faces of the musicians I, my parents, and most of the world revered, looking ready to break into their signature melodies—Willie Nelson, Elvis, Frank Sinatra, Dylan, Elton John, Aretha, Johnny Mathis, Dolly Parton, the Three Tenors, Kiss, Alice Cooper, and so many more.

Silent, as if in a chapel, I didn't hear the footsteps behind me.

"Thought you might like it," Mateo said.

I started but didn't take my focus from the images. Some in color, some in black and white, all ready to sing, nearly alive. Some of the images seemed as old as the eras the singers came from, others were recent additions. "I don't just like it. I love it. This is a treasure."

"Yeah. Who woulda thought something like this could exist in a Podunk town in northern Arizona?" Mateo came around and leaned against a display carrel.

I'd been holding my breath. Dizzy, I inhaled, catching a musk of dust and cardboard. "This is totally amazing," I said in the hushed tones reserved for funerals and museums.

"My boss is a multi-talented guy. Glad you're here in time to meet him."

Mateo tugged at my sleeve. "C'mon."

Towed by my brother, I twisted my neck to look back at the mural. I'd return and spend more time with it before my visit here ended.

Odd how innocent plans can be twisted.

On our way to the counter, we passed carrels of LPs, old and new, DVDs, and sheet music. I knew from Mateo that the shop also handled instrument sales and rentals to music students throughout the Verde Valley, the valley that sheltered Cottonwood, Sedona and a few tiny towns.

Between us and the counter were a couple of high, freestanding bookshelves holding books about everything music-related—early history, the rise of the industry, the people who grew wealthy from it, and those who fell from glory. I slowed to take a look. Books meant treasure. Mateo shrugged. He knew I took delight in bookstores of any kind.

A man's voice broke into my rapt absorption. "I can't talk about that now, Violet. In my opinion, and you know this, when a person makes a promise, it should be kept." After a brief pause, the man continued, his tone curt. "No, I don't agree. Not at all. I have customers. I have to go."

Mateo tugged on my arm and drew me toward the counter that ran along the wall opposite the front windows. A man stood behind the register. He wore his gray hair pulled back in a short ponytail, the tail hanging curly below a balding pate and a high, receding hairline. His white beard was trimmed short and looked spruce instead of scrubby.

When he saw us, he blew out a puff of air and squared his shoulders. I had the briefest sense of an actor or a public speaker calming himself before the next appearance. He smiled at me, revealing two chipped incisors in a mouth of teeth no longer white. The smile was broad and compelling. "I'm delighted to meet Mateo's sister at last," he said. "I've heard so much about you." His magnetism drew me closer, and I smiled.

"Madrone, meet Ross Zelinger, my boss. Ross, Eva Madrone Guzman Hunter." I shot a quick glance at my brother. I rarely used my full name and for an instant didn't recognize it. Was he trying to impress Ross? "You two have a lot in common," Mateo continued. "You're both artists. Only Madrone's an artist in the kitchen."

"So I've heard." Again with that captivating smile.

"My baby brother kept your artistry a secret. That mural is awesome . . .

beyond words."

He smiled, his eyes crinkling. "Sometimes hobbies spiral out of control, you know?"

"A hobby? Much more than that. I'm in awe. Do you do other art? Sell commissions?"

He shook his head. "As I said, a hobby. Has Mateo invited you to tonight's concert in Jerome? I went ahead and reserved a table for dinner for your group."

Concert? Nope. Something my baby brother forgot to mention. "Sounds like fun," I said. "I love all kinds of music."

"Wait till you hear me on the ukulele," Ross said. "That awe at my artistry will disappear, for sure." He came around the counter to shake my hand, and I thought I caught a whiff of cannabis.

"I'm sure that's not true. I confess I've never heard a ukulele concert."

"We're a mixed group of beginners and old pros. I'm rather new at it. But we have fun and so does the audience."

A dark-haired woman walked in from the back room, smiling, and put her arm around Ross's waist. Ross introduced me to his wife Helen and assured us we'd see more of her at the concert. She seemed several years younger than Ross.

"Do you also play?" I asked her.

"Not the ukulele. You have to be a little crazy to try that."

Ross turned and hugged her. "And my wife is definitely not crazy."

"Crazy for you," she said.

Mateo pointed to the phone. "Was dear old Violet giving you grief, too?" he asked Ross.

Helen stiffened and a frown darkened Ross's face. He shuffled some papers on the counter. "It was nothing. Trying to encourage her to back away from the day-to-business in her shop. She needs to trust Kirsten."

"Amen to that, boss. I couldn't agree more," Mateo said.

RK and Erin arrived and after they met Ross, I dragged them to the mural. Even Erin, who'd spent much of her life in close proximity to the masters in the Louvre, expressed awe. When she went to Ross, to express her awe, he blushed and stammered something unintelligible. With long, black hair streaming down her back nearly to her waist, an almost pearl-like complexion and the slightest tinge of an accent, Erin might have been a visiting French film star, not a contractor's daughter who worked in his Durango offices.

We promised to catch up with Ross during the concert's intermission. "Promise you won't escape before the second half, when our audience tends to shrink," he begged us, his eyes twinkling with humor. Then the five of us climbed into the Adventure Calls van and headed up the hill to Jerome. Roadkill had permission to drive the van for his week off after the last trip before he headed south to Phoenix to pick up another group of ecotourists.

Assuming that he still had a job. Of course he would. Violet's complaint meant nothing against the satisfied reviews of all the others. Despite my best efforts, worry crept into my thoughts and lingered like the smell of boiled cauliflower.

6

Ukulele Night Hits a Sour Note

Jerome proved a good choice—a chance to relax and to get to know Erin and Kirsten better. RK parked the van in a spacious lot. A prominent sign warned visitors that the lot might well slip a few inches down the hill while we shopped and explored and spent money in their wobbly town. We looked at each other dubiously, and then shrugged and continued.

The five of us set out. RK doted on every word from Erin's lips and Kirsten and Mateo walked hand in hand. Sometimes I trailed behind, sometimes I surged ahead, always feeling like a unicorn in a basket of pears. Alone.

We wandered the streets of the former mining center, a town that rebuilt itself on tourism. In 1920 Jerome was the third largest town in Arizona. The mines beneath the hillside town yielded a variety of ores—copper, gold, and silver, eventually dwindling, until the final mine closed in 1954. In 1976, the town was declared a national historic landmark, and tourism gradually became its largest source of revenue.

But tourism in Jerome is not for the couch potato. Shops, restaurants and hotels are scattered along steep, winding, streets, with daunting wooden staircases providing pedestrian access to the upper streets. Even the lowest part of Jerome lies at an elevation of 5014 feet, nearly 2000 feet above Cottonwood.

I concluded that the stores got much of their traffic from tourists who wanted to catch their breath on a level surface. "Let's pop in here for a bit," or "Look, that entire shop is dedicated to kaleidoscopes," seemed better than gasping out, "Stop. Wait. Can't breathe."

Eating out, tasting the creations of other chefs, is something I always look forward to. The Bordello boasted a rich history and a menu offering Greek food beside mouth-watering hamburgers, followed by the ukulele concert.

The food was delicious, the art colorful and eclectic. The ukuleles? I concluded it was great the players enjoyed themselves and tried hard to maintain an interested expression and not wince.

At the intermission, Ross and his wife Helen joined us in a smallish gravel parking area behind the building. She'd been seated at the front of the room. I admired her courage, wondering if she might be a little deaf. She was of average height, curvaceous and elegant. His arm around his wife, Ross said, "You and Helen have much in common. She, too, is a culinary artist." He patted his stomach, which remained surprisingly flat for a man in his seventies. "Fortunately, my hiking and bicycle riding help work off the products of her art, because playing the ukulele doesn't burn many calories." He chuckled. "No doubt the act of covering your ears provided some small exercise for you," he said to the group at large.

I wasn't sure how to respond. Did he want us to gush over their fumbling efforts? Laugh?

"I've heard the ukulele is an easy instrument to learn but only a few masters can make it sing at its best," RK said. Sometimes my Idaho friend's tact—and breadth of knowledge—astonished me. I gave him a ten for that save. Maybe he was working on "urbane" to impress Erin. The couple I'd considered mismatched fit together better than their outward differences predicted.

"None of us has reached Jake Shimabukuro's level, but it's something to aspire to," said Ross, smiling. "In my dreams."

Erin asked for a closer look at the instrument Ross still held, and she and RK huddled with Ross as he pointed out the uke's features. Mateo and Kirsten seemed lost in their own thoughts, holding hands and exchanging small, secretive smiles. I was alone and worked on not feeling like a fifth wheel. Mostly I failed.

When feeling like a social misfit, I tried to force myself to befriend someone else. Ross's wife stood by herself. Maybe Helen needed a friend? Had she noticed her husband admiring Erin? I edged closer to her and she looked up and smiled. She had a friendly face whose wrinkles looked comfortably in place. At five-eight, I loomed over her. While that might be an exaggeration, I definitely had a few inches on the older woman.

"If you're wondering how I can listen to their amateur squawks, you should know that I'm pretty much tone deaf," Helen said with a smile that took any sting from her words.

I shook my head. "I'd never admit to a thought like that."

She grinned. "If I can support Ross in this small way, it's worth it. He loves it. And I love him. It's simple." She gazed at her husband as if he were a chocolate éclair in a box of ginger snaps and she was a chocoholic.

Would I ever be as willing to sacrifice an evening for the man I loved? More to the point, would I ever be that much in love?

Helen stiffened and her expression turned icy. I turned to see what or who had caught her attention and her anger.

A shrill voice broke over the muted rumble of the relaxed concert goers. "I knew I could find you. Leonard brought me," Violet announced. She shot a coy smile in Leonard's direction. "I may have misled him a teensy bit when I told him I'd missed my ride to the concert." A tall, slender man about Violet's age lagged behind her, looking bemused.

The old woman marched up across the dirt lot to Kirsten. "Since you were out gallivanting, I went to the shop and took a good look at the books. I knew you were stealing from me, you little vixen. After I put my trust in you. We'll talk about this tomorrow. You can't get away with stealing from me, even if I am your grandmother."

Kirsten crossed her arms and glared at Violet. "You're imagining things, Nana Vi. How can you come up here and make such an accusation? In front of my friends?" Kirsten's gaze shifted from person to person, her expression frantic. Mateo tightened his arm around her shoulders.

Violet turned away from Kirsten to where RK and Erin stood beside Ross. "As for you . . . How dare you prance around and enjoy yourself while I'm still shaking from your terrible driving? I saw your van in the lot, and I'm surprised all of you made it up the hill with a maniac like you at the wheel. I spoke to your boss, and I might even go to the police. Your driving scared me spitless on that trip, and I will have your license."

RK stared at her, mute, his mouth hanging open. She turned to her companion. "Leonard, I fibbed to you but I had to come here and give these two a piece of my mind. I will not be discounted because I'm an old woman. I went on vacation to escape that attitude and they turned on me. Even you, my lifelong friend, think you can force me to sell my land, so you can build more ugly buildings and those dang wine-tasting rooms. My dear Chet and I worked hard to see this town grow and yet keep its small-town, cozy character. It's a disgrace what our town is coming to. I miss him, but I'm glad he can't see Cottonwood today."

Leonard clutched Violet's forearm, his expression morphing from confused to frustrated. "Vi, now's not the time for this. Let's go—"

She wrenched out of Leonard's grasp and headed toward me. "As for you, you traitor. I'm sure you're disappointed I found you yesterday before you could twist the minds of my daughter and her no-account husband. Trying to prevent the truth coming out about your incompetence during our tour."

Yesterday Violet seemed closer to normal than I'd seen her for several days—although still tossing out untruths about RK and me. Now she chose to track us down and call us out in public? I don't call that normal. And why tonight? In such a public arena?

I pressed my lips together and noticed that beside me Helen shook her head. To warn me how useless arguing would be? Or had she seen Violet like this before? I knew better than to argue with any Adventure Calls guest. I dug deep for some empathy and patience, because Violet was obviously unstable. I blew out a breath. Then I spoke anyway. "I know you had some issues with the trip, Violet, and you have every right to address them with the company, but the other guests seemed satisfied." I cursed myself inwardly for even trying to refute her.

"Ha! They were all too well-mannered to express their true feelings." Erin opened her mouth to speak, but Violet waved her off. "I know my rights. I'll get my money refunded and chalk up some more for damages. It's no way to treat an elderly woman, is it, Leonard?"

Poor Leonard remained speechless, looking thrown for a loop by Violet's outburst. Ross put a hand on Violet's arm. "Even if you have a dispute with

Madrone's company, this isn't the place to have it out with her, Vi. We came up for a relaxing evening." He flashed her the peace sign. "Remember what you used to stand for."

Violet's eyes widened, and she backed away from Ross. "Stay away from me. I know what you're capable of, and you have no shame, no shame at all. It's time to let it all out. Shame on you. Shame on me." Sobbing, she threw herself into Leonard's arms.

What if Lavender were here to see Violet's emotional roller-coaster? Would she consider it standard behavior or would she think something might be off-base, even for Violet? In my mind, Violet had morphed from a curious tourist who chatted and joked with our Navajo guides in the first days of our tour, to this weeping fountain of emotions. But she wasn't my mother and I'd only known her for a few brief days.

No. No daughter should have to witness this evening, and sadly, Ven would hear about it from Kirsten. Secondhand would be painful enough.

Leonard patted Violet's back. "Hush now, Vi. Calm down. Let's not make a scene. No one's out to get you." He spoke to Ross. "She led me to believe she'd arrived too late to drive up with your group and that it was urgent she join you. Not that she had bones she wanted to pick. I'm so sorry." He shrugged. "I should have known better. When Violet's sweet and anxious, she's up to something. I'm sorry." He looked at me, then shifted his gaze to Kirsten. "She's your grandmother. Can you calm her down? Then I'll take her home."

Violet jerked away from his arms. "Stop talking about me as if I'm not here! I am not a child. I am a grown woman. No one can tell me how to behave or what I can or cannot say. I'm responsible for my actions, and I intend to make amends for my sins anyway I want. It is my life to live." Her voice rose in pitch and volume as she went on. "My store, even if you're trying to steal it from me," she screeched at Kirsten.

I cast a glance around the grounds where we'd exited for the break. By now, most other concert goers who had ventured outside with us were bunched together at the opposite end of the lot, observing this new performance with interest. So much better than the squawk of ukuleles in amateur hands. My skin crawled. This had to stop, soon.

Without flinching, Kirsten strode up to her grandmother and took both her wrinkled hands in her smooth ones. Her voice soothing, her expression caring, she said, "No one's telling you how to live or how to run the store, Nana. I promise we'll talk first thing tomorrow, but right now, the rest of us are here to listen to Ross and the other ukulele players."

Totally impressed by Kirsten's calm, measured response to her grandmother's rage, I let out a breath I hadn't known I was holding. Would the old biddy listen? Heed her granddaughter's request?

Leonard stretched an arm around Violet's shoulders. "Let's go, Violet."

Violet said nothing more and surprisingly let Leonard walk her away from the group and down the dirt street. She stumbled once but he held her close.

Our small group returned to the concert hall, aware of the eyes of the rest of the audience on us.

"We could have charged admission for that show," RK murmured in my ear as we returned to our seats. He was close enough I smelled his pleasant aftershave. Our rowdy activist was smoothing out the rough edges, and I was certain Erin had no clue of the extent of his efforts.

* * *

I barely listened to the rest of the concert, too worried about the fallout from Violet's anger. I'd let Gabe and Tripp, the co-owners of Adventure Calls, know about her accident and about her dissatisfaction, but heaven knew what kind of horror story she'd spun them. Mateo nudged me when Ross had a brief solo, and I struggled to pay attention. He really should stick to his art.

As we left the concert hall, a woman in her fifties with long gray hair streaming around her face engulfed RK in a hug. "Roadkill? I thought that was you. What brings you to Arizona? To Jerome, for pity's sake?" She backed a few paces away. "Don't tell me you don't recognize me. It hasn't been that long."

Roadkill's expression transformed from puzzled to delighted. "Fig?" His grin widened. "I can't believe you're here. In a ukulele band, of all places." He introduced her to the rest of us, explaining that they'd been on several forest protest events some ten years prior in Idaho. "You're looking absolutely fabulous, as usual."

"I'm Fiona these days, dear. Otherwise, it might be Prune instead of Fig." She winked at the younger man. "We need to get together one day soon if you're living here now."

After RK and his old friend exchanged phone numbers, we left Jerome, everyone declining a post-recital drink. Maybe Fiona could be a character witness for our driver if Violet went ahead with a lawsuit.

I stewed most of the way home, seeking some way to either make Violet's concerns go away—fat chance of that—or to provide evidence that she was ill and that her complaints came out of her dementia, not reality. I doubted it would be easy to do either.

7

Where Is She?

Some people believe that our dreams sort out the problems we face in life and that we wake up with answers. My dreams are all too often a jumbled replay of the worst parts of my day, with any solution missed when I jerk awake, my heart racing and drool running down my chin.

I've tried finding calm through meditation. I sit quietly, following my breath, in, out, in, out. I never make it past a few minutes before I'm asleep.

My most successful meditation comes when I bake bread. When I'm really stressed, I have to pay attention or I over-knead the dough, even though I knead by hand. The ritual of kneading, folding, turning, repeating, becomes my mantra and my racing brain rpms eventually slow.

The morning after Violet's dramatic outburst in Jerome found me in the cottage's kitchen, measuring, stirring, and eventually kneading. Before the dough rose for the wheat bread, I had baked two pumpkin quick breads and three batches of pumpkin chocolate chip cookies. Fall, after all, means pumpkins.

I called headquarters and after wrapping up a mini-tour outside Tucson, Gabe would drive up to speak in person with Violet.

In this moment, all was well. In the next, it would be well. That was all I could control. I took several breaths. After the bread baked, I'd find somewhere to explore. Maybe Dead Horse Ranch State Park? All would be good.

Maybe.

Dead Horse Ranch State Park, a few miles outside Cottonwood, was small but filled with fun surprises, like three lagoons. I saw a great blue heron and quite a few red-winged blackbirds as I circled the lagoons and wandered the other paths in the park.

Feeling more at peace than I had in days, I returned to my car and listened to my messages and read my texts.

Every message conveyed the same fact: Violet Brock was missing.

I messaged Mateo, asking what was going on.

My phone rang. "Where the heck have you been?" Before I could reply, he added, "Have you seen Violet? Is she with you? Although I can't imagine how that would happen."

I cleared my throat. "One: I've been hiking. Two: No, I am not with, nor have I seen Violet. As you said, I doubt she'd seek me out and I'm staying clear of her until Gabe gets here and exercises his charm. What's going on."

"It's a total mystery. She was supposed to meet with Kirsten this morning—"

"A not-to-be-missed event," I said, remembering last night's fireworks.

"She didn't ever come to It's All Goods this morning. Kirsten waited a couple of hours before raising the alarm."

"Aren't there lots of places she could be? Maybe she forgot an appointment? Is sulking at home? Decided to give everyone a break from her nasty accusations?" I swallowed. Way too harsh, Madrone. "There could be any number of reasons she didn't go to the store." Not a proud moment for me. Because I was angry with Violet Brock, I was too ready to disregard my brother's concerns.

"Kir's thought about all of them. She and her mother checked Violet's cottage and called the hospital and her doctor. Zilch. They checked with Leonard, who swears he dropped her off at her cottage in perfect health and a slightly better attitude about 9:00 last night. She doesn't drive anymore, so that's out. You were our last hope, even if a faint one."

"Surely she has other friends she'd go see. I'm not on her good list." And she wasn't on mine.

I heard a woman's voice in the background and Mateo spoke again. "Ven says that since Violet's a vulnerable adult, old and upset, the police will mount a search right away." He lowered his voice so I had to strain to hear him. "In my opinion, Violet's off her rocker, but Ven won't hear any of *that.*" In his normal voice he said, "Ven used to be a 911 dispatcher so she's been in touch with some of her old friends already. No dead bodies, no one in the ER. Now she's on the line with them to let them know Violet's not with you." He paused. "Say, have you heard from RK this morning?"

"He and Erin had plans. Don't go blaming him for Violet's disappearance. I'm sure there's a good explanation."

"Ven says old people wander off all the time. And maybe she's with someone we haven't thought of."

But Ven won't consider that her mother could be in dementia? *Do not say that, Madrone.* "I hope she shows up soon," I said, with what I thought was admirable restraint.

"If it's not too cold, and if the person doesn't come across a snake or trip and fall, they're usually found. The police and the town's Search and Rescue team know what to do." He again lowered his voice. "If you ask me, she went to commune with other witches, maybe put a curse on me. But don't let Kirsten know I said that."

8

Beside the Stream

After ending the call with my brother, I drove to my temporary home. As I pulled into the driveway that led to the tiny garage out back, it came to me that Violet might have come to see me, maybe holler at me for some other terrible thing I'd done during the tour. With Violet, you had to expect almost anything.

Maybe she was still waiting for me on the comfortable front porch. As if. When I'd mentioned where I'd be staying, Violet knew where it was and launched a tale of its history. Leah's cottage was one of many small homes built during Cottonwood's heyday. I doubted Violet's proclamation that Leah's home had been a brothel. How many wicked women could one town boast?

Anyway, if Violet had wanted to speak with me, she knew where I was staying. I entered the back of the cottage and went directly to the front. No one on the porch. I opened the door to reassure myself no one had left any messages or nasty notes—possibly a notice of legal action—taped to it.

Where might my former client be?

What were Violet's favorite hangouts? We chatted a lot in the early days of the tour. At one time, she'd been an avid river rafter, but those days were behind her. She'd also hiked and climbed throughout Sedona, but that kind of rigorous activity was also mostly in her past. Had she mentioned any friends?

I stood and considered the few options facing me. Sit here waiting for word of Violet's whereabouts. Ignore the concern others had about her and chalk this disappearance up to further inconsistent behaviors. Twiddle my thumbs until Gabe arrived tomorrow. Bake more bread.

Ignoring the situation never worked for me. Violet may well be unpredictable, but despite last night's outburst, it was clear from all she'd said about her granddaughter as we traveled together that she loved Kirsten. She'd want to settle her concerns about Kirsten's management of the store, possibly her second greatest love, as soon as she could.

She was a woman in her seventies whose behavior of late had been erratic. I had to help find her. Some would call it meddling; I thought of it as helping out as best I could.

At least I'd be doing something, moving. How much bread could I bake?

First, to Violet's cottage and see what came to mind. Sure, I'd be on ground already covered by others, but at best I'd stumble on a clue, and at worst, keep myself occupied. Waiting was a non-option. I believed in action. The more people out looking for Violet, the better.

Water bottles filled, boots back on, I pulled on a fleece sweatshirt, grabbed my backpack, locked the cottage and headed out.

It was a short walk down the few blocks behind Main Street. I stopped a few houses up from Violet's home, noticing a police car parked in front. Where would Violet have gone, if she indeed wandered off this morning? Her shop, It's All Goods, was only up Pima and in the center of Old Town. I strolled toward town. I didn't want to encounter any of the family in Violet's home or in the shop. They didn't need another person to worry; I'd be more help on the streets. I headed toward Main but instead of turning right, strolled the other way, to the Lion's Club Park, empty save for one young woman watching her daughter do cartwheels. I paused long enough to ask if she'd seen an elderly woman wander past. No, but her eyes had been on her active child.

I walked the perimeter of the small park, checking behind every bit of scrub brush. Next I headed to the Community Garden, barren at this time of year, but a place Violet had mentioned when she talked of her beloved hometown. I opened the latch on the fence and walked up and down the garden paths.

What had we talked about? In the first part of the trip, Violet and I had shared our love of the outdoors and all things natural. I'd mentioned The Loop, Tucson's 125 mile-plus bike and walking path that skirts our rivers and washes and circles the community. Violet boasted about Cottonwood's very own Greenbelt, called the Jail Trail because it began near the former jail house. The walk followed the Verde River to Dead Horse Ranch State Park. Surely that would be one of the first places the search team would investigate when seeking a vulnerable adult like Violet. However, Violet mentioned that she sometimes turned off the trail instead of following it back into Old Town or heading toward the state park. She'd once seen a rare yellow-billed cuckoo there among the cottonwood trees that lined the Verde River.

I had little chance of finding her, but maybe I'd see some wildlife and soothe the endless worries dive-bombing my brain.

* * *

I walked back to Main Street and to the women's clothing boutique that now occupied the old town jail building. For a second, I wanted to skip the hunt for Violet and simply wander inside the little store, maybe finding a new outfit for when Gabe arrived in town. *Idiot!* He wasn't coming to see me, but to try to unsnarl the mess I'd made of our last tour. A new outfit would not help. Besides, when did I become a clothes horse? My typical outfit consisted of shorts or jeans and an Adventure Calls T-shirt, short or long-sleeved depending on the weather.

I headed into the woods toward the Verde River Greenway. The Jail Trail was a flat, easy hike along the Verde River. The river became wild enough for rafting downriver; here, it was a gentle stream, at times a trickle. The graveled walkway started at a sign that touted the benefits of the omnipresent cottonwood, without a mention of the tree's remarkable sneeze-inducing power. I followed the greenway until I reached a point where the path veered south.

Violet had mentioned she often turned off the path here, enjoyed heading upriver along a tiny trail occasionally too muddy to be passable, but that lured fewer tourists and walkers. Maybe she'd gone there to consider how she'd deal with her granddaughter's embezzling. Could it be true? Kirsten, stealing from her grandmother's beloved shop? The cloud of doubt made me shiver. I really didn't know anything about Kirsten except my brother's infatuation with her.

"Not possible." Violet imagined Kirsten's theft the same way she'd imagined RK's ill intentions. Even though she'd seemed angry and vengeful the previous night, if Violet really believed Kirsten had stolen from her, she surely also felt betrayed by the granddaughter with whom she'd entrusted her beloved store.

If I could find Violet, maybe I could calm her, help her realize it would be better to resolve her problems with Kirsten with reason and discussion, not with words that might soon be regretted, not with angry threats. I snorted. As if. Violet was an angry old woman, and from what I'd heard from Mateo and Kirsten, she'd never been much for exercising reason or caution.

Still. It looked like an easy, pretty meander, even if not part of the maintained walk. I pulled out my phone to see if it had a signal here then texted Mateo to keep me apprised of the search and turned left. I'd seen a number of birds at Tavasci Marsh near Tuzigoot. Maybe I'd spot a cuckoo or a golden eagle here. My way of pushing back my worries with good thoughts.

Shoe prints appeared when the soil turned from sandy to muddy, indicating I was on a human footpath. After only a few hundred yards I saw a flash of color beside the narrow stream bed, some thirty yards ahead.

I broke into a jog, aware that one wrong step on this unfamiliar ground meant a fall. Violet had worn a brilliant orange jacket during our recent tour, boasting that no one would miss her if she fell off a cliff. RK had muttered to me, "Too right. No one would miss her."

As I got closer, it was easy to make out a body, clad in an orange jacket, lying half-in, half-out of the trickling water, causing a small pool above it. Then I saw the bright colored sneakers that Violet generally wore. I worked up enough spit in my dry mouth to call out, "Violet," even though the awkward twisted position told me this person was at best unconscious.

I ran to her and threw myself to the ground beside her, ignoring the rocks that gouged my knees. "Violet, can you hear me?" I grabbed her shoulder and shook it as they'd taught us in CPR training. No result. I tried again. And once more. Nothing.

The next step was to start compressions, but it appeared obvious that my efforts would be futile. Her skin was gray and when I touched her cheek, cool. Violet's eyes were open slightly and clouded over. I stood and backed away, my own heart pounding enough for two people.

I stumbled farther away, certain I was about to puke. My body crumbled in on itself. I hunched over, panting. Concentrating on slowing my breathing, I counted in, out, in, out. It wouldn't help Violet if I fainted. I pinched the skin on my forearm. A scream tried to force its way out, but not as a call for help—in frustration and rage. How could this have happened? I fumbled in my pocket for my cell phone. Less than a bar, too weak to get through to anyone. I spun around and ran back up the trail toward town, checking every twenty yards or so for a signal.

9

"Just the Facts, Please"

When I finally got through, the 911 dispatcher was aware of the search for Violet Brock, and calmly asked me for my location and walked me through a series of questions to ascertain that Violet was not conscious or breathing and had no pulse. "I had to run back toward town before I had a signal," I told her, "but I checked for a pulse and breathing and it seemed clear she was beyond my help." On that I choked on a sob. "Is there anything I should try? I can run back."

The dispatcher suggested I make sure Violet wasn't in the water and that I cover her, in case she was still alive, to prevent further shock. After giving the woman on the phone detailed directions, I said, "It's not far. How long before someone gets here?"

The dispatcher assured me help was on its way and urged me to remain calm. Fat chance. All that emergency first aid training we'd undergone at Adventure Calls couldn't help me remain calm and unaffected. What it did do was allow me to do what was necessary, despite being plunged deep in this horror.

I ran back to Violet, way too fast for the rocky path. But what if the poor woman was alive? What if I could help her? I ran faster.

I tripped on a wobbly boulder and fell, hands hitting the gravel first, then knees, and barely missing hitting my chin and knocking myself out. The cell phone I hadn't bothered to return to my pocket flew out of my hand, hit a rock a few feet ahead and bounced off the trail. Tears came, from pain and from the sheer frustration of knowing how dumb I'd been.

My phone lay under a graythorn. Pulling it out, I scratched the back of my hand, but the phone seemed intact. Count that a blessing. Also a blessing that no scorpion or snake had been resting beneath the bush.

I leapt to my feet, palms bloody and gritty, jeans ripped. When I got back to Violet, I dumped my backpack on the ground and extracted and unfolded the emergency blanket stuffed into the bottom of the pack. I slid my arms under the elderly woman's frame and pulled her out of the trickle of a stream, my cut hands agonizing as they scraped along the gravel. Poor Violet's body was not at all flexible. I'd watched TV—rigor mortis came to mind. I also wondered about moving her, but if it could help Violet, I was all in. A gash on her head had stained her white hair, but was no longer bleeding.

This was not emergency training. This was real, someone I'd spoken with—argued with—the previous night. My stomach's contents roiled upward and I staggered away and vomited behind a snakeweed bush. I'd touched a dead body. Moved a dead body. Violet Brock's body.

I returned to sit on a rock near Violet. The sun warmed my back but still I shivered inside my fleece. It seemed glaringly clear that Violet was dead, had been for some time, but on the slim chance she clung to life, I talked to her. It seemed the best thing to do while waiting for help. I could try to clean the wounds on my hands and knees, but surely one of the EMTs would be able to do that, better than I could.

"Violet," I said, "What made you decide on a hike today? Or worse, last night? You were supposed to meet Kirsten. She's waiting for you now, so hang in there, Violet. You have a family worrying about you." I shivered again, and rinsed my mouth with some water and spit it out to rid it of the residue of vomit. "Distraction, Violet. I need a distraction. Not to mention the arrival of the EMTs."

I examined the ground around Violet. It was sandy away from the creek, and the earth that had been beneath her showed the tracks of Violet's small sneakers—my, what tiny feet she had. Then I wondered, were they really all Violet's prints? There were so many. Other, larger tracks had been smeared when I dragged Violet out of the stream. The sand beside me was strewn with my larger boot prints, and I couldn't see others. I'd scuffed around, trying to find a signal before I ran back toward town. But the absence of other tracks seemed odd.

My thoughts turned to Violet's family. Lavender would now be the oldest in the clan, unless she had siblings. I didn't recall Violet mentioning other children. I flashed back on the devastation I'd experienced when the police had come to the house to inform Mom that Daddy had been struck by a hit and run driver. It seemed worse that he'd died alone, without his family. And now Violet had died here on the Jail Trail, alone, without her family. If she had a stroke or heart attack while in a care center, she might have been saved. At worst her family could have spent those last moments with her.

But would it have been better for Violet, or simply less traumatic for her family? Being saved from death didn't mean returning to good health or a stable personality. For truly, she'd been falling deeper into dementia, even if her daughter denied it. Her behavior had been totally off kilter.

Were her accusations the previous evening a sign of her deteriorating mental condition? Or were they correct? Was coming here alone yet another sign of dementia, or had she come with someone else, someone she trusted?

I thought about how I might figure out if Violet had been alone or with someone else. A really good dog or a brilliant crime scene investigator might be able to tell, but no clues jumped out at me. They'd have to bite for me to discern much. Even so, I scanned the path above and below where the body lay. Looking for what? A cell phone? A bloody rock?

The thought of discovering some kind of weapon made me think of Gabe when he found a dead man who'd been stabbed with Gabe's own hunting knife. Let the experts take over. When I took off on this ridiculous hunt for Violet, I hadn't thought through how I'd feel if I found her, except perhaps to launch into another argument with the poor woman. Now that wasn't going to happen. I let out a breath. Once the officials came, would I be off the hook, or, as I suspected deep down, would it be the beginning of lots of questions and even suspicions?

Not off the hook. EMTs arrived, followed soon after by two Cottonwood police officers. I wanted to go home, be anywhere but out there, but the patrol officer fired questions at me. Had I moved the body? Touched her?

Turned her at all? Seen anyone on my way there or as I waited? What motivated me to walk this direction, on this undeveloped path? Had I known the dead woman? Known her well?

I answered his questions readily, willing to help, but when a detective arrived and launched a series of very similar questions, I fidgeted, worried that my story might change, that I might leave some vital detail out. The policewoman was kind, short and strong-appearing. "I'm Sergeant Willa Doughty with the Cottonwood Police Department. Like most folks in town, I knew Violet Brock. One of our town characters. Eccentric, but focused on Cottonwood's success."

The detective probed my relationship with Violet. "The tour was over two days ago, yet you're still in town?" I told her I was visiting my brother, but decided against adding anything about his relationship with Violet Brock or her granddaughter. It wasn't my business.

"Ah, yes, Mateo Hunter. He's dating Violet's granddaughter Kirsten, right?"

So much for discretion. Did everyone in this small town know everyone else's business? Know about that heated argument on the street? I nodded. "Yes. Kirsten's a nice young woman, they make a good couple. This will be hard on her."

The detective bit her lip. "On her daughter Ven, as well. Ven's a friend of mine, we met back when she worked dispatch." She adjusted her belt. "I've heard your brother and Violet had a few . . . issues. Care to elaborate?"

"That was really between Violet and Mateo, but I'd say he didn't like her overbearing attitude toward Kirsten." I paused. "And she didn't like him dating her granddaughter." I wasn't sharing anything the detective and eighty percent of Cottonwood residents didn't already know. "Your questions make me think Violet didn't die from exposure."

The woman's face closed into an expressionless mask. "I like to explore every possibility. It's way too early to determine the cause of death. Thought I'd ask you a few questions, since you're here."

I remained silent for a period that might have been too long, trying to decide how much to share with this representative of the law. Aware I shouldn't babble on, that I should simply answer questions honestly and succinctly, I pondered telling the detective that Violet planned to sue

Adventure Calls. That Violet blamed me and RK for her bad experiences during the tour. Imagined or not, Violet had believed she'd been badly treated.

Oh, for heaven's sake. They were bound to find out, if they talked to anyone who'd witnessed Violet's eruption the night before. "I need to tell you that Violet was not satisfied with the tour she took with Adventure Calls. In fact, she threatened to sue us, called my bosses with a number of complaints. My boss Gabe Ramsay will be here tomorrow, planning to discuss her dissatisfaction, and I'm sure he would have been able to pacify her. If you knew Violet, you know she's been exhibiting some . . . paranoia lately." Oops. Too much information, Madrone.

The detective straightened like a hound finding a good scent. Did her nose quiver? "I've heard she's been more vocal about some things recently. But still, must have ticked you off, her spreading tales about your company."

I inhaled. I wasn't about to step into that trap. "Our mission at Adventure Calls is that every client will come out of every tour completely pleased with every aspect of the trip. Nevertheless, there are frustrations and everyone has different expectations. It's important that their concerns are respected and dealt with."

She raised an eyebrow. "Someone definitely dealt with Violet."

"If, indeed, it wasn't a terrible accident."

Doughty nodded. "As you say. Too early to tell."

I massaged my right shoulder, the one that carried all my tension, always. Not surprisingly, it was rocklike and aching. I forced my shoulders down. "When do you think I might go home? I told you where I'm staying . . . at Leah McCall's home. And you have my cell number."

"A couple more questions. I can see you're wearing thin, and I understand this has been stressful. Have you lost other clients?"

So much for her sympathetic words. Another trap? I smiled. "We try to keep it to one per trip." I threw my hand to my mouth. "Forgive me. Warped humor. No, I've never lost another client. And strictly speaking, Violet was no longer a client."

"Was she angry with anyone else from Adventure Calls?"

The woman was a questioning demon. Her queries were never going to end. I would be here when snow fell, answering Sergeant Doughty's incessant questions, never getting the chance to pee, or eat or. . . . I shook my head. "Sorry. I really am whipped. In answer to your question, Violet had issues with our driver, Cliff Mustard. No one else found any fault with his driving. In fact, I'm sure he'll get rave reviews."

"I'd like to talk to your boss tomorrow, and to this Mustard guy, if he's still around."

Oh, thank goodness. My shoulders dropped at her words. Tomorrow. She was through with me. At least for today. Every inch of me felt drained of energy.

I gave the detective contact information for both men and was given the okay to leave. I hadn't walked far up Jail Trail, but my return to town felt like the Bataan Death March.

At home, I showered for much longer than a good environmentalist should, trying to scrub off the aura of death. Dressed in leggings and a huge sweatshirt, I scavenged for food, ending up with toast and cashew butter and some apple butter. I phoned Mateo, who was at Ven and Wes's home with Kirsten. He assured me there was no need for me to join them. When I asked him about Kirsten and the store, he cut me off, saying, "You're a star for finding her, Sis. Thanks." And clicked off.

Drat. I wanted to talk to them, find out if Violet's death was natural or not, find out more about Kirsten and the store. Wait. What do people, especially in small towns, do when someone dies? They bring food. Yes!

The perfect reason for a visit. If they'd let me in the door.

10

Morning After

The next morning, after sleeping like a sloth, I found several text messages. I'd been so exhausted the previous evening, I'd turned my phone off before heading to a very early bedtime.

Before I crashed, I phoned my boss Gabe to give him the news and was relieved when I got voicemail. I apologized for delivering bad news in a voice message and told him why he wouldn't be meeting with Violet. I suggested his presence here was a good idea, PR-wise. He could discover Sergeant Doughty's request to speak with him once he arrived. I didn't mention that I, and possibly RK, would appreciate his moral support. Too needy.

Mateo texted that Wes and Ven and Kirsten would like me to drop by this morning. My shoulders slumped. At least they didn't expect I'd already be in police custody. I'd take that traditional bereavement offering of food anyway, even if I did have an invitation.

Mateo left a voicemail that he'd be going to work today. As an afterthought he added, "Cops are sure asking a lot of questions for a natural death." RK texted he'd be talking to the cops sometime this morning but "under protest." Since he'd told me he'd become friends with the sheriff and his deputy in Hancock, Idaho, I'd harbored hope he'd shed the activist's kneejerk reaction to the police. Apparently not.

Gabe messaged that he'd be in Cottonwood before noon.

Then, while I dressed, the phone's beep announced another text. This one told me that Tripp, Gabe's partner—and my other boss—had fallen while on a rock climb on a tour and that Gabe was now driving to New Mexico to take over. "I know you can handle whatever happens, Madrone," he wrote. I guess he thought that was more reassuring than, "I'm hanging you out to dry up there." I was alone, searching for strength to handle things.

My stomach, always eager to be fed no matter how dire the situation, growled. I sliced and toasted some of the bread I'd made the previous day and slathered some avocado on it. After scarfing down the toast, I wrapped a loaf of pumpkin bread, inhaling its spicy fragrance, to take to Violet's family.

How to find words of comfort for the grieving family? "She wasn't all that nice" didn't cut it. "At least she won't be suing my employer" struck out as well.

"Whiner, Madrone. You haven't lost your mother or grandmother. Suck it up." Leah's appliances apparently had no opinion because the kitchen remained silent.

Lavender and Wes Sturgess lived in a small bungalow style home in Clarkdale, another former mining town north of Cottonwood. We'd passed the turnoff to Clarkdale on the way to Jerome. Was that only the day before yesterday? Driving the car Leah had offered me during my visit, I found their home in less than fifteen minutes, time that left me no more ready to face bereavement.

I crossed the front porch, forced to ignore the invitation from the broad glider swing to the left of the door. I would much rather spend my day on that beckoning refuge than face the task ahead of me.

When Ven Sturgess opened the front door, I batted away my worries about saying the right thing and let my heart speak. I hugged the woman I'd met only days before as if she were my sister—the loony sister who'd tried to convince her that her mother was bat-shit crazy. Her hair had pulled from its braid and her clothes smelled musty, as if she'd never gone to bed. She allowed me to hug her but remained stiff and pulled away too quickly. I pulled back. "I am so sad for all of you."

"It's tough," Ven said, "maybe even tougher since she so often made me angry." Her honesty surprised me. Given Monday's tense conversation, I considered myself the last person she'd want to confide in. Ven stepped back.

"Please, come in."

Ven took my gift of food to the kitchen and we joined Wes and Kirsten at the table by a bay window overlooking a small backyard. "I am very sorry for your loss. I'd hoped to find Violet alive and well," I said.

Wes looked at me across the table. "After what she put you through, after what she threatened, and after we doubted your accusations the other day, I'd say it's mighty generous of you to offer condolences." He rubbed his chin. "Still, funny you'd know right where to find her."

"Dad," Kirsten murmured at the same time her mother said, "Wes, really."

My ever-present appetite fled, replaced by shock mixed with anger. I tried not to hate Sturgess for his accusation, telling myself he was in mourning—not that I believed for a second he mourned his mother-in-law, at least from his statements the other day. I pasted on an awkward smile. "Despite my concerns about her accusations, I didn't wish bad things for Violet."

"Making you a better person than me," he said. "Sometimes I wanted to wring her scrawny neck. Who wouldn't want to off the person who might cause them to lose their livelihood?"

Either Wes Sturgess meant his words or he meant to draw me into some kind of confession. I pushed the thought away as uncharitable. I wasn't that person, or at least I tried not to be. Most likely Wes was a man who spoke before he considered the impact of his words.

Kirsten looked like she might explode. "Good job keeping your thoughts to yourself, Dad."

Ven glared at her husband. "Violet was my mother. Give her a little respect."

"Like she gave me respect? The old broad never had a good word to say about me. Never trusted me." He poured himself coffee from the insulated server on the table. "Now I'm supposed to go all 'boo-hoo' 'cause she got herself killed?" He lifted his head and sniffed the air. "What's that scent? Oh, yeah. Hypocrisy."

Silence seemed the best response to Wes.

Ven cleared her throat and took a long, slow sip of her coffee. "I'm relieved it was you and not some tourist who found her. I'm grateful," Ven said. After another pause, she added, "Although . . . why did you think of that part of the Jail Trail to search?"

My face flushed. Both of them were considering that I might have killed Violet. Whoopee. And did Kirsten think her new boyfriend's sister capable of murder? Sheesh. I was a pacifist. "I couldn't simply stay home and do nothing, and it was a place I recalled her mentioning when we chatted."

"I should have thought of it," Kirsten said, "but I was too worried to think straight. Nana Vi loved her little walks, and she liked secluded places that tourists didn't know about." She waved a biscotti at her father. "She wasn't always cranky, you know." A tear rolled down her cheek. "If only I could have explained to her . . . ."

Her father sat up straight, his shoulders stiff. "She knew you loved her, knew you did your best in her precious store."

I remembered all the platitudes people had spouted when my father was killed. "We never have enough time to talk with those we love" was one of the better ones. "He's in a better place now" definitely had not helped me at age thirteen. So I stuck with "I'm so sorry for your loss. All of you." Why had they allowed me in their home, since they clearly had some suspicions? I picked up a biscotti and nibbled on it. "This is delicious."

"Food started streaming in the moment news got out Mom was missing," Ven said with a sad smile. "Small towns."

"Big hearts," I said.

"Bigger mouths," Wes said, earning glares from his wife and daughter. Interesting comment and responses.

"Violet had an exciting life," I said, in an attempt to relieve the tension. "She told me she used to hitchhike throughout the West. Then became an activist. Was her husband an activist, as well?"

Ven grinned. "Pops? No. A wanderer who fell in love with Mom. She convinced him to move back here, where she'd grown up. Neither of them had a plan for what to do with their lives, so they settled in, got jobs, and eventually opened the mercantile. Saved their earnings and bought land. I'd say they got rich more by accident than plan."

"He worshipped her, and I gotta say, she loved him, too," Wes said. He gazed at his wife. "Their marriage gave us something to live up to. Both Violet and her daughter had some indescribable power over men." He winked. "Sometimes it's easy to forget the good stuff."

Ven shot him a huge smile and said, "It was horrible for Mom when Daddy died. She's never been the same. But she loved this town." Her gaze went to Kirsten. "And you. Always wanted the best for you."

Tears leaked from Kirsten's eyes, and she wiped them away. "I know she did. I loved her, too." She blew her nose, and I noticed both Ven and Wes swiping at tears.

Ven rose and offered to make more coffee, but all of us declined. She sat again and said, "You may be wondering why we asked you here this morning. Not merely to thank you for finding Mom and staying with her, despite your injuries." She nodded at my bandaged hands.

"Anyone would have done the same," I replied.

"Still . . . I'm grateful. We all are," Ven said. "From what I hear from my old pals at the dispatch center, they're thinking Mom didn't die of natural causes. Or at least they're treating her death as suspicious, which means we're all suspects."

"You? She was your mother, your grandmother. No way," I said at the same time I thought about Wes's angry words and the accusations Violet had made about Kirsten.

"She hasn't exactly been generous with us, and you saw the way she tore into Kirsten up in Jerome."

"Mom," Kirsten said. She brushed her hair back from her face and waved a hand in a circle, a 'get on with it,' gesture. "Your point is?"

"All right, already." Ven chewed on the end of her long braid. "The thing is, I'm pretty sure the cops will want you to stay around, maybe longer than you'd planned." I speculated on what she had in mind. You and I can plan Kirsten and Mateo's wedding? Plant a garden together?

I forced myself to keep a half smile on my face.

Wes put his hand on Ven's. "If we're all suspects, it's best if we carry on as if we aren't. Act like one big happy family. Ven wants you and Mateo to come for dinner, maybe in a couple of days."

Given the comments the two of you made earlier, I'm thinking you're trying to keep me close, keep an eye on me. Hmm. I can do the same, my new friends. "I have no reason to suspect any of you. Why should the cops? Still, that's a kind invitation."

"What about Mateo?" said Kirsten. "Lots of people, including a police volunteer, saw him in a shouting match with Nana Vi the other day. They asked me about it. And so many people heard her accuse me of stealing and know Mateo didn't like it. Not to say I liked it, either."

I stood. Kirsten didn't have to voice every worried thought I'd had. If she wasn't stealing from Violet, who was? My brother? If he was, why? Surely he wasn't doing drugs again. Was he? I didn't share any of my fears. "If none of us killed her, then none of us has anything to worry about. I appreciate the offer of dinner, and if Mateo agrees, we'll certainly join you. I do want us to remain friends."

Wes burst into a humorless chuckle. "If you think because you're innocent, the cops won't suspect you, won't probe into every aspect of your life, then welcome to the ostrich club, my friend. Hide your head and nothing bad happens."

"Please see to the dishes, sweetheart," Ven said, with no indication she felt anything like sweetness toward her spouse at that moment. After Wes headed for the kitchen, she took my arm. "I understand how you feel, like this can't possibly be happening."

I let her steer me to the door. "I'm sure we all do," I said. "Not only are you suffering the loss of your mother, you're concerned about suspicion falling on one of you. Again, all I can say is how sorry I am. Things will work themselves, out, I'm certain."

I wasn't at all sure, but Mom taught me about positive thinking.

11

Call It Investigating, Not Snooping

After leaving the Sturgess home, I drove around the little town of Clarkdale, aimlessly heading up, then down, the streets. Eventually I parked along the central square, in front of a church, and turned off the engine. I considered entering the church but feared I might run into someone. I had no desire to make small talk or to unburden myself on someone else. Right now, I needed to think.

What had I learned from Ven, Wes, and Kirsten? Certainly there was tension in the home, tension fiercer than grief for Violet. Under Kirsten's tension, I sensed anger—but at whom? I had no clue, but I didn't get the sense it was directed at me.

Three days ago Ven and Wes had scoffed when I told them Violet was exhibiting signs of dementia. Today they told me her death was suspicious and I'm among the suspects. Poop on a platter. If I'm a suspect, and they said we all were, then so is Mateo. And RK.

The Sturgess family wasn't my problem, not even Kirsten, despite her relationship with Mateo. But Mateo? He'd had enough problems in his life. I'd promised our mother I'd look out for him. RK was a grown-up, old enough to defend himself. But . . . I'd recommended RK for the job at

Adventure Calls, and on this last tour, I'd been his supervisor. I should have found a way to protect him from Violet's fury, and I didn't.

I had to prove the innocence of myself, RK, and my brother. I had no idea how, but I'd approach it the same way I did a new recipe—step after step. Only this time I had no recipe, no written instructions, no path to follow.

I took a deep breath. "You are *not* the kind of person who panics, Madrone Hunter. You are calm, in control, intelligent. You can do this." Right. First step: try to believe that statement. Second step: hope no one heard you talking to the parking meter.

Real second step: find out more about Violet and who might have wanted her dead. I almost chuckled at that huge leap, but looking into Violet's death might keep me out of jail and might also keep me from fretting about the whole situation. My darkest concern? If Mateo was back on drugs and needed cash, where better to find it than in Violet's shop?

"No. Do not go there." He was straight and we were all innocent.

I started the car and headed back to Cottonwood. I needed to know more about Violet Brock.

I drove past Violet's cottage and parked several houses down the street, then walked back to the alley behind the homes. Violet's backyard had a gate leading to the alley, conveniently unlocked. This was, after all, a small town in rural Arizona, not a big city like Manhattan or Tucson.

I skulked toward her back porch. Halfway across the tidy yard, I realized my skulking would look suspicious to anyone who could distinguish it from casual strolling. My head swinging back and forth, peering into every innocent, barren corner of the yard, my shoulders hunched as if that would hide my identity—might be considered skulking. I stood up straight and headed for the back door. Grasped the handle and gave a twist. Nothing happened because the door was locked. Drat. Maybe she'd hidden a spare key.

A small patio table held a Talavera pottery planter with a weary-looking cactus. I checked under it first because pots on the ground likely sheltered cockroaches or scorpions, neither of which I relished encountering. No luck. I continued to search, nudging the pots out of place with my shoe.

I struck gold—brass, really—under a flattish piece of slate that lay beside the back steps, on the concrete patio.

I paused on the porch when I heard a noise inside. Voices, voices I recognized. My mouth went dry and I whispered a curse. Why couldn't the cottage be empty? I leaned in close to the door, hoping I couldn't be seen through the side window. I couldn't make out what was being said, but it wasn't sweet nothings. Fortunately the window was caked with dust.

I wanted, no needed, to know what they were arguing about. The voices were not close, so I turned the key in the lock and pushed the door inward.

I stopped in the doorway and peered into the empty kitchen. To my left was a door that must lead either to a pantry or a basement. I crept across the old linoleum floor and opened the pantry door, thrilled when it didn't screech at me. Now I had somewhere to go should the couple enter the kitchen.

The voices seemed closer. I stepped into the pantry, a tiny room lined with shelves filled with canned fruits and vegetables in glass jars. I left the door the tiniest bit ajar so I might hear the arguing couple.

"It was kind of you to help me gather up the cats, Mateo, but I've had enough of your advice." Kirsten Sturgess did not sound at all like the sweet young woman I'd spoken with earlier that morning. Nope. She was ticked off, and the target of her anger was my brother.

I inched closer to the door.

"I wish you'd listen to me, Kir. Lots of people heard Violet accuse you of taking funds from It's All Goods the other night. Like they heard me fight with her. The cops will be looking into all of us, and it won't take a financial genius to figure out she was right—you did steal from the store."

"Borrowed, not stole."

"Whatever. All the same to a number cruncher. And now you don't have to pay her back."

"But—"

"Your father should see that, too. But he's not going to stop gambling or admit the theft without good reason. He's an addict, like me."

I gasped and threw my hand over my mouth. Wes Sturgess?

The couple fell silent. Had they heard me? I backed against the far wall of the pantry and bumped into several aprons on hooks. I squatted beneath them, pulling one down so it draped over my head.

"Did you hear something?" Kirsten said.

"Probably the cats are getting anxious in their carriers."

"Daddy would never let me go to jail." She sniffed and blew her nose, as if she'd been crying. After a while, she added, "Now they can make this place into their dream restaurant."

"If Violet left enough cash for them to renovate. Let me take those."

Their voices had grown louder. They were entering the kitchen.

"My nana had enough money for that and more. She owned lots of property around town."

"Ah. I'm dating an heiress."

"Right. Not." Pause. In a lighter tone she added, "Or maybe yes, and I'm too rich to date a working guy like you." After a moment, I heard her blow out a sigh. Right next to the pantry door. "Okay, grumpy pants. I'll think about talking to Daddy. But I'm sure everything will be okay once they find the real killer."

"Sure it will."

Maybe Kirsten didn't know Mateo as well as I did. He was lying to reassure her. "Let's get the cats to your folks' house. They're not happy," he said. "Come on, you little furballs."

I heard the back door thump open followed by the yowl of an angry cat. Then Mateo said, "I'm gonna pop these babies into your car. You get them settled at your parents' and I'll wait here. Maybe start on these dishes and tidying up."

"Don't you have to be at work?" Kirsten said.

"Ross told me to take all the time I need to comfort you and help out. He's a good guy."

"Okay, then. I'll be back in under an hour."

Their voices faded more quickly than the angry cat noises. Did I have time to sneak out the back door? I had no desire for them to know I'd heard the awful secret. Things were far worse than I'd imagined. However, if I left now, I'd miss my chance to check out Violet's cottage.

I stood and massaged my thigh, which had cramped from my prolonged squat. Did I have time to get out of the pantry? Find somewhere else to hide until my brother left?

The back door thumped shut. Seconds later, the pantry door swung open, and my brother said, "You might as well come out of there. And don't try anything. I'm armed."

I stepped out of the pantry with care at the same time I called out, "It's me, Mateo. Madrone."

My brother stood outside the open door, hefting a cast iron skillet. I giggled. "Potted, not armed."

"Not funny. What the hell are you doing here?" He set the skillet on the counter, positioned himself to block my escape out the back door, and crossed his arms.

I chewed at my lip and tried out a sheepish grin. "How'd you know I was there?"

"I heard a noise and figured someone was hiding in the pantry. I didn't want Kirsten to confront them, so I hustled her and Beans and Smokey on out to the car."

"Beans and Smokey? Cool names. Wish I'd met them."

"No stalling, Sis. Why are you here?"

"Duh. Not to wash the dishes, although since you offered, we ought to do that before Kirsten gets back." I returned to the pantry and grabbed an apron. "I'm here to find out why someone wanted Violet dead. As I imagine you are. But I also do dishes."

12

A Nose Too Long

"Why no crime-scene tape, no cops searching this place?" I asked while we speed-washed the few dishes in Violet's sink.

"Not certain. They searched yesterday when she went missing, and there's no hint she died here, I guess. They did come back last night and took a few things away, Ven said. They let her in to feed the cats and told her she could pick them up today."

"We'd better take a quick look before Sergeant Doughty changes her mind."

When we washed up I saw no signs of a coffee cup, so guessed that Violet had died the night of the concert, or been lured from her home before breakfast the next day. "Violet treasured her one cup of "real" coffee as soon as she was up," I said. "I'm betting she died the night before."

"I'm betting the cops already know that," Mateo said. So little respect for my skills of deduction.

"I heard Kirsten tell you Violet owned property around town. Wasn't she raving about people trying to get her to sell her land when she waylaid us in Jerome?"

Mateo slammed a cupboard door shut after stacking the last dry plate. "You have a lot of nerve sneaking in here and listening in on a private conversation."

"I thought the cottage was empty until I heard you two arguing. I had no clue it was you."

I edged out of the kitchen, but Mateo grabbed my arm and spun me around. "That is a bad answer, in so many ways. First, you shouldn't be snooping around Violet's home. Second, why the hell would you walk in, not knowing who or what awaited you? Third—"

No way was he going to intimidate me, his older sister. I moved close enough to smell the coffee on his breath. "I came here because you and I are prime suspects in Violet's death. If we're going to get suspicion off us, we need to know more about who disliked Violet." At his disgusted look, I added, "Disliked her enough to kill her."

"I arrived here four months ago and didn't start dating Kirsten until a couple of months ago. You met Violet on the tour. There must be a boatload of other people who've known her longer and have way better reasons to kill her."

I stared at his hand on my arm. My cold, deadly stare that always did him in when he was little.

"Like 'the look' is gonna stop me, Sis." He let go of my arm but kept up the argument. "You're overreacting. The cops will look at you and me, sure, but they've got other suspects."

Talk about naïve. "We're the outsiders, dummy. Outsiders are always the best ones to blame, even to frame, because we don't have all the connections, all the history and friendships. I had a great motive for getting rid of her, and you publicly announced someone would get rid of her. And don't forget you have a record. Police look first at people with a record." I crossed into the small dining room, a room dwarfed by an oversized cherry sideboard. I opened the top drawer. Real silver. People still had that? Used it? I closed the drawer. "Nobody in this town wants to put the finger on Kirsten or Lavender or Wes." At the look of horror on his face, I softened my harsh tone but the words were harsh no matter how delivered. "We have to be ahead of them, that's all I'm saying."

He crossed his arms. "I'm not saying I agree with you, but what's your plan?"

"Plan?" I am more a seat-of-the-pants person, except when baking, and my brother knew that. But maybe this situation did indeed require a plan, possibly more than "Discover who really killed Violet Brock, so neither of us will take the fall."

Wait. That didn't sound so bad. "Discover who really killed Violet Brock, so neither of us will take the fall." This time aloud.

"I'm sure it wasn't Kirsten, but her parents should stay on our list." He looked past me, out the back window, but I doubted he noticed the oversized acanthus with its fall blooms or the redbrick fireplace.

"To be fair, the list should include all of us until we find a way to get ourselves off it. Once we know for sure when she died, and if it wasn't natural causes, that will help." I shuddered. I didn't like the clinical, cold way I spoke, but being pragmatic was the only way we'd find out the truth. "In the meantime, we can take a look-see here."

Mateo nodded, a slow nod with his lips drawn tight as if his agreement was reluctant. "You take the bedroom. I'm uncomfortable doing this at all, but pawing through her lingerie like some pervert? Too creepy."

"I'm champing at the bit," I said. I headed toward the hall, cringing at the thought of digging through my late client's personal belongings.

Two rooms sprouted off the short hallway. In between was a small, old-fashioned, charming bathroom with black and white tile and a small shower/tub.

The back room, with windows to the peaceful backyard, was obviously Violet's bedroom, and the one in the front was a multi-purpose sewing room, office, and storage center. I made a cursory search of Violet's bedroom, noticing the eclectic mix of art, some that reflected an older matron's taste—or my idea of it—prints of Georgia O'Keefe flowers and landscapes, along with some modern art prints that featured fiery splashes of orange and red and black. I couldn't bear to grope through her lingerie, so instead checked the closet shelves and the bedside table. If I'd hoped to find a diary displaying who she met the previous evening or a list of her most recent enemies, my hopes were foiled.

Violet's bed, a double, was to the right of the door. It was made, more evidence that she'd died at night, not in the early morning. I sniffed and caught the faint odor of lavender. The clock on the nightstand reminded me that Kirsten promised to return within the hour. I needed to move fast. The wall opposite the bed displayed a number of black and white and color photos, some striking landscapes, most showing forests denuded by fire, leaving a few stately pines overseeing charred land. I was soon distracted by a jewelry box on Violet's dresser. It was the work of an artist, made from several different kinds of wood, with two drawers faced with contrasting wood. I opened the lid and saw a jumble of earrings and necklaces of varying quality. The top drawer was filled with a variety of buttons—political campaign buttons, old and new, a button for The Notorious RBG, another stating "You can disagree without being disagreeable," several with peace signs, one for Earth Day, another with the sun symbol, and lots more, jumbled together. The bottom drawer held a few pieces of finer, older silver jewelry, some inlaid with turquoise.

I shivered, whether with sorrow at Violet's death or guilt over my intrusion, I couldn't say. I simply could not paw through Violet's dresser. The office beckoned, as more promising and perhaps less personal. At least it lacked the intimacy of her bedroom. File cabinets lined the side wall with a smallish desk in the middle. A bulletin board behind the desk displayed dozens of photos, mostly of Violet's family, but some artistic outdoor shots of flowers and red rock country. Beside the bulletin board was a calendar, one of those cheesy ones of firemen in various sexy poses. I wished I had time to thumb through the pages. Eye candy would be a nice distraction. The date squares for this month were empty, dashing my hopes of discovering whom she met the previous night.

There was a small, neat stack of boxes beside her desk, the top one containing old photos. What was missing was a computer of any kind, and I thought Violet owned one, although I wasn't sure why I thought that. Not as simple as thinking everyone had a computer. Not true, particularly in Violet's age bracket.

Ah, yes. She'd told me at some point that she was writing a memoir, "letting it all hang out," was how she put it. I looked around for a bit longer, because the room was not as tidy as the rest of her home. Nope. No laptop nestled amongst the stacked papers.

I scanned those papers when I looked under them. They seemed typical of any household—bank statements, bills, solicitations from charitable organizations. Not much of a surprise that someone Violet's age preferred paper over electronic. Given the three tall file cabinets, I'd wager she kept papers from years past—many years past. To one side of the desk was a bound notebook, leather or faux leather. I opened it, using a tissue in case the cops weren't done with their investigations, and saw a list of addresses. Properties she owned?

I straightened and looked around the room. Yes. On the wall beneath the front window a small printer sat on a low table. She did indeed have a computer. But where was it?

I slapped my forehead. Possibly Ven or Kirsten had taken it, or the police had confiscated it. Maybe they sought a calendar to find out if she'd met someone, or simply wanted to see who she'd been in communication with recently. Was this standard procedure? I had no clue. If Sergeant Doughty had been here, she'd been very respectful of Violet's home and belongings, but she seemed that kind of person. Tidy and respectful.

Squatting to peek into another box, I saw it held more photos, lying unsorted, helter-skelter. Another carton held maps, another yellowed, crisp newspapers and newsprint guides to parks. Clearly, Violet had been working on her memoir. I swallowed and shut eyes that threatened to overflow. Given Violet's long and varied life, it would have been a engrossing read and it was a shame it would now go unfinished.

Perhaps when Lavender got her mother's laptop back, she'd discover a nearly complete autobiography. One could only hope.

I unfolded from the deep squat, wandered over to the first filing cabinet, and tugged on the top drawer pull. Locked. I wasn't sure what I hoped to find. Violet had been wealthy, owned several properties in Cottonwood and perhaps elsewhere, and rarely discarded a piece of paper. Not unlike many people her age, save for her wealth and property ownership. I used a pencil eraser to page through the journal. Tabbed pages were labeled with addresses. Most held a number of names and dates. Blackmail subjects? More likely a list of rental properties and renters. Wowza. She did have a large number of properties. Who was suggesting she sell them? And why did they want them? For the land?

I've always been able—sometimes after a hard internal struggle—to keep myself from opening other peoples' bathroom cabinets and drawers. Looking at Violet's personal papers made my skin crawl in the same way. Except that she was dead and would never know. Still, I didn't belong in her office, in her home.

I'd make a terrible burglar. What I was doing felt an awful lot like burgling, except I had no intention of stealing anything. Peeping from the inside? Whatever. I rubbed my arms. This wasn't right.

I replaced her journal, trying hard to get it in the same place I'd found it. Then I left the room.

Mateo met me in the hall. "I didn't find anything of interest in the kitchen. No big wads of cash in the freezer or in cookie jars. Nothing in the living room except a lot of books, many of them large print, and stacks of magazines. The woman had eclectic tastes—Forbes, Arizona Highways, E."

"You lost me at eclectic—who are you and what have you done with my baby brother?"

He puffed himself up in mock outrage. "I am much smarter and better read than you give me credit for."

"Which might not make you smart or well-read." I grinned.

"Muchisimas gracias. Now you'd better leave before Kirsten gets back and finds you here. Anything in the office?"

I made a beeline to the kitchen, glad to shake off my voyeur's shame. "Other than me feeling like a thief? Her computer is gone. There's a printer, so I'm pretty certain she had one. I'm thinking the cops took it. Unless . . . Could she have taken it to the shop?"

He shook his head. "I doubt it. She really had left handling the store to Kir. Which is why it's odd she . . ." His voice trailed off.

"She what? You know I hate when you stop mid-sentence."

Mateo's face looked the same way it had when I'd caught him with a neighbor kid's bike when he was seven. Or with Mama's biscochuelos she'd made for a party. Guilt and defiance rivaled for dominance.

I knew my brother, and I knew how to make him fess up. I crossed my arms, pressed my lips together, and said nothing. This time "the look" worked.

"What I meant was it was odd that she suddenly took a look at the store's books. She'd stayed out of Kirsten's way, trusted her."

He had grown up and we'd grown apart. I couldn't read his thoughts. But his guilty look had not cleared. He had more to tell me, if I pushed the right buttons. "And was she wise to check?"

"It was her store. She could do whatever she wanted." He pulled out his phone. "It's time you left. Kir will be here any minute."

"Don't try to bluster your way out of this. Was Violet right? Did Kirsten take some money? Embezzle from the store?"

"Don't call it embezzling. She borrowed some money, okay? But it wasn't for herself."

I shook my fists loose to prevent a gloating fist pump. He'd folded like a soggy graham cracker. "If not for herself, then . . . "

"Then none of your business!" Kirsten said. "What are you doing here?"

Oops. Kirsten had arrived and neither of us had noticed. She didn't seem pleased to see me. I didn't see an easy way to explain.

13

Dynamite and Girlfriends are Volatile

Kirsten pointed to the back door. "Leave. Now."

"Let me explain," Mateo said. "Madrone wants to help."

Continuing to point at the door, Kirsten said, "Both of you. Out." She glowered at Mateo and added, "I confided in you and you decided to tell her everything. I know where *your* loyalties are. Get out." As she spoke her volume rose.

"But he didn't tell me anything," I protested. "And he didn't invite me here. I came on my own."

She marched up to me and put her face way, way inside my personal space. "I heard him. I heard you. I can't trust either of you. Get out of this house right now or I will call the police, who will not be pleased that you're here."

I got. Mateo followed on my heels. When we got out to the sidewalk, I said, "Wow. She definitely inherited Violet's temper."

He stopped and stared at me. "Thanks, Sis. Thanks. You've ruined my relationship with my girlfriend, not to mention any possible chance to find out more about who killed Violet, and now you want to bad-mouth Kirsten? You always think you know what's best for me, don't you? Well, I'll tell you what's best. Leave me alone. Leave this town. I do not want or need your help. I'm not sure I can stand to look at you right now."

Hmm. I wanted to argue with him, to convince him that we needed each other, but possibly this wasn't the best time.

After hurrying back to my car, I let out the tears that I'd been choking back on the way. I sobbed for so long I feared a watchful neighbor might report me loitering there. Part way through my sobfest, I realized I was crying for Violet as well as over my brother's anger. I knew we would patch things up, somehow, as we always did. He had a short temper but he'd get over it. He had to.

I prayed he'd get over it. He'd lost his girlfriend, even if temporarily. She'd proven a strong support during his recovery. Without her and with his being furious with me, would he turn to the pills for solace? I prayed he'd forgive me soon and that Kirsten would let him apologize and resume their relationship.

But Violet—Violet was gone forever, with no chance for her family to say their farewells, no chance to apologize for hurt feelings. I missed her, missed the long talks we'd had when our tour started, missed her offbeat humor and her endless curiosity and her stubborn determination to keep up with the younger tour guests. I sobbed until my eyes throbbed and my nose felt raw.

I swigged some water, wiped my eyes, blew my nose one last time and started the car.

Mateo and Kirsten had clearly told me to butt out, but it wasn't possible. I had to figure out who'd killed Violet. Somehow finding her made me even more responsible. Warped logic, I know. Was it an advantage or a disadvantage that I was neither family nor family friend? People might share opinions with an outsider more readily than they would with Violet's family or even with the police.

Or at least that's what I told myself.

Google informed me that the Yavapai County Recorder's Office was in Prescott. A drive sounded like a terrific idea. Good ol' chatty Google told me it was a little over an hour's drive. The road trip would cheer me up and I might be able to find out more about Violet's Cottonwood and Verde Valley land ownership in the county seat.

The drive took me past Jerome and wound upward, the landscape changing from cactus to chaparral to piñon pines and juniper and eventually to stately Ponderosa pines. The two-lane highway through the mountains had turnouts to allow passing. At one point I looked out at hillsides scattered with grey and blackened pines, the remains of a not-too-long-ago fire. Concentrating on my driving freed my mind from spooling and respooling my discovery of Violet's body. It didn't seem long before I descended into Prescott.

Prescott, twice the capital of the Arizona Territory, lay a couple of thousand feet higher than Cottonwood. It was often used as an escape from the heat of the lower communities. I'd never been there and knew little about it, except that it hosted an annual rodeo that billed itself as the world's oldest.

I pulled into the parking lot in front of Yavapai County Administrative Services, housed in a new redbrick building that looked clean and functional if not very exciting.

My phone let me know that people had been trying to reach me while I was out of cell service. A text from RK said, "Phone me. Now." He'd added an angry emoji and one of a javelina. What did a half-blind, smelly peccary as an emoji imply? Okay. I checked my voice messages and found one from Sergeant Doughty, asking me to drop by the police station to file a written report and answer a few additional questions she'd neglected to ask me on the day I found Violet.

RK answered after only two rings, a record for my normally technology-averse friend. "What's up?" I asked. "And what's with the javelina? Too cute."

"Javelinas will gore you if they feel surrounded. Just sayin.' The cops think I offed Violet. Will Adventure Calls pay for a lawyer?"

"Oh, please. It's not like you to panic. To overreact, sure, but you sound panicky." I tried to keep my voice soothing, because he truly sounded shaken.

"She hated me. Shouted that I'd tried to kill her on the tour. Threatened my job. That sergeant sweated me for hours. Filled me with coffee and then wouldn't let me take a piss."

"Um, I'm pretty sure she wouldn't do that. Plus, it's only 11:30 and you texted me you'd be going in this morning."

"Seriously, Mad," he whined, "she was like a mountain lion on a fresh antelope."

"Don't call me Mad." He knew I hated that ridiculous nickname.

"I'm barely recovering from a grilling and you're worried about a nickname?"

"Did she really lock you in? Not let you go to the restroom?"

"Well, it seemed like it. She got a call and left and I didn't want to be caught wandering around the halls of justice."

I laughed until I snorted. His reaction was typical for him. Way over the top. And what I needed to put things in perspective. "Have you been returned to freedom yet?"

"Well, yes, but they want me to stay in town or let them know if I leave. It was awful." He sounded closer to three than thirty-something.

"Poor, poor baby. Did she tell you anything more about how Violet died after you dried off from the waterboarding? When?"

"Make fun if you want, but she was too busy putting me through the wringer. I'm exhausted. Where are you?"

"My day hasn't been great. Sergeant Doughty wants to see me, too. And Mateo's not speaking to me. I'm in Prescott, trying to find out more about Violet's property ownership in Cottonwood."

"So you're a sleuth now? I'd call you nuts, but maybe it's not such a bad idea, given our history with Violet. I wish you'd taken me with. I'm getting stir crazy."

I asked him why he wasn't spending the rest of his day with Erin and he told me she and another woman from our tour were on a spa retreat day in Sedona. Left on his own, he was at loose ends.

"Here's a thought," I said. "Violet used to be an environmental activist. You know lots of them. Like that woman from the ukulele group. Maybe she has some dirt on Violet." I cleared my throat. "Information, I mean. Like who she knew, any recent things she's done that might have stirred someone up."

"That shouldn't be hard. The woman stirred everyone up."

"But not enough to want her dead. You know what I mean."

"Gotcha, boss. Am I on payroll for this?"

My mouth fell open until I realized he was teasing me. "Staying out of jail enough?" We ended the call.

Marching up to the counter at the Recorder's Office, I hoped I didn't need lots of data on Violet and Chet Brock.

Turned out I didn't. The clerk, a bouncy brunette with a streak of gray at her right temple, greeted me with a smile. When I told her I was looking for information about property owned by Violet Brock in Yavapai County, she spent a few moments on her computer and laughed. "Might be easier if you searched for what *isn't* owned by her. That woman must be one savvy investor. Her name pops up a lot."

"How about the names Wes or Lavender Sturgess."

"Hmm. Somebody's fond of flowers. Violet? Lavender?"

"Lavender is Violet's daughter."

"I'm Robin and my sister is Ursula, for the bear. My mom was a nature freak." She turned back to her keyboard. "Wes and Lavender Sturgess own property in Clarkdale. I don't see anything else. I won't see title transfers for a while, so there might be a few transactions not yet recorded. Anything I print out costs a buck."

"Another animal name," I said. I shook my head. "Nope, I have that address. But could I get a list of the properties Violet owned?"

"Owned? Is she deceased?"

"Would that affect my getting the list of properties?"

"No. Clerical curiosity." She returned her focus to the monitor.

"She died Monday."

"I'm sorry. I gather the vultures are circling."

I jerked upright. "Vultures?"

"People anxious to get their inheritance. We get that a lot here." She frowned. "You a lawyer? Work for one?"

"I'm a chef."

"Oh, wow. A good one? Should I visit your restaurant?"

I smiled but flinched inwardly. If only. "Yes, I am an excellent chef, but I don't have a restaurant. Yet." But I will, dang it, I will.

Her face fell. "I'm always up for new restaurants. We have some good ones in Prescott, but there's always room for another."

All the talk about chefs and restaurants made me hungry. Before I left, I'd ask Robin for a recommendation for lunch. "I gather this is also the place I'd find records of property that changed hands, like sales or transfers and stuff?"

"Same database, different query. Let me add that and we'll see what we get. But remember we might not have newer transactions."

I strolled out of the Recorder's offices with a small stack of papers and a recommendation for lunch. And even more questions about the motive for Violet's death.

14

Comfort Food and Conversation

I arrived back in Cottonwood at 4:00 and decided I'd have time to do some fishing. For clues, that is. So far, I confirmed that Violet owned a big batch of property in and around Cottonwood, some of it commercial, some of it residential, some of it zoned for agriculture. The documents didn't tell me who occupied those properties, nor did they tell me who might want Violet to sell them. When she'd crashed the ukulele intermission, she ranted about people who wanted her to . . . What? Give up her land? Sell her land? Was she talking about her kids, and how Lavender and Wes wanted to turn her cottage into a café? Or was it something or someone else? Someone with a desire for revenge for some ancient slight? Someone jealous of her wealth and power?

If the reason for her murder were as vague as long-held anger or other emotions, it might be hard to find. And why bother? Violet was old and her influence in Cottonwood was likely to fade.

My focus had to be on more tangible events, or on statements Violet or others had made.

People wanted to turn everything into wine-tasting rooms, Violet said.

True, the main street of historic Cottonwood boasted a wine-tasting room in every other building, and they all seemed to be bustling when I walked by. If so, the town council approved of the transition to wine and the accompanying tourism as the community's main source of income. Sedona had Cottonwood beat for hiking, vortexes and spiritual wellness, but Cottonwood and the surrounding area were reaping the benefits of its agricultural nature.

What were the reasons people killed? Love, twisted love, that is. That would include jealousy. Rage. Revenge. To keep a secret. Greed. Greed, the desire for money or profit, covered a lot and would be easier to investigate than people's emotions, which they could hide.

I decided to try one of those wine bars Violet detested, partly in search of a good lead. Maybe I'd encounter someone with information about Violet, someone willing to share that information, because I truly needed a lead. I had no clue who might have wanted the elderly woman dead.

My phone buzzed as I'd found a seat in the Merkin Vineyards Tasting Room and Osteria. I slipped back out the front door, because I hate seeing people on the phone when I'm in a restaurant.

Sergeant Doughty. I explained that I'd been out of cell reach and missed her call. She agreed I could come in the next day to sign my statement and answer a few more questions. The tendons in my neck tightened as if they were strings on a ukulele. I thought I'd answered every possible permutation of questions after I found Violet's body. Apparently not.

Was RK right? Were the cops eager to place the blame on out-of-towners? Specifically, on me? The sergeant had sounded cordial, but that was no doubt a ploy to lure me into a confession.

Seated again, my appetite gone, I ordered their special mac and cheese. I needed my strength and I deserved comfort food. Plus, I wanted to grill my server. She was a petite woman with spiky hair. Each time she reached for a dish from the prep kitchen's counter, her shirt pulled up and her pants inched down and I could see a tiny tattoo of a saguaro on her lower back.

Was the tattoo a conversation starter? Or would she think I was from the health department? If I'd had any, we could have compared tats, but I still hadn't gotten around to getting an ankle tattoo, mostly because I couldn't decide if I wanted a climbing rose, a cactus or a hawk.

I decided to go for it. If she cut me off in a conversation about ink, I could ask about a real estate agent, say I was considering moving to town.

After she brought my meal and a glass of rosé, I said, "Love that saguaro ink."

She yanked her T-shirt downward. "Sorry. I'm too short for the darn counter."

I smiled. "No worries. I like your tattoo. Wasn't commenting on anything else." When she stared at me in silence, I added, "I'm not from the health department or anything, just someone who keeps thinking about getting a tat and doesn't."

She stared at me a moment longer and then broke into a grin. "Thanks. When I asked the manager for a larger T-shirt, he told me I didn't need it, but he's always on my case if someone mentions the stupid tattoo, or that my skin shows."

"I'm no seamstress, but maybe you could sew a strip from another T on the bottom of that one."

"Next paycheck, I'm taking it to a seamstress here in town. I have no clue how to sew. Took all the science and shop classes in high school."

The bell rang for her order up, and she left to deliver it.

I needed more time with the server, so I ordered gelato. Okay, maybe I also sought a bit more comfort. I asked for coffee, as well. As she served me, I asked if she was new to town.

"To this café. I've lived here or in Sedona most of my life."

"Nice place to live," I said. "I'm thinking about it, but don't know if I can find something I can afford."

She shrugged. "Better here than Sedona. I used to have a trailer on the river, but they tore out the park and built more homes for the rich folks."

Our conversation continued between her taking and delivering orders, and me enjoying my gelato and coffee. We exchanged first names—hers was Lola—and I eventually asked if she knew a good real estate agent. "Depends on what you want, but there's a really nice guy who comes in here pretty often. Older fellow, in great shape. I think he's honest."

"And he knows Cottonwood well?"

"You can bet on that. Ernie, that's Ernest Whipple, seems to know every person who walks in here, too. Very friendly but polite." She winked at me. "He'd never mention my ink or the cut of my T-shirt." Her smile erased any censure. "I might have his card, but I'll bet he stuck one in the cork board in the hallway."

"Good suggestion. Anyone I want to steer clear of?"

She squinted. "I'm not sure I know you well enough to badmouth any of my customers. But most folks here in Cottonwood are cool."

As she placed my bill in front of me, she said, "You could visit the Cottonwood Chamber of Commerce. They know everyone and have lists of businesses and stuff. My aunt volunteers there."

I thanked her and left a generous tip before heading to the cork board to gather info on local services. I hoped "Miracle Worker" would be among them. Definitely something I needed.

I reminded myself to bring some fliers from Adventure Calls to post here. Tripp Chasen, Gabe's partner in Adventure Calls, the lead sales and booking guy at our company, continually reminded all of us guides to "always be closing," the ABCs of sales. I'd rather "Always Be Cooking."

The cork board told of a town with lots of entrepreneurial spirit, or at least with a lot of entrepreneurs. Cards for massage therapists—ooh, I longed for that one—personal chefs, psychics—maybe that would help—tax accountants, gardeners, upholsterers, meetings to recover from every addiction imaginable, roommates, and lo, real estate agents, cluttered the board.

I took photos of several interesting cards, including the massage therapist's and the psychic's cards. Who knew when one or both might come in handy? There was also a card for a mortgage broker, someone who might know a lot about who was buying up, or wanting to buy, property in Cottonwood. How I'd convince her to share that information was an unknown.

Back at the cottage, I checked out Ernie Whipple's website. His business covered the entire Verde Valley, with the majority in Cottonwood. I guessed that the lower-priced properties he bought and sold turned over more quickly than the million dollar-plus homes in Sedona. But what commissions those must bring. I decided to visit his office the next day.

15

The Perfect Agent

The next morning, I dressed conservatively for my police interrogation-slash-conversation. I put on black jeans, a deep blue short-sleeved shirt and a lightweight grey blazer. Ironing the blazer, which had lain too long at the bottom of my bag, was a bear, but worth it. I'd had it for ages and it remained my go-to topper when I wanted to look sophisticated. I looked so dull, I added a multicolored silk scarf one of my Adventure Calls clients had sent me when she visited France. Proof that some people valued my skills. It boosted my dragging spirits. The police department was on 6th Avenue quite near the library and other public safety buildings, not far from Old Cottonwood. The building, an attractive two-story sandstone brick structure, however, was obviously built quite recently. I passed the senior center on my way. I hoped I wouldn't have to stay in Cottonwood long enough to take advantage of that facility.

Sergeant Doughty was efficient and focused, perceptive and persistent. Also unfailingly polite. She started by informing me that she was now considering Violet's death suspicious. "Violet Brock's death was not from exposure or an accident. There was trauma to her throat indicating she'd been choked and the wound on her head seemed deeper than we'd expect if she'd fallen on the rocks. We have concluded that she went to the stream voluntarily Tuesday night, either with someone or alone, and was assaulted there." She paused and added, "Both the trauma to her throat and the head wounds were severe enough that she lost consciousness immediately, and didn't suffer."

I said nothing for several moments. My pulse beat in my forehead, and my breath suddenly became scant. I leaned forward like we'd learned in first aid, putting my head between my knees, to forestall fainting. Eventually I asked, "Am I still a suspect?

"We're pursuing all avenues." Did I mention her answers were annoyingly vague?

"So the person had to be pretty strong? More likely a man?"

"I can't comment on that."

"How about the man who brought her to Jerome when we all went to hear Ross's ukulele group? Leonard Something? No one told me his last name or anything about him."

"Hmm. They've been friends a long time," she said. Really very little, but I grasped that nugget because she'd thrown me so few.

"And he lives here in Cottonwood?"

"We're talking to all of Violet's friends and acquaintances, like we're talking to you and your fellow employee at Adventure Calls, Mr. Mustard. Interesting character," she added with a smile. And then she launched more questions about the tour, about Violet's anger with Adventure Calls, about her fall at Canyon de Chelly, until I considered seeking sanctuary at the senior center.

After I signed my typed statement and she'd come back into the quiet room where we'd talked before, I stood. "Look, am I or am I not a suspect in Violet's killing? This is getting to me."

"You're not going to like my answer, but here it is: We're exploring all avenues and talking to a lot of people. I knew, and liked Violet Brock, but there were times when I wanted to throttle her and I'm a cop. Therefore, I understand and, if you have anything more to tell me, I'm here to listen. If not, please let me know if you need to leave town and where you'll be."

"So. . . I'm not a really big suspect?"

She smiled, but I couldn't tell what the smile indicated. Either the woman enjoyed being enigmatic or it was her job to keep all suspects nervous. "Cottonwood is a small town. I gather you've been asking questions. That might be dangerous for you, but I can't stop you as long as you stay away from my crime scene." The hairs on the back of my neck prickled. Did she know I'd snuck into Violet's home? Surely Mateo had no reason to tell her and only Kirsten knew. I couldn't think why she'd tell the cops. I hoped. Besides, that wasn't where she'd died.

"Maybe Leah told you about the community barbecue we hold every Friday? It's a lot of fun, an opportunity to meet lots of people. It's this evening. I'm sure you'd be welcome to join us."

Was the detective asking me to do some sleuthing for her? I smiled. "That sounds like fun. I'll bring some bread. I bake when I'm nervous."

She laughed. "Never tell an investigator you're nervous." Her expression sobered. "I expect you to share anything you discover, Ms. Hunter. You have my number."

"And you have mine." I shook her hand, worried that mine might be sweaty, an indicator of guilt. But if I didn't shake her hand, that might look suspicious. Aieee. I strode out, trying for a jaunty, confident stride. I walked to the glass door leading to the lobby, turned and waved to her and pushed on the door. I bashed straight into the inward opening door with a loud thunk. I backed away, rubbing my bonked hand and tried again with better luck.

The receptionist at the front of the building almost succeeded in hiding her smirk. I stumbled to my car.

I found a coffee house called the Jerona Café and treated myself to a breakfast burrito and coffee before going in search of the realtor. Lola at Merkin's said that Ernie Whipple knew everyone, so maybe he knew Leonard the escort. Or I could ask Ross, Mateo's boss, if I was allowed inside the music store by my angry brother. Despite the police detective's warning that snooping might put me in danger, I needed to pursue this to the end. And hope the end was not mine.

The office was in the new part of Cottonwood, in the neighborhood of the Chamber of Commerce according to Google. I walked into Verde Properties and was greeted warmly by a woman about my age. Compared to the realtors whose photos adorned the entry, she was not imposing—pale blond hair in a short bob, pale skin, pale blue eyes, pants and blouse in forgettable neutral tones. If she aspired to become a realtor, she'd need a major makeover. But her smile was warm.

"Welcome to Verde Properties. How may we help you find your perfect home today?"

I imagined the greeting was a canned one dictated to her by one of the stars on the wall, but she delivered it convincingly and as if it were as fresh as newly baked bread. It elicited a spontaneous smile from me. I held up a finger and took in the displayed portraits. After a moment, I said, "My name is Madrone Hunter. I'd like to speak with Mr. Whipple."

Her smiled broadened. "Lots of women would like to do more than speak with him." She threw her fingers to her lips and cast quick glances in all directions. "I cannot believe I said that. He's my boss and he's a wonderful guy and that was *so* inappropriate."

"People tell me I sometimes bring out the worst in them," I replied with a grin. "I didn't hear a word, I swear."

She put her hands together as if in prayer and gazed upward. "Thank you. Let me try again." She heaved in a deep breath. "I'm sure Ernie can fit you in, but you may have to wait a bit. Is there someone else who might help you?"

"No, thank you. He was recommended to me. I can wait."

She rose with smooth grace from behind her desk and said, "Let me pop in his office and check his schedule."

I'd have thought a modern real estate agency would have digital calendars, but what did I know? Maybe this woman had trouble keeping tabs on all seven of the people whose whitened teeth glinted from the wall behind me. While I waited, I ran through a mental checklist of my investigative tasks for today.

I wanted to ask Ernie Whipple about Violet's properties in town. I had to find out who Leonard was—last name, occupation, relationship to Violet, and I needed more info about Ven and Wes Sturgess. How? I could do some sleuthing on social media, and I would definitely attend tonight's BBQ. Maybe RK would get some good background on Violet from his friend Fiona, as well.

I thumbed through a couple of magazines that lay on the table beside me and discovered that home prices in the Verde Valley ranged from reasonable to out of this world. Cottages like Violet's could sell for half a million dollars on the right street, in the right condition. Planned developments were springing up in Cottonwood and Clarkdale. People who couldn't afford five million-plus for a home in Sedona could find floorplans under 2000 square feet in the three hundred thousands. Still seemed like a lot to me, but I had never shopped for a home. I'd spent some dreaming time looking at spaces for a restaurant, so I knew more about price per square foot for commercial properties, and I was betting even Cottonwood would be beyond my budget.

A man in his fifties, possibly sixties, with steel gray hair and a well-trimmed white beard, approached me, hand outstretched. "I'm Ernie Whipple. Pleased to meet you, Ms. Hunter." His grip was perfect—dry, firm but not painful. He kept my hand a few seconds too long, stared into my eyes, and . . . My breath caught. This man was definitely a silver fox. The receptionist winked at me from behind his back, obviously saying, "Told you so."

"If my luck is with me, you're a house Hunter," he continued. "Get it?"

How an innocent name like Hunter could have caused me so much grief over the years is a mystery to me, but it has. Kids who can't remember their multiplication tables were exceedingly clever about coming up with ways to tease another child about his or her name. I'd heard most of it, from what I might be hunting for to unsavory rhymes with my last name. But this man's smile erased any annoyance. What a charmer.

"I might be, one day. But not today," I said. This honest approach might have been a mistake. I could have imagined hours, maybe even days of pleasure in Ernie Whipple's company, in search of the perfect place to light. "I'm told you're someone who knows a lot about Cottonwood."

He grinned. "Houses, land, people, some politics, I'm your go-to guy. History? A little. Geology? Not so much." He gestured toward his office. "Come on in and ask away. I'm free for a while." As we passed his threshold, he said, "Cynthia Ann, could you bring some coffee, please? Or would you prefer tea or water?" he asked me.

"Coffee, black, but I could do with a glass of water, as well."

Once we were settled, drinks at hand, I explained who I was and why I needed information about Violet Brock's property holdings.

He gave me an assessing look. "Ah, yes, poor Violet. I'm guessing you're afraid they'll lay the blame on you because you found her. Or on Mateo."

That silenced me. I hadn't mentioned Mateo more than to say I was in town to visit my brother. Whipple was well-informed. Not sure how to respond, I said nothing. Most people dislike silence.

Whipple didn't disappoint. "I've known Violet my whole life, with some noticeable gaps when I was away. She and my parents were contemporaries." He grinned again. "I'm old, but not that old."

"Not old at all," I assured him. I rolled my hand to encourage him to continue.

"Violet's always been outspoken, but honest. Didn't tolerate fools. Her husband was a softy, but a good businessman. Those two had a lot to do with Cottonwood's success, with the revitalization of Historic Cottonwood. Until the council decided to focus on wine and wine tasting. Grapes are a relatively new crop around here, and until recently, the wine wasn't much to speak of." He tilted his head. "Some maintain it will never be like the Napa Valley, Oregon, or southwestern Idaho, but tourists do love to taste wine."

He sat back in his chair. "Violet and Chet started out with a grocery store but expanded, bought property, turned the store into a gift boutique before folks in this town knew how to spell it." He chuckled. "Truth be told, I'm pretty sure there's still a lot of folks who can't spell boutique. The Brocks had vision. She mourned him, but never lost her grip or that vision for what they wanted Cottonwood to be." His eyes darkened. "Her outspokenness turned more into bitterness as she got older. Not sure why. She's—she was—opposed to all the wine-tasting stores. I don't think she was a teetotaler. I guess we don't need reasons for what we do, but hey, it can help."

"I gather she made a lot of people angry with her opposition to . .

. What? The wine tastings, other innovations in Cottonwood?"

Whipple's eyes narrowed. "Good question. One thing that irked a number of people, myself included, was her adamant refusal to sell any of her property, even when the offered price was way above market. Her stubbornness put the kibosh on at least one development and forced a couple of others to change their plans, downsize." He paused. "Which means people lost money and no one likes to lose money, myself included."

I leaned forward. This might be a bone big enough to chew on. "I gather this wasn't a one-time thing, but can you tell me who might have lost the most because of her refusal to sell?"

He smiled and pursed his lips. "I'm thinking that would be . . . me."

I leaned back. Drat. Yet another suspect, this one suave and kinda sexy. I gave him an interested but non-accusatory look. I hoped.

"I focus mostly on residential properties," he continued, "but I was a partner in a housing development company that had to backtrack big time because of dear old Violet." He drained his coffee. "But not enough to kill her. If I killed everyone who annoyed me, or even those who bilked me on a real estate deal, I wouldn't have time to sell property or go hiking. Have to become a serial killer."

"Really." I cocked my head. "I'd heard real estate was cutthroat, but not that bad."

"You'd be surprised the shenanigans people will get up to when they see riches in their future."

"Would you be willing to tell me who your partner or partners were in the development company?"

He smiled. "If I don't, I'm sure you'd be able to find out. So let me save you some time. Although, let me add, I don't see either of them killing Violet. She's been a thorn in their sides, and in mine, for years, with her refusal to part with even an acre of land. And none of us has killed her yet. To be perfectly honest, she's getting on in years, and developers know everything about patience. I'd be happy to show you the development. It's a gem, even if a bit smaller than we'd hoped," he added with a twinkle.

I gave him my best "I'm waiting patiently" look. Sort of like our old Golden retriever hoping for a walk.

"Leonard Anderson and Isabella Garcia."

Leonard? Surely not a common name. I tried to keep my expression neutral. "Is that the same Leonard who took Violet to Jerome the other evening?"

I hoped my neutral expression worked better than Whipple's attempt at innocent. "They're friends, but I don't know if they're dating."

"I'm sure it was merely a friendly gesture." I paused. "But remember, he *was* the last person to see Violet alive. By his account, he dropped her off around 9:00."

"Leonard's a great guy. Always ready to help out. And Isabella lives in Sedona, when she's not globe-trotting." He steepled his fingers. "Any bad feelings any of us had are forgotten by now. Water under the bridge. Or maybe I should say that bad feelings about it are as scarce as water in Arizona."

I remained silent, hoping he would fill it, but the man was in sales. Knew that trick very well. I wasn't going to get anything more out of him about that little cabal, so I ventured elsewhere. So far, Ernie Whipple had been forthcoming, even if I suspected he was hiding a few things. I'd have to figure out how to investigate the development more thoroughly. "What's the name of the development? I'd like to drive by." At his smile, I added, "I'm a Tucsonan through and through, when I'm not traveling with Adventure Calls. But you never know."

"Vista Rioja." He handed me a printed prospectus on the development. "I'd be happy to give you a private tour, anytime. A couple of the models are still available."

Even though I'd told him I'd never move here? You had to be an optimist to be in sales, I guessed. Or . . . was he interested in me as a woman? Or was flirting simply a hobby for Ernie Whipple? I decided to savor it and smiled at him. "If I'm not arrested, I'll let you know."

"Surely you're kidding? They can't seriously think you'd be angry enough to kill poor Violet."

"I hope not." I leaned forward. "But I believe in being proactive. Who else should I be talking to? Can you think of anyone who'd gain from Violet's death? I gather her daughter and son-in-law had hoped to make use of her cottage. And her granddaughter would get the store, I assume."

He leaned back in his chair, no doubt anxious to distance himself from my suppositions. So much for flirting with me. "That's absurd. Have you met Lavender Sturgess? She used to work as a communications dispatcher. Saving lives, helping people. She'd never harm anyone, let alone her own mother. I've known her since she was tiny and I have nothing but admiration for her. And Kirsten is an angel to work with Violet in the store. She simply has no mean bones in her body." He stood. "Now, if there's nothing more . . . I do have some work I need to focus on."

I stood and offered my hand. "It was a pleasure to meet you. Thank you so much for your time, Mr. Whipple."

Kinda weird. First he's flirting and offering to show me his latest development, and then he's hustling me out the door. I must have hit a sore spot, but I had no clue when. Sigh.

I left the offices of Verde Properties, pondering the interesting omission in Ernie Whipple's response. He had not sung the praises of Wes Sturgess. Had not uttered his name.

I reached the street and heard my name being called. "Ms. Hunter. Madrone. I know you want to learn all you can about Violet Brock and her family. We have a potluck barbecue each week at a local park and a lot of townsfolk show up. Folks who used to work with Ven at the Communications Center, cops, Town Council members. It's this evening. I would enjoy being your escort."

Was the silver fox asking me for a date? Flirting with a murder suspect? I smiled. "I would enjoy going with you."

"The pleasure will be all mine." We agreed to meet at Riverfront Park at 5:30 that evening.

I shook my head. That had been a confusing encounter, sort of like fencing. Advance, parry, advance farther, retreat. I had learned Leonard Anderson's full name and occupation, along with the name of another possible suspect, Isabella Garcia. And of course Ernie had reason to dislike her, although somehow I doubted he did. Hard to know where you were with Ernie Whipple. Still, I looked forward to seeing him again. I told myself it was only for the introductions he could make for me, but myself wasn't buying it.

16

It's That Easy!

I slid onto the stool at the bar counter at Crema at 1:15. They closed at 2:00. Not too late if I ordered quickly. I was surprised to see my server of the previous day, Lola, behind the bar. She greeted me like an old friend when she placed the menu before me.

"We close here at 2:00, and I work the late shift over at Merkin's." While I scanned the daily specials, she painstakingly peeled hard-boiled eggs. "They're for our Haunted Bloodys, Bloody Marys with a whole hard-boiled egg. Very popular and a huge pain prepping enough eggs."

"I'll have the BLTA. I need some spoiling. And when you get back, bring a spoon and I will demonstrate a potential solution to your eggs-traordinary problem."

She gave me a puzzled look and shrugged. "Whatever. Good choice in sandwiches."

Once back, she offered me two spoons—one a teaspoon, the other a soup spoon. "If you show me how to speed up the egg prep, I'll be your friend forever. And I'll even forgive your fibbing to me yesterday."

I flushed, head to feet, I swear. "You saw through me? And here I thought I was the new Sherlock Holmes."

"What we do not need is one more Sherlock Holmes, or even a female version, say Shirley Holmes." She smiled. "You forgot this is a small town, especially Old Town. You ate breakfast here with your adorable brother and another interesting guy. No way I wouldn't have heard about it. I like Mateo. In fact, if he and Kirsten don't make it . . ."

"If you think I'm a bad detective, you should see my matchmaking skills. Non-existent. However, I am an excellent chef and I do know how to peel hard-boiled eggs lickety split."

She stood at the ready. "Hit it."

"No," I said. "*You* hit it. Crack the egg all over. Rolling it works. Then take the spoon, probably the teaspoon, you decide, and edge it under the shell, under that inner skin. I like to start at the air pocket at the top." I waited until she caught up to me. I wanted to snatch up an egg and demonstrate but the health department might object. "Okay. Now wiggle the spoon, and work it around the entire egg. It usually works like a charm." I watched her do three eggs before the bell signaling an order up rang. "Good work."

She retrieved my sandwich and coleslaw and placed it before me. "You are a total lifesaver. Why have I never learned this technique before?"

"We Cordon Bleu chefs rarely share our secrets," I said.

Her eyes widened. "Get out of town. Cordon Bleu? For real?"

I laughed. "Nah. Wanted to see if my lying skills totally sucked."

"You got me. So, what did you think of Ernie?"

I focused on my lunch to hide my discomfort. My cheeks burned. After I chewed and swallowed, I said, "He invited me to the town potluck tonight."

"Whoa. Fancy chef and fast worker, too. You're gonna have to share more of your secrets with me. Want something to drink? Our espresso bar is open and the creme brulée latte is to die for. Or I could make you a cocktail."

"I'll go for the latte. This half-witted sleuth needs every brain cell working, so no cocktail."

She spun around to the espresso machine and within a few minutes placed an aromatic cup of foam-topped coffee in front of me. She lifted a jar of cinnamon, raised an eyebrow.

"That's it, cinnamon. I could become a regular here. So far, I've loved breakfast, lunch and latte."

She shot me a smile as she raced through half a dozen eggs. "It's a good job, for now. So how can I help you stay one step ahead of the long arm of the law?" She paused. "Which has to be a mixed metaphor or something."

"Metaphors, espresso, cocktails. You must be a mixologist. I'd love to hear more about the 'for now,' but I'm gonna take you up on the offer of help. I'm looking to find out about Violet's investments, her properties, and who wanted her to sell. No one at a bank's gonna share—they'd be breaking the law. I don't know, maybe a financial advisor? Investment guru?"

"For sure you need to visit the credit union. I have no clue if Violet banked there, but the manager is a hottie, and he used to date Kirsten Sturgess. For my money, he wishes he still did, but your brother aced him out. No love lost there, I'll bet. He might not share financial info, but he might know about the family from when they dated." She gave me directions to the credit union, then paused to write up my check. "We're closed and I need to finish up. You can pay me."

I jumped from the stool. "I am so, so sorry. I hate people who overstay closing."

"Big tips make up for anything." At my expression, she added, "Gotcha! I was the one doing the talking. It's not a problem. The guy's name is Greg Yarborough. He's an insatiable flirt, but I think he's harmless, unless you work for him. Kind of a hardass boss, I hear from a friend who works there."

"This has been fun, Lola. If I'm not arrested, I'd like to buy you a cocktail or a beer before I leave town."

"Get out of here, nobody's gonna arrest you. Especially not before the barbecue, if they find out you're a chef. Bring something wonderful. I'll be there. You can catch me up on your detecting."

I left Crema, thinking I could squeeze in a visit to The Whistle Stop after a conversation with Greg Yarborough at the credit union. I yearned for Mateo's forgiveness and had to find a way to earn it. I was glad he was living in this small, friendly community. I liked Lola and looked forward to seeing her again. However, she was a friendly and chatty person. It would take no time for any of Cottonwood's populace that didn't already realize it, to know I was looking into Violet's death. At least those who weren't already certain that I had murdered my former client.

17

Stop, You're Chilling Me

I walked into the main office of the credit union Greg Yarborough managed and joined a line of harried people. The woman in front of me turned and said, "Can you believe it's happened again? They'd better fix that dang ATM pretty soon or I'll have to move my account. And I'm sure as heck gonna let Greg know it."

Uh oh. The odds of my finding Greg Yarborough in a chatty, receptive mood were narrowing. I gave the woman what I hoped was a conspiratorial shrug and smile. Can a shrug be conspiratorial? I don't think she bought it. I perked up my ears and heard several other muttered comments about the ATM sprinkled with curses.

The credit union was in a one-story, modern building of concrete blocks and stucco. It had a dark plate-glass window and double glass entry doors. Its design was like a restaurant and I wondered if it did serve as one in an earlier decade. Like any banking institution, tellers stood behind barred windows and customers waited in line for the next available teller. Given the angry atmosphere, I thought the tellers might be grateful for those bars today.

I didn't want to conduct any banking, so there wasn't a reason for me to wait in line, but I feared for my safety if I tried to bypass the queue. "I'm not an actual customer," I said to my angry friend in front of me. "I'm here to meet the manager."

She smirked. "If you're looking for a job, go somewhere else. This place is always having problems. Still, their fees are lower and the puny interest on savings is a little higher." She pointed to a man seated at a desk almost hidden by the teller's cages. "Greg's back there, hiding from me and several other irate members." She waved me past her.

Oh, yeah. People joined a credit union and became members. In the past you had to belong to a certain group, like firefighters or a school district, to join, but the membership requirements were more lax these days. Do you breathe? Walk upright? Have lungs instead of gills? Maybe live in the same county?

I edged past the angry line of customers and stepped toward the desk in the back. I deduced, good sleuth that I was, that it was Greg Yarborough, since the nameplate said so. He waited, hands clasped on top of his desk until I had stood there some long, countable seconds. Eventually he stood and extended his hand, which slipped in and out of mine in seconds, as if he feared contamination.

"Well, well, it must be the older sister. You're the spitting image of Mateo, except in better shape." He let his eyes trail down my body, making me want to puke.

"You know my brother?" I asked with a forced smile.

"Sure do. You planning to move to town and take over someone else's relationship, like baby bro'?"

I squinted at him. "Whoa, there. Stop with the venom. I have no idea what you're talking about."

He didn't just roll his eyes, he rolled his head in a one-eighty. "You'll hear soon enough. I'm the jilted lover. Kirsten's ex." He let that sink in, and apparently recognizing that I didn't know the story, he oh-so-kindly clarified. "I'm the one who'll be waiting to console poor Kirsten when your brother gets arrested for killing Violet Brock. Not that I'm shedding tears over the old witch's demise."

He hadn't offered me a seat but I took the one in front of his desk. It was clear that charm wasn't going to get me anything from this vengeful man. "You might want to cool it with the accusations," I said. "And if Violet was a customer here, her family won't be pleased to learn what a spiteful person you can be."

"Threats? From a woman who faces losing her job? I'm shivering in terror." Even with the nasty smile, his face was put together the right way. Strong, rugged cheek bones, narrow nose, dark blond hair styled perfectly. In his late twenties or early thirties, and well-dressed, Greg Yarborough looked like someone on his way up. In his opinion. To me, he was a disgusting worm who wished both me and my brother ill because he couldn't hang onto his girlfriend.

An older, stout woman with spiky gray hair sat at a desk that I hoped was in earshot of our conversation. I raised my voice. "Sour grapes are not an attractive feature, Mr. Yarborough. And I thought you were here to serve the customer, not insult her."

"You are so not a customer. And not planning to be one, I hope. Come to think of it, why are you here?" Clearly, he wanted to convince me to leave, soonest. Yarborough curled his lip at me as if he smelled something off. I prayed that gray-haired woman was a gossip with the ears of a bat.

I returned his sneer with a bland smile. "I had thought to discover a little about Violet's property holdings in Cottonwood."

"Even you should be aware that I cannot share any information about our clients." I must have given something away, because he added. "Or even if Violet was or was not a client. Everyone in town knows that Violet was wealthy. If you were looking to con her out of some money, it would have been better if she stayed alive. Shame your brother wasn't aware of your plans." He tried to stare me down, but I stared right back. What a creep. If Kirsten had fallen for him, then she lost points from me.

"Since neither my brother nor I killed Violet or had our eyes on her fortune, I find your accusation insulting, not to mention slanderous."

"That's a load of crap. Your brother has eyes on her fortune. Why else woo Kirsten?"

That was so priceless I couldn't stifle a laugh. "If Kirsten had any regrets about breaking off with you, that comment puts the end to them." I rose from the uncomfortable chair. "It has been an incredible pleasure meeting you, Greg."

I made my way past the still long line of customers and left the building. I needed a shower after chatting with that scum. But I would have to postpone that pleasure. I wanted to talk with Mateo, if I could convince him to break his angry silence.

All I'd learned from that encounter was that Kirsten might not have the best taste in men, in the past, at least. Also that I hoped never to encounter that creep again. But I couldn't see why he would want Violet dead or injured, even though I'd love to pin any crime at all on him.

Another theory came to mind. What if Violet had been as opposed to Greg dating Kirsten as she was to Mateo? And what if Greg thought he could capitalize on Mateo's animosity toward his girlfriend's grandmother and frame him for her murder?

Possible, but lame. If Greg wanted to frame Mateo, he would have left clues, pointed the spotlight on him. Of course, I don't know what the police found.

18

Whistling Dixie

After my growling match with Greg Yarborough, the jealous jilted lover and a barely-possible suspect, I deserved a margarita or at least a Modelo Negra. But saint that I was, I postponed pleasure for duty. I had to see Mateo, get him to talk with me, to cooperate in our search for the real murderer of Violet Brock before one of us was arrested for murder.

Sure, Sergeant Doughty had been pleasant, and didn't seem to be targeting me or Mateo as potential killers. But small towns can be small-minded and focused on protecting their own. My brother was new to town and I was an outsider. It would be a lot simpler for their community if one of us, or RK, another outsider, proved to be the culprit. And, darn it, we all had reason to want Violet stopped.

None of us, however, would consider a permanent solution to the Violet problem. I'm all for negotiating, talking things out. RK would avoid the situation as long as possible and then hope his charm and humor could win her over. He had a deep reverence for all things living that he would never violate.

Mateo? How had we grown so far apart that I wasn't certain of my brother's reaction to Violet's opposition to his romance with Kirsten? He'd always had a temper and a violent reaction to injustice. He'd come home from school bloodied fairly often after calling out bullies or liars. I admired him for that. Violet had verged on bullying in her insistence on controlling Kirsten, not only at work but in her personal life. Mateo hated that, disliked Violet. However, my brother was a gentle soul with a kind spirit. I knew this in my heart, even if my brain spun out a few wild possibilities of what he might have done if Violet had succeeded in destroying their relationship. I told myself those were thoughts and thoughts were not reality.

Reality was that Mateo Hunter had an innate goodness that had landed him in trouble before.

Reality was that he'd been arrested for possession and use of opioids. Reality was, he hadn't narced on his friends. Friends who convinced him to steal from the pharmacist he worked for while a student at the local community college. Torpedoing any chance of a career in health services. Reality was that he owned up to his addiction and took the punishment and treatment and that made him an ex-convict, a surefire person of interest for the Cottonwood police. My reality was that he was my brother and I would do whatever it took to help him. Uh-oh. Making me another person of interest, even without my antagonism toward Violet.

Reality was, I had to convince Mateo we'd both be better off by cooperating with each other to find out who wanted Violet out of the picture. But first I had to convince him to even talk to me. Maybe I could find an ally in Ross Zelinger, his boss. I knew how stubborn Mateo was. I had to get him to forgive me. So, if Mateo wouldn't see me, maybe Ross would help.

I walked into The Whistle Stop and saw my brother dusting shelves near the register at the back of the room. He looked up when the brass bell sounded someone was entering the shop. The welcoming smile fell off his face faster than a pancake dropped from a spatula. He turned toward the back of the store and entered the area marked "Staff Only." In moments a smiling Ross greeted me with a wave and "Hey, Madrone, how's it hanging?" Yep, aging hippie. I was pretty confident I had nothing hanging.

We met and shook and I said, "Not very well, if my brother left because he saw me come in."

His face flushed. "He, um, had some errands to run and was afraid the shop might close if he didn't hurry?"

"Nice try, Ross. You might want to stick to ukulele or art instead of improv." I sighed. "I need to talk to Mateo. Did he happen to tell you why he's avoiding me?"

He extended both hands, palms up. "I assumed you'd know."

"He might be a little irked at me for getting him in trouble with Kirsten." I moved my gaze to the LPs in the carrels beside me. I didn't want to share my family issues with this man, with anyone for that matter.

"Ah. That's why he's been secretly texting madly all afternoon. Without the answering pings he thinks I'm too old to hear."

"I was hoping you'd become a sort of father figure, someone he'd confide in. And you could convince him I have only his best interests at heart."

His raucous laughter bounced around the store. "Me? A father figure? To your brother? That young man is far more mature than I." He wiped tears from his eyes. "And besides, I'm his boss. You don't confide in your boss."

I fumbled for words, not sure how much to tell Ross. "Not in some bosses. But you seem like a good guy. Willing to give him a chance, even when he's on parole."

His eyes widened. "Mateo is on parole?"

Wait. No. He had to know. Didn't he? Could the floor open up and suck me down? Should I crawl out now or later? "Umm. You're kidding, right?"

He shot me a huge smile. "Kidding. But your little brother is not a typical jailbird. He is an excellent employee and a model citizen."

If he's not a murderer or back on opioids because of me. I took a deep breath and let it out. "I know he's one of the good ones and that he's been very happy here in Cottonwood. But . . ."

"You're concerned that the first person the cops will suspect is a convicted felon and former drug addict."

I nodded.

"In Tucson, maybe. In fact, most places. But our police force is honest and hard-working."

"The ones you know, maybe. But he's the easiest target."

"It's possible. I'm gonna assume they want to find the right person. I assured Willa Doughty that Mateo's one of the good ones."

"She talked to you." I swallowed. "About Mateo."

"She's talking to everyone close to Violet." He laughed. "Even me. Even though we've been friends forever. Trust me, forever is a long time. She was an outspoken proponent of what she believed in, never afraid of disagreeing, always ready to defend what she thought was right. I admire that in a person. That's one of the things I like about Mateo. He's loyal. He will not let anyone speak ill of Kirsten, even the girl's own grandmother. When it comes to his friends, Mateo is loyal. To a fault? I don't know."

I examined the floor. "Yes. He is loyal." I knew that too well. Wait. Was Ross implying he thought it possible Kirsten stole from her grandmother? A suspicion I definitely did not want to confirm. "I'm, umm, trying to find out more about Violet's life here in Cottonwood, maybe people who were angry with her? So far, I've found one man who really, really, dislikes Mateo. And I'm not sure he's all that fond of me, now."

"Ah. You've met Greg Yarborough. Jealousy is such an ugly emotion. Poor lad." He cleared his throat. "It enraged Greg when Violet pulled most of her finances out of his credit union. She didn't like his relationship with Kirsten any more than she liked her granddaughter seeing Mateo."

I tilted my head. "Really? I wouldn't have thought Violet could have been that petty."

His expression darkened. "Petty? You have no idea. Violet truly believed she knew what was right and that those who disagreed with her should be mowed down. Her weapon of choice was usually money, sometimes property. I guess it was her way of controlling things. We all want to be in control, no?"

We do? I tried to remember what stoic philosophers say about control—we should focus on what we can control and accept what we cannot change. I remembered it, but didn't always practice it. Did I ever? But Ross made a good point about Violet—she had control issues. Maybe losing her husband made her recognize the fragility of life, but instead of enjoying each day, accepting that she couldn't control anything except her own reaction to events, she tried to control events and people. And maybe, like a lot of people, she assumed that wealth means power over people. True only if they're willing to give you power. Which, if you continue that thought, meant that I shouldn't worry about losing my job. I'd do the best I could to find the truth in this sad situation and then accept whatever decision Gabe and Tripp made.

I could not control the future, only my response to it. How heavy was that?

"Earth to Madrone?" Ross said. "You there, my dear? You seem lost in thought."

I shook my head. "Sorry. Sometimes I do drift off. Guess I'm feeling sad that Violet felt that way, felt she had to use money to control people. Kirsten loved her, and I gather her daughter did, too." Totally off subject, totally drifting from the "line of inquiry" I needed to follow to absolve myself, my brother, and RK from a charge of murder. I asked Ross, "Do you have children?"

With every good reason, Ross shot me a look of total confusion. "Helen has a son and a daughter from her first marriage. She'd tell you they were the best things to come from that relationship. They're grown now. The boy lives in Phoenix and we see him often. The daughter lives in Boston." He smiled. "What might that have to do with your investigation into Violet's death I have no idea."

"Neither do I. My brain wanders sometimes. I was considering Leonard, the poor man Violet coerced into taking her to Jerome the other night. What's their relationship?"

"Ah, Leonard. He's another old friend, a long-time resident of Cottonwood. He invests in land, but is usually wise enough not to try to convince Violet to sell her property to him. He and her late husband were great friends, used to play chess and hike together."

"I'd like to talk with him. He was so embarrassed that night." I forced a small chuckle. "Poor man."

"We're all accustomed to Violet and her occasional tantrums. Leonard wasn't embarrassed enough to kill, I'm sure."

How can he be so sure? Because he killed Violet? Or because he had faith in an old friend? My neck hairs rose. No one really knows the unexpressed thoughts of others. "Still, I'd like to talk with him."

"I'll give you his contact information. Come back to my office."

I trailed Ross to his office in the back of the store and was treated to a few small works of his art on the walls. He gave me Leonard's phone number and politely told me he had some inventory work to do before closing up for the night.

"One more thing," I said. "I understand Leonard was a partner in a development that Violet tried to stop. Do you know of other times when she stalled people's plans?"

"She owned a lot of property here in Cottonwood. And when she was on the city council, people often asked her to recuse herself on certain votes. That amused my old friend, who went ahead and voted as she chose. But I don't know any specifics, at least I can't think of any right now."

"Thanks, Ross. If you get the chance, maybe you can put in a good word for me with my brother. We all do things we regret. I'd like a chance to apologize."

He frowned. "I'll relay your message, my dear. But I'm his employer, not his counselor. I make it a policy not to become too involved with my employees' personal lives."

I left, realizing I hadn't gotten much from Ross. If I intended to discover Violet's killer, I'd have to become a better investigator or get darn lucky. I drifted home for a quick shower before I met Ernie, hoping I could throw together something to take to the potluck and still meet him in time.

19

Grilling Time

If you imagine Arizona as one big, dry, hot desert, you've forgotten its water. The Grand Canyon has the Colorado River and Cottonwood has the Verde River. In Cottonwood, the Verde River that runs beside Riverfront Park is a placid, wide, slow-moving stream, at least in September. It's a great river to raft in the spring and has wild water up to Class 5 in some places—but those are south of Cottonwood. Here, beside Riverfront Park, cottonwoods—surprise—lined the creek banks. The park had a lot of fun features for a small town—a disc golf course, an inline hockey rink, an adjacent dog park, even a skateboard park.

Several years of drought in Arizona and throughout the West had reduced water flow, but as I gazed at the water meandering past me, I imagined myself paddling along in a tiny kayak. I'd much prefer that solitary activity to my present—watching four of the park's five ramadas fill with Cottonwood denizens. They seemed to enjoy themselves—eating, gossiping, eyeing their kids on the swings, listening to music from a small bluegrass group. But there were so many of them.

Dizziness swept over me, whether from the loud music blaring with raucous abandon from the nearest ramada, the lingering heat, or my determination to sort through this crowd of people and find a killer, I wasn't certain. I sat on an accommodating, low cement bench and chanted to myself that all was well, I was well. Sometimes it worked if I started soon enough after I felt queasy or dizzy. Not that it happened often. I was a healthy woman.

My companion/escort—I refused to consider Ernie, who was, after all, on my list of suspects, my date—was off to deposit our contributions to the potluck supper at the central ramada. I'd wrapped three loaves of pumpkin bread, one with chocolate chips, and threw together a quinoa casserole and he'd brought a case of Corona—not a six-pack, a whole case of twenty-four bottles. Considering how many people I saw toting similar amounts of beer, I hoped most folks lived near or watched out for one another like the folks in my mother's neighborhood in Tucson.

I gazed at the people wandering around, hoping to see someone I knew. Lavender and Wes Sturgess arrived from the direction of the parking lot, stopped every few feet by people offering condolences. Had Kirsten warned them away from me? Told them I'd been snooping around Violet's home? They were joined by Ross and Helen Zelinger, Helen engulfing Ven in a lengthy hug. I hoped by now that Kirsten had forgiven Mateo. Even though it worried me to see two recovering addicts together, they seemed well-matched—and happy, until I messed things up.

Ernie returned, carrying two beers and a plate of finger foods. I hadn't mentioned my dizziness, so I accepted the beer with thanks and a smile and stood. "I bet you want me to point out likely suspects, or at least people who had business dealings with Violet," he said. "I feel like stroking a luxurious mustache and speaking with a Belgian accent, if only I could."

"I hope you're kidding. I would appreciate being introduced to Violet's old friends and possible frenemies, but I don't want you to get involved. I'm glad you invited me." I gestured widely with my arms.

He beamed at me. "Truth be told, I'd take any excuse to spend time with a lovely lady like yourself."

I twinkled back at him, as much as I ever twinkled. "Wow. Silver tongue to match your silver hair. No surprise you're great at real estate."

"Born to be a salesman, they say. If only I could succeed so well with women."

I laughed, relieved I'd lost my dizzy feeling. "From what I hear, you're pretty good in that area, as well."

Ernie blushed, a reaction I'd assumed he'd long ago overcome. "Since my wife died, I do enjoy the company of a variety of women, but no one compares," he said softly. "Still, you gotta keep up the image."

I touched his arm. "How long has it been?"

"Eight years. You'd think I'd be over it, but she was a gem."

"Do you have children?"

"A son, who lives in Los Angeles, pursuing 'the dream.'"

"Acting?"

"No. Graphics art for film. Maybe he'll be the next George Lucas and will support me in my dotage."

"Stranger things have happened." We clinked beer bottles. "To dreams," I said.

He raised an eyebrow. "Some dreams are shorter term," he said.

"And yet, they're still dreams," I said. We both sat on the bench and after a short time I asked him, "If you see Leonard Anderson, could you introduce me? I have his contact information, but we haven't caught up yet."

"If you'll be okay on your own, I have a bit of schmoozing to do. If I take you with, everyone in town will think we're shacking up."

I smiled. "A compliment to me, but I'm fine on my own."

We agreed to catch up later by the barbecue, where burgers and dogs were being grilled.

* * *

When I stood up and decided to do some obligatory mingling, the dizziness threatened again. I began some serious self-talk. "I am perfectly healthy, perfectly capable, perfectly functioning, perfectly human." I repeated the mantra, alternating with sips of my beer.

I jumped when an arm encircled my shoulders. "You must be dead serious about solving this case if you show up at a party," my brother said.

Only Mateo and a few very close friends know how nervous big parties make me. I hate trying to remember names of people I haven't seen for years, remember which facts are public knowledge and which are privileged information. Hate being nice to people I really despise and hate not having enough time for a good conversation and to get to know intriguing new acquaintances. And because of all that, I want to drink too much and have to keep a strict eye on myself. Not an easy feat. Big parties for me are a form of torture. But sometimes they're a necessity.

I don't know why none of that bothers me when I'm guiding for Adventure Calls. Maybe 'cause I'm paid to do it? In reality, because I'm there to share with my guests something they may have never before seen or experienced. I wear a guide/public relations hat so much better than a party hat.

I cuddled in closer to Mateo and asked, "Does this mean you're starting to forgive me?"

"Maybe. Starting. A little. But why subject yourself to this?"

"I could pretend I'm circulating and trying to dig up business for Adventure Calls." Which, come to think of it, wasn't a bad entrée into conversations. And an important aspect of my job.

He tilted me away and looked into my eyes. "But?"

"But maybe you don't realize how much at risk you, I, and RK are, as prime suspects in Violet's murder."

"Even if I do, and that's only a maybe, we should leave it to the cops."

"Is Kirsten still mad at you? At me?" I hastily added, "Which would be far better, if she were mad at me, not you."

"You're right, that would be better," he said. "She's still mad at both of us, but mostly me, because I let you control me and that's not something addicts should do. Therefore, I need to stay away from you for a while, Sis."

That took it out of me. I hadn't even considered that it wasn't a good idea for Mateo to agree to my crazy schemes, that he needed to be his own person. Because, face it, he'd always followed along on whatever zany adventure I proposed. I hadn't thought about how that might have shaped his personality. "Oh," I said, very subdued. In controlling my brother, in becoming almost a surrogate mother when Mom worked long hours at the bakery, had I stifled his chances to learn to make the right decisions?

I knew tears were slipping out, even though I squinted, trying to hold them back. I bit my lip.

"Stop with the guilt, Madrone. I know you love me and I'm the one responsible for my bad choices. Kirsten's mad at me a lot more than she is you. We surprised her, that's all."

I shot him a weak, tentative smile. "So?"

"So. I'm working on forgiving you and I'm not working on being a sleuth. And you shouldn't either." He shrugged. "But I won't try to control you. I can only control myself and my reactions." After a moment he added, "I need to tell you, since nothing's a secret in this town, that the cops want to see me again tomorrow." He grimaced. "I appear to be in first place on the detective's suspect list. Wish I'd kept those fights with Vi inside."

I wished he'd not fought with her at all, but bit back my words.

I flashed to the argument between Mateo and Kirsten that I'd overheard. Was it only yesterday? Kirsten was letting her father and his gambling addiction control her and not confronting him with how it was affecting her. I chewed my lip, determined not to mention it.

"Thanks for talking to me," I told my brother. "I truly suck at huge parties. Thought I was getting better."

My date/not date, Ernie, returned. "Thought I'd lost you to a younger man, but then I saw it was your brother." He stuck out a hand and said, "Mateo, we haven't met yet. I'm Ernie Whipple and I like your sister. That okay?"

This guy was definitely a silver fox. A suave and kind fox. I laughed. "Wait a minute. Why do you think you need my brother's permission to hang out with me?"

"Why not?" Mateo and Ernie said in unison.

"Let's go get something to eat," I said to Ernie. I had no appetite but I needed a distraction from my worry about Mateo.

"Care to join us?" he asked Mateo.

"Wouldn't think of cutting in on your action," he said with a wink.

I sought help in the sky. "You two are too much for me. Thanks for the chat, Mateo." I hoped neither of them could tell how frightened I was for my brother.

20

Into the Madding Crowd

Ernie put a friendly hand on my arm and steered me into the crowd of townspeople. He had a smile and a greeting for everyone.

"Ever think of going into politics?" I asked him. "You'd be perfect."

He gave a low chuckle. "I *was* perfect. The job was not. I served as mayor of this little town for eight long years. Vowed never to do it again. I was like that Gumby kid's toy, stretched in all directions until I was ready to snap. Some folks there's no pleasing and some folks are plain annoying."

"So that's why you know so many people."

He nodded. "Most of them I like. Like the beautiful woman I see now." He led me to Ven Sturgess before I could warn him that I might not be on her favorite's list. In fact, if Kirsten told her I'd been snooping, I might be on her "toss out with the tired potato salad" list.

"Lavender, my love, I've been looking for you," he called.

Ven smiled a warm welcome at Ernie and gave me a cool nod. Let's see. I'd said her mother was a fruitcake, then I was the one who found her mother's body, and I'd also seen her, Wes, and Kirsten snipe at each other. She also might know I'd been nosing into her mother's life and financial dealings. Maybe not her bestie.

Ernie expressed his condolences to Lavender. "I gather you've met Madrone. You may wonder why I have such a delightful young woman in tow tonight," he added.

"Not really. She seems to show up in lots of unexpected places," she said.

Ernie carried on blithely, although it was clear her cool response surprised him. "Like all of us, Madrone wants to know who did this terrible thing to your mother," he said. "I offered to introduce her to people who knew Violet."

She focused a cool stare on me and then answered Ernie. "Since she and her brother are two of the key suspects, I guess it makes sense she's looking for a scapegoat."

"Oh, come now," Ernie said, "You can't seriously believe this young woman is a killer."

"Someone killed my mother and Mom wasn't at all happy with her trip with Adventure Calls."

Ernie raised an eyebrow. "Really?" He laughed. "Recently, Violet was rarely happy with anyone or anything, Ven, even you know that."

"What do you mean by that?"

"Oh, let's see. I heard she accused your daughter of theft, she pissed off my business partner over not selling her land—and making such a scene about it, at a party, what's more—so much Isabella now avoids most social gatherings in town, and your husband rarely stops complaining about Violet's stinginess." The angry expression on a face I'd only seen as genial surprised me. Possibly Violet had also done something to piss off Ernie, the happy-go-lucky real estate agent. It seems my list of potential suspects was growing like mold on old cheese. I wanted to ask how I might meet up with Isabella but it didn't seem the right time. "Shall I continue or do you promise to be civil to my companion?" he concluded.

Ven's face paled under Ernie's diatribe. "Mom had some issues." She looked at me. "And possibly she'd been getting worse lately." I shot her a tight smile at this concession. "Ernie," she continued, "I'm very sorry about the way Mom attacked Isabella. You're right. No one deserved that."

"No one did. Isabella can be abrupt, but Violet totally overreacted." His face relaxed somewhat. "I know what it means to lose a loved one. But pain doesn't excuse flat-out rudeness. People remember our words, even those we regret and apologize for."

Ernie Whipple, philosopher and counselor. I squeezed his arm.

I thought about my mother, and how gut-punched I would be if something happened to her. "Losing Violet has hit your family so hard. Believe me when I say I can only imagine your pain." I needed to escape this woman and looked at the crowd for some possible excuse. I understood Ven's pain and her mixed feelings toward me. She had enough on her plate that she didn't need to apologize to me. "I see Sergeant Doughty. I'd like to have a word with her. Can I catch up with you, Ernie?"

"You bet."

I nodded goodbye to both of them and headed for the police detective. As I passed through the crowd of townsfolk, I noticed quite a few of them staring at me, some nudging each other and pointing me out. I doubted they had me confused with J-Lo, but it puzzled me that they knew who I was. Either they'd heard I'd found Violet or they wondered who was trying to snag their former mayor. Or?

I caught up to the police sergeant and touched her shoulder. She spun around so fast I stepped back in surprise. She chuckled. "Never a good idea to sneak up on a cop," she said. "But I'm glad to see you. I wanted to talk to you."

I ducked my head like a Cooper's hawk. Crud. I'd wanted to ask her about the investigation but I hadn't considered she'd subject me to yet more grilling. Wasn't there enough of that here tonight? "Then it's good I caught you," I said weakly. "What's up?" Was Mateo in more trouble? Had she found out about his past? Mine? No, wait. My record was clear of arrests and surely no one ever told about that crazy night six of us drove to Willcox and liberated a basket of apples. Had they? Sweat dripped down the side of my face, but I ignored the tickling evidence of my anxiety. I hoped Doughty wouldn't notice.

"I'm told you're the one who brought that pumpkin bread. It's scrumptious. I must have the recipe," she said, with a kind smile. She knew she'd scared me. "I'm glad you came tonight. Ignore the curious faces—people in our town are always hungry for a little vicarious drama. And you found poor Violet."

"Does that mean I'm no longer on your suspect list?"

"Nope, that's not what it means. She was a powerful woman with lots of money. She could have ruined your tourist company and from what I heard, that was exactly what she planned. You're on my list. Until I find whoever murdered her, everyone's a suspect. Well, I'm not, since I know I didn't do it, but the list of people who had a reason to be upset with Violet Brock is long, and my name's on it, as well."

"It is?" I hated the way my voice squeaked.

"She wrote a lot of letters to the mayor and the city council, complaining about the police, and she fought the building of the skate park my two sons adore." Before the sweat dried in my armpits, she added, "That said, she did a lot of good in our community and I *will* discover who killed her."

"I heard she stirred up a lot of trouble," I said. "If I hear any specifics, I'll be sure to let you know."

"If you hear something in passing, you can email me or call me anytime. But I'm not anxious to have amateurs putting their noses in my investigation, Ms. Hunter." She smiled again, but it was tight-lipped and didn't reach her eyes. "Stick to baking. You do it very well. Me? I'm an excellent investigator. My email's on my card. I won't get in trouble if you use it to send me a recipe or two."

I went to find Ernie. I slumped, mulling over Doughty's reasonable assumption that I was a better baker than sleuth. It stung, because I couldn't equate the two. Smart enough to read a recipe, but not to find a killer. Which provided more value? Violet had not always been vindictive—she'd helped the community of Cottonwood grow and prosper. She deserved better than a merciless death. And what could I do about that? Pfft. Bake some pumpkin bread, share the recipe.

On the other hand, my pumpkin bread *did* kick butt, like most of my cooking. I dug deep and told myself we each contributed to the world in our own way and we each had value. I strode across the park, this time simply smiling back at the gawkers, my shoulders back and my head up. If I was to be gossip fodder, I'd stand tall. Mateo had faced down our friends and neighbors after his release from prison before finding a job in Cottonwood. Neither of us had anything to be ashamed of.

When Ernie and I found each other, he said, "I see Leonard and Isabella. They may have some information for us amateur sleuths."

Ahh. Now he'd caught the Sherlock syndrome. Drained after facing the throng, I wanted nothing more than to head back to the little cottage, take a bath and chill.

"Ernie, much as I want to meet Isabella and Leonard, I am whupped." When I get exhausted, particularly party-exhausted, I can barely get my words out straight. "Is there a chance we could arrange to meet with them tomorrow? Maybe for breakfast? If you're free, that is."

He displayed a broad smile. "How could I turn down the opportunity to see you again? You sit here and wait for me and I'll see what I can do."

"I'll be indebted to you," I said as I sank onto a nearby bench.

He waggled his eyebrows. "And I'll see that you pay."

21

Help Wears Many Faces

I watched Ernie politic his way through the crowd to the man who'd escorted Violet to Jerome on Tuesday. Making him the last, or second-to-last, person to see Violet alive. I wanted to talk with him, but, as I'd told Ernie, I doubted I had a coherent question left in my exhausted brain. Isabella Garcia was a petite Latina who looked especially small next to the lanky Leonard Anderson. They both greeted Ernie warmly, Isabella with a hug, Leonard a little less boisterously, but with a smile. After a few moments they both looked my way and I gave them a little wave. Instantly I worried that it looked like an arrogant prom queen gesture. But the stress of the party and the past few days had felled me and I had no strength to walk the short distance to them.

Ernie returned after another hug with Isabella and a handshake with Leonard. "We're all set. At the risk of insulting your beauty, you do look worn around the edges. A good night's sleep will fix you. I've arranged for us all to meet up at Crema at nine tomorrow morning. It's a café not to be missed while you're here."

I didn't have the heart to tell him I'd already become a Crema regular. "Sounds good."

I begged off getting a ride back to Leah's from Ernie. "Walking soothes my soul. I really appreciated your picking me up on the way, especially since the casserole was still warm." His face pinched with concern, but he didn't argue. Patted my shoulder and told me he'd see me in the morning.

When I retrieved the empty casserole dish, I noticed the pumpkin bread had also disappeared. Yep. I could cook and I could bake.

It was about a mile from the park to Leah's cottage, an easy walk. Getting through the remaining crowd at the barbecue posed the most effort. It seemed like a dog show. I smiled and nodded at the gawkers, pretended not to notice the pointers, made my way past the retrievers bent on finding their dishes amidst the leftovers, smiled at the workers still positioned near the grills, and nearly tripped on a terrier bent on sniffing my ankles. That last one was an actual dog.

Once back on the road outside the park, I wiped the sweat from my face with a napkin and paused to look at the kids in the skateboard park. Were any of them Sergeant Doughty's sons? Finally alone, I breathed much easier.

I mosied along 10th Street toward town, enjoying the solitude broken only by the whoosh of cars passing. Most of the cottonwoods had turned a brilliant yellow and scattered firs provided pops of deep green contrast.

Could I live here, maybe open a restaurant? Or was my destiny in my hometown of Tucson, or simply to wander with the guests of Adventure Calls for as long as they'd have me?

Gravel crunched in the street beside me. I looked over and saw Mateo and Kirsten's friend from The Tavern Grille. He slid his bicycle to a stop beside me, and I noticed it had both head and taillights and his jacket had reflective stripes. I tried to remember his name, but I'd been introduced to a gazillion people already this evening.

"Hey, you're Mateo's sister, Madrone, right? We met the other night?" He flashed that unforgettable smile. "Ash Coretti. I'd hoped to see you at the barbecue earlier."

"I was there," I said. "It was a little crowded."

"Oh, not like sometimes. It's 'cuz you're new here. Everyone wanted to meet you."

"Or stare at me." That sounded way too arrogant. "At least, it seemed that way. Plus, I went with Ernie Whipple and he knows a lot of people."

"That Ernie. He's some fast worker for an older guy."

I blushed. "It wasn't a date. We met earlier today and he suggested it was a good place to . . ." I trailed off. I didn't know this man, didn't need to confide in a stranger that I was investigating Violet's death.

"Oh, I get it. Looking into who might have wanted poor Violet Brock dead. Besides Mateo."

I didn't reply, merely kept walking, but he'd brought his bike to the sidewalk and strolled beside me as if he'd been invited.

After a few minutes' silence, he said, "The money where I work is on Mateo as the killer, even though I've tried to explain he's as gentle as a pussycat. I hear the cops have him high on their list. It's not true and I want to help, I can help. I know almost as many people as Ernie, plus I might have more dirt on them than he'd be willing to share."

I stopped and stared at him. "Why would you want to do that? And what makes you think I can't find out things on my own?" I gulped. How gullible could I be? I'd stepped right into his snare.

He smiled back, all innocence. "Just trying to help my friend and his sister."

I shrugged. It was silly to turn down help, especially from a local. "Got any ideas?"

He grinned at me. "Oh, I have *lots* of ideas. On the subject of Violet Brock? I have contacts here and in Sedona that may be able to help."

Cheeky, but endearing. "Why do you think that? You're a lot younger than Violet, and I doubt you run in the same circles. I think I'll have better luck with Ernie." And besides, Ernie's charm didn't make my toes curl like this one did. I needed to keep my distance.

"I grew up in Sedona and have lived around here my entire life. I know a lot of people, in a lot of different circles."

"How can you stand living in a small town like this, where everyone knows your every secret, your every thought, for goodness' sake?"

"Maybe 'cuz my mom's a psychic. Used to the mind-reading stuff."

I laughed until I realized I laughed alone. I swallowed. "You're serious."

"As a chakra." Another grin.

"You believe in what she does?"

"It's what I've known since I was a kid. My mom helps people find their spirit guides, does yoga on the vortexes. She makes a pretty good living at it."

"Not only did I insult you, I insulted your mother. I apologize."

"My skin is thick and hers is thicker. You have no idea what people say. You're a rank amateur."

"I'm glad. My tongue gets me in trouble sometimes." He shot me a tiny smile and I reddened more. "I can't seem to get anything right. I should refuse to talk to you, but . . ."

"I'm so cute you can't resist. I get that a lot."

"Not what I meant. I'd appreciate any insights you can give me. I'm pretty much at a loss."

We walked together, Ash, me, and his bicycle, and I filled him in on what little I'd discovered so far. Told him about Violet's unhappiness with the tour and about the encounters with Ven Sturgess that had almost turned into confrontations. Ash was a good listener.

He didn't offer many suggestions, but promised to be in touch after he did some research. I wished he'd invite me along, but kept that wish to myself.

Once again, I considered how he knew Mateo and Kirsten. Okay, worried that they were connected because of their addiction issues. I concluded that no matter his link to my brother, Ash's willingness to help me gave him points, lots of points.

* * *

Back "home," I fell onto a stylish buttery tan leather sofa after carefully removing my Tevas. I checked my phone and discovered I had a text from Gabe and two from Heather Begay, a guide for Adventure Calls who was on a leave of absence to deal with some family issues.

Heather's text said: "Hey, girl—make that woman—I heard about the prob in Cottonwood. Flagstaff's less than an hour away. Want me to come kick some ass?"

In a second text, she added: "Or I could give you a hug. I'm good with hugs. My people know about clearing your chakras, but I don't, so you're out of luck. Kick ass or hugs. Your choice." She added a couple of cute emojis of a donkey.

I shivered. How bizarre that two people today had mentioned my chakras. And when Leah returned, she'd no doubt want me to do a sweat to clear away all the recent bad stuff. I didn't want to mock any of it. For one, those were the deep held beliefs of others. Second, I thought they might well be right. Third, I *wanted* them to have the ability to clear away the bad stuff.

Gabe's text also gave me shivers—the good kind. "I miss you—your smile, your voice, your gorgeous hair. I know you can handle things up there, but I wish I were with you. Darn Tripp. If you decide you need me, let me know. I'll figure out how to get there." No emojis included, none expected.

I brushed aside any tiny twinge of guilt about my reaction to Ash Coretti.

Like I told Gabe after his first encounter with Adventure Calls as its new partner, I could get used to having him around. Awkward that he's my boss, but good that so far, we remained friends. Friends who might become more. But why oh why did it have to involve a murder?

22

Co-conspirators

I arrived a few minutes early at Crema the next morning, hoping to run into Lola and catch up with her. I headed to the outside patio and the bar and asked for a table for four.

She winked at me. "Ernie phoned ahead. You work fast, girlfriend."

Where was that deadpan expression when I needed it? "You know I've asked his help to investigate Violet's death. Although he is sweet as Crema's brownies."

"If only you meant that," came a voice from behind me, accompanied by Ernie's low chuckle.

I spun the barstool around and stood to give Ernie a quick hug. "I mean it. You have been nothing but sweet to me," I protested.

"You may not be so pleased with me when I confess that I may have stretched the truth a little to convince Isabella and Leonard to meet with us." He hung his head.

"Wha—"

Before I could find out what he meant, the tiny woman I'd seen last night swept into the patio and engulfed Ernie in an embrace. "Cariño," she said. "We are here. Let us meet your new friend." Leonard shambled in seconds later, with that awkward, humble gait that belied his profession as a successful real estate developer. Was it intentional, a guise he'd developed over the years to convince people he was the salt of the earth kind of guy? It had worked for me on that terrible night in Jerome. I'd never have pegged him as a deal-maker. Isabella, on the other hand, looked every inch, albeit not that many inches, the polished developer. Well-dressed, black hair streaked with gray so artfully I suspected a stylist helped, a face possibly a plastic surgeon's pride.

Ernie completed introductions and we followed Lola to our table. As I trailed behind Leonard, I noticed he wore expensive boots that might well have been Lucchese and his jeans were definitely not Levi's. Humble apparently worked for him. He'd fooled me the other night. Could he have escorted Violet home and then forced her to take that one last walk with him and killed her? The question was not only could he have done so, but why? Another question was why the heck I believed I might be competent to pry out those secrets.

At the table, Isabella peered at me, her expression avid, almost voracious. The pleasant scent of an elegant cologne wafted across the table. She toned her expression down to what I guess she thought was sympathetic concern, her slight frown indicating she'd had more than a few Botox injections. "You sweet thing, it must have been terrible for you to find poor Violet."

Violet had been easier to deal with dead than alive, but that didn't seem the appropriate response. And I never wanted her dead, no matter the grief she gave me. I gave Isabella a sad little smile. "It wasn't a good experience, but I was glad to have found answers for her family."

She tilted her head. "Answers?"

"That she wasn't out somewhere, wandering around frightened and alone, or injured," Ernie said. "At least I think that's what Madrone meant."

"Ah, I see." She cleared her throat. "But we're not here to discuss Violet, but to talk about your potential move to Cottonwood."

We were? What the heck had Ernie told them? I glanced at him. He raised his eyebrows and smiled, tight-lipped and tense. The light dawned. He hadn't embellished; he'd downright lied to get them to meet me. My choice was to go along with his story or to lose my chance to learn about the relationship Violet had with Leonard and Isabella. And possibly be forced to eat alone.

I laughed. "It's only a dream so far. Ernie may have exaggerated my interest." Or made it up out of whole cloth. Or he'd read my mind after we parted the previous day and perceived that I might consider moving here. Sly fellow. I sipped my coffee. "Who wouldn't want to live in this part of the state? I adore Sedona, but could never afford it, and Cottonwood has the charm of a small town. I've always wanted to own a restaurant, but it's beyond my reach in Tucson. Here?" I smiled. "Anyway, I don't want to mislead you or waste your time. I'll be working for Adventure Calls for many years."

Leonard cleared his throat. "Unless they're forced to fire you. Ven and Wes are considering the lawsuit Violet threatened. We all hope they decide against it, though."

The coffee turned from pleasant to bitter acid in my mouth. "This is the first I've heard of that."

"I thought you knew," he said. "I'm sure they'll change their minds. The pain of losing her is still raw, I guess."

I didn't want to argue with this man, but I couldn't hold back the words. "I had nothing to do with that. And right now I wish I'd never found her."

Isabella put her soft hand on my arm. Her nails were polished an oyster-shell pink and she wore two silver rings, both delicate, one bearing a gorgeous turquoise stone. Prominent veins on her hands told me she was closer to Violet and Leonard's age than she'd at first appeared. "Regrets are wastes of our energy and our life spirit, my dear. All will work out as it is meant to."

Oh, criminy. One of those. Was Ash's mother her guru? My appetite fled.

Isabella clapped her hands together and held them beneath her chin. "No more bad thoughts or words. Let's talk about finding you a place to live here in Cottonwood. I know you're staying in Leah McCall's place. It's a designer's playground—gorgeous."

Great. Everyone in this town knew more about me than I did, it seemed. I did not want to chirp back a pleasant response to Isabella, but I still wanted to learn about her and Violet's business clash. Or clashes, if there were any. "I'm lucky she let me stay there. It's a great little place. And she's a talented designer, as I'm sure you're aware."

Lola, who'd already brought coffee for us, came by for our orders. I started to decline, then realized I needed fuel to keep my spirits up and my brain working. Not to mention those chakras chugging. I would find Violet's killer and I would not be forced out of my job. Isabella wasn't the only one with mantras. I ordered the daily special and silently chanted, I will survive this. I will arise, stronger, from this.

When Lola left to place our orders, Ernie leaned close to me. "I'm proud of you," he whispered in my ear. "A lesser woman would have left. You'll get through this." He patted my hand, and instead of feeling patronized, I felt comforted. Not only a charmer, Ernie was becoming a friend I could rely on.

Isabella, who had predictably ordered an egg-white only omelet with fruit, pointed her fork in my direction. "Vista Rioja has a few homes being finished. You could have Leah help you decide on the interior colors, the flooring. You'll want LVP, everyone does these days. Leonard, are the bathrooms and kitchens finished in those, or could Leah decide on the counters and backsplash?"

LVP? Was that flooring or fuel?

Leonard grinned at me. "She'll have you moved in within the month. I think you ought to take a look at our development and see if new is what you want, or if something closer to Leah's home meets your needs." He turned to his partner. "Not everyone shares our dream."

"Did Violet?" I asked, knowing full well she did not.

Ernie raised his eyebrows. I feared the peacekeeper would speak up, but he remained silent.

Isabella sat back in her chair and sighed down to her no doubt well-pedicured toes. "I'm beginning to wonder if you have any interest at all in Vista Rioja or only want to know if Leonard and I were angry with Violet." She leaned toward me. "I'll tell you this. She often did things that made me want to throttle her. She wasn't logical and it was getting worse as she got older. But she had a right to fight our work, like we had a right to go forward, or shall I say, around her. But I for one didn't care if she lived or died. You should be looking at people who would benefit from her absence now."

I backpedaled. "I am interested in the development, although as Leonard observed, I'm more of the Old Town kind of person. I grew up in an historic barrio in Tucson, and still call it home when I'm not on the road. But it may be time for a move, if I can get myself and my brother out from under suspicion of murder."

"I'll take you for a tour whenever you give the word," Leonard said. "And

I'm betting Ernie has some houses for you to look at." He swallowed some coffee. "As to Violet, I'm under suspicion, too. I was plenty upset that she had me drive her to Jerome only to put on a scene worthy of the theater. But it wasn't the first time, and I had no thought whatever that it should or would be the last. Violet never hesitated to voice her opinions—strong ones— and she was getting worse. But believe me or not, I didn't kill her. Sergeant Doughty is looking into things. She's clever—give her more credit."

We finished our meal, treading carefully and sticking to pleasant topics. All the better for my digestion, if my mind hadn't been silently exploring why and how Isabella could have killed Violet. Why couldn't I simply admire her polished good looks, expensive jewelry, and obvious business acumen? Instead of the sisterhood I wanted to feel for a talented Hispanic woman, I battled envy, that nasty asp of an emotion. She probably had no clue about cooking or baking.

I gave Ernie a grateful hug when we parted and shook hands with the others. I tentatively set up the next day for a visit to Vista Rioja with Leonard. Isabella, alas, was booked. Maybe my luck was changing.

23

At the Chamber

The Cottonwood Chamber of Commerce was located off the main drag on a road that curled east away from the highway that led to the intersection leading to Camp Verde and Sedona. A woman came to the door when I paused outside to look at the flyers in a box. "Come in, come in. We're more interesting than those pieces of paper."

Since her hair was a mix of gray, silver and pink, she did indeed qualify as interesting. I moseyed behind her into a two-room office. Tall and sturdy-looking rather than heavy-set, she headed behind the low counter and I settled in front of it, amazed at the number of opportunities that appeared to await me in Cottonwood and its vicinity. Shelves lined the walls, filled with flyers promoting places to stay, places to eat, places to raft, hike, run, play, swim, and otherwise totally exhaust yourself.

The woman with the multi-hued hair wore a tag with the name Nora. She smiled broadly at me and asked how she might help. Fortunately, I'd had the foresight to bring along some flyers for Adventure Calls.

"I'm Madrone Hunter, a guide for Adventure Calls Ecotouring."

Nora's smile widened. "Of course you are. I saw you at the barbecue, with dear Ernie Whipple. We didn't get a chance then for introductions. I'm Nora but my name tag gives that away." Nora might have been in her fifties or sixties, but she had bounced into the Chamber like a gymnast warming up.

"What's going on? You looking for Violet's killer? That would be exciting."

"I was hoping you could find a place to add some of our flyers for Adventure Calls." Tripp always tells us to repeat our name as often as we can, so it sticks in the "prospect's" mind.

Nora's smile deflated somewhat. "I'll have to clear that with Mary-Margaret, but it shouldn't be a problem." She pivoted and bounced toward a doorway behind the counter. "Mary-Margaret! Assistance needed," she bellowed. She turned back to me. "She's the only paid one around here, so we let her make a few decisions," she said. "Makes her happy."

A tiny woman somewhere in her seventies bustled from the back of the building, dusting her hands. "I've been sorting. An endless task, it seems." She nodded at me. "How can I help you?" She blinked and stared more closely at my face. "Oh, heavens, Nora, you don't want me to help you grill this poor young woman. I imagine she's had enough prying from others."

Nora threw her hands in the air. "I'd never do such a thing. Besides, her aura is clear. It would be murky or black if she'd committed murder. I'd hoped she was on the hunt, but she says she's looking to leave some flyers."

I smiled. "Nora's being very helpful. I wanted to see if I could leave some flyers for Adventure Calls Ecotouring. I'm confident other visitors to Cottonwood would have an interest in our company's tours."

"I'm glad you visited our Chamber. You're welcome to leave flyers, and if you leave extras, we'll keep the shelves stocked. I imagine a lot of people will be interested, given current events. Right now, too many of them might be looking for the vicarious excitement. When things settle down, though, I'll bet you'll get some good leads. We get lots of visitors here."

When the little woman paused for a breath, I took one, too.

Nora burst out laughing. "She's a pistol, isn't she? Wears me out, too." She turned toward Mary-Margaret. "I truly wasn't 'grilling' her, only chatting. You were good friends with Violet, weren't you, Mary-Margaret?"

Mary-Margaret shot her a severe look that anyone could tell had little force behind it. "You know better than to sass the boss, Nora, let alone laugh at me. What ever will I do with you?"

"You could try cutting my pay for starters, but it might be tough."

Mary-Margaret shook her head. "These dang volunteers think they can say anything to me," she told me. She chuckled. "And it's true. They walk all over me, but if we didn't have them, the Chamber would fold." Her expression turned pensive. "Violet was a dear friend. I'd known her all my life. She was such a beauty when she was younger, and oh, so headstrong. All the boys were putty in her hands. And we girls? Well, we were jealous but we admired her. Back then, girls were supposed to be quiet and mannerly and hide our intelligence. Things I'm sure you can't imagine. But Violet would have none of that. I guess she was Cottonwood's first feminist." She smiled, seemingly lost in youthful memories. "Then Vi decided to save the environment."

"She took off on her own?" I asked.

"Oh, no. A couple of the boys went with her. Said they had to take care of her, but she was perfectly capable of caring for herself." She gazed across the room, and I imagined she was recalling life as a young woman newly out of high school. "Leonard and Ross both fancied themselves in love with her. So did some of the other boys. She let them go with her, but also let them know she was fine on her own. Back then, we were pretty independent. No one thought it was a good idea, but girls hitchhiked everywhere. It was the time of sexual revolution, long before anyone worried about AIDS or herpes. Well, anyway, they all headed up to Idaho. Me, I went as far as Phoenix and called myself an adventurer."

I smiled, imagining this tiny woman taking charge in the Phoenix of the 1960s, a town then, as versus the freeway-striped metropolis of today. "And I'll bet you were."

"Mary-Margaret's always been a take-charge person. She even ran against Ernie for mayor, way back when." Nora apparently didn't want to be left out of the conversation.

What did these women know about Violet that could help me? Well, every morsel of information was a puzzle piece. I could assemble the pieces later. Maybe. And the more they liked me, the more they were apt to help. "I really like Ernie. But I'm hoping you beat him." I grinned.

Mary-Margaret shook her head. "He won, but I had him running scared for a while. And I served on the Town Council and gave him what for when he needed it."

"And Violet? Was she ever on the Council? A candidate for mayor?"

"She was on the Council a couple of years, but mostly she wielded power in different ways. I imagine Ernie filled you in, but Violet and her dear husband Chet made quite a lot of money, what with their store and then with what I guess we'd call real estate speculation nowadays. In Cottonwood, they were real moguls." She shook her head. "After Chet died, he wasn't there to soften her harsh edges."

"And she had plenty of those," Nora said.

With a tilt of the head and a pat of the hand, Mary-Margaret silenced Nora. "Poor Violet suffered greatly when Chet died. She'd already lost one daughter, Rose, and then Chet . . . Well, it could have crushed her. Instead it hardened her. Made her plum angry at the world. At God, I guess." She paused and looked down at the Adventure Calls flyer. Pretty obvious she wasn't reading it, but looking much farther away. "Took out a lot of that anger on poor Lavender and Wes. Became less trusting, if that was possible. But she did love poor Kirsten. When the child got into trouble, Violet took her on in the shop, gave her lots of leeway. That's why we were all surprised to hear she accused her granddaughter of embezzling. Not like her to air dirty family linen in public, even if it was true. But I can't imagine that sweet thing stealing from Violet, after all she did for her."

I floated an idea, not sure whether it would crash and burn or be accepted. "I know you don't know me or my company, but the things Violet accused us of were not true. I tried to tell Ven and Wes that I suspected she had early dementia, but they thought I was simply trying to protect myself."

Mary-Margaret took time to look around the small room, as if answers lay in the racks of tourist brochures. "Well, she had been acting a bit off lately. At one of our town pot lucks, she rambled on to me about the importance of facing the consequences of our actions. At first I thought she was accusing me of something and I admit I got a bit huffy, but no, she said she'd done something she regretted and that she planned to get it off her chest. I didn't want to hear some family dirt, so I made up a lame excuse about having to meet another friend. My land, that set her off and she hollered at me about not being much of a friend." She sniffed. "It hurt, because we'd been friends since our school days, and she and Chet and my Walt and I played Canasta together for years."

"Do you think she got angry with other friends? Or told someone her secret?"

Nora edged Mary-Margaret aside, ever-so-gently. "You bet other folks were ticked off at her. Like Leonard and Isabella. She refused to let them buy her land for their new development. I'm sure that cost them a pretty penny. And she could be a beeeitch at town council meetings. Acted like she was queen of Cottonwood."

"But that was vintage Violet," Mary-Margaret protested. "She valued her land higher than the most generous appraisers, and she bargained well and got the best prices for it. You had to admire her business savvy. I'm sure Ven and Wes weren't angry. Violet was Cottonwood Queen, way back in high school, back when we had a parade and floats. I doubt anyone would hold a grudge that long."

From her expression, I gathered that Mary-Margaret was considering the girls Violet had beaten out in the race for Cottonwood Queen. And the depth of their resentment.

Nora tilted her head. "That's your opinion. I'm letting this poor thing know as much as I do about Violet. If she doesn't find the real killer, she might be arrested for it herself."

If Nora could have hummed eerie music, she would have. I might have chimed in.

"I appreciate both your help. I imagine it has nothing to do with anything that far back in Violet's past, but I'm looking at every possibility. What I wish is that people knew I could never take a life—I usually trap scorpions and put them outside."

"I'm sure you're innocent," said Nora, "but I happened to see Violet and your brother having it out a few weeks ago. They were both spitting mad. People can surprise you."

I took a deep breath. So Tuesday morning wasn't their first public spat. Oh, crud. "Can you tell me more about that? Do you recall what they were discussing?"

She chuckled. "I wouldn't call it a discussion. I can't recall when it was, but I was picking up a gift for my nephew at The Whistle Stop. Violet and Mateo were standing at the counter. She was yelling so loud neither of them noticed me come into the shop. I decided to come back later."

"Did you hear anything?"

"Same ol', same ol'. She told him she didn't want her granddaughter to—

how'd she put it?—'dally around' with some foreigner. Kind of insulting. He's as much an American as she was. I bet that burnt his biscuits."

I let out my breath. At least it wasn't on the streets of Cottonwood that time, but I was afraid Nora hadn't kept that juicy encounter to herself. "It sounds awful, but no matter what, my brother could not harm Violet. Someone else did, and I'll simply have to find out who."

I gave an internal eyeroll. Up to now, I'd asked questions, hinted to Ernie that I'd like to know more. I'd never vowed before a complete stranger that I would solve Violet's murder. But, darn it, if people thought Mateo or I were capable of killing her, or if they found out about RK's sometimes dangerous pranks up in Idaho, they'd for sure be glad to have a scapegoat.

I wasn't about to let that happen. I know my expression was verging on stubborn-angry when I said, "Ladies, thank you so much for your time and information. I will be sure to drop more flyers by later this week."

24

Ross Tells a Story

The Chamber women had provided me with more information about Violet and her relationship with the town, and that was a good thing. Nevertheless, I felt mired in mud that could easily become quicksand like the kind we'd seen in Indian territory. This time it was me slowly being sucked into the earth, not an animal. Our Navajo guide had told us about lassoing people on horses who'd disobeyed his orders to stay on the marked path. I wished I had a guide to pull me out of this muck. I also wished I knew where the path was. I could call Heather Begay and she'd be here, as would Gabe. But I didn't want to call on any of them. I needed to prove I could solve this, that all my skills weren't in the kitchen or the wilderness.

I'd driven to the Chamber of Commerce since it was in what I'd come to think of as "new" Cottonwood. Instead of finding parking in Old Town, I parked in the cottage driveway and walked toward Main. I needed to work off my anxiety and didn't have time for a hike. I'd hoped to spend time hiking in Sedona, even bought a book on hiking trails in Red Rock country before I'd left Tucson. Those hikes began to look like fantasies, but I tried to visualize them to raise my flagging spirits.

The Whistle Stop had a new display in the window of a variety of ukuleles. I'd already learned at the concert that there were several varieties of ukulele. The one I was used to seeing was the soprano or standard. For this display, Ross had gathered together a passel of ukuleles and provided with identifying labels. I paused to look at concert, tenor, and baritone ukuleles, and one shaped like a banjo, called a banjolele. At the concert they'd shown us an electric uke and a miniature one, called a sopranino or a bambino. Who knew?

Mesmerized by the beauty and variety of the ukuleles, I stood for some time staring at the display. When it became clear that what I was really doing was stalling, I forced myself to walk through the door. I understood and wanted to support Mateo's decision to steer clear of me for a while, but maybe he knew something about Violet that would help me resolve her murder. By now, he'd had time to cool off and might be willing to talk. After all, he'd stopped to talk to me at the community potluck.

Ross Zelinger stood alone behind the counter. His broad smile beckoned, drawing me in. The man had charisma. I made my way to him, glancing down the aisles for a glimpse of my brother.

"He's not here. He's down at It's All Goods helping Kirsten sort inventory." He snickered, but it wasn't cruel. "If that's what they call it these days."

I chuckled. "Haven't heard it called that yet. Although, when some men ogle women, they're certainly taking inventory." After a moment's silence, I added, "I'm glad he and Kirsten are back together. I'm the reason she got mad at both of us. At least they patched things up."

He strode around the counter and leaned back against it, arms crossed. "Things are still shaky, I gather. But there's a magnetism between the two of them that a little spat can't damage. Sisterly love's not as powerful."

I chewed at my lip. "He doesn't realize the jeopardy he and I are in. We're outsiders in Cottonwood and we both had reason to be furious with Violet Brock. I'm only trying to figure out who else might have had it in for her."

His laughter boomed throughout the shop, bouncing against his mural, maybe startling the musicians on it. "Sweetie, by now you should know that *everyone* had a bone to pick with Violet. You saw her in Jerome. She was getting worse, making offbeat accusations, ranting. Kinda scary to someone like me, who's the same age as Violet. Made me start to worry, think I should get my shit together."

"Did you have a bone to pick with Violet?"

He didn't meet my eyes, but gazed around his shop. "Violet owned this entire block. She was my landlady. Not a terrible one, not a perfect one. I don't get enough traffic in here. Don't make a bundle, except on instrument rentals, sheet music. Violet intended to raise my rent starting in January when my lease comes due. I'd hate to lose this place."

Higher rent seemed a poor reason to kill, but losing your livelihood, somewhere you invested love and a lot of creativity in? I turned around to look at his mural.

Ross cocked an eyebrow. "I love this shop and I'm proud of what I've created, including the mural. But it's not worth killing someone for." His eyes looked sad. "Poor Violet. The woman you met is not the one I've known for years."

"I'd heard she was a beauty. Did you date her in high school?"

"I knew her. Everyone knew everyone back then. It was a long time ago."

I wouldn't have guessed that Ross was anywhere near as old as Violet Brock. Genes, exercise and good eating had served him well, I guessed. The man was in great shape.

"I'd love to chat more," he said, "but without my employee, I have a few things to tend to. Please excuse me."

A woman's voice came from the back room. "Don't forget you have me." Helen sauntered up to the counter and waved a greeting. "I'm happy to fill in whenever he needs me. This store is important to both of us, and to the community of Cottonwood."

"One more question," I asked.

An emotion—anger? Frustration?—crossed Ross's face before he pasted a smile on. "Yes?" Which translated to, "It had better be one, no more."

"With all her property holdings, Violet must have been an extremely wealthy woman. Which means Lavender and Wes stand to inherit quite a lot. Unless she had other children I don't know about?"

Ross's face flushed an unappealing red. "So someone's mentioned Rose, have they?" He glared at me. "Rose left town years ago. I imagine she's dead. And as for Lavender killing her own mother for her inheritance, that's absurd. Violet was elderly. She didn't have many years left. And now, you're out of questions and I'm out of patience."

"Thanks for your time, Ross," I said, in a feeble attempt to pacify him.

"I'll tell Mateo you dropped by," he said. I might have been exercising my optimistic side, but I heard less anger in his tone. Beside him, it seemed that Helen's smile expressed more than farewell. Maybe triumph that her placid spouse had put me in my place? Relief that I and my questions were leaving?

I walked home, passing It's All Goods on my way. It was dark inside and a sign on the door said, "Closed for Family Emergency."

I didn't knock.

25

Neighborhood Watch?

Ross had filled in some details about Rose, the sister who'd left town. From what Mary-Margaret at the Chamber said, I'd assumed she'd died young. Ross had also admitted that Violet planned to raise his rent. Would he have told me that if he'd killed her?

If Ross were a sworn witness, he'd agree that Violet was well into dementia, but I was aware that few people in Cottonwood would come out and say such a thing about Violet if they knew her daughter didn't want to hear it.

But what about her neighbors? Had they noticed anything the night Violet had died? Sure, Sergeant Doughty and her minions had no doubt canvassed the neighborhood, but had they asked about other things going on with Violet? Everyone I'd talked to, save Lavender, had mentioned that Violet had become more volatile in recent weeks. Maybe she'd done something to enrage one of her neighbors.

Maybe they'd be more likely to confide in an unofficial person, someone who had no power to arrest or harass them. Me. Or possibly one of them was a murderer, hiding out, ready to pounce on anyone who poked her nose where it wasn't wanted.

Violet's home was not far from her shop. I power-walked the few blocks, mulling over the best approach with her neighbors.

A dusty pickup truck, full-sized with a gun rack on the rear window and a huge tool chest in the bed, sat in the driveway of the house to the north of Violet's, so I decided to start there. The truck and the house had seen better days. The contrast with Violet's tidy, freshly-painted casita, with its neat front yard of native plants, was almost painful. This little house needed a power wash and a paint job and the yard needed a miracle. I picked my way through dog do and wobbly pavers to the front porch and knocked. I hoped the dog doer was inside and not as large as the piles indicated.

Said dog barked and scratched at the door after my knock. Maybe I was wrong and no one was home.

I heard slow, ponderous footsteps inside, and some muffled words. Then, sharper, "I said sit, Frisco. Sit your ass down."

The door swung open. I looked up. And up. A very tall, very wide man stared at me. He wore a dirty T-shirt that stretched over a large gut and huge biceps. His dirty brown hair hung long and lank and he smelled a little like an Arizona passionflower. Not a good smell. His lip curled a little and he said, "Yeah. Waddya want?" Behind him, I heard a dog whine and pant. It wanted to eat the intruder on the porch.

What I wanted was to turn around and make tracks. I swallowed. "Hi, I'm Madrone Hunter. I knew Violet and well, since I'm the one who found her, I'm looking into her death. I don't know, I feel responsible somehow." I gave him my best sweet young thing smile, one I hadn't practiced for a while, if ever.

The smile must have been rusty because it didn't make any inroads with this guy. He glowered at me. But he didn't slam the door. "So?"

"Violet was your neighbor. I'm sure the police asked if you'd seen or heard anything . . ." I let my voice trail off, hoping he'd fill in the blanks.

He didn't. "Yeah. They asked. I didn't see nothin' and if I had I can't see no reason to tell you." He started to back away, ready, I was sure to do the door slamming thing.

"Wait. Had Violet seemed different to you? Angry? Did she confront you about anything? People are saying she seemed a little odd lately."

His mouth twisted. "Odd, huh? People, or you, trying to make up bad things about Miz Brock? I heard you been asking questions. Snooping around. Miz Brock was a good neighbor to me. A good landlord when she wasn't being picky about my landscaping. She was a pitcher of this community. I won't hear you say bad things about her. Fact. If I hear you were to blame for her death, if you hurt a hair on her head, I would be plenty mad." He stepped toward me. "And Frisco here, he'd be mad, too." He turned and the dog took a menacing step toward me. Growled, as if he'd absorbed his owner's animosity toward me.

I backed away, slowly, trying not to spur either of them into jumping me. I felt like wetting my pants. "No, I didn't hurt Violet. I'm not that person. Thank you for your time. I'm real glad Violet had such good neighbors. I'll be on my way." I blathered on, edging backward, until I tripped on one of those loose bricks and fell on my butt. I put out a hand to stop the fall and it landed in dog poop.

His laughter was as scary as his dog's growl. When he closed the door, I struggled to my feet and boogied to the sidewalk, where I finally sucked in a breath.

Was the giant dog owner telling the truth? I couldn't see Violet enjoying his yard and possibly the barking of that huge beast. But he seemed to hold her in high esteem, or so he said. Whether or not he lied about his relationship with his landlady, I wouldn't get anything more from him, except maybe a dog bite.

Maybe a neighbor across the street had seen something the night Violet died. And maybe if I were across the street, I could escape Frisco if his burly owner saw me and decided to sic him on me. I love animals and they generally like me, but Frisco's growl had a hungry undertone.

I stooped and wiped my hand on the grass, successfully getting rid of most of the dog poop, but not all the aroma. I knocked on the door directly opposite Violet's home. No one answered. I debated but discarded the idea of leaving a card with my number. The police would not be pleased to learn I continued to snoop. I'd come back at another time. I tried the house to the north, catty corner to Frisco's place. A frail, friendly looking, white-haired man answered and gestured to me to wait until he put in his hearing aid. So much for him hearing a disturbance across the street. He did tell me that Violet had sold the home to him and his late wife many years previously. He invited me in for coffee and a little chat. It was obvious that Perry, as he introduced himself, was lonely. I couldn't refuse.

Since Perry seemed a kind host, I asked if I could use his bathroom to wash my hands. He pointed to a door down a short hall and I scrubbed my hands with soap and enough hot water that I hoped he wouldn't be bathing soon.

After he'd seated me in the tidy but musty living room, he bustled around in the kitchen and returned with two mugs of coffee and a box of Girl Scout cookies. "I'm not supposed to eat too much sugar, but I found these in the pantry."

"I'm not much for sweets, either," I lied, eying the box with trepidation. He opened them despite my protests and I waited for a flock of pantry moths to emerge. They didn't, but I decided to pass on the cookies anyway.

"Was Violet a good neighbor?" I asked.

"Oh, sure, sure. Sometimes got a little testy, but we're all getting along in years. She was well-respected in Cottonwood."

I could tell that this kind man didn't believe in gossip, which was exactly what I was searching for. Rats. "Did you ever notice any arguments? Disagreements with other neighbors?"

He frowned. Picked up a cookie and put it down. I waited. Something weighed on his mind. "Well, now, I'm not one to tell tales, but like I told little Willie Doughty—she was a student of mine a lot of years back—Violet and her son-in-law Wes never hit it off. I know he thought she should let him and Lavender turn her cottage into a little café, but she didn't agree. Mind you, I think it might be nice to have a small eatery across the street, but I didn't get into the argument. The neighbors here all have different opinions on the impact of something commercial like that on the street. Feelings ran kind of high for a while."

Aha! "How high?"

"You ever see Verde Creek after a monsoon?" He chuckled. "Our little spat was like that. People were riled up but calmed down fast so you wouldn't think anything had happened." He paused. "Now that you bring it up, one couple did move after all the kerfuffle and that may be why there weren't any more heated arguments."

Arguments? People forced to move out? Or angry enough to move? Finally, something to chew on! I picked up a cookie and bit into it before I remembered its probable age. Gulp. I wanted to spit it out but that would be a terrible insult to my host. I chewed and swallowed and smiled. And hoped I wouldn't puke in the next few minutes. My phone vibrated in my pocket, but I ignored it. I needed Perry to feel good about me, good enough to share what he knew. "You happen to recall the name of the people who moved?"

He pondered that, rubbing his chin. "Can't say as I do, but you could check with Martha, the woman who bought their place. Don't know her real well. Flower, one of them had a name like a flower, which my wife and I thought was funny given, you know, Violet lived next door. Daisy? Marigold? Nope, it's not there anymore. My memory banks are shrinking."

Maybe my investigator's luck was changing. If I could catch Violet's northside neighbor at home, she might be able to send me to some people who were truly angry with Violet Brock.

I rose, thanked Perry for his hospitality, and left. Without cookies, despite his urging them on me.

I took a circuitous route to the house next door to Violet's, walking down Perry's side of the street a few houses, then crossing and walking back down the street. I didn't want to run across Frisco or his unfriendly owner.

The house next door to Violet's was enchanting. A white picket fence straight from Tom Sawyer skirted the front garden, which boasted a patchwork of colorful flowers, many still in bloom even in September. A tall ocotillo still grew green leaves closer to the porch. If you were going to squander some of Arizona's precious water, better here than some golf course. A freshly painted bright green wooden bench sat in the shade of a tall desert willow. The tiny garden charmed me.

The gate was latched and a brass bell hung from the side post. A small brass plate was engraved with the notice to "Ring Bell Before Entering."

No way would I ring that bell and announce my presence to Frisco and his owner. I reached under the bell and clutched the clapper between my index and middle fingers to keep it from hitting the side and walked through the gate. A brick path meandered through the garden to the porch.

I'd made it about halfway to the porch when I was drenched with water. A stout woman came around the side of the house, holding a hose nozzle aimed straight at my face. When she saw me, she lowered the spray to my legs. Now I was well soaked from head to toe. "Stop that," I spluttered.

"The sign says Ring the Bell. You didn't." She turned the spray away from me, but it didn't matter, since I was drenched, head to foot. "Unless you're blind, you have no excuse."

"I could be blind from the power of that spray," I said. "I was trying to be quiet, so as not to warn Frisco."

"That darn dog knows better than to come in my garden." She smiled. "And now, I guess you do, too."

I gathered up the dregs of my dignity and said, "May I ask you a few questions?"

"You're dumber than the dog. At least he has an excuse. I know who you are. You're who killed that cantankerous Violet Brock. She might have been testy, but she didn't deserve killing. I'm not talking to a murderess." She raised her hose but didn't spray me again.

I turned and trotted out the yard. So much for small-town, neighborly Cottonwood.

26

The Warnings Begin

I slogged homeward, waterlogged. My hair dripped down my face, my socks squished in my also soaked shoes. The only part of me that had stayed somewhat untouched by the water cannon was my back, and that meant my backpack had stayed dry.

"My phone," I yelled halfway to Leah's. I tried to pull it out of the pocket of my formerly nice khaki slacks, but the sopping fabric pulled tight against my thighs. I'd already caused quite a commotion as I walked down Main, and no doubt my shouting convinced passersby that I was well and truly nuts. Most people hurried by, trying not to stare.

By the time I turned onto Leah's street, I was convinced that Cottonwoodians were harsh and cruel. Not to mention at least one was a murderer. Then a woman about my age, who'd been sitting on her porch, trotted to the sidewalk. She stopped in front of me. "Did you fall into the river? Are you all right? How can I help? If you wait, I'll grab a few towels."

"I'm fine. Didn't fall. Fortunately, the weather's not cold." She still looked concerned, so I went on. "I got squirted by a protective homeowner."

"Protective! That's way out of line. Maybe arrest-worthy. Want to come in and call the cops? Get dry?"

"You are too sweet. I'm staying at a home down the street. Leah McCall's?"

"Still, you're soaked. I could get a towel and you could bring it back, whenever." She patted my arm. "I'm Dolly Gardiner."

"Dolly, you've restored my faith in the people of Cottonwood. I got quite a soaking, but I'll be fine. I'll get home and take a nice long bath. Warm. Thank you for your kindness." I felt tears spilling over and brushed them away.

"You're in shock. Have some tea when you get home. Relax and, well, I'm sorry you were treated that way, especially if you're a visitor to our town."

I smiled at her through my tears and a few last drips of water. "I promise to follow your orders. Are you a doctor?"

"Nurse practitioner. Seriously, if you get chills or feel worse, you should drop by the Urgent Care Center. Or knock on my door. Poor baby."

She patted me on the back and I walked on home, feeling better for the kind human contact. Although I wouldn't be knocking on doors for a while, or if I did, I'd wear a raincoat.

I staggered up the front steps and opened the glass door to get to the locked wood door. An 8 x 10 piece of cardboard slid to the porch. I bent over to pick it up before I dripped on it. Glued to it were words cut from a magazine or a newspaper, some made up from cut out letters: SNOOPING'S NOT HEALTHY. STOP PRYING.

Perfect. And for a few moments there, I'd believed my day couldn't get worse.

Then it struck me—someone thinks I'm getting closer to finding the killer. If only he or she knew how wrong that was. I decided to go to sleep with thoughts of what I'd learned. Maybe I'd wake up with the answer. Fat chance. The going to bed thing looked good, however.

Truly a rotten day. It would be a lot worse if my cell phone didn't work. I sighed, opened the door, and walked inside. Maybe I should have worried that whoever left the note was inside, waiting to harm me, but I was too exhausted to care. Besides, I reasoned that anyone who'd stuff a note in the door wouldn't then wait inside for me. This was a quick, early warning and, with luck—in short supply today—the last.

I staggered inside, threw my pack on the floor and stripped off my slacks. Then I pried my phone from my pocket. Three text messages, one from my mother, and two from Gabe.

My text from Gabe read, "I'm missing you and worrying about you, even though I know you can handle whatever comes your way. I'm going to find a way to get up there soon. Take care of yourself." Gabe was confident I could stay out of trouble and keep his company out of the grip of a lawsuit.

I burst into tears and ran for the bathroom. On the way I wadded the note as best I could and stuffed it in a trash can. If I couldn't see it, it didn't exist.

27

Ven Dishes

I rarely take time for a bath. Always seems to me I have something better to do. But I took a good long soak after being drenched by that hose-wielding senior citizen. While the tub filled with bubbles stolen from Leah's stash, I poured myself a glass of wine and fixed a small plate of cheese to go with it.

The way my day had gone from downhill to the depths of the sewer, the cheese would end up in the tub with me, the wine would spill, the glass would break and I would cut a major artery in my foot and bleed to death. I had no idea, incidentally, if there were indeed major arteries in the foot. However, none of those disasters occurred. I simply luxuriated in soothing, lavender-scented bubbles.

I arose from the tub feeling much better. I hadn't been hit by paint balls or shotgun pellets, after all. It was only a little water and the September day was balmy. A couple of cranky people and a growling dog weren't so awful.

The note warning me off wasn't as easy to shrug off as the hosing. Whoever had placed that note on the door knew where I was staying. That thought made me want to dive under the covers and stay there.

No! Hunters don't give up and they don't scare easily. Someone worried I'd stumble into—make that discern—the truth behind Violet's death. Worried enough to try to get me to stop.

Well, a note calling me names—a snoop!—wasn't going to stop Madrone

Hunter. No way. However, since I had no clue what had triggered the angry warning, I needed some help. I might be able to convince Mateo to be my partner in detection, but he'd warned me about the effect on his recovery should I try. I believed him and I trusted him. I would not, could not, ask for his help. If he offered them, I'd accept his insights.

I decided against calling Sergeant Doughty. This was only a note, nothing that serious. Focused on figuring out what this unknown person thought I might have discovered, I didn't consider that receiving a warning might take me off the suspect list.

I had another friend not that far away. Not Heather. I liked her but I didn't want to involve her in this mess. She was young, barely twenty, and she might charge into the midst of this without thinking. Unlike me with all my grown-up wisdom and discretion.

No, I was thinking about RK. Maybe he could help me figure out what I knew that had scared someone into warning me.

Maybe, maybe. . . I was meddling in something unrelated to Violet's death and angering someone. But what?

I dressed in a pair of black jeans and a white silk blouse. Very professional. My good leather shoes were drying on the back porch so I slipped on my sneakers. Maybe no one would notice my feet.

I texted RK and asked him to meet me at the bar in The Miners' Choice Hotel, the one managed by Ven and Wes Sturgess. He responded in a few minutes, adding, "I need cheering up. Erin flew out today."

I'd forgotten Erin was heading back to Durango today. I decided a tiny fib wouldn't hurt and texted back, "What are friends for?"

The man was nobody's dummy. He immediately replied, "Oh, dunno. Maybe helping solve a murder?"

I couldn't wait to see my friend. I hoped he'd learned some good stuff from his activist friends.

I ate some cheese, an apple and some turkey jerky before I left, in case the bar didn't serve food. I had to hang onto my brain cells tonight.

I arrived a good half hour before I expected RK. I had a few questions for Ven Sturgess before he got there, if I could convince her to talk to me.

Ven was working the bar. My shoulders lost half their tension. She would be polite, even if she told me nothing. Her husband? Maybe not so much.

She smiled when I slid onto a stool at the bar, but it was a poor imitation of the grin I got when we first met. "I see you're still in town."

"Yes, but not in jail. In fact, I don't think I'm considered a suspect these days." I had no clue if that was true, but no harm in positive words and thoughts. I asked for a draft beer, amber or red, and Ven pulled me a pint of Railhead Red by a brewery in Flagstaff.

"I hear you're doing some sleuthing." Without any intonation, I couldn't tell if she approved or disapproved.

"Look, I'm afraid my brother's still under suspicion."

"So is my daughter, but that doesn't mean I'm going around town asking questions. What some folks might think are too many questions."

"The only people it should bother are those with something to hide," I said. Tension returned to my back and shoulders and above my right eye I felt a headache coming on.

"Everyone has something to hide, unless they're saints. And I've heard even the saints weren't always pure." She paused to pour a draft for a waitress. "I heard about you snooping around in Violet's home. My thought is the cops wouldn't like to know that."

I jerked backward at her words, then forced myself to lean forward. "Are you threatening me?"

She shook her head. "No way. If you can figure out who, among all the people my mom ticked off, lost their cool, you'd be doing me and my family a favor." She served a new arrival at the end of the bar. While she was busy, I noticed a menu chalked to a big board on the wall. Mostly sandwiches and burgers, but definitely enough to keep me sober.

Ven returned to me. "Kirsten wasn't happy about your sneaking into the house. I told her you loved your brother. People do strange things for love." She stared at me.

"Strange, but not murder. Mateo and Kirsten have something special, and he definitely didn't like the way Violet treated her—or him—but my brother is not a killer."

"I agree with you. But then, who? Mom was getting old. People who were anxious to buy her property didn't have that long to wait. They'd be aware that Wes and I would be ready to sell. Are ready to sell, come to think of it."

That made me think. "Has anyone come to you to talk about the land that's yours now?"

She looked at the bar and then the ceiling. "Who would be dumb enough to murder Mom and turn around and ask me to sell her land?" Her expression changed.

She had a point. But, "Desperate people do dumb things. That's why most killers get caught."

She raised her eyebrows. "You sound like Willa—I mean Sergeant Doughty."

"You knew her and lots of law enforcement people when you worked in dispatch. Have you heard any gossip?"

She laughed. "The best gossip is about you and who you've been hanging out with." She checked off on her fingers as she spoke. "You're having hot sex with Ernie Whipple, you've got a thing for Ross at The Whistle Stop, you're making the move on Lola at Crema—or the scones there, no one's sure, and you have a nice pair of legs, according to the old guys who hang out by the library."

"And I thought Tucson was a small town."

"You're something new, and most people don't want to talk to me about Mom's murder and the investigation, even when I ask. Afraid I'll shatter." She sighed. "For pity's sake, I worked Dispatch. I heard horrible things, and I'm aware of the bad things people can do. It is hard to consider that someone was willing to kill my mother. For all her abrasiveness, she loved me, and Kirsten. And Wes."

The pause between Kirsten and Wes was way too long for me to ignore, but what could I say? Ask? I simply said, "Families are tough to understand." I sipped at my beer, telling myself chugging it might make my brain cells sluggish. I needed every single one in top form. I needed to get back to the question she hadn't answered. "Has anyone else—friends of Violet's, neighbors—said anything odd? Unexpected?"

After taking time out to fill another drink order for a server, Ven turned back to me. Was she stalling? Buying time to think up a reply? A lie? "I'm answering your question, but you have to know I've already told Willa Doughty the same thing, and she's better qualified to pursue it. She's a cop and you're snoop—curious. But I can tell you have the same tenacity that your brother has—which I find part annoying and part admirable. Ross dropped by earlier. He asked that we consider extending his lease as it is. He hinted that Violet planned to up his rent. And Leonard Andersen asked if we might consider selling the parcel of land next to their new development that Violet had refused to part with."

"Hmm. Do they fall into the category of innocent, stupid, or cleverer than we'd imagine? Seems a bit soon after Violet's death to discuss business," I said. "Did you tell them that?"

She gave me a half-smile. "Only with a raised eyebrow. Maybe it wasn't as rude as it appeared. But I guess everyone needs to watch out for him—or herself." Her implication was clear.

"Or her brother." Time for a subject change. I said, "I'm expecting a friend to join me for dinner. Do you recommend anything tonight?"

"Everything's excellent, but the carrot-beet soup is special and we don't serve it often. Shall I put an order in for you?"

"No, I'll wait till my friend arrives." I looked at my phone. "He's late."

She smiled, her gaze focused beyond me. "He's here. Attractive man."

Roadkill? I mean RK? I almost told her it couldn't be him, but took the high road. Maybe she was teasing.

A tall, beardless man with dark brown hair parted on the side and brushed back on the other, slid next to me. For an instant I thought someone was making a move on me, and then I recognized my old friend. My mouth fell open. He grinned.

28

New and Improved Version

RK winked at me. My scruffy anti-establishment, activist friend had been replaced by a smooth-shaven hunk.

I closed my mouth. What to say? Went with, "You look pretty good for an Idaho country boy." I turned to Ven, who remained behind the bar, and introduced them.

"You're the scruffy driver my mother complained about?" Her broad smile took the sting out of her words.

"The very one." He smiled. If I hadn't known better, I might have thought he'd had his teeth whitened. Maybe they'd always shone that bright, but been hidden beneath his beard.

"You clean up nice, friend," I said. "I take it you were trying to impress Erin?"

"Erin likes me the way she met me, but her father threatened to fly down to get her and I wanted to make a good impression. What're you drinking?"

"She's having Railhead Red on draft," Ven supplied. "Pint?"

He nodded. He got his beer, I got a refill, and we found a table after saying our goodbyes to Ven Sturgess.

Seated, I said, "Someone might think you're a metrosexual."

"Say what you will, you will not get a rise out of me. Erin likes the new me. But I'm not sure I'll keep the look."

"You might not have scared Violet if you'd looked like that."

"Violet was on the verge of a nervous breakdown. Wonder why they don't call them that anymore."

"Not PC, or medically accurate. But you're right. As she grew physically exhausted her rational thinking ability was depleted."

"Maybe we all do that, but not to Violet's extreme. But she was rested up when she came to Jerome and chewed you, me, and Kirsten out. It's a puzzle."

"One we are going to solve. After we eat."

We ordered, both of us starting with the carrot-beet soup. He opted for a burger, medium rare, and I decided on a Reuben sandwich. Like clam chowder and tiramisu, I consider that sandwich a measure of a good restaurant.

I was avid to hear more about Erin and Gabe's father. Gabe rarely spoke of the man. "Tell me all about Erin's dad."

He grinned. "You mean, 'What's Gabe's father like?'"

"Whatever. Spill."

He shook his head. "He didn't come. She flew back on a commercial flight today. She didn't want him to make a fuss over her. Or that's what she said." He stared at the table. "I'm afraid she didn't want him to meet me. Like you said, she considers me a week's fling."

I patted his hand. "You'd like it to be more."

He gave me a little half-smile. "I shaved and cut my hair for the woman. That should tell you something."

"If you keep working for Adventure Calls, you're bound to see her again."

"If I'm not arrested for murder."

"None of that. I'm a suspect, too. Which is why I need your help."

As soon as we gave the server our order, I asked, "What did you learn from your old friend Fig?"

"I called Fig—Fiona—but her roommate said she was rafting. She promised to get the message to her as soon as she got back."

"Why not once she leaves the river? How long will she be gone?"

He reached over and patted my hand. "It was a day trip. I'll hear from her soon. Now, what have you found?"

I caught him up on my investigations, concluding that I still had no clue who'd killed poor Violet, or if I was even looking in the right direction. Still,

I wasn't going to give up. Not my way. While I talked, our food arrived. The soup was artfully prepared, the beet and carrot creating a yin-yang effect. My Reuben looked perfect—almost too big to get my mouth around and dripping dressing and sauerkraut. The aroma of garlic, cloves and other spices made my mouth water.

"Nope. Your tenacity is world class." He sipped his beer. "This food is excellent. I can see why Ven and her husband want to open a bistro."

"Not enough to kill her mother, though," I said.

He shook his well-coiffed head at me. "Obsession does not become you."

We'd finished dinner before I told him about the nasty note I'd received, and about why Mateo was avoiding me. I brushed off his concern about the note, assuring him it hadn't bothered me, and that it told me someone thought I knew a lot more than I did. "But I hate that I might have been one of the causes of Mateo's addiction. I didn't realize love can become control too easily. At the community BBQ, he asked me to keep my distance. But at least he spoke to me. I guess that's a step forward."

"Backing off right now is a good idea, okay. But thinking you're a cause of his addiction? That's bull crap. You were a loving big sister, trying to guide him. You didn't introduce him to pills. Or encourage him to steal. Thinking that takes away power from your brother, and I'm pretty sure he wouldn't like that. You two will be okay soon."

"Love that optimism, Doctor Mustard."

"Truth." He chuckled. "Back to the important stuff. What's on for dessert?"

I chose cheesecake, he chose black bottom pie. We both ordered coffee. "Share?" I asked, indicating our desserts.

He waved his fork. "My sacrifices for you have no end."

As we ate our desserts, he said, "I can tell you want me to do something. You're nervous. Tell me the plan, oh brilliant investigator."

My mind was filled with thoughts about who hated Violet, who hated my snooping, what was important enough to kill about, I didn't know where to begin.

"The shplan?" he said, his mouth so full of pie his words were garbled.

"Okay, like I told you, Violet left Cottonwood in her late teens, I think, and wound up an activist in Idaho and Oregon, maybe other places. I want to know if any of that history is what caused her death."

"That was what, more than fifty years ago? And you think it's relevant today?"

"I have no clue. Two men who still live in Cottonwood and still associate with her followed her when she left town. I want to know what happened to her while she was gone. Activism can be dangerous, as you know. You make friends for life, you make bitter enemies on the other side." I sighed. "It might be far-fetched, but I haven't gotten anywhere on figuring out what happened recently to cause someone to kill her. It seems to me that we need to spread the net, go deep and wide. We're looking for any reason someone would kill her and I haven't found anyone with a good motive yet."

"Besides you, me, and your brother."

"Yeah. Did you kill her?" I peered at him over my coffee cup.

"No. Did you?"

Maybe I imagined that my buddy watched me closely. "No, I did not."

"That leaves Mateo," he said.

Every muscle in my face and neck tightened. I glowered at my former friend. "It absolutely does not. I know my brother and I know he did not kill anyone. If you feel that way, I don't need or want your help." And yet something niggled at me. Was it something Mateo said? Or someone else?

He patted the air in front of him. "Cool your jets, big sister. I was testing the strength of your faith in your brother. I'm not proposing this as truth, but some people might say that his refusing to see you, to even talk to you, means he thinks you'll see through his denial." He threw up a hand to stop my angry retort. "I'm telling you what others might think, not that I do. You say your brother's solid, he's solid."

His faith in me undermined my own. Isn't the family of a serial killer always the last to know? After all, Mateo was in love, or at least in the throes of new love, with Kirsten, and Violet treated Kirsten little better than a slave, a slave whose love life she could control, whom she'd accused of embezzling.

"Stop doubting your conviction. He didn't do it."

"Am I that transparent?"

"I've known you a long time, Madrone. I know you love your family and are loyal to your friends. You're smart and perceptive and tenacious. We will figure this out." He shrugged. "Well, mostly you, but I'll do what I can. Fiona will get back to me soon. She knows other folks who've lived here forever. I'll get some dirt."

I stood up, trotted around the table and hugged my good friend, and kissed his smooth cheek. He stood and walked out and I watched him, regretting not telling him how nervous the warning note made me, not asking him to spend the night in the cottage.

29

The Comfort of Friends

I walked away from the hotel and toward home, telling myself I was silly to take the warning note seriously. It might have even been a prank, not from the real killer. Or from someone else, with another secret to hide. Surely lots of people had secrets, even in a small town where secrets seemed hard to keep.

A hand clasped my shoulder from behind and I jumped, yelped and spun around faster than a shot putter. I jerked my arm back, palm cocked backward, ready to strike.

Ash Coretti displayed one of his patented broad smiles and I swear his eyes twinkled. "Whoa! You're as spooky as a feral cat. Who put the burr in your posterior?"

I did not smile back. "You did. What gave you the idea to sneak up on me like that?"

"I wanted to catch up with you. See how your day went. Maybe buy you a beer?"

First time he'd caught me, after the barbecue, I'd consider normal interest. Twice? Was this guy a stalker? Some other kind of weirdo? "Puppy dog eyes won't work on me today. I already had dinner and a beer. Now I'm headed home to take a load off." Inspiration struck. It might have been lust—those eyes were deep and compelling—but I'm calling it inspiration. "You may walk me home and tell me stories about your day."

He bowed, making as sweeping a hat off. "It would be an honor. Might I have a glass of water when we get there? I'm kinda parched."

Someone to search for monsters in my home without my having to phone for help. Hoorah. "Water for sure. Beer or wine if you are polite while we walk and maintain your distance." I wrinkled my nose.

"Deal. You're right to keep your distance. I was on a hike, a long, steep hike. I was heading in for a quick draft when I saw you and decided to scare the pants off you."

I gave a reluctant smile. This guy had charm. Must be something in Cottonwood's water.

He grinned back and we headed toward my temporary home. "I've been reading about your company on the website. Nice concept. I'm into nature. Otherwise, why live here?"

"Maybe to find your inner self?"

"I've found and lost it dozens of times. I warn you—don't try to insult me. I've developed thick skin as the son of a Sedona seer."

"That's quite the tongue-twister. Son of a Sedona seer. Son of a Sedona seer."

He winked at me. "Second time you've brought up your tongue. Trying to tell me something?"

I blushed. And could think of not one response that wouldn't dig me in deeper.

"I heard your pumpkin bread and the casserole were hits at the potluck. Sorry I missed them."

"Who told you?"

"I don't know—Ven, Kirsten, not sure who. You're becoming famous in Cottonwood."

"Yeah." I lowered my voice and tried to imitate a radio newscaster. 'Is she a cook or a killer? Who knows the real story?'"

He chuckled. "Something like that." We walked along in pleasant silence, and then he asked, "How is your detecting coming along?"

I flopped my arms out to the side. "I'm pretty much a dud at it so far. Only . . . it seems someone thinks I might be getting somewhere." I told him about the spooky note, trying but failing to sound casual.

He stopped, clutched my forearm. "You got that today? Have you called the police?"

"Not yet. I found it this afternoon. Didn't want to overreact."

"Seems like something I'd worry about. I wouldn't call it overreacting."

I shook off his arm and walked away. "I have a burly guy walking home with me. You can check the place out before I go in, if you want to."

"Moi?" He turned to stare at me. "I'm a lover, not a fighter. And I know that's a terrible cliché, but it's true. Remember, son of a Sedona seer, seeker of peace and light."

I stared back. "Look. I didn't want to phone the cops or a friend because I didn't want to admit I was scared. But I don't know you well enough yet to care what you think of me. I'm scared. Please go into the house with me. We'll face the bogeyman together. Waddya say? And then I'll give you a beer."

He crooked his elbow for me to grab and sauntered onward. "Deal. I wish you had a baseball bat, but we'll cope. I'll even go in first, if you have any of that famous pumpkin bread left."

My chest felt lighter and my steps quickened. "It is so a deal." I paused. "Thank you, Ash. I was almost desperate enough to offer kinky sex."

"Something I would love, but I'd suggest you phone Sergeant Doughty if you're that frightened."

This was a good person. I grinned. "She's into kinky sex?"

We laughed our way homeward. Ash told me more about his mother and growing up in Sedona, living for most of his life in a trailer by the river. Like Lola of Merkin's and Crema fame. "The woo-woo people in Sedona were my extended family. I do have a younger sister, Blaze." He peered at me from his position by my side. "Do not laugh. We got enough of that growing up. And no, my mom's name is not Ember. It's Serena—formally changed from Mary." He chuckled. "I love her, but it's a challenge having her as your mother. Blaze took off for California years ago. I expected her to move to Boston or Missouri, someplace where they'd never heard of a vortex. But after she lived in LA for a while, she ended up owning a store outside Joshua Tree National Monument, another spot known for its vortexes. Mom insists she missed the energy. Me, I have no clue."

"I always feel different, more centered, when I spend time in Sedona. So maybe there's something to it. I'm not ready to scoff."

"I knew there was a reason I liked you."

I could see the house when Ash ruined the mood with his next comment. "Your brother told me the Sturgesses might continue with Violet's lawsuit against Adventure Calls."

I stopped in my tracks. My brother told this guy my worst fears. "Perfect. Not sure why he felt like sharing that."

He shrugged. "We're friends."

"Which reminds me. How are you friends? How did you meet?" Please don't say you're also an addict.

"Through Kirsten. We've known each other forever."

30

This Chef Is Shakin'

We reached Leah's cottage. "We're here." I turned onto the entrance path and he followed. Leah had upgraded her home everywhere and the motion sensor lights went on when Ash and I neared, because dusk had become dark while we walked. I paused on the steps, digging for my keys in my backpack, and Ash proceeded to the porch.

"Well, crap," Ash said, "How'd that get there?"

I looked up at his shocked face and my triumph at finding my keys dissolved. He pointed toward the doormat, an elegant coir mat with "Home" stenciled on it. Plus a huge dead frog, not stenciled. I gasped. "Oh, my sweet Lord," I whispered. "No more."

I froze, my keys dangling from my hand. The frog was another benign but nasty warning. I was perfectly safe. I was a big girl who didn't need the protection of some male I'd met days earlier. Still, I was glad Ash had already agreed to go into the cottage with me. "Ready to make good on that promise?"

He took my hand. "I'm betting this is merely another nasty warning. But it seems an escalation from the note. Let's do this," he said. He bent down and picked up the door mat. "Do we need to save it as some kind of evidence?"

I wilted. My shoulders sagged and my hands shook. It was a frog, poor thing. Dead when whoever found it. But in its presence, I felt menace and I hated the fear that threatened to overcome me. I cleared my throat. "Maybe put it in the corner of the porch?"

"If it's evidence, we need to put it someplace safer than out here. Let's go inside and find a plastic bag or something. And then we can talk about calling the cops." He laid the mat down beside the door and put his hand out for my keys. I handed them over. A voice inside my head said that I was a wimp and a betrayer of feminine power for letting Ash take over. I told the voice it was for no more than a few moments, until I pulled myself together.

He unlocked the door, mentioning as he did that it was for sure locked before he opened it. I started to pass him to enter the hall, but he held me back. "What kind of a hero would I be if I let you go in that dark house first?"

"Umm. It's not dark, Ash." Another of Leah's modernizations, the entry light went on as soon as someone entered the hall. I couldn't have loved my friend more at that moment. Still, I let Ash lead the way in.

Once inside, we walked side by side through the house. I pointed out my favorite features of her decorating, on the pretext that this was not a safety check but a simple, gracious tour of a stellar home decorated by a successful designer. I chattered on, aware nerves were making my tongue race but unable to slow the flow. We ended up in the kitchen and I went to the refrigerator for wine and pumpkin bread. "I'm surprised you haven't met Leah," I said. "You two would get along. Wine or coffee with that bread? Maybe Leah has some port. That would be good with the bread."

"Got tea?"

I nodded and started the kettle. I liked him even more. This guy didn't hang onto his masculinity with a beer opener. While the tea steeped, I rummaged and found an old plastic butter container. Ash retrieved the frog corpse from the porch and set it inside the container and then beside the front door.

We settled with our tea and pumpkin bread at the kitchen table. I'd finally stopped babbling by distracting myself with the tea preparation.

Ash took a few bites of the bread and deemed it a winner and then leaned back in his chair. "Truth time. Why didn't you call Sergeant Doughty when you got the note?"

I hung my head. "I didn't want to call attention to it. Wanted it to go away."

"That's what my dear mother would call magical thinking. Maybe if we find it and burn it, we'll be able to find who wrote it by the burns on his hands."

"Or hers," I corrected him. "I know I should have called Sergeant Doughty. I will, as soon as we finish our tea." I hoped she'd take me seriously. Especially when she saw the note I would need to drag from my trash.

I phoned Sergeant Doughty after we drank our tea. She promised to drop by after she fed her family, rather than sending a patrol officer to collect the note. And the frog? She didn't tell me to save the frog, but it remained where Ash had put it. I had a mental picture of a CSI tech taking great care and dissecting the poor creature, checking for what? DNA? Organ donations? Fresh enough legs?

Ash tried to get me to phone Mateo, even offered to do so himself, but my pride stopped me. Darn it, my brother had told me he needed me to stay away from him, needed to work through things by himself. So did I!

Ash refused to leave until Doughty arrived and I didn't argue. It felt good to have someone watching out for me. I tried not to feel guilty about my wimpiness.

We went out on the back porch to talk and wait for the sergeant. We watched the night hawks and bats swoop after insects and heard the birds settling in for the night with low, reassuring sounds. A frog croaked and I wondered if it was mourning its dead companion. For heaven's sake, Madrone, can the drama.

I let out a sigh, releasing with it some of the day's tension. Who was I kidding? The week's tension. I knew tea was better for me than my typical go-to prosecco, but boy oh boy, I could use a glass of wine. Why didn't Leah have a nice double glider? I pictured my head on Ash's shoulder and quickly shook the image away. Absent that inviting glider, I took a seat in a cushioned wicker chair and indicated with a sweep of my hand that Ash could choose his place.

"Maybe it's karma catching up to me," I eventually said. "When our tour started Violet seemed like a charming and fascinating person. I made the mistake of confiding some of my dreams about eventually owning a restaurant to her, private dreams she later shared in a loud voice to everyone on our tour. Including my boss's sister. After that, I had some pretty nasty thoughts about Violet Brock. Thoughts I'm ashamed of now."

"If everyone we wished bad things on encountered those things, the world wouldn't be so overpopulated. Or so my mother advises her clients."

"Or as I've always heard, 'if wishes were horses, beggars would ride.'"

"Your bad thoughts didn't kill Violet. Another human being did. And that's an ugly thing."

My brain registered a crackling sound like fireworks, followed by a loud crash from inside the house. I jumped up to investigate. Ash leapt in front of me and pushed me back into my chair. He wound up lying across my body, blocking all movement except the wild thrashing of my legs. "What the hell do you think you're doing?" I shouted.

He pressed one arm against my legs to stop my kicking. I braced my lower arms against the chair's arms. I could escape this monster's attack with a good heave. But I waited. He sucked in two or three breaths. "Did you hear that?"

"The backfire? For sure." Maybe he was a veteran, with PTSD. I summoned my tolerance. I'd hear him out before I tossed him off my lap. Besides, it had been a while since a man threw himself at me.

"That wasn't a backfire. It was a gunshot. From in front of the cottage."

I leaned forward and my breasts pressed against his side. I leaned back. Had Sergeant Doughty arrived? Caught someone breaking in and shot them?

When I concluded I'd as soon stay beneath Ash as investigate what the noise was, I pushed up and away from him and stood. Quivering like a dog in a bathtub. "Well, then," I said in my chipper Adventure Calls guide voice, "Let's go see what's going on."

Ash snorted. "Faker. Mind you, there's nothing wrong with faking when things get scary." He stood. "Don't turn on any lights when we head inside. We should be able to see okay, since we've been outside."

I nodded, stifling my annoyance at his bossiness. For all I knew he'd been a Navy Seal while I practiced my cooking skills. Still, my house, my battle. I picked up a ceramic ashtray that Leah used when she smoked cannabis. Even that small weapon bolstered my courage. I led the way into the house, sliding the glass door open as noiselessly as I could. Ash followed. I noticed he left the door open behind us. It popped into my head to hope that mosquito season was over. I squashed that thought. Good Lord, we'd heard gunshots and I was worrying about mosquitoes?

We pussyfooted through the kitchen. I paused at the archway that led into the small dining room. Nothing in that room. I crossed it, avoiding the chair at the near end of the table. Next was the living room, the front door on this side, with a large picture window centered on the front porch wall. The porch light was on in expectation of Sergeant Doughty's arrival, and light spilled into the living room. The room was empty but for the shattered glass that adorned the tile and the area rug. And a mango-sized river rock, wrapped in paper held on with several rubber bands, the broad, flat kind that grocery stores use to bind vegetables.

My knees and quads ached as they did when I ventured too close to the edge of a high cliff. My heartbeat pounded in my ears. I leaned my head against the wall.

Ash touched my arm and I flinched away, wondering how my heart could beat any faster. How much more of this I could take. I took a few stiff steps to the front door and gripped the knob. Still locked. "I don't think anyone came in," I whispered.

"I'm going to do a quick check," he said. "Let's not touch anything until Willa gets here."

Willa? Was this guy friends with everyone in Cottonwood? I ignored his order disguised as a suggestion and crunched through broken glass until I could squat and pick up the gift-wrapped rock. I had to know how much my enemy had upped the threat. I had to know now.

The note was bound up with pieces of string and rubber bands. I pulled on one string.

Ash cleared his throat. "It would be easier to see it in the kitchen, where we could turn on the lights."

Silently blessing him for not giving me grief about picking up the rock, I headed for the kitchen. I flipped on the light. "Someone could sneak out back and shoot at us in here," I said, my voice shaky.

"Yeah. But I'm guessing that this was another warning. At least, I'm hoping."

I forced out a fake chuckle. "You're hoping whoever it is won't get serious till you head home."

He grinned. "Caught me. I'm no Superman."

I removed string and rubber bands from the stone and smoothed the note on the table in front of me. "I suppose I shouldn't have touched it, but nobody's going to bother to do forensics on a stupid note."

"Too late now."

"Now I have a witness that I'm not creating these threats to get myself off the suspect list."

"'Sergeant Doughty, Madrone couldn't possibly have tossed it through that front window. We were out back, messing around.'" He'd raised his voice in a bad imitation of himself speaking to the police.

I had to smile. "We weren't messing around. We were talking."

"Yeah, but I'm working on my rep."

"I doubt it needs work." I braced myself and sat down to peer at the note. "Digging too deep will get you hurt. Stop or those you love will feel the pain. Like the frog." This note was printed in a thick marking pen, all caps. All scary.

"Holy heck," I muttered through numb lips. "Things get worse and worser." Goosebumps covered my arms. Grateful I was sitting, I looked across at Ash. I leaned my head on my hands. "I'm not sure I can take any more."

He reached his hand to pat my arm. "You're strong. And Willa will be here soon. She's smart."

"I feel like making a public announcement: 'I don't have a clue who killed Violet. Except it wasn't me.' Maybe I'll take out an ad."

Although the threat chilled me, it also puzzled me. The police considered me a viable suspect, but being threatened away from "snooping" made it seem less likely that I was the killer. So who wanted me to stop? The killer, or someone with another, different secret to hide? Aieee. Too much for my tiny brain to consider.

The front bell rang and we both yelped. I jumped up and my chair fell over backward. Ash rose and righted the chair while I went to the door. "Be sure you know who's there," he reminded me. No reminder needed, but I decided against calling him on it. No use stomping on that protective male urge, no matter how annoying it could be.

Sergeant Doughty—it was her and not a maniacal killer at the door—exchanged warm hugs with Ash and a handshake with me. "We're distant cousins," she explained, "and nothing I do seems to get him removed."

I stared blankly. "Cousins, twice removed," she said. "Get it?"

"Sorry. My wit fled sometime this week, along with my sense of humor." I handed her the first note I'd received and later retrieved from the trash can in Leah's bedroom.

Doughty listened without interrupting me while I told her about the evening's events. Ash couldn't help himself and added a few details, but since they were important, I forgave his butting in.

The sergeant sat back, sipping the tea Ash had made. I gave him points for that. I suddenly had no energy at all, as if some energy pipeline had drained me. I yawned. She smiled. "Adrenalin rush is fading and so are you. I won't be long. I'd like to take both notes, but we're not likely to get prints from them. We have an officer who's trained in fingerprint analysis, but I'm thinking our bad guy used gloves." She tipped the last drops of her tea into her mouth and rose. "There's good news in this, you know."

Good news in being terrorized in my own, well, my borrowed, home? I gave her another empty stare.

"You're looking less and less like a suspect in Violet's murder." Something that had already occurred to me, I didn't say.

Swiping my brow dramatically, I said, "What a relief. Off one hook and onto another."

"I'd say that includes her brother, too," Ash said. "He was still on the list until someone threw that rock. And I'd swear I heard a gun fire."

Doughty rose. "Could be. Now I'd like to look in the front room."

Ash and I trailed after the sergeant into the darkened room. I flinched when she switched on the lights. Could I pay for the window repair and keep Leah ignorant of the damage to her home? My shoulders slumped. No way. Even if I could get away with a lie—something I'd never mastered—she'd hear the whole sordid tale as soon as she set foot in Cottonwood. Maybe before. Small town gossip travels faster than political tweets.

Doughty stood and pulled on a pair of latex gloves. She surveyed the room, as methodical as I remembered from our first meeting by the river. And the body of poor Violet Brock. She must have mentally blocked the room into sections as if cordoning it with crime scene tape. After a few moments she crisscrossed the room, using her flashlight even though the room was well-lighted by the ceiling lights and two lamps on end tables that I switched on.

I raised my chin. "Doesn't all the light make us great targets?"

"At this point, I don't think our bad guy wants to hurt you, but simply scare you off investigating. Which is not a bad idea." She squatted amidst the broken glass and scanned the room from that angle. She stood, walked a few steps, and swooped to pick something up. She put whatever it was in a small paper bag she took from her purse. "Like I said, he or she isn't out to hurt you—yet. These are BB pellets. Ash was right about the gunfire. With a BB gun, you'd have to stand pretty close to be injured. Not that it can't happen. Witness my sons."

Her sons? Are cops' kids like preachers' children? More likely to get in trouble? I shot her a small smile and shrugged, as if I were well aware of the trouble kids could get into.

"Anyway, they want to frighten you. Convince you being an amateur sleuth is not a great idea." She grinned. "If it wasn't against the law to shoot up someone's home, I might have tried it myself. It's definitely time you stop nosing around, Ms. Hunter."

"Madrone," I said reflexively.

"Madrone. The note mentioned those you love. That means your brother, maybe others, as potential victims. Please, leave the investigating to me and my team."

"I'm convinced. I'll keep my nose clean." She didn't have to know my fingers were crossed behind me.

She nodded, her expression skeptical, and continued to examine the room. After a while, she went outside and looked on the porch, then returned. "I'm not going to send techs out here. We can't afford their time. You can go ahead and clean up, but I suggest you talk to Leah before you decide on a window replacement company. I know her, and she's pretty selective."

I laughed out loud, feeling myself thaw from the chill that had taken over my body since the rock went through the window. "Come on. Is there anyone you don't know in this county?"

She smiled. "Between me and the rest of my team, possibly not, unless they're newcomers. This town has big ears." She paused. "One reason I—and our bad guy—knew you were being nosy, and will know if you continue to pursue this." She let her gaze trail around the room. "I doubt anyone will come back before you can get the window fixed. Let's see if there's something we can use to block it with."

We wandered around the house and eventually settled on propping two extra table leaves we found in the entry closet in front of the window. We shoved the sofa against them and then pulled the drapes.

"They'll have to find another way in," Doughty said. "But I'm sure they know you've gotten the message," she added when she saw the shock on my face.

"I really appreciate your help. I don't think that's in the police procedures manual. Would you like more tea?" I asked.

"Happy to help. As to the tea, no offense, but I'd prefer to have it at home. How about you, Ash? Are you heading out?"

"Hey, are you suddenly a chaperone?" Ash asked her, eyebrows raised.

"I'm a detective, a wife, and a mother," she said. "I can take on many roles." She strode to the front door and turned, spreading one arm out to the side as if to guide Ash from the room.

He glanced at me and I said, "I feel like wet toast. I'm headed for the sack. Goodnight to both of you." Before he left, Ash drew close and kissed my cheek. Sweet and brotherly.

I touched my cheek, working to dismiss my attraction to this man I barely knew. Nerves, nothing more. I closed and locked the door behind them, forced to remove my hand from my cheek to accomplish it. Then I traipsed around the house assuring myself that all doors and windows were locked.

I saluted my teeth with a damp brush, donned a big T-shirt and hit the bed.

31

House Hunting with Leonard

If my goal in this visit to Cottonwood had been to meet the maximum number of residents, I was on the right course. I'd intended a relaxing few days on my own with lots of hiking. I hadn't planned on finding the dead body of one of my tour group members, nor had I dreamed I or my brother would be considered suspects.

Plans change. Mine now was to track down a killer, one with the nerve to threaten my family and friends. I brewed coffee, strong, and scrambled eggs to eat with some toast. I needed energy. And courage.

Waiting on my porch for Leonard Anderson to pick me up for our visit to Vista Rioja, I considered my strategy. I had no intention of buying a home here, but I'd googled the comparative costs of living while I ate breakfast. Shoot. Everything cost more in Cottonwood than it did in Tucson. The price of being a bedroom community to Sedona.

I hoped that by spending time alone with Leonard, I'd be able to find out more about Violet's younger years and evaluate Leonard as a murder suspect. Some might think that spending time alone with a man I considered capable of murder was foolish, but I had an excuse. People generally have a reason to kill someone, and Leonard and I were strangers. Of course, if he *did* kill Violet, and he suspected I was only meeting with him to interrogate him, he might revisit that violent streak. The thought made my palms sweat and my breaths come faster.

Remorse hit me for taking up Leonard's time with me, who had little desire and fewer means to buy a home in Cottonwood. I sent that emotion down the street. I was not the first to waste his time and wouldn't be the last. Maybe I'd see something adorable and recommend it to a friend or client who might be able to afford a home. I wanted to plan a subtle way to pry into Leonard's knowledge of Violet's life but my fickle brain decided to dream of finding a small casita here in Cottonwood with space for a huge, well-furnished kitchen and an outdoor cooking area where I could open my restaurant. I'd serve Mom's recipes and my modern adaptations of them. And the presentation—each plate would be served with Madrone's signature flair. Once I discovered it. And could afford to implement it.

The arrival of a silver sedan brought my dreams plummeting to earth and left me without a plan for investigating. Well, I'd ask him about Violet. After all, she was what brought us together, and he knew from yesterday's breakfast that I was curious about her death and her past. I grabbed my pack and trotted to his car. Leonard got out of the vehicle and opened the passenger door for me. Old style courtesy always made me feel special, with that twinge of feminist guilt for not being outraged.

"Welcome, Madrone. Another crisp fall morning in Cottonwood, ordered up for you."

"I had no idea you were in charge of the weather, Leonard. Thanks! And good morning to you. I appreciate your taking the time."

"I'm all yours until 11:00 or so. I have a lunch meeting. Do you want to stop for a coffee before we head to the development?"

"No, thanks. Maybe after?"

He tipped a hand to his head and nodded. "You're the customer." He reached into the back seat and handed me a flyer.

As we headed toward Clarkdale, Leonard commented on places of interest we passed. "That's the Clemenceau Heritage Museum. Used to be a school, but it closed and now it's a museum. It's worth a visit, especially to see the model railroad."

"What's Clemenceau? A town? A famous settler?"

"Used to be a town built by James Douglas to house employees. Company town. He named it Verde, but there were several towns called Verde in Arizona, so the post office asked him to rename it. Douglas was a big fan of the French and named it after their premier. Apparently, they were friends."

"The rich and famous hobnobbed together the same way they do today, I guess."

"Yep. Nothing's really new. The quest for money and power. "

"Did you go to school there?"

"Nope. I'm a proud Marauder of Mingus Union High School."

"In Cottonwood?"

"Yes. The school was pretty new when I started. Sadly, like me, it's getting on in years."

"But still going strong." Trite, but what could I say?

"I knew I liked you. And, while I'm happy to show you Vista Rioja because I'm proud of what we created there, I seriously doubt that's why you arranged to see me today. We can stop for coffee after and you can ask me about Violet."

I flushed from the tip of my head to my toes. No idiot, Leonard. Possibly I was, for thinking he wouldn't see right through my ruse. "That would be great. And I really do want to see the development. I'm not in the market right now, but I have friends and lots of wealthy clients."

"Which is why I never say no." He paused for a significant time. "To a chance to show property."

We both chuckled.

I enjoyed the tour of the model home and the drive through Vista Rioja. It had been well plotted, with views from most of the homes, and a walking path. I would recommend it and I told him that.

We ordered coffee and pastries and sat outside a cute bakery in Clarkdale. I needed to get out and hike soon. All this sleuthing and schmoozing was fattening. Leonard insisted on paying, assuring me it was a business expense.

"First," Leonard said, "let me apologize for my dear partner Isabella's touchiness. We've had some rather nasty encounters with Violet through the years that Isabella *says,* and probably *thinks,* she's dismissed, but when Violet's name pops up again, in the news or on a legal document—"

Or in an obituary.

"It stirs up memories of past disputes, slights. Cottonwood's not the place for socialites or snobs, but Violet and her late husband had influence in Sedona, as well. Isabella and Violet never got along. Maybe jealousy. Because you see how lovely Isabella is, and Violet once was a stunner, as well."

I didn't know what to ask, but I wanted to keep Leonard talking. If I learned enough about all these people and their rivalries, maybe a motive for Violet's death would jump out and bite me. Possibly chew my ass. At that moment, I so wanted to talk to Gabe about this killing in Cottonwood. He and I had uncovered the murderer of a developer during Gabe's first training assignment near Tucson. We could solve this, too. But then, chirped the little voice in my head, you would have invited a man in to solve your problem, something you vowed long ago not to do. Nope, this one was up to me.

"I heard from Mary-Margaret at the Chamber that Violet stirred up jealousy even when she was in her teens."

He smiled. "Oh, yes. All the guys drooled over her, but she was a spitfire. Did Mary-Margaret tell you she took off right after high school, determined to save the world? At least its trees."

"Were you one of the guys who followed her?"

He flushed. Looked over to where the train sat in the station. Focused, I guessed, on anything but me. "Yes, I was, but at the end of the summer, I gave up and headed off to college. Got a degree in architecture. Decided I'd see the world. And then ended up back here in little old Cottonwood." He looked immeasurably sad to me. "By the time I decided to come home, Violet was married to Chet, and Ven was a toddler."

"And you were still in love with her," I whispered.

He nodded, sent me a lopsided smile that didn't reach his eyes. "Guess I still am," he said.

"You never found anyone else?"

"Oh, sure. Had lots of hot romances, some that lasted a while. Even got married for a couple of years. But she hated small town living and left for Seattle." He shook his head. "I think she knew my heart wasn't in our marriage."

"But Chet's been gone for years. Surely you could have rekindled the romance after a while?"

"Violet considered me a friend. Always. Nothing more. So, I took what she offered and settled for friendship." He tilted his head. "Not that it wasn't getting harder to be a friend recently. She had grown brittle, I'd say bitter.

Pretty volatile and moody. Spouting off stuff like the need for atonement. Believe me, she wasn't a religious person, no bead-counter. If that's a PC term." He drank his coffee. "And that's my sad tale of a bruised heart. It's hard to say how I felt when she died. I miss the old Violet, but not the one she'd become. Which somehow makes it even sadder."

Yes, it did. And although my heart surged with pity for this man who'd loved and lost, the doubt niggled at me. Could he have lost patience with the changes in Violet? Tried to choke the bitterness from her? When you hold inside a deep emotion, like the love Leonard said he had for Violet, couldn't that emotion turn to hatred after years of being bottled inside?

32

A Not-So-Musical Encounter

Filled with gratitude that our ride back to Cottonwood would be blissfully short, I struggled for a neutral topic. Then I settled on something that might bring a smile to Leonard, the story of our tour of Canyon de Chelly and how, before her near-disastrous fall, Violet had spoken with our Navajo guide in Diné, his native language. True, he'd been more amused than amazed at her facility, and teased her that she needed to practice more, but the rest of us had been impressed. "When he told her that her Diné was dusty, she laughed and said it wasn't the only thing about her that had gathered dust."

Leonard smiled and it lightened my heart. "Violet had an ear for languages, even back in high school. I wanted to bum around Europe with her after high school, but she was determined to fix America's problems first."

I had Leonard drop me at the Whistle Stop. I wanted to check in with Mateo, and I needed to tell him about the threats I'd received. After all, the last one had included those I loved in its warning. I definitely loved him and knew that even when I ticked him off, my brother loved me.

I entered the store behind Ross's wife, Helen, and held the door open for her. She toted a wicker picnic basket. Its weight almost tilted her to one side, even though she appeared muscular. Although I'd had coffee and a pastry, I wanted to know what was in the basket. I told my voracious appetite to cool it, not that it helped. Ross had mentioned what a great cook his wife was.

"Hi, Helen."

My nose must have twitched because she smiled over her shoulder. "I've got plenty. Join us."

Ross walked out from the back, either heeding the call of the brass entry bell or guided by an excellent sense of smell. Mouth-watering, enticing aromas came from Helen's basket. "Well, well, two beautiful women," he cried. "We shall indeed have a delightful repast." Maybe he was studying for a role in some Shakespearean comedy. "Mateo, come join us," he called.

Mateo stalked from behind the curtain separating the office from the front of the store. My throat caught. Ached. I so didn't want him still determined to keep his distance from me. But his face, when he saw me, immediately tightened. He slowed, then paced across the store to stand in front of me. "How could you?"

"Umm, how could I what?" Was he still angry about my intrusion into Violet's home? Or had I committed some other big no-no in my brother's book of sins? How could I tell what he meant?

"You were threatened and you did not let me know. I am your brother."

For some reason my mind flashed to the Princess Bride. "You killed my father. Prepare to die." So much conviction in my little brother's voice. I breathed easier than I had in days. He still loved me.

I sent him a tentative smile and walked a few steps his way. "I'm sorry?"

"You're sorry? That's all you have to say for yourself?"

"I thought you were still angry. And . . . I came today to warn you."

"To warn me. To warn me?" Okay, he was shouting now. I got it. He was not happy. But he was talking to me.

I didn't try to stop the little grin that slipped out. "How'd you find out?"

"For heck's sake, Madrone, this is Cottonwood! I'm dating Ven Sturgess's daughter. I knew by 9:00 this morning."

Ross gave Mateo a sidelong glance and then focused on me. "Scary stuff." After a moment he added, "So do you intend to heed the warning? Stop snooping?" He peered into the wicker basket Helen had placed on the counter.

Mateo burst out laughing, but his laugh held no joy. "Stop? Stop? You're asking my sister to stop?" He wiped his face with a forearm. "Madrone

Hunter is the most persistent person I know."

"Persistence can be a good trait," I said.

"In many cases, that's true. In this one? Not so true." He shook his head. "Look, Kirsten's joining us for lunch and she's still sore at you. I'll come to your place tonight. In the meantime, try to stay safe." His voice had dropped below screech. There was a chance that by tonight he'd be more willing to discuss my investigation than try to stop me. At least we would continue to "dialog." I despised the term, but if it meant my baby brother would talk to me, I'd dialog through the night.

"Come for dinner? Eightish?"

Kirsten walked in from the back and stood next to Mateo. "We'll both come," Kirsten said. "Maybe together we can get you to stop. And to understand the meaning of keep out of your brother's business."

"I look forward to seeing both of you," I said. I tried and failed to keep the elation out of my voice. They were both coming to see me tonight. The three of us could go over what I knew and solve this case. I'd call RK before dinner and see if he could join us. "Helen, Ross, thanks for the invite, but I think I'd better go now."

"Please, stay," Helen said. "I'd like to hear your progress on tracking this killer."

"Yes, join us," Ross said.

I looked from the scowl on my brother's face to Kirsten's tight-lipped expression and knew they still needed time. Likely more than the few hours until dinner, but they'd promised to be there, so I'd take that offer. "You are very kind, but I'll let the four of you enjoy lunch. I need to work on getting dinner ready." My voice chirped like a cactus wren. I cleared my throat, working on the mature, sedate older sister look.

I accepted the cookie Ross offered and backed away from the group. Right into a standing rack of greeting cards. It fell over. Mateo helped me right and restock it and I slunk out the front door. He flipped the Open sign to Closed as I made my exit. Instead of feeling shut out, I was exultant. My brother would forgive me and work with me to solve Violet's murder!

I am nothing if not an optimist.

33

Ven Shares a Secret

I trudged down the street to a small barbecue restaurant and ordered comfort food from the young guy who staffed the counter—a pulled pork sandwich with pickles and raw onions. And onion rings on the side. I pulled out a tiny notebook to try to wrestle my thoughts together. My wayward mind strayed to what I might fix for my brother and Kirsten for dinner. Thinking about menus soothed me and kept the fear of what my "threatener" might have in store for me. A new thought arrived. How did this person know what I was up to? Was it someone I'd spoken to, asked about Violet?

Really? I should have considered that before, but it hadn't occurred to me. The fact that someone knew who I talked to, was aware that I was still looking into Violet's death, and might discover too many secrets, had to reveal something.

The server at the little café laid my food before me and after sliding the ketchup my way, asked, "How's sleuthing?"

My mouth fell open. I had never been in the café before, never, as far as I knew, met the redhaired young man. Had he been reading my notes upside down? I gaped at him. "Have we met?" I asked.

"Nah. But my mom works at the Call Center, used to be friends with Ven Sturgess. I saw you at the Cottonwood potluck." He lifted a brow. "We don't get a lot of hot women at the potluck." He flushed bright red and I felt a smidgeon of sympathy for his redhead's complexion. But for goodness' sake, if he was a day over twenty, I was ready for retirement. He stuck out his hand. "I'm Eddie."

Please. Notes on my car, stones, not to mention BB guns. I did not need a teenager gawping at me and calling me hot. I poured a small dollop of ketchup beside my rings. "Pleased to meet you, Eddie. Right now, I'm not sleuthing, I'm trying to eat this delicious looking food."

His expression crestfallen, Eddie said, "Sorry to bother you. It's . . .we all knew Violet—we all know the family—it's really a shame."

Another information source? Woot. "You know the family?" I asked and popped an onion ring in my mouth. It was hot and crisp, perfect, except for the hot part scalding my mouth. With young Eddie gazing raptly at me, I couldn't spit it out. I gulped down some water, which doesn't go well with onion rings.

"Yes, it is a shame," I said once my mouth cooled. "Is there anything you can tell me? Do you know Kirsten well? Or her parents?"

"Nah, Kirsten's way older than me. But she's always nice when she comes in. My mom always liked Kirsten's mother. And Violet was a good person when she wasn't acting all high and mighty. I admired her 'cause she said what she thought."

"Yeah, I liked that about her, too. She'll be missed." Deciding that Eddie knew local gossip, like Lola at La Crema, but didn't have any new insights on why Violet died, I added, "Thank goodness, Sergeant Doughty is smart and experienced. I'm sure she'd be interested if you know anything about what happened to Violet." There. Washing my hands of the sleuth role. I. Am. Not. Investigating. If whoever threw that rock and left that frog had eyes everywhere, as he or she seemed to, maybe they'd hear my proclamation of uninvolvement.

"Whatever. I don't think I know anything everyone else doesn't." Eddie wandered out to the tables and made a show of wiping them down and paying no attention to me.

I was finishing my meal and ready to pay when my phone rang. Leonard.

"Can you meet me at Violet's house? Ven will be there. We want to talk. And listen, don't tell anyone you're coming here. It's private." A chill ran down my back. I liked Leonard, but then again, I'd liked most everyone I'd met in this town. With the exception of Kirsten's ex, Greg. One of them was a killer.

Leonard continued, asking me to meet them as soon as I could, and I agreed.

I thought for a few moments. I jotted a very short note on a piece ripped from my notepad and folded it. "Eddie, I told you I wasn't snooping into Violet's death, and that's pretty much true. But I can tell you're a person I can trust. I'm headed to meet someone who knew Violet well and I'm sure nothing will go wrong. But if I don't call you within the next hour—"I gave my watch a quick look—"get this to Sergeant Doughty." I put my finger to my lips. "Please don't look at the note or tell anyone else about it. I really don't want to get anyone into trouble. This is between you and me." I laid my hand on his arm. "I'm putting my faith in you, Eddie. Should I?"

His eyes wide, Eddie said he would do as I asked and not tell a soul. After he gave me his cell number, I patted his arm again as I left. If the kid thought I was hot, I might as well take advantage of it. Didn't happen all that often.

* * *

I sauntered up the walkway to Violet's casita, wondering if I was sauntering into a trap. Sauntering while looking everywhere for a rabid dog named Frisco and his perhaps more rabid owner is no easy move. Maybe I should have asked Leonard to let me speak to Ven, but then he'd have known I didn't trust him. By now he should realize that I was hard put to trust myself.

It wasn't hard to trace my steps in this small chatty town, particularly Old Town. Whoever wanted me to stop my snooping likely knew I hadn't yet given up. Which brought to mind the idea that I might try a disguise. I loved wearing costumes, for Halloween or other festive events. I reserved a drawer in my tiny room of Mom's small home for costumes, and I was pretty creative at coming up with ideas. My shoulders sagged. Most of my costumes easily allowed people to recognize me. Not to mention they were in Tucson. It would take quite a bit of work to come up with a costume that hid my identity and allowed me to fit into Cottonwood life. People might notice a pirate or an alien entering Crema. *Bad idea, Madrone.*

Once I took the steps onto Violet's porch, the door swung open and Leonard stepped out, smiling. "You came. We weren't sure you would."

If they knew how badly I wanted to get inside Violet's home and snoop some more, he'd have had no doubts about my arrival. "It did sound mysterious. By the way, I left a note that will only be delivered should I not return safely." Figured I might as well be open.

His face fell. "I'd hoped you trusted me, but I understand. It's been scary here since Violet's death. Please, come in."

"Violet's murder," I corrected. I followed him inside.

Ven waited in the front room. She leaped up from a sofa upholstered in a southwest motif. "I'm sorry about the secrecy," she said. "I imagine you're wishing you'd never met my mother."

"You're wrong about that. I enjoyed much about Violet. I regret she got angry with Adventure Calls. And I regret she died in such a terrible way. I was upset about her lawsuit and her rage, but I wished her no harm, believe me."

"I do believe you. And I'm beginning to believe Mom might have been ill, not simply growing more outspoken, as some older folks do. What I used to think of as her 'little fits of anger' were coming way too often."

I gave a half-smile. "If only I'd recorded those words. I understand you're considering continuing with Violet's promised lawsuit."

"Wes thinks it's worth considering, but honestly, I'd like to drop it. You meant well."

"I did. So did our driver. We are not bad people."

"I'm sure you doubt it, but neither are we."

"And yet, we're all suspects in Violet's murder." I looked over at Leonard. "Including you."

His normally benign expression hardened. "Watch your accusations. She was my friend."

"The accusations aren't mine. Sergeant Doughty told me we're all suspects until she says we're not."

Ven stared at me. "She can't suspect me of killing my own mother."

Tired of being the nice girl, I said, "Your very wealthy mother. People have killed for far less money."

"True. All the more reason I wish this was over." She indicated two leather chairs opposite the sofa. "Sit, please." She clasped her hands together and then began to alternately rub first one, then the other. Either she was nervous or had painful arthritis. I voted for nervous.

I sat. Ven perched on the sofa and Leonard took the other chair. I waited. Kept my mouth shut and my expression expectant through a lengthy silence. These two invited me here. I wasn't going to put words in their mouths. However, if either of them said, "You're probably wondering why I asked you to come here," I might go ballistic.

"I don't want Wes to know what I'm telling you. I love my husband, but he. . .has some issues and well, he might not go along with my plans."

Talking about her husband's "issues" might be hard on Ven, but I had little sympathy for her. Hadn't the woman heard of codependency? Enabling? "He's a gambling addict. I heard. Your daughter's been enabling him. She lied to her grandmother to help her father. At least that's her story."

Ven's face paled to a pasty gray. Then she sat forward and pressed her palms together. "I didn't know about it until she confessed to me this morning. Wes should never have done that to her. If she'd come to me, I would have advised her not to bail him out."

"And yet here you are, asking me to keep what you plan to tell me from your husband." I could only hope that my brother's relationship with Kirsten wouldn't last. This was not a functional family.

She looked at me with soulful brown eyes that were a lot like my mother's. Or maybe an Irish Setter I once loved. "Love makes us idiots sometimes."

That I could not deny. I smiled, trying to show the empathy I felt with her. "Yeah, it does."

"My mother never trusted Wes, and as she grew older, her dislike became more open. He, as you heard the other day, was not her biggest fan." She turned to gaze fondly at Leonard. "Poor Leonard heard way too much about that, I'm sure."

He raised an eyebrow. "Friends listen and try not to judge. But she was getting angrier and more vocal about a lot of things in the past several months."

"I know. Maybe Madrone's right and she *was* suffering from dementia. But I have to believe it was clear thinking that led her to gift me with one of her homes."

I gaped at her. "She gave you a home? To live in? By yourself?" Not a smooth way to pry into the state of her marriage.

Her smile forgave my gaffe, at least I decided to assume that's what it meant. "I planned to make the house into a café. I have construction plans and permits in place already. Mom's death might mean I'll change my plans, maybe start here."

"But . . . Wes didn't know about the home . . . or your plans?"

She shook her head. "Mom gave me the house and loaned me the development money but made me promise not to tell him, and I knew she was right. Wes has a problem with money."

Yeah, he spends it. Or gambles with it. I'd call that a problem. I'd also call that a darn good motive for getting rid of Violet.

Okay. I don't have a poker face. Ven frowned at me. "I knew you'd jump to that."

I grimaced. "Jump to what?"

"My husband is a gambler. He is an addict. But he is *not* a murderer. Therefore, I want you to find who really killed Mom, before Willa Doughty jumps right along with you to the wrong conclusion." She stood and paced around the little coffee table to touch Leonard's shoulder. "Leonard told me it was true, that you were still looking into her—death, despite those threats. And that I ought to come clean with you about the house and such."

"And since your mom's death, have you told Wes about the other house? About your plans?"

"He's excited to begin planning what to do with this place. He . . . doesn't know about the other place yet, but I'll tell him soon. I have a dream to have two or three eating establishments, maybe a small boutique hotel-slash-casita. I know he'll love them, but I'm worried about his gambling."

"Has Kirsten told the police? You know at some point she'll have to. I'm sorry, but your husband had every reason to kill Violet. He had more at stake than I did." And so did Kirsten, but I'd already accused her husband. Her daughter? No way. I shook my hands out, working to calm myself. After all, what Ven was telling me didn't give Wes more motive to kill Violet. Unless. Unless. "You're sure Wes didn't have a clue about your other house. From what I've seen, Cottonwood is a very small town, and gossip travels faster than swallows at Tuzigoot."

"That's true, in most cases. But any of my friends who knew about it also recognized how important it was to keep it secret. And Wes kept busy at the bar and hotel." After a long pause, she added, "And the casinos."

Ven stood and wandered to stare out the front window. "I know you're thinking that if Wes found out, he might have flown into a rage and killed my mother." She shook her head, not looking at me. "More likely he would have taken all the money I'd set aside for remodeling and gambled it away. Maybe sold the house. I had another account, but if he'd known, he'd have found it and spent it." After a pause she added, "He didn't know."

How bad was the state of their marriage, keeping such enormous secrets from each other? I considered the level of anger Wes nursed against his mother-in-law. It went against my nature not to blurt out those thoughts, but I pressed my lips together. Realizing my expression revealed my thoughts, I shook my head. "I'll let you know what I find out. I don't have the forensic information the police can get, or even access to all the paperwork they have. I'm simply relying on gossip and what people decide to share. You'd do better than me." An idea came to mind. "Kirsten and Mateo might be able to dig up more than I can, if you can convince them to help me." If someone else did the dirty work, then I wasn't trying to control my brother, right?

"They seem to be thawing toward you. Dinner's a good first step, I'm sure, especially with your cooking." Ven's expression seemed more hopeful than when I'd walked into Violet's home. "And I'm sure I can convince Wes to drop the lawsuit."

"I hope that's true. As I said before, we did our best. As to finding a murderer, I said I'd try, no promises." Time for a diversion and for another step toward solving Violet's murder. "Violet told me about her casita. I'd love a tour, if it wouldn't be too hard on you."

Ven smiled weakly. "Didn't see enough the first time?" I cringed and Ven added, her smile a little stronger, "Kirsten told me. Maybe you're right about the impossibility of keeping secrets in Cottonwood. Maybe. With most people." Something mysterious about her tone hinted that she herself had more secrets, but I'd have to use thumbscrews to get them out of her. And I had no idea how to use thumbscrews. Have to settle for patience. Oops. Something else I had little experience with.

Leonard shot me a lopsided smile. "We've searched everywhere for clues.

But you should give it a go. Besides, this is a terrific casita. Ven, you could show her, and tell her how you and Wes plan to make it into a bistro."

I trailed Ven around Violet's well-designed small home. Even though the police, Violet's family, and Mateo and I had spent time here since her death, it still had that musty, unlived smell, like homes get after even a short vacation.

In each room, Ven paused to tell me her plans for transforming the casita into a lively bistro. I enjoyed this leisurely, guided tour far more than my earlier furtive and hurried search for clues. The casita was well-lighted for an older Arizona home, with a couple of skylights and a large number of ceiling mounted spotlights highlighting a variety of art. Most were landscapes, but whether original or good copies, I didn't know. Two large, striking images of forest fires dominated the smallish dining room. I hadn't noticed them in my last visit, but Mateo and I had divided the search in this room and I'd been paying more attention to my brother than the room.

Ven's voice lightened and her steps transformed from halting to brisk as she proceeded. When we reached Violet's bedroom, I stopped in the doorway, feeling suddenly like a trespasser. In the rest of the home, I'd simply been curious and open to Ven's plans. Here I was an invader. Yet here was likely the place I had the best chance of finding clues to Violet's state of mind before she died. On my earlier search, I'd skimmed over the room, too guilt-ridden to do a thorough search.

As I hesitated in the doorway, I looked across the room to an entire wall of photographs of forest fires, many black and white and stark, several in full and frightening color. I'd noticed some of them before, but been distracted by the beauty of the jewelry box.

Ven turned back to me. "Come on in. It's hardest in here, but I tried to look for a diary, and letters, that might have given us answers. The saddest things I found were brand new towels in the linen closet, brand new underwear in here. Saving for what? For when? I went home after that and opened up a new set of sheets I'd set aside. I vowed to enjoy the nice things now." Tears traced her cheeks. "I haven't given her clothes or anything else away—it's too soon. Except those darn towels. I made Kirsten take them, and promise to use them right away."

I blinked to get rid of my tears. I took a few steps into the room and ran my fingers over the colorful handmade quilt on Violet's bed. The soft lumps of quilting and hand-sewn patches felt comforting beneath my fingers. "Was she a quilter?" I asked.

Ven shook her head. "No. She bought that in a charity auction."

I nodded toward the wall of photographs. "A photographer at one time?"

"In her younger days, she was quite the amateur photographer." Ven choked on the words, sniffing.

Time to deflect her sorrow. "On the TV shows, people hide diaries and stacks of cash in their freezers. Did you find anything?"

She shook her head and smiled, a small result for a big effort. "No packages of cocaine, either. I found copies of her will in her office, and bills and other paperwork, but no blackmail letters, no copies of threats she made or warnings to people. She did have quite a few renters, but most were managed by someone else, and Violet had little or nothing to do with them." I gulped. I'd seen that list of renters on my previous foray into the home, but I decided not to share. Ven continued. "Mom was an old woman who was occasionally cranky, but didn't hurt anyone. Except with her tongue. It doesn't make sense."

I closed the distance between us and patted her upper arm. "I don't think murder makes sense, but someone had a reason to want to silence Violet. I promise I'll do my best to find out who, and why." Brave words from someone who'd hours before sworn she was not continuing her investigation.

Sheeze. I cry at sappy movies, especially those about lost dogs and cats, and occasionally about lost—and—found loves. But why was I offering to help the woman who, despite her claim to the contrary, might still sue me and my employer?

My guess? Ven's tears. Or, possibly because I wasn't fond of being threatened. Most likely, my insatiable curiosity. Not the first time it had gotten me in trouble.

The rest of the tour revealed that Ven had a designer's eye and a great plan to transform the casita into a bistro. It would take cash and labor, but I imagined she would succeed. She had her mother's grit and determination. And now she had her money.

As soon as I was on my way home, I gave Eddie at the barbecue place a quick call and told him to get rid of the note.

34

Sideswiped

That afternoon, I paced inside and outside the cottage, trying to predict Mateo's behavior when he and Kirsten arrived. Would he be ready to join my investigation? Determined to stop me? More worried than angry or more angry than worried? He'd told me he couldn't let others control him. So that in turn meant that neither should I allow that behavior from him. Didn't it?

I had to stop the squirrels dashing around in my brain. My brother and Kirsten were due for dinner around eight, so I had way too much time to kill after returning from my visit with Ven and Leonard. Those dratted squirrels threatened to make me physically ill.

Earlier that morning I'd spoken to Leah before Leonard came by and filled her in on her broken window. Like the good friend she was, she expressed more concern about me than her window. She gave me the go-ahead to call for a replacement, and I insisted on paying her deductible, which would become a deductible from my savings account for my restaurant. I couldn't worry about that today. Too much of that dish on my plate already.

Leonard phoned a window replacement firm and used his connections to schedule a repair team late that afternoon, so I had to remain at home once I got back from Violet's casita and await their arrival. I stopped on my way home to buy food to prepare that would keep me occupied and pacify Mateo when he arrived.

Chopping veg and prepping simple but satisfying hors d'oeuvres calmed my nerves. Everyone loved hummus, didn't they? After the prep, I devoted a couple of hours to cleaning Leah's place, starting in the front room, thoroughly vacuuming the remnants of broken window glass, following with mopping the tile areas. I vowed no shard would remain waiting for the next unsuspecting bare foot, mine or Leah's.

Then I turned to preparing the simple but delicious meal of *calabacitas*, one of Mateo's favorites, with oven-roasted pork tenderloin, and pan-smashed potatoes. The tenderloin and the potatoes would make a mess of the kitchen, but I was not only a great cook. I knew how to clean kitchens. Soon the aroma of sauteed onions and peppers filled the kitchen and calmed my soul.

I wasn't sure if Kirsten was a vegetarian, or even a vegan, so I kept the cheese separate until I could ask. If she preferred veggies, there was plenty of the zucchini and corn dish. I'd braise the tenderloin right before they were due, but put it in the oven after they arrived, because no one enjoyed overcooked tenderloin. Tough instead of tender only worked for cowboys. And tender often worked better for them.

Once everything was ready, I hopped in the shower and put on fresh clothes. I hadn't spent much time with Kirsten, so I wanted to put on my best face for my brother's new girlfriend. I even put on mascara and blush. The girl didn't know how special she was. I decided not to worry about how old that mascara was and what germs the wand harbored.

At 8:15, I opened the wine I'd chilled for dinner and had a glass. I had an extra bottle, so one small glass wouldn't hurt, and it might calm my nerves. Mateo wasn't the kind to avoid confrontation, and he was generally prompt. He'd said he'd come for dinner, so come he would. Unless Kirsten refused to speak to me. But no. She'd invited herself along. It was in all our interests to talk and resolve Violet's murder, if we could. I'd make sure we were all subtle in our enquiries, so whoever wanted us to butt out might not know we continued to snoop.

I wandered to the front porch with my glass of wine, smelled the aroma of someone's barbecue. My stomach growled. In the distance I heard a siren, faint and fading. Was the cottage near a hospital or fire department? I went inside and snitched a few crudites to stave off my hunger.

I was persuasive when I wanted to be. Mateo and Kirsten would join my quest. Things would work as planned. But they were late. Why?

At 8:30, I texted my brother but heard nothing back. At 8:45, I phoned him and the call went directly to voice mail.

By that time, I'd found plenty of room on my plate for more worries. Where were my brother and his girlfriend? How could he have transformed into someone that unkind? Mateo wouldn't do this to me, no matter how upset he was with me. By 9:00 my worries fought with my anger. How the heck could my brother be so heartless?

Shortly after 9:00, finally, someone knocked on the front door. About time. My ire rose and I felt like a worried parent when a child gets lost—relieved to breathe again at last, but furious about the behavior.

I trotted to the front door, then paused, cautious, and peeked through the viewing hole. Instead of Mateo, Sergeant Willa Doughty stood before me, her expression sorrowful.

I flung the door open, my heart pounding. I could not take more bad news.

Or so I thought. Willa Doughty reached out to me as she would one of her own children, arms outstretched. I fell into them for the few seconds, maybe twenty, that it took to recall she was the person who considered me and my brother capable of killing an elderly woman.

I drew back and crossed my arms, my lips pressed tight. I swayed the slightest bit, like a desert willow branch in the wind. Then I steadied myself. "Tell me what happened. Where is my brother? Did you arrest him? Or . . .?"

Doughty put a hand on the door frame and started to step inside. I could either block her entrance and look like an idiot—and entertain a neighbor or two—or invite her in. I backed away in silent invitation.

She came in. "Mateo's fine, Madrone, or he will be. So is Kirsten. But—"

"What happened? A car wreck? Bicycles?" I glanced outside at the dark night. Hoped they hadn't been riding their bikes after dark. I sucked in a breath and shut up so the sergeant could talk.

"Let's sit down and I'll tell you everything I know, I promise." She touched my upper arm lightly and guided me toward the sofa. "Let me get you some water."

I sat on the edge of the cushion. "Tell me what you have to say now. Then water. I'll be fine."

She must have believed me because she lowered herself onto an easy chair opposite me. "They were headed here, as I understand it, to eat dinner with you." I let out the breath I'd held for too long. So at least one of them was able to speak. I fixed my gaze on Willa, who continued her story. "They were walking together on a side street, not far from here, when they were sideswiped by a car, a hit and run. Fortunately, someone was sitting on their porch, saw what happened, called 911 and ran to help them."

I felt myself deflate. It never stopped. All the pain of so many years ago struck me. "Hit and run?" I managed to squeeze out.

The police detective nodded. "And the person who saw the accident couldn't identify much about the car, except she thought it had no headlights on. And didn't stop."

My chest contracted against the pain, current and ancient. What was wrong with me? People I loved—I shook off the direction my thoughts were headed. *Focus on now. Focus on now.* I rubbed my cheek. "How bad was it? Where are they?" I jumped up. I should go to him. He can't be alone.

"They will both be fine. But they're out of commission right now. You can wait a few more minutes and I'll take you there." She must have noticed my eyes widen, because she added, "Or you can drive yourself. It's not far from here. Give me a moment to explain." She rose. "And I'm going to get you that water. Sit there and I'll be right back."

Her voice persuaded me to sit, although I inwardly chafed at being treated like a dog. Sit. Stay. I'll bring you a treat.

My body was still, but my mind raced. How bad was it? Who had done this? Could the person who threatened me already—

"Here you go," Willa said. She'd brought two glasses. "I got myself some, as well. It's been a long, interesting day."

She thought my brother being nearly killed by a rampaging car interesting? What kind of monster was she? I wrangled my thoughts back to reality. She was a cop, doing her job, working to keep me calm. I needed her on my—our—side. "How badly were they injured? Have you found the hit and run vehicle? Was it kids?" In Tucson, kids stole cars for joyrides that too often ended without any joy.

She leaned back in the chair and drank some water. "You can get more details from the ER doc at Verde Valley. She's a good doctor, treated my sons way too often. As I understand it, Kirsten's in surgery for a broken leg and Mateo injured his shoulder and possibly broke some ribs. He was unconscious for a while, so they took a series of x-rays or whatever they do these days. Madrone, it's a good hospital, with good facilities. I wanted to get in touch with your mother, but Mateo insisted it wasn't necessary, that you were in town and not to call her. It's fortunate someone saw them, or it might have been worse."

My mind immediately envisioned my poor brother and Kirsten in the middle of the road, causing annoying thumps to countless drivers striking them again and again. "I'd like to meet them. Thank them. But first I need to go to Mateo."

"Yes to both those. Very soon. Mateo's under sedation and was asleep when I left his room." She saw my mouth open and threw a hand up to stall me. "Believe me, I would have sent someone for you but I only spoke to him for a few moments. Then I came straight here. I wanted to be the one who told you, Madrone. We need to consider the possibility that this wasn't an accident."

"Possibility? Are you kidding me? You surely don't doubt that this was the work of whoever left those notes. Slaughtered that frog. Threw that rock. Shot that BB gun. This is no coincidence." My face flushed. My voice had risen to top volume by the end of my rant.

"It's a dark, moonless night. I checked their clothes and they weren't wearing reflective clothing. It would have been hard to see them. And it was around a corner."

"Where someone could have waited for them. Was there a place to hide a car and wait?"

"Yes. *If* that's the case. I'll be checking tomorrow as soon as it gets light."

"Don't you have lights for that kind of thing? I could check tonight. I have a flashlight. A good one. Someone could get rid of any evidence tonight."

"Someone's on the scene, we've got roadblocks up. You absolutely should not try to go there. You need to visit your brother. I do not want to find you in a ditch by the side of the road."

A vision of Mateo's crumpled body lying in a ditch flashed to mind. Tears that I'd postponed earlier leaked from my eyes. "They were in a ditch?" I croaked.

She smiled and patted my leg. I flinched as if her hand were a hot branding iron. No more pain. "No, Madrone. Our witness-slash-Samaritan dragged them off the road to the side and covered them, keeping them from going into shock. It didn't take long for the EMTs to arrive, anyway. But please, please don't try to find the scene. As I told you, some of my team members are out there right now with lights, checking with the neighbors for other witnesses. I promise I'll be there as soon as we're done here and again at dawn when we can see more."

Since she hadn't told me where the incident occurred, I agreed with her restrictions. I doubted I was trained enough to recognize anything of significance. "As long as you admit this is most likely tied to the person or persons who've been threatening me, I promise I won't visit the scene."

"Narrow promise, but I'll take it. Believe me, I'm taking this seriously. Our witness believed that the vehicle swerved to hit them." She paused. "Purposefully." She touched my hand. "It could have been a lot worse, Madrone. If it wasn't an accident, as I'm pretty certain it was not, then our suspect is upping the ante. Watch yourself very carefully. In fact, it might be time to get your friend RK to keep watch on you. He's a big guy."

RK? I chewed on that for a moment. Then gave a mental head slap. Roadkill's new nickname. Rattled, Madrone? Thinking about my friend made me wish he were here. I'd phone him from the hospital. "Good idea. I'll see what he's up to as soon as I check on Mateo and Kirsten. I imagine Ven and Wes are there already."

"The Verde Valley grapevine is possibly faster than dispatch. They beat me to the hospital. Not a good week for any of you."

I hoped the universe would see fit to grant me a better few days.

"I need to get over there." I wanted to nudge her out the door like a Border Collie herding sheep.

She glanced at the nearly empty bottle of wine. "It might be best to wait 'til morning."

"It might, but no. I'll grab a cup of coffee and eat some of the dinner I prepared for them." I crossed my heart with one hand and held the other behind my back, fingers crossed.

She nodded, the skepticism plain on her face. "I'll check with you tomorrow morning, let you know what we've discovered. And I'll have some of the guys drive by tonight. Give your friend a call and watch yourself every minute. Danger—and often, accidents—come when you're rushing toward something else."

I wasn't sure what exactly that little nugget meant but I nodded as if I had absorbed the wisdom. "Thank you so much for coming here, for filling me in. It's good to know you're on the job."

She smiled. "For a possible suspect, that's saying a lot. I appreciate your attitude and will appreciate you even more if you keep me informed and," she paused and looked directly into my eyes, "if you don't try to solve this yourself. That's my job and you know now how dangerous it can be for an amateur."

And for the people said amateur loves. But I didn't say that. I herded her closer to the front door, repeating my gratitude for her help and for her trust in me.

35

How to Ask for Help

Recognizing Willa's wisdom, I trotted to the kitchen, where inviting aromas of pork and sage and onions mocked my dinner plans. I wrapped the half-cooked pork loin in foil and stuck it in the fridge. I might salvage some hash from it. The calabacitas were an equal disaster but I choked down a few cold bites along with a hunk of cheese and then tossed it in the fridge. Maybe I could come up with a soup or something from the squash or at least use it to flavor that hash. "Work with me, universe. Bring Mateo and Kirsten here for breakfast someday soon."

While I chewed on the dead dinner, I heated water to make French press coffee. I'd put it in one of Leah's insulated travel mugs. While it brewed, I headed to the bathroom to splash my face and wipe away the streaks of mascara. How often did I put on eye makeup? Almost never. Maybe it was bad karma.

I shook my head. No. Not bad karma. Bad person, one who not only thought it okay to kill an elderly woman but one who worked very hard to scare me away from the case. If indeed, as I'd considered before, it was really the killer trying to scare me off or someone else, someone with a secret they urgently needed to protect. Either way, bad person or persons. Very bad and amazingly determined and well-informed of my activities.

I could rule out anyone who knew me at all well. When people try to push me around, I dig in my heels and push back. As Mateo had told Ross earlier today.

I blew my nose and headed to the hospital.

* * *

The older woman at the reception desk in the ER made a call and suggested I sit while I waited to talk to the emergency room physician. "Dr. Wygand is with a patient, but she'll see you as soon as she can. Your brother is in a room down here, but he might be relocated if we get an influx of new cases."

It smelled of disinfectant and sweat in the room. Not even disinfectant could dispel that taint of fear. I found a chair and sat. Immediately popped up and started pacing. Then I noticed I wasn't alone—a young woman and a woman who might have been her mother huddled together in one corner of the waiting area. They hadn't had time to wipe away the mascara streaks. The younger woman's legs were crossed, one foot pumping up and down, up and down. But where were Ven and Wes?

I asked the clerk, who told me that she couldn't give me information about Kirsten, but said, "Generally speaking, if someone needs surgery, they are transferred to the surgical suite." In other words, I'd find Kirsten's parents in the surgical waiting area. Something to do after I talked to Mateo's doc and had a chance to see my brother. Even if he were asleep, I needed to see him, touch him, if possible. Assure myself he was alive.

I forced myself to sit. The two other women in the room didn't need my nervous energy polluting the waiting room air. I pulled out my phone and texted RK. It was 10:30. I had no idea where he'd be but if he got my message, he'd respond.

Sure enough, my phone buzzed in under ten minutes. "What's up, boss? Need bail?"

"Not funny. I'm at the hospital with Verde Valley Hospital. Mateo and Kirsten were brought her after someone tried to take them out with a car while they walked to my place tonight."

Silence. A long silence. "Do you want me there or do you want me to go to Leah's? I'm in Sedona but I can be there in half an hour, maybe less."

My shoulders lost some of their tension. I had a friend, someone I could rely on. "The cops think you should spend the night with me. They don't think this was an accident. And . . . those threats, and . . . I'm scared." That last came out like the squeak of a toddler.

"I'll come to the hospital. How is he? And Kirsten?"

"I haven't talked to the doctor yet, but Sergeant Doughty said they'll both be okay. Could have been much worse, but someone saw it happen and called for help. I think Mateo's sedated, so I'm going to take a peek after I talk to the doctor. But . . . text me when you get into Cottonwood and I'll tell you where to meet me."

"Done. Hang in there, Madrone. You've got friends. Should I call Gabe?"

"No! He's got enough on his shoulders, filling in for Tripp." I giggled. Who giggles when her brother's in the hospital? I was losing it, fast. "Must be something in the air. I gather Kirsten has a broken leg, too. Shoulders. Legs? Get it?" I tried and failed to stifle another giggle.

"Breathe, sweet stuff. You're getting hysterical. I'll be there as soon as I can."

After I waited what seemed hours but in reality was around twenty-five minutes, a petite blonde woman in bright turquoise scrubs and carrying a clipboard strode toward me. I stood. I had four, maybe five inches on her, but her stance and muscled arms told me she could take me out in a fight. Despite the late hour, she radiated energy and stamina, and I immediately felt better about my brother and Kirsten.

"I'm Janet Wygand. You're Mateo Hunter's sister?"

I nodded. "Yes. How is he? Can I see him? Will he be okay?"

She smiled and held her hands up, palms facing me. "Yes, you can see him, but he's asleep. Yes, he'll be okay, if all goes as expected. He's doing better than most pedestrians who take on vehicles." She gestured me to sit and then joined me, rubbing her shoulders and neck. "Your brother and his friend are quite lucky, even though right now I'm sure you don't agree."

"If being alive after taking on something as big as a car is good fortune, I guess."

"The EMTs said if they'd been hit much earlier or a bit later along that street, it could have been worse. They were pushed into brush along the road instead of the creek bed or against a barrier. Your brother's shoulder is torn up and he has a few broken ribs. He'll be in pain, but he'll heal."

"And Kirsten?"

She smiled. "I can't tell you about her condition, but I can tell you she was sent to surgery. Her parents are there, so you can see if they want to talk with you. Both your brother and his friend are young. That's always on their side."

"I'll peek in on Mateo and then go visit with them. Any idea when he might wake up?"

Her smile lost wattage. "He was awake and refused strong medication. Said he had a problem with drugs. That said, he'll possibly wake sooner than I expect." She paused. "I can ask a nurse to bring a cot in for you so you can be there when he does wake up." She cleared her throat. "Sergeant Doughty will want to speak to him. I gather this might not have been an accidental hit and run."

I nodded. "Yes, a cot would be good. Thank you for what you've done for my brother."

She rose, stretching. "We'll be keeping an eye on him, but we may move him upstairs if we need the room. Not tonight, but tomorrow. Those rooms are larger, at any rate." She started to head back into the denizens of the ER, but turned before she hit the doors. "I hope they find whoever's responsible. I see enough mayhem here. Don't need the on-purpose kind."

The nurse led me to Mateo's room and promised she'd send for a cot and some blankets. My brother slept fitfully, little moans and starts disturbing his sleep. Those small noises kissed my ears. I touched his chest and whispered reassurance to him. Then I squared my shoulders and left the room. I asked the nurse to let RK know where I'd gone and headed to the surgical suite, following her directions.

* * *

About the only thing that my visit with Ven and Wes Sturgess did was confuse me. Both wept when they caught sight of me and rushed to embrace me. Their relief that both of our loved ones would be okay spoke loudly. They loved their daughter and wouldn't endanger her.

However, as he embraced me, Wes muttered, "She never told me she was going to your place. My little girl. I can't believe this happened." So, he didn't know his daughter would be there, but maybe he wanted to ambush Mateo to warn me off? No, Wes, you're not off the hook yet.

My joy about Mateo and Kirsten dimmed when I considered again who might have attacked them. Could it have been Wes, expecting Mateo to be alone? I didn't want it to be Kirsten's father, but who else knew he was coming to see me? Everyone in this town, it appeared, where news had wings.

Someone was following through on their threats, making me more determined than ever to find out who was behind all this, who was trying to stop me from investigating, who had hurt my brother and the Sturgess's beloved daughter.

Ven whispered to me when Wes had once more peeked in on his daughter in the post-op room, "You need to keep searching. We have to stop this monster. Please."

I hugged her and whispered back. "We will. We definitely will." Then I turned to sit vigil by my brother.

36

RK on the Scent

Despite it nearing midnight, my adrenalin spiked. Thinking exercise might calm me, I decided to walk down the stairwell instead of taking the elevator. Wired, I headed up the outside stairs before spinning around and trotting down to the ground level of the ER.

I walked out of the stairwell and into RK's chest. We both jerked backward but when I recognized my dear friend, I leaned into his now wide-open arms for a long, silent hug. Tears streaked down my cheeks and I sniffed up. He reached into a pocket and handed me a bandanna that I proceeded to soak with tears and snot. I am not a beautiful weeper.

RK patted my back.

Eventually I stepped back and looked up at his rugged, kind, face. Now that his hair was shorter and his beard shorn, he was a total babe magnet. Obviously Erin had perceived that sooner than I had. To me, he was my good buddy. Strong, sure, agile, yeah, but hot? Shocked me.

"Hey, cute stuff," he said, "How ya doin'?"

"Mateo's okay, so I'm fine. Exhausted and really, really pissed off, but I'll get over the exhausted part."

He led me to the least scruffy sofa in the ER waiting room. "Tell me everything."

I caught him up with recent events but fell asleep on his shoulder before

I could finish.

* * *

I awoke the next morning, muscles complaining, unsure for a moment where I was, but with a feeling I wasn't alone. I opened my eyes, yawned and looked around. Two pairs of eyes peered at me. My own brown eyes were gritty and my mouth tasted foul, like last night's coffee. I was on the cot in Mateo's room and RK had dragged his sleeping pad in and was sitting up, leaning against the wall beneath the window, drinking coffee.

"You snore," Mateo said. "And you drool."

"And if you weren't already laid up in a hospital bed, I'd get you for that, baby brother," I said. It was hard to snark when all I wanted to do was sob with relief that he was awake and talking. "Hey, RK, can you track down any more of that nectar of the gods?" I asked. He nodded and left the room and I swung my legs around and stood, rolling my shoulders. The cot was not a Serta perfect sleeper. I staggered into the bathroom, splashed my face and took care of another urgent item. I couldn't totally avoid looking in the mirror. Wished I had. My hair hung around my face in limp brownish strings and my clothes bore evidence of a night tossing and turning on the narrow cot. But Mateo was awake. All was right with the world.

I emerged from the bathroom and spent the few minutes RK was gone reassuring my brother that Kirsten would recover from her injuries and that I would keep RK nearby for protection. I tried but failed to convince him the hit and run was an accident unrelated to the threats I'd received. When he asked me to swear I'd stop investigating Violet's death, I lied. After all, worrying about me would only hamper his recovery. After he was better, we'd work on forgiveness for my deception.

My skin itched and I needed a change of clothes and someplace RK and I could talk undisturbed. "I'm headed home for a shower, brother of mine," I told Mateo. "You get some rest. That's how the body heals itself."

"Have you called Ross? I'm supposed to work today."

"I'm sure he's already heard, given this is Cottonwood, but I'll phone him from home as soon as I clean myself up and get something to eat." He opened his mouth and I added, "And I'll bring you something good when I come back."

"When we come back," RK corrected. "I'm sticking to you like a burr on a horse blanket."

"And just as alluring," I said.

I gave my brother the gentlest of hugs and we left.

37

Really Bad News

Back at Leah's, I showered and changed while RK used her guest shower.

We regrouped in the kitchen while I threw together a couple of omelets and sliced and toasted some strawberry bread. We ate and downed the good coffee I'd brewed, sitting companionably at the comfortable corner table.

"I am a totally new woman," I said. "I haven't thanked you yet for coming so fast last night."

"No thanks needed. We're friends." I silently thanked all the goddesses for friends like RK.

"Still . . ."

"You'd do the same for me." And I knew his statement to be true.

My shoulders relaxed. "Tell me what you found out from your old friend. Fig?"

He frowned and pulled a newspaper from his backpack. "Um, later on that. I saw this last night but didn't want to give you more to fuss over. Now that you've had some sleep and a good meal, maybe you can read it without reacting." His expression told me he doubted that. He handed me the *Sedona Red Rock News.*

"Police No Closer to Finding Slayer of Elderly Cottonwood Woman"

Police in Cottonwood are seeking information about the last night of Violet Brock, prominent Cottonwood elder, whose body was found by an employee of Adventure Calls Touring, Madrone Hunter. According to Sergeant Willa Doughty of the Cottonwood Police Department, several persons of interest have been interviewed regarding Ms. Brock's death, but investigations continue. Hunter, who said she noticed Ms. Brock's declining health during the recent tour with her company, vowed to help find the person or persons responsible for Brock's death.

The byline read Ash Coretti.

Ash Coretti was a reporter. Ha. News to me, bad news. I stared at the article, unaware of my tightening shoulders and neck until RK stood, moved behind my chair, and began to knead my already board-hard muscles. "It's not that bad," he said. "Towards the end, he says you're determined to find the murderer."

I shoved the newspaper across the table, jumped up and began to pace. "Not that bad? Not that bad? He betrayed me, and then he opens me up for even more danger. Me and my brother and you and who knows who else? He's supposed to be Mateo's friend. How could I have been so stupid? So naïve?"

"You didn't know he was a reporter? He didn't tell you?"

"Not only did he not mention his profession *or* his plans, he flirted with me. Led me to believe he was interested in me. Flattered me, made me consider . . . you don't want me to go there. Talk about dumb." I squeezed my eyes tight shut, as if I could will myself not to cry. Didn't work.

RK grabbed my shoulders as I walked and turned me around to hold me in a warm hug. "He's the dumb one. Not to mention unethical. You should report him . . . to someone."

I swiped away the tears. "Report him to whom? I walked right into it. Flirted back, told him more than I've told anyone else except you. Ooh, I hate him, but I hate me and my big mouth more."

I turned back to the table, grabbed up the vile page and reread the story. "He left out a lot about what I said about Violet, and who my suspects are."

"So maybe it's not that bad," he said. But his voice held doubt.

"Yeah, he's saving those juicy details for the next edition. How could he do this? Really, he seemed like a nice person."

"A nice person doing his job, maybe. I bet he didn't notice you thought he was coming on to you. Maybe he comes on to all the pretty women."

I glared at him. "I suppose you're trying to make me feel better, but trust me, it's not working." I paced more, tried to shed enough of the anger that I could think clearly, move forward, listen to the information RK had gleaned from his friend. Eventually I went to the sink, poured and drank a large glass of water, and took a seat at the table. "Nothing I can do about Ash Coretti, until I see him and gift him with a black eye. Let's get to work."

RK took my hands in his. "That statement about your determination to find the killer worries me. Whoever it is will be more dangerous than before. I want to be your American Express card. Don't leave home without me."

"I promise to be extra careful. I'm not convinced yet it was the killer who tried to scare me off. It takes me off the list of suspects and you'd think he—or she—would want that list to be long."

"Don't know if I agree or not. Maybe you've got two different threateners?"

"Oh, please. Don't make it worse than it already is." I chewed on my lip. "I should call Mama, no?"

"Maybe this evening. It will take her a while to drive up here. Mateo begged me to stop you from calling her, but I didn't promise. I don't see that she'll help his recovery."

I smiled, a tiny one, but a smile. "But she'll bring *biscochuelos.* They cure all ills." I took my hands back, rubbed them together and said, "Onward. We have the answer. We haven't seen it yet."

"Sure. That makes sense. Not. Anyway, on to what I learned from Fig—Fiona. She got me together with a couple of other women. They call themselves retired activists, but they're all active in bringing Jerome back to life, in cleaning up the mining damage, and in working with young people. A couple of them are working with native Americans on fire stuff—you know, starting controlled fires to encourage regrowth of the shrubs and trees they have used in their traditional crafts for, well, forever. And training the younger generation on peaceful actions. Good stuff."

Although RK excelled at his job with Adventure Calls—most recent tour notwithstanding, and really, *most* of the guests loved him—his heart wasn't in it. At soul level, he remained an eco-activist, someone who wanted to save Mother Earth from all the damage we humans had been inflicting on her for eons. It was obvious he wanted to share more about his friend's current activities. Another time, I'd have been all ears. This morning it was time to find a killer and perhaps the very person who'd run my brother and Kirsten down last night. I tamped down my urge to shout that we had to focus on the important thing.

I poured more coffee for both of us. "Did Fiona and her friends know much about Violet? The young men who followed her from Cottonwood?"

"Yeah. Something. One of them had known Violet for a long time. She said that the loss of her daughter Rosie devastated Violet. I'd asked them all to think about things Violet might be regretting and ready to talk about, and the woman reminded me that Violet had lived a long life with opportunities for many regrets. Said that Violet was "strong-minded," and that Chet and Lavender were able to deal with it." He grinned. "She said that Chet and Lavender and Rose were like the old Confucius quote: 'The green reed which bends in the wind is stronger than the mighty oak which breaks in a storm.' Chet and Ven bent from the storm that was Violet. Rose, or Rosie, as she was called, broke. Ran away. They never found her, never heard from her again. Fiona's friend imagined Violet regretted the way she treated her daughter. She never spoke of her again, but her grief and suffering were apparent. She and Chet spent a lot of money on private detectives, searching for her. But they got nowhere.

"That woman's point to me was that everyone has regrets, makes mistakes they wish they could fix, especially as they face their old age, their own mortality."

I rolled my tight shoulders. Despite my intention to focus on RK's information, an image of Ash's smile flashed to my mind. He'd seemed so . . . kind, so . . . understanding. I shook my head. I had to dispel any good memories of my betrayer. "Okay. I get that. However, something Violet planned to do or announce upset someone who lives here in Cottonwood big time, enough that they killed her to stop her. Which makes me think it has nothing to do with regrets about long-ago parenting gaffes."

"Being the cause of your daughter running away seems like more than a parenting mistake," he said. "But I get your point. Her plans to make amends for something in her past affected someone today. Someone who discovered those plans and decided to stop her, no matter the cost."

"Exactly. I keep thinking if I'd paid more attention to her on our tour, she might have told me. Or maybe she did, and I didn't listen. Chalked it up to the rants of an old woman."

"Then let's go back there, visualize it, try to remember what she was most interested in, talked about. Maybe the clue is right in front of us and we missed it."

I cringed. "I thought I was way past being one of those people who don't see old people. I like to think of myself as caring about everyone. You know, a nurturer, a cook, a compassionate Capricorn. And yet, I let her whining get on my nerves to the point I shut her out, stopped listening. How could I do that?" Tears clouded my eyes and dripped down my cheeks.

RK stood and tracked down a box of tissues, which he held out to me. "Don't let your regrets, your concerns about what you might have done differently, cloud what we've got to do now. Find a killer."

I chuckled, grabbed a tissue, and swiped away tears and snot. "In other words, 'Suck it up, Madrone.'"

"Got it in one." He stared out the window. "Violet talked a lot to me about forest activism. And once, she asked me if I'd ever done anything I regretted." He scoffed. "Who hasn't? I said something lame about the good things outweighing the bad. I noticed she didn't seem convinced, but she dropped it." After a moment he added, "Or more likely I got distracted by something more interesting than an elderly woman's random thoughts."

"Okay. No more pity parties for either of us. We'll figure out who killed her as our way of making amends."

"I asked the woman who'd known Violet the longest about which men in town went with her when she took off after school. Maybe who came back first, who seemed different from when they left, that kind of thing. She said she wasn't sure, but thought it might have been Leonard. She said he attended college after he got back, like he'd planned, then went into construction work after the war, then real estate. Ross took a different path and enlisted in the army. If you didn't go to college back then, you got drafted. Lots of guys went to college to escape the draft, or enlisted in the Navy, but he joined the Army even before he had to. A lot of young men left for Canada if they were against the war—or wanted to stay alive. She said a woman who works at the Cottonwood Chamber might know for sure, or we could check with the high school alumni association. They might have records or know who keeps tabs on the other alums."

"Good idea. I spoke with the woman she likely meant at the Chamber, Mary-Margaret. I'll phone her and see if I can find out anything else." I stood and paced the kitchen. "What we need to learn is if anything bad happened while Violet was out being wild and crazy. Maybe I can get Sergeant Doughty to check for any arrest records for Violet, or for that matter, for Ross or Leonard. But I want to check in on Mateo before I do anything else. He wants me to call his boss, so that's on my list, too."

"I think I'll head to the library and check old files for around the time she graduated high school. And online, I can check the places she visited. She did tell me she'd been in Colorado and in Idaho and Wyoming way back when."

We agreed to meet at the hospital for lunch, even though I grimaced at the thought of their cafeteria food. I am such a food snob.

38

Whistling Up Some Clues

I phoned Ross. He already knew about the hit and run, of course. He wanted details so I told him I'd drop by. I walked to The Whistle Stop. It took less than twenty minutes, long enough to clear my thoughts and tamp, if only a little, my fury with Ash Coretti. I postponed calling Mama until later, telling myself I needed to know more about Mateo's prognosis before worrying our mother. Like he told RK, Mama would smother him with love until it was hard to breathe.

Violet's murder and the attack on Mateo and Kirsten had to be related, that was obvious. I *might* have blamed bad driving if someone had not sent me that warning about danger to those I loved if I kept snooping. The only odd part was that the attack had followed so closely after the threat. I hadn't had time to investigate further. Well, not a lot.

Perhaps odder was the fact that whoever was warning me off was well aware of my activities—who I met and talked with, what I'd learned. The issue was that he or she knew the facts I was slowly gleaning around Cottonwood might lead me to Violet's killer.

Was it a good thing to stir up this evil person's worries? And what the heck was I learning that was of such value? Whoever sent those threats had more faith in my deductive powers than I did. Everyone says there are no secrets in a small town, but I was fast learning that wasn't true. Secrets thrive everywhere.

The brass bell announced my arrival at The Whistle Stop. Helen Zelinger bustled out from the back room, hoisting a large box in front of her, a smaller box atop it. "You're in time for a scone," she called out to me. "Ross is brewing the coffee. We want to hear all about what happened to poor Mateo."

Ross emerged from the back room bearing a coffee pot. He laid it on the counter and dashed to his wife's side. "I've told you not to try carrying those heavy loads, dear. It's far too heavy for you." He snatched the pastry box from atop the larger one, tossed the small box beside the coffee pot and hefted the larger box from his wife's arms. I didn't think she looked strained by anything except her husband's excessive concern. She shot me one of those woman-to-woman glances that conveyed, "Men are such geese," and shrugged.

As soon as he'd deposited the box, which, I now saw, contained LPs—so it was indeed hefty—beside a carrel, Ross rushed to embrace me. "My poor dear. You're not seeing the best side of Cottonwood." He held me and I felt comforted, until a question niggled in my brain—had he been the driver who so ruthlessly cut down my brother and Kirsten the previous night? Because Violet threatened to raise his rent? Absurd, but I had to allow for absurdity. I shivered.

"You're shivering. Did you walk here? You must have been up all night. Coffee's the answer." Ross, acting more the fussy mother duck than my brother's employer, pulled away and led me to the counter. He dragged a third stool from the back room. "We heard. This is Cottonwood. Everyone in Crema and Violette's Patisserie could talk of nothing else."

Helen pulled three mugs from beneath the counter and poured, with a raised eyebrow in my direction. I nodded my acceptance and asked for it black. People often add that fake powdered cream, which is, in my opinion, close to poison. "Now tell us everything," Helen said, "Starting with how they're doing. I phoned the hospital, but they wouldn't give me any details."

I sketched in the story of Mateo's and Kirsten's injuries and assured them they'd both be fine. "In fact, I imagine Mateo will be wanting to come back to work as soon as he can."

Helen frowned. "With that shoulder you described, he won't be able to do much. I can fill in."

"But that's why I hired someone, so you wouldn't have to work so hard," Ross protested. "I'll find a temp until Mateo's back. You have your cooking, your charities, to attend to."

"I said I could handle it and I can." Helen's face reddened and she glared at Ross. "I handled it before Mateo came. And my group can get along fine without me, believe you me. I'm not an invalid, sweetheart." She swallowed, her lips tight, obviously trying to hide her frustration with Ross. "I don't want Mateo to worry about his job. Now, Madrone, tell us more. Did they see anything? Hear anything? It must have been so frightening."

"From what I gather, it happened too fast for either of them to be scared. Fortunately, they were at a spot where the brush prevented the worst. They're both pretty scraped up, and poor Kirsten broke her leg. I hate to think how bad it would have been had someone not seen them and called for help right away." I sipped my coffee, which was much better than I'd hoped for, and picked up a scone. "I'm at a loss as to why someone would do this to them." I definitely wasn't going to share anything about the escalating warnings I got, but I imagined the Cottonwood gossip line would spread that news soon enough.

Helen pushed a scone my way. "I saw the article in the *Re• Rock News*. Noticed he said you were determined to find the murderer. Maybe it's time to leave those things to the police, dear. I worry about you."

"There are a few loose ends I wonder about. I hate to pester you, Ross, but I know you and Violet were friends in high school."

He stroked his short white beard. "Oh, yes, and after. I trailed after that girl like a puppy. Even when she wasn't very friendly to me." He looked off into the distance. 'It was the best of times, it was the worst of times.'"

Helen headed for the box of LPs and began to unload it onto the carrel. "There's lots to do without our employee," she said to Ross.

We both ignored her pointed look and I asked Ross, "You enlisted in the Army when you came back to Cottonwood, as I heard it. Why the Army?"

He smiled but I could tell he was still in the past. "Why not? Nothing like a few firefights to heal a broken heart."

"Oh, for heaven's sake, both of you," Helen said. "That was then, this is now. It wasn't enough Violet drove us all to distraction when she was alive, she's *still* making our lives miserable. Can't we focus on something positive for a change?" She shot a glance around the shop. "The mural. Have you even noticed the superb mural my talented husband painted, Madrone?"

I'd been staring at Ross, still apparently back many decades, and it took me a minute to return my focus to his wife. "Yes, Helen, I got that pleasure the first time I visited Mateo. It's a masterful work of art. Has anyone photographed it? It should be documented. I'd love that honor, but I'm a mere amateur."

Helen transformed from grumpy to beaming. "A few people have tried, but it's hard to capture the essence of it. I'm sure Ross would welcome you and your camera, wouldn't you, dear?"

Ross seemed to struggle to return to the present and his expression remained sad and distracted. "Sure, sure. Any time. Light's best in the afternoon. It's better in spring. Maybe your next visit to Mateo," he added.

A vision of me visiting Mateo in jail or him visiting me there sprang into my mind. First things first, dang it. "Thank you," I murmured. "I know it's uncomfortable to discuss these things, but it's urgent for me to get some answers."

"I don't know why. For heaven's sake, you've been threatened and your brother's been attacked. Surely the police don't still consider you a suspect," Helen said. "Do they?"

"I don't know. All I know is, it's important to find answers. Ross and Violet were close a long time ago. We all heard her announce she wanted to get things off her chest the night of the ukulele concert. I'm trying to find out what."

Ross reached for the pot and distributed the remaining coffee to our three cups. I sipped at mine, but it was lukewarm. Ick. "Violet, all of us, I guess, had regrets," he began.

Helen pushed forward, putting her body between me and Ross. "That woman was always carping on about one thing or another. Who knows what she was babbling about that night? It's not like it was anything new with Violet."

"Somebody thought it was," I said. "I'm speculating." I pressed my lips together. "What did you mean by the Dickens quote, Ross?"

He chuckled. "Oh, you know. In the time we spent together, Violet and me, good things happened. And bad things. I always hoped the good outweighed the bad." His face filled with sadness. "And they did. Until they didn't, for Violet." He looked at the floor. "I would have understood if she'd killed herself," he whispered.

But she didn't kill herself. Someone else did. "Why do you say that? Do you think her death was caused by something that happened way back then?" I asked.

He inhaled and paused before he replied, his voice again vibrant. "Can't see why. Don't see how it could have. That was a long, long time ago. Some day you may understand. I'm old, Vi was old, but inside, deep inside, we're still the crazy young firebrands we were decades ago. The body dries up, gets wrinkled, but the soul? Mostly undamaged, mostly the same."

"What a load of hogwash," Helen said.

"Well, except for *your* body, my dear. You're as lovely as you were when we met."

It was true that Helen retained a youthful appearance. I wondered how much younger than Ross she was. Her long black hair remained glossy and rich-looking, made memorable by the streaks of silver. A bit taller than Ross, and in good shape like her husband, she was a striking woman who obviously adored her spouse. Her eyes tracked him constantly.

"When *did* you meet?" I asked. I regretted the question instantly, because it gave them something besides Violet to talk about. But, heck, I was curious.

Ross laughed. "I courted the schoolmarm. Typical story of the Old West."

Helen giggled, and I could see the young woman Ross fell in love with. "Silly old coot. The truth is, I moved here to teach school and I could see we needed to improve our music program. I came to Ross to see about lending the students instruments, and—"

"She swept me off my feet," Ross interjected.

"He wouldn't take no for an answer," she said. "I'd been through a pretty ugly divorce, you see, so I'd sworn off men. Off the myth of true love. But he persisted, and—"

"She couldn't resist me. In reality, I wore down her resistance. I'd given up on finding my true love after Violet spurned me. Helen and I healed each other, and here we are, more than thirty years later—"

"And still in love," Helen concluded. "Now, I must unload that box of LPs." She returned to the open box of albums.

I pounced on Ross's comment. "You say Violet broke your heart? Can you tell me more about that?" Ross followed his wife with his eyes. "Not a lot. I wanted to get engaged. She wanted to be free and on her own. No attachments, she said. We were too young, she said. So I came on home and enlisted. When she came back to Cottonwood, with good old Chet tagging along, everyone could see they were fated to be together, even though I'd harbored some hope she'd come home and admit I was 'the one.' Write love letters to me over in Nam. But it wasn't to be. I wish I knew who wanted Violet dead," he said in a low voice. "Too many people, for too many reasons. She'd made enemies, she had secrets that she threatened to spill, she was a rich widow. I'm afraid she was a prime target." He squared his shoulders. "You tell Mateo he has a job whenever he feels up to it. Although I think he may have to share it with Helen. I was only trying to relieve her of some stress. You love someone, you have to help them any way you can."

I thanked him, walked toward the door and then had a final thought. "One last question, Ross. Violet donated a new fire station and I heard she sponsored a few firefighter calendars. Any particular reason you knew of?"

He paused for a long beat, then laughed. "What healthy woman doesn't enjoy ogling a fireman? I guess Violet did, too. Not much else I can tell you."

Helen had paused her task to stare at me. I thanked both of them and took off.

I had some time before I met up with RK, so, seeking time alone, I wandered back to the place I'd found Violet. I shivered when I reached the shadow of the cottonwoods. Maybe I shouldn't be here, alone. The wind rustled the cottonwood leaves. These trees had lived many years and seen grief and joy and silliness and sorrow. More than one person had died beneath their branches, or those of cottonwoods before them, but they only whispered in the wind, not sharing their secrets. Like Ross and Helen and Violet's family, hiding secrets from me and the rest of their neighbors. How could I possibly find the truth? Close to the spot I'd found Violet, I spotted a sitting stone, a rock large enough and flat enough to perch on comfortably.

I lowered myself onto the stone and released the tears I'd been holding back—tears for Violet, tears of terror mixed with relief that Mateo and Kirsten would be okay, tears for my father and brother, lost long ago but always in my heart. I knew too well that some deaths are never resolved, but this one, this one, could not join those others. Somehow this one I would solve. I felt my determination tighten. "No damn threats are going to stop me," I said in a strong voice. And immediately hoped there were no walkers nearby to overhear my vow.

39

No News Is Good News

Back in town, I sat on a convenient bench to call Mary-Margaret at the Chamber of Commerce. She had little to add about Ross and Leonard's returns to Cottonwood. When I asked if either had done anything unexpected on their return, she said, "Who knew what was expected of us back then? It was the Age of Aquarius, of free love and birth control pills. The war in Vietnam was taking a lot of our young men away. Maybe Leonard came back a few months before Ross, and then went off to college. I do remember one odd thing: Ross enlisted as soon as he got back. Who knows if he'd have been drafted, lots of fellas were, but most tried to get a college deferment, find some way out. That's why so many tried for med school or some kind of graduate school."

"Did he seem different? Moody, before he enlisted?"

"I wasn't that close to him. Rumors flew when he enlisted, since most guys had no desire to go to war. I'd guess that activists like Ross and Leonard felt that more strongly." She paused. "Say, you should talk to Leonard. He might know more about Ross and why he enlisted. We were all thrilled when Ross came home from the war uninjured. We lost several guys over there and others who came back were never the same."

I needed to talk to Leonard, but if I weren't careful, he'd sell me one of those homes. I needed to figure out how to ask him a few more questions in a neutral environment.

I headed down Main and turned right, in the direction of the hospital. Deep in thought, I pondered the information I'd gleaned so far and how to tie the strands of information together.

A hand grasped my shoulder. I swung around, prime to fight off my attacker, my right hand fisted. There's a chance my nerves were the slightest bit taut—close to a drawn bowstring.

That fist hit Ash Coretti's jaw hard enough that it hurt. My fist, that is. I hoped it hurt him, too.

"Ouch! Hold it," he yelped. "It's just me."

I backed a few feet from him, feeling no remorse about my overreaction. "Just the liar who turned my sad tale into a great news report? Who never bothered to tell me he was a reporter? What would your editor say?"

He rubbed his jaw. I was thrilled to see it was red. Nope, still no remorse. Too bad I didn't get his eye. "She told me it was a great story and wanted more. Believe me, Madrone, I filed that story before Mateo and Kirsten were attacked. I'm so sorry they were hurt. I want to help."

I swiped at my annoying leaking eyes. "How could you betray me like that? Pretend to be a friend? You want to help? Stay away from me."

"I wasn't pretending to be a friend. I like you. Reporting is my job. I assumed Mateo told you what I did."

"Like heck you did. You were happy I didn't know and happy I chose you to confide in. You rat." I turned to go.

"I want to help you find who killed Violet."

I spun around and lunged at him, punching him in the chest with my finger. Close enough to catch that familiar spicy scent of his. "What a great story that would make. Reporter turned sleuth."

He stared at my finger, then at the ground. His voice meek and quiet, he said, "I want to help *you,* Madrone. I don't care about a story. In case you hadn't noticed, I didn't write word one about who you suspected."

"Huh," I scoffed. "You were worried about libel, not about my feelings."

"You're wrong," he whispered. "I do care about your feelings. I do want to help. If I find out anything, I'll text you. That way, we don't have to talk."

"Don't bother yourself on my account," I said. I marched off down the street.

As soon as I turned the next corner, I slowed my pace and let my shoulders slump. I had not wanted to run into Ash. He looked contrite, but his betrayal was too much to forgive, despite my earlier fondness for the man. I shook my head, trying to rid myself of the memory of our encounter.

I checked the time and decided I could run by the cottage and pick up some pumpkin bread for my brother before meeting RK for lunch in the cafeteria. I drove there and stayed in the car long enough to and phone Sergeant Doughty and thank her for her support the previous night. "I'm not sure I'd have made it without your strength."

"I'm sure you would have been fine. You have amazing wells of strength in you. I don't want you to have to tap into them anymore. Are you staying out of trouble?"

"I'm struggling. I spent some time with Ross and Helen Zelinger this morning. Thank goodness, Mateo still has a job. It was good of Ross to hire him, because according to Helen, she didn't need any help. Did Ross maybe have a criminal record or something in his past that created his empathy with Mateo?"

"Oh, for heck's sake, Madrone, you're still poking your nose into things. Since I can't seem to stop you, be sure you let me know if you find out something interesting. And keep that Mustard fella close to you. As for Ross, he doesn't have a criminal record and neither does Leonard Anderson. Because that was your next question. And that's all you'll get out of me, even with bribes of pumpkin bread. And recipes."

Drat. I needed to send her that recipe. "For sure? Because I was wondering about Greg Yarborough."

"Ah, you've met Greg. Not a pleasant man, and he very much dislikes Mateo. He has an alibi for last night, although I can't see him hurting Kirsten, even if she did dump him for your brother. And before you ask, I checked his alibi for Violet's murder. There was little love lost between those two. She took her money from the credit union and badmouthed him to Kirsten and let him know it. But he was camping with a Scout troop. So no luck there, Sherlock."

"Not for the Scouts, either."

My comment made Doughty burst out laughing and we ended the call with both of us in slightly better spirits, especially when I promised to send her the pumpkin bread recipe soon.

* * *

I hurried inside the hospital to Mateo's room. He woke from a doze when I entered and was healthy enough to carefully open the bread and break off a chunk. He thanked me while chewing. I hugged him and headed off to meet RK. My stomach growled. "Don't get excited. We're meeting him in the hospital cafeteria."

My old friend rose and waved when he saw me enter the cafeteria. I trooped into a line for the salad bar but changed my mind and tried an enchilada scooped out for me by an employee. It dripped with cheese. How did they justify serving something that rich at a hospital? I guessed it qualified as comfort food and this was one place where comfort was a necessity.

RK frowned at my plate. "Not brain food, that's for sure."

"As if you're a gourmet."

"I know what's healthy. Don't always choose it. I checked in on Mateo's floor and he's doing pretty well."

I told him I'd stopped by, too. Then I dug into my comfort food. Not bad. Nothing like what Mom or I made or even that from any of the many Mexican restaurants in Tucson, but it tasted like it was made fresh, not poured from a can or even a freezer bag.

As he ate, RK caught me up on his library research. "I checked the places Violet mentioned she'd been—Colorado, Idaho, Wyoming. For sure she went to Oregon—it was a must-see place back then, according to Fiona." He stumbled over his old friend's name as I did when calling him by his initials. But we were both trying to honor our friends' wishes. "The sixties were pretty early for most forest activists—Earth First! wasn't founded until 1980. Finding news about fires is easier, but unlike these days, there were fewer fires in Oregon in the sixties. I narrowed my search to Colorado, Idaho, and Wyoming. There were quite a few forest fires back then, and that was when they almost universally tried to put them out. No controlled burns, even though the Native Americans lobbied for them, and sometimes got in trouble for setting them. Nowadays the Forest Service is admitting that those burns are what keep certain plants and even animals plentiful."

Fascinating as all this was, he could go on for hours, so I nudged him. "Any bad fires? Lives lost?"

"Have you read much about the great fire of 1910?" His eyes widened. "It was a doozy."

I waved him on. "Fill me in on that one another time. Way too early."

He grinned at me. "Well, there was the Sundance fire in the Selkirk mountains in 1967. Another in my territory. And another big one."

"And likely too late. I'm guessing she graduated in 1963 or '64, and headed for the hills soon after that."

"Right around the time attitudes toward fire suppression started to change. In fact, in 1964, they passed the Wilderness Act, that included allowing prescribed burns. I couldn't find any major fires, but there were quite a few smaller ones. Most are lightning caused. Far fewer are caused by humans than most people think."

"We need specifics, my friend. Maybe Ven knows where her mother visited, or we could ask Leonard and Ross. Your research is good but too general."

We headed to the ward where Kirsten was recovering from surgery, and where I hoped to find her parents.

40

Nice Likeness

Ven nodded off in a chair beside Kirsten's bed while her daughter slept. She jerked awake when we walked in, and jumped up, looking pleased to see us. Since I'd most likely been the cause of the attack on Mateo and Kirsten, I'm not sure I would have been glad to see me, had I been the one sitting by Kirsten's side.

Ven scrubbed at her face and bent over to retrieve a box from the floor beside her chair. She crept out the door and motioned us into the hallway. "Wes left to tend bar. We have good employees, but they can't handle everything. He was up all night keeping watch on our baby," she added with a fond smile. "I'm glad you're here. I found something at Mom's place last night that might help your investigating." She led us to a lumpy sofa in the nearby waiting room. Once settled, she passed the box to me. "It has a bunch of old photos of Mom from her activist days and the early days of her marriage."

"We're trying to figure out who was with her when she first left Cottonwood, and who came back first. Kind of get a picture of those days. Because as you know, she was talking a lot about regrets. I'm not sure the regrets were that old, but she was talking to Ross and Leonard, and we know those two were old friends of hers."

"I think she and Leonard became more frenemies as they grew older. You know, when she tried to stop him and Isabella from creating that new development."

"Still, they were close enough that he drove her to Jerome the night of Ross's ukulele concert."

She smiled. "Mom could be persuasive and fun-loving. You only saw her crabby side."

RK grabbed a stack of photos from the box and began to go through them. "Violet was quite the storyteller, especially early in the tour. I imagine we wore her out."

Ven flushed. "You're too kind." She gazed at the box. "I dug around in there. Saw a few photos of a very young Mom and a very young Ross, both of them looking starry-eyed."

RK held up two photos. "These look around the right vintage. Can you identify the people in them?"

Most of the photos I take are labeled img-dot-something and I have no clue where they were taken. I have to rummage through my calendar to figure out where I was, when. I have great hopes of becoming one of those organized people who files everything in its place. Shortly before I die.

Ven peered at the photos for a few moments. "Okay, that's Mom, looking pretty cute way back then. The guys must be Ross and Leonard—Leonard being the taller, skinny one, Ross the more muscular one with darker, curly hair. We'd look at the photos together sometimes, and Mom teased Ross about how he had to lose his wild curls when he enlisted."

I didn't see how this helped much. All of them traveled together after high school. Ross came home and very shortly after that, enlisted in the Army. Leonard went to college to escape the draft.

"Oh," said Ven, "here's a couple of me and my sister as toddlers." She sniffed. "My sister Rose."

Needing to tread cautiously, I said, "Someone mentioned your sister went missing. As a teenager?"

"Yes. Mom and Dad searched for her for several years, but they had no luck. We were so close. I miss her," she said, ending in a near whisper.

"Things are different these days, with the internet and social media. Have you considered renewing the search? Or . . . is there a chance Rose is alive . . . and—"

Ven jumped up from the sofa. "You think Rose came back from—wherever she might have been all these years—and suddenly decided to kill our mother? That is totally ridiculous and a disgusting thing to think."

I went to where she stood. "You asked me to look into your mother's murder, and I need to consider all the reasons someone wanted her dead. People do terrible things for greed, or when they are desperate." I thought hard, seeking more justification for my oddball theory. "Maybe Rose had decided to come back and someone didn't want her to see your mother."

"Lovely." She turned away from me and stared out the window. "First you want to pin a murder on my long-absent sister, then on who? Me? I can't tell you how glad I am I asked for your help."

Something was off in Ven's last sentence, besides her justifiable anger with me and my theories. Before I could gather my thoughts, RK unwound his frame from where he'd been sitting, cross-legged, on the floor. "Hang on." He fanned out several 4 x 6 black-and-white photos in front of us. "These are shots of a fire, and of burned trees and grassland." He flipped them over, one at a time. "No label, no way to tell where or when they were taken. But Madrone, you said you saw several pieces of art that featured fire at Violet's home."

I stared over his shoulder at the photos. "Yes. I'm beginning to think she had an obsession with fire. Particularly given her heavy donations to the local firefighting organizations."

Ven leaned in for a closer look at the photos. "She even paid for the construction of one of their training towers. I remember Daddy complaining that they didn't have that kind of money, but Mom insisted. I was in my teens, so her fascination with fire didn't begin recently."

Yes! The photos confirmed my suspicion that the reasons for Violet's murder had their origin in her past. I stifled an exultant yelp, because I was still in the land of suspicion without any proof. Moments earlier, I'd been ready to pin the murder on a long-missing sister. Lots of straw snatching, Madrone. Still, this looked like a strong lead. "We need to ask Leonard and Ross if anything happened when they were traveling, anything to do with fire or firefighters," I said. "When she was ranting at us up in Jerome, she seemed almost frightened of Ross, and determined to atone for her sins. I sure wish she'd told us what they were, but maybe she said something more to Leonard when he took her home."

I had my doubts. I'd asked Leonard before and he denied she said anything, but by now maybe he'd remembered more about that horrible night. Or was more willing to help my investigations. What set Violet off that night, why did she trick Leonard into taking her to find us? She'd found evidence that Kirsten was stealing. But couldn't she have waited until the next day to confront her granddaughter? Was there something about that night? That date?

I took out my phone and checked the calendar. "Ven, Violet had what I'd call a breakdown on the day of the ukulele concert. Is there anything special about that date?"

Ven peered at my phone and spent a few minutes thinking. "I don't think so. Certainly not the folks' anniversary or anyone in the family's birthday. But it could have had significance to her. Who knows?" She started to tear up.

Time to back off. "Thanks for sharing the photographs with us. It gives me something to talk to Leonard and Ross about. Any chance I could borrow some of the photos?"

"You can borrow the whole box. I want you to find out what happened to her. Return them, please."

"I can share with anyone? Even Sergeant Doughty?"

"Sure. I looked through them and there aren't any shots of Mom nude in Oak Creek Canyon. She used to tell me that was a fun outing when she was a teenager."

From behind me, a woman said, "Is someone telling tales of sins in Oak Creek?" I turned to see Isabella Garcia stride into the room. "Now that they have an official park at Slide Rock, it's a lot tamer," she added with a smile.

While Ven rushed to engulf the exotic developer in a hug, I imagined a much younger Violet and Isabella, frolicking naked on the smoothing rocks in Oak Creek. I may have blushed.

"I'll bet you would have been sliding with her," Ven said.

"Maybe not," said Isabella, a slight frown marring her smooth forehead.

"She was a few years older than me."

Ven raised her eyebrows but said only, "Thanks so much for dropping by. I know you're busy."

"Never too busy to check in on our dear Kirsten. How is she doing?"

"She'll be okay. Her leg will take a while to heal, but she's young."

"And you, my friend? What a terrible week it has been."

Ven smiled through tears. "I'd call that an understatement. Have you met Madrone, Mateo's sister? And RK, her friend and coworker?"

Isabella smiled at RK, who nodded and leaned against the wall, holding the box of photos and evidently trying to become wall art. Then she turned a much cooler gaze on me. She was so well-preserved, pampered and groomed, it was hard to imagine she was nearly Violet's age. "Madrone and I have met. She took the opportunity to grill me about Violet's and my topsy-turvy relationship. Something better left to the police, don't you agree?"

Ven sighed. "I want this nightmare over, the sooner, the better. I've encouraged Madrone to continue looking into it."

"It seems to me snooping into a murder could be dangerous," Isabella said, her cool gaze turning frosty.

I shivered. "Since my brother and I are in danger of being arrested, it seemed a good decision."

She shrugged. "I guess it's your choice to put those you love in danger."

My mouth dried. I didn't think anyone knew that the hit-and-run had likely been intentional. "What are you saying?" I asked, trying to be vague and lure her into a mistake.

"Oh, please, next you'll ask me where I was last night. Leonard phoned and told me the so-called accident was on purpose." She shook her head, her smooth, shining hair barely ruffled. "You do not understand small towns, my dear."

This woman and I rubbed each other the wrong way, so I had little to lose. "Now that you mention it, where were you last night?"

Ven put her hand to her lips. "Madrone! Isabella is a dear friend."

"It's likely that someone you consider a friend killed your mother and ran down your daughter. I know I'm being direct, but sometimes the direct way is the shortest route."

"And sometimes the shortest route will lead you off a cliff," Isabella said.

"I ate dinner with friends at Elote in Sedona. What happened later in the evening is my business alone."

"Thank you. I hear that's an award-winning restaurant. I hope you enjoyed yourself." We both knew I meant doing whatever "her business alone" was. I doubted we'd ever become best buddies. I turned to Ven. "I need to visit my brother. Give my love to Kirsten when she wakes."

She wiped her eyes. "Really, you can't know how grateful I am that you're pursuing this. But be careful." She focused her gold-flecked brown eyes on RK. "Promise me you'll stay with Madrone until all this is cleared up. And by stay, I mean within ten yards. I rarely have premonitions, but my gut is telling me things will get worse before they get better."

My pal made an X across his heart. "I'll be a thorn in her side."

41

Leonard on the Grill Again

"Okay," I said, jaw iron. "You can go with me. Although it's ridiculous. I'm thinking Ven's gut was queasy because of all the hospital food she's been eating while keeping watch over Kirsten. You should be guarding Mateo. He's vulnerable. I can take care of myself." I lifted my right arm, fist clenched, in the traditional I've-got-muscles pose. Apparently my courage came out in daylight.

RK swatted my arm down. "Right. Call Leonard and set up an appointment for me to look at one of those houses. Who knows, I may buy a villa in Cottonwood."

"Why not Sedona while we're dreaming?" I couldn't afford a trailer house in upscale Sedona, if they still allowed such affronts to the rich.

I phoned Leonard and agreed to meet him at the development. When I told him I was bringing a friend, he said it was a good idea. "Young people often share homes out there, and I'm sure you're beyond the party-all-night-with-loud-music phase."

I laughed. "Not sure I ever went through that phase." During my late teens and early twenties, family crises had crushed the party right out of me.

"See you soon," he said.

RK followed me and I dropped off "my" car and joined him in the Adventure Calls van. I confessed I felt guilty about leading Leonard on. "I should have told him I had a few more questions about Violet. You know he was in love with her for years and years."

"You told me. That doesn't mean he couldn't have killed her. He said she'd changed, turned strange on him. Maybe was about to reveal something he didn't want her to."

"I think we should have been upfront with him, poor guy. He needs to sell homes, not waste time with us."

He cleared his throat. "I didn't tell you this, but Erin's not happy working with her father. It's not totally out of the question that she moves down here. I'll tell him I'm scouting for her. It's off the road to Jerome, right?"

"Yes. Okay, you tell him that. Why not? One lie's as good as another."

He shot me a glance and then directed his concentration to the road. "It's not complete fiction. I'm tired of Idaho's cold and the 'heat' up there's getting tired of me." He winked at his play on words. I grimaced. "I'm enjoying this gig with Adventure Calls," he continued, "and I can't sleep in my old truck forever when I'm not working." After a pause, he added, "I really like her, Madrone."

I stared at him. In all the years I'd known him, RK had been a perennial flirt, rarely dating one woman for more than a few months. "*Madre de Dios,* you're serious. Go slowly, my friend. That's my only advice."

He smiled. "I doubt that. You're full of advice."

"And you're full of—take a left up there."

* * *

We waited at the gate to the development for Leonard Anderson. He arrived soon after us, making me wonder if he'd been in his office or if he lived nearby. We followed him into the development and he parked by the sales office.

"You were fast. Do you live near here?" I asked him after making introductions.

"I was in my office, which is in the new part of Cottonwood. I have a condo near it."

"Considering living here?"

"If we sell enough properties, fast enough. Otherwise, I could be sleeping on the sofa in my office."

Which told me that Violet's opposition, which caused delays in construction of Vista Rioja, had been costly for him and Isabella Garcia.

"We're here for a friend from Colorado who's considering a move south," RK said. He smiled. "If I can persuade her."

Leonard beamed at him. "We've built several homes here with divided floor plans. You could be a platonic roommate and then do a small amount of remodeling and voila, a cozy home for two!"

RK's boisterous laugh bounced off the wall of the sales building we were headed for. "A man with a plan and an answer for all purposes!"

"I was hoping Madrone had changed her mind, but I'm open to all comers."

After showing us the development's layout, Leonard led us through the model and then took us to a completed home with the floor plan he'd mentioned. RK wandered ahead of us, peering in the front windows, and I took the chance to ask a few questions. "Ven found some old photos in Violet's things. Of you and her, and of you and Ross and Violet."

"And then of Ross and Violet, after she told me to scram."

"Yes. Also a lot of photos of scorched grasslands and burned pine trees. Do you recall any fires while the two of you were together?"

He climbed the two stairs to the porch and looked down at me. "Does your friend really have any interest in these homes? I could have answered your questions on the phone."

I blushed. "RK is truly hoping Erin will move to Arizona. He told me he's starting his campaign with finding affordable homes. But no," I confessed, "I need to consider Tucson my home as long as my mother's there. And I doubt she'll be moving soon."

"Thanks for your honesty. As to fires, there were always small lightning-caused fires, but they usually went out by themselves or were easily controlled. That was around the time when the idea of prescribed fires was catching on. Native Americans had practiced that for years, but few white folks took time to learn from them." He opened the door when RK joined us. "Take your time," he said as my friend brushed past us.

"I've been to Violet's home, seen all those paintings that deal with fire," Leonard continued. "And I know she donated to firefighters' associations, but as to the why, I asked her once and she told me she enjoyed the view—of their buns." He grinned. "Maybe she did, but I saw her stare at that art many times and I don't for a minute believe that's the whole story."

Leonard and I trailed after RK. "Why your interest?" he asked. "Do you see a link? Did you ask Ven? Ross?"

"Ven had no clue. I'll ask Ross next time I see him. One last question: What do you know about Ven's sister Rose, the one who ran away as a teenager? No one's been in touch with her? No proof she's dead, or hint she's alive?"

Leonard tried hard to keep his expression neutral, but I'd spent time with him for a couple of days. He refused to look at me, instead played with the house key. "I can't tell you anything about Rose that Ven hasn't already shared with you. It affected Violet and Chet very badly, and Ven, as well, when she disappeared."

He was hiding something, but he wasn't going to share. Darn. That family had too many secrets. "Thanks for your frank answers, Leonard. Now let's have a look at this home. Are you selling many with this floor plan?"

We kept to the topic of homes for the rest of our visit.

As we parted from Leonard, RK armed with fliers, floor plans, and Leonard's card, Leonard said, "I know you won't stop looking into this and I guess it reveals character—you promised Ven. But be careful. Someone doesn't want you to continue your snoop—sleuthing. I'm glad you have a friend with you, a hefty friend. But still . . . Watch your back."

42

Love May Find a Way

RK tossed me the keys when we neared the van. "I've gotta make a phone call."

Elected designated driver, I drove straight to the hospital, where we would visit Mateo. Knowing my brother, he'd check himself out if not handcuffed to the bed, unless I assured him I was staying safe and keeping my largish buddy with me at all times.

RK tried turning the radio on to muffle his conversation, but I punched it off. "Your secrets are my secrets," I said as he swiped at his phone.

He shot me an ugly face—the kind where you scrinch up your nose and wrinkle your eyes—and turned toward the window. It wasn't his true angry face—that one was cold enough to freeze custard—so he'd let me listen in.

"Hey, got a minute? Free to talk?"

I heard a feminine voice say something unintelligible.

"Listen, this might be kind of sudden, but I know you were thinking about leaving Colorado and before you decide that France is the answer, I have a suggestion."

He listened, then said, "Look, people move to where they have family. I understand that. But Gabe's moved to Tucson and he's family. I was thinking you might not want to be that close to him, and I toured an affordable house here in Cottonwood. Remember I told you my brother and I sold our parents' place and I need to invest somewhere, so I was thinking . . . I'm not there that often. . . Maybe we could . . . share?"

Oh. My. Goodness. He was asking her to move in with him? After knowing her for two and a half weeks? My buddy had lost his mind. I could only hope that Erin had a better grip on her sanity.

When he launched into an enthusiastic description of the home we'd seen, I gathered that their time together had made mush of Erin's brains as well as RK's. A sane woman would have hung up long ago.

Fortunately the hospital wasn't far. I sped up. *Don't say anything you'll regret, Madrone.* I hung a right into the hospital parking lot a wee bit too fast, so we both bounced as the van sped up and over the driveway. He didn't drop the phone, though. Dang.

"Yeah, well," he said as he shot me a lethal look, "we're at the hospital. I have to stay with Madrone, keep her safe. Although she's wearing thin right now. Give it some thought and I'll phone you tonight." After a moment he disconnected and turned to glare at me.

"Have you lost your freakin' mind, *bufón?* You've only known the woman a few weeks!"

"You're jealous that I'm thinking of settling down," he said.

I jumped out of the van and only stopped myself from slamming the door when I remembered it was a company car. "You are so wrong. I am not jealous, I am simply worried about your sanity. You do not buy a home with a woman you've known less than a month. You do not ask a woman you barely know to move in with you."

"Are you saying you don't like Erin?" He looked like a pouting toddler.

I stopped and took in a few deep breaths. "I like Erin. She's pretty, friendly and gets along well with others. I could say the same for a dog I adopted at the shelter, or a Brownie Scout. You don't know her yet!" I screeched. Obviously, the deep breaths had not calmed me.

His face closed down. "Thanks for being supportive."

"I am supportive. I love you, I like Erin, I'm fond of Gabe. I don't want any of you to be hurt. And trust me, when you include money matters in all this, like buying a house, someone's bound to get hurt. I'm not saying no to the relationship, but please, please, take it slower."

"You're suggesting I phone her and say, 'Oh, never mind. Madrone doesn't think this is a good idea'?"

"No. Chat tonight, tell her you love the house and that you really like her, but maybe it's too early to talk about living together. For all you know, she can afford it on her own. For all you know, she was leading you on about considering a move." Why oh why I added that last 'for all you know,' I didn't know. Only that I shouldn't have. I put a tentative hand on his arm. "You are a good friend and I am truly happy you have found someone like Erin. Someone you might fall in love with. But give it some time. If it's meant to be . . ."

"Not the 'if it's meant to be' speech. That one's the property of my dear brother up in Idaho."

"Forgive me for butting in, but you did phone her in front of me."

"You're right. About the phoning in your presence. I won't do that again." He turned to walk away and then turned back. "But you are my good buddy and I value your advice. I'll think about it. Promise."

My shoulders lost much of their tension. "Forgive me?"

"You're forgiven. I know you said what you said for the right reasons." His voice had lost that angry, tense tone. Hallelujah.

"Now let's go see Mateo and I'll see if I can piss him off, too."

"I'm sure you can, with no effort at all."

43

Sometimes You Make Me Sick

We walked into Mateo's room to find him ensconced in a rowdy game of poker with Ross Zelinger. His color looked enough better to make me breathe easier.

RK pulled two chairs close to the bed and we both plonked ourselves down. "Who's holding down the fort?" I asked Ross, after hugging my brother long enough to make him squirm away.

"Helen opened the shop. I told her I could hire a temp, but she insisted."

"We might drop by and give her a hand. I could be the brains, and RK here, the muscle."

RK curled his lip at me, but I could tell he was no longer angry. Irked, maybe. Probably.

"That's considerate of you. Wes dropped by earlier on his way to his bar. He hated to leave Kirsten, but work is a hard taskmaster. Or maybe it's his wife," he added with a wink.

After some awkward hospital-don't say-anything-to-raise-the-patient's-blood pressure chatter, silence cloaked the room. "We spoke with Leonard this morning," I began.

"You're still snooping!" Mateo shouted, rearing up in the bed, scattering playing cards on the floor. "I thought you'd back off after," he waved at himself. "What kind of an idiot are you?"

So much for keeping his blood pressure normal. And there went my hope that he'd help me figure this crime out. "We went to see Vista Rioja," I said, my voice smooth, soothing, calm. "RK's considering buying something."

He settled back. "Yeah, like I buy that crap. You do need her in the shop, Ross. She can really fling the BS. Should be great at sales."

"She's not lying," RK said. "Not totally. I am interested in that development. She did snoop the tiniest bit, but she was safe. I was right next to her. It's cool, Mateo." He squatted and picked up cards and I joined him.

After my tantrum about Erin, I didn't deserve his support, but I appreciated it. I shot him a grateful smile. "Thanks, friend. I did ask Leonard a couple of things and I wanted to verify with Ross."

Mateo crossed his arms and scowled but said nothing further, so I continued. "Violet seemed to have a strong interest in forest fires and firefighting. Did anything happen while you were together that might have caused that interest? Might there have been some significance to the date of the ukulele concert? She really went ballistic that night."

Ross was already shaking his head. "I told you, Madrone, that was a long, long time ago and my memory's not sharp. I think you're headed down the wrong path. For all the right reasons. Losing Violet was a blow to all of us." After a moment, he added, "I appreciate the help with the shop. Helen claims she can handle everything, but neither of us is getting younger." He patted Mateo's bed. "We still have a game or two to finish."

I savored the idea of getting Helen alone to ask her a few questions about Ross. "If it saves the job for Mateo, I'm happy to help out. And I'm sure he finds you much more interesting than me." I eyed Mateo.

"Don't make me choose, Sis. Way awkward." He squirmed upward in the bed, careful not to disturb the cards that again lay on his lap. "Sure wish I knew when I can fly this coop and get back to work. Maybe you can chat with the docs, Madrone?"

RK chuckled. "You don't want Madrone talking with the medics. She'll suggest they keep you for weeks and weeks. You're her baby brother."

"Days or weeks, the job's yours, kiddo," Ross said. "I've never found an employee familiar with all genres of music, who could steer people in the right direction, and who was fun on top of it." Ross looked uncomfortable at his revelation. Suspicious me wondered if he lied or revealed his true feelings.

"He is a keeper," I said. "Even if annoying at times."

We chatted for a while and then I rose. "Well, if you're willing to keep Mateo entertained, I'm ready to head to the shop. RK?" I leaned over Mateo to give him a kiss.

His focus moved to the doorway. He smiled. "Hey, Ash. Not sure you're my sister's favorite person right now. That was some story in the paper."

I spun around to snarl at Ash Coretti. "Got your phone on record? Wouldn't want to miss a single intimate second of my time with my injured brother."

Ash stayed in the doorway, hands up as if to calm me. As if he could. He'd suckered me, and being suckered doesn't appeal. But I shut my mouth, allowing him to speak. "I come in peace," he said. "I want to help. Reporting news is my job and for a small-time paper in a small community, I'm not half bad. But I didn't trick Madrone. I assumed she knew I was a reporter. And, as I already told Madrone, I submitted the story long before you and Kirsten were injured."

I glared but remained silent, backing up against the side wall of the room. My entire body remained tense, in attack mode, even though my brain knew Ash was no physical threat to my brother. He wasn't, was he?

Mateo waved his friend in. "What you need to know is that I'm far more forgiving and understanding than my older sister." His face clouded. "We have some bad memories connected to hit-and-run incidents."

Incidents? Bad memories? How could he speak so blithely about the vehicle that ran our father down, killing him instantly? The police eventually termed it a regrettable accident and gave up trying to find whoever murdered our father. I knew in my heart that it had to do with his reporting a drug house in our barrio to the police, but it wasn't a subject we discussed. Without proof, we had nothing but the huge hole in our family my father's death caused. And for me, a never-ending hatred of drugs and drug dealers, intensifying when my brother got snared by them.

I struggled, but managed to keep my face expressionless.

Or so I thought. RK rose and walked to my side, lightly touching my fist. Ross looked my way, something like pity or understanding in his eyes. Mateo, the rat, barely looked at me, and waved his friend into the room.

"Come on in, Ash. Kirsten got hurt worse than I did, but we'll both survive. That's what counts. And it kind of knocks me out of the running as a suspect."

Ash ignored the resentment emanating from me and moved to Mateo's bed. "Well, that's one piece of good news." His head jerked back toward me. "This is all off the record. I'm glad you're both okay."

"Okay is relative, but we're alive," Mateo said. "If you can find anything out that clears this up, maybe it will keep my big sister out of the hospital. Or the morgue. Nothing else will stop her snooping."

I glared at my mouthy brother, but said nothing, because he spoke the truth.

"As I tried to tell Madrone, I really want to help. I plan to do some online sleuthing. I have access to some databases through the paper that most folks don't have. But I would like to speak with you, Ross, on the record, sometime today. As I understand, you and Violet went way back, and you were there the night she lost it with Kirsten."

Ross grimaced. "Seems like everyone wants to chat with me about Violet. To be honest, I'm mourning an old friend, and although I realize some people like to reminisce, I'm finding it tedious."

Ooh. I got the feeling Ash wasn't Ross's favorite person. Something we agreed on. Maybe, on the other hand, Ross truly was tired of my—and no doubt others'—endless questions about Violet and was sending me a message. Seizing the moment, I said, "You know, Ash, you really ought to do some kind of story on Ross's art. Have you seen the mural in The Whistle Stop?"

He smiled at me, maybe pleased that I deigned to speak to him. "Obviously you haven't been a regular reader of *The Sedona Red Rock News.* We do some sort of piece on it every year. Ross is a rock star in Cottonwood."

Ross looked at the ceiling tile. "Right. Big frog in a miniscule pond."

Mateo, perhaps irked that he no longer was the focus of the room's interest and sympathy, said, "Speaking of that art, you should take some photos, Madrone. While you help out in the shop. Helen can give you the deets."

"Great idea. I've been planning to, and today's a good day. Is there a chance you could help me, Ash? You know more than I do about design and layout stuff. And I might want to take some from a ladder." Had I laid it on too thick? Or should I have batted my eyelashes? I wanted to know what he learned from searching the paper's databases, long before it hit the press.

Ash looked at me, no doubt questioning my motives. Hours earlier I'd practically decked him, minutes before I'd sneered at him, and now I was asking for his help. He was no dummy and saw right through my ruse. But if I stuck close to him . . .

After a lengthy pause, Ash shrugged. "Sure. I'll meet you there after I stop by the office for the good camera."

Roadkill, who'd vowed to stick to me like molasses, shot me a questioning look. He could easily help me with the photos of Ross's mural. But, bless his heart, he stayed mum.

"If you're off to help Helen, I'm going to run some errands, once we finish our game," Ross said. He patted Mateo's leg. "We miss you, kiddo. It isn't easy to take up the slack."

"That mean I'll be getting a raise when I'm back?"

Ross chuckled. "Don't press your luck."

"Good grief," I said. "He's keeping your job open."

Mateo smirked. "Chill, Big Sister. I was kidding and Ross knows it."

"If you think I'm smothering you, wait. I have to phone Mama tonight or she'll kill us both as soon as you recover."

He waved me away. "On your way. All this visiting is wearing me out. I know you have to call Mama. Thanks for giving me a little breathing time."

Ross followed us out to the hall. Keeping his voice low, he said, "I'll see what the doctor says when she makes her rounds and report back to you." Even quieter, he added, "Helen's worried about appearances—didn't want me to spend too much time visiting with 'a murder suspect. What will people say?'" He shook his head. "Why worry what people in Cottonwood think, I told her. The thing is, your brother has grown on me. I've had some fine employees in the past, but Mateo's more like—a son, if I might be so bold. The one I never was blessed with."

With my usual lack of restraint, I gave him a hug. "He's learned so much from you. Maybe it's a blessing he got sent up here. Thank you for placing your faith in him."

"He's a good kid, and he's lucky to have a sister who loves him and trusts in him. Now scoot. Tell Helen she should spring for lunch for you."

We scooted. I liked this man, liked his affection for my brother. I'd really hate it if he proved to be a murderer.

44

Musical Snares

Helen greeted us with a lukewarm smile. "Ross texted me that you were heading over. I appreciate the help, although we're not all that busy. That man fusses over me way too much." A lightening of her mouth told me she liked his fussing.

"I'm happy to do what I can, but I'm no music whiz like Mateo."

At the mention of my brother's name, I thought I detected a shadow cross Helen's face. Maybe, as Ross mentioned in the hospital, she was concerned about her husband hiring a recovering addict, or an ex-con. Although it wasn't as if he'd spent years on a chain gang.

"RK can do the heavy lifting, if you need it." RK flexed his muscles and a big grin.

"What are you, her bodyguard?" Her smile seemed strained. "I guess she needs one."

"Not a real bodyguard, or even like those in the movies, but I am watching her back," he said. "After what happened to Mateo and Kirsten, even Sergeant Doughty thought it was a good idea for someone to keep an eye on Madrone. We're old friends, and she does have a tendency to get into trouble."

She nodded at his explanation. "Mateo did share a few of his sister's exploits. Good idea. I'll keep an eye on her, too."

"And so will all those folks up there," I said, staring at the mural.

"Someone's dropping by later to help me take some photos. You must be so proud of Ross."

Her smile erased all stress from her face. "He has his moments. He's underrated in this town."

"Why didn't Ross move elsewhere to pursue his art? It really is an incomparable talent."

"I could never convince him to leave Cottonwood. He tells me he loves it here."

"Do you? Love Cottonwood?"

She looked away, her distant gaze telling me she was thinking of other places. Lost opportunities? "I like the town. Most of the people are good sorts. When I retired from teaching, I suggested we leave, pursue his art in New York City, Paris. He wouldn't leave dear old Cottonwood. Ross could do whatever he wanted, but he doesn't give himself enough credit. If he wanted to, he could be mayor, maybe even a state representative. But rumors fly fast in this town, and appearances count for a lot." Ahh. She really didn't like Mateo working here. She'd lost her animation of moments before and her entire demeanor had stiffened.

"Has Ross ever been asked to do a commission like the mural somewhere else?"

A little shake of her head said a lot. "Oh, yes. For big bucks. But he couldn't leave dear old Cottonwood." After a moment, she added in an undertone, "And its dear old residents."

I detected bitterness in her tone, mixed with regret and sorrow. "What held him here?"

"He said he liked being the big fish in a small pond, but I believe he hated to leave his friends." Her expression darkened, as if she were brooding some old resentment.

"I guess in a small town like this, they still consider you a newcomer."

"Ha! You said it. It wasn't easy to make friends, especially before Ross and I started dating. Then all my 'best friends' came out of the woodwork."

"Ven showed us some photos she found at Violet's house this morning," I said. "Some fun ones of Ross in his virile youth. I'll bet you can get copies."

Her expression darkened. "I love Ross the way he is now. No need to dig up the past. That was Violet's obsession."

RK tilted his head like a curious roadrunner. "Obsession?"

She shrugged. "I'd call it that. She wouldn't or couldn't let the past stay in the past. Became quite annoying about it as she got crazier and crazier."

"Wow," I said. "I could have used you when she started flinging accusations about me and RK and our touring company."

"Her daughter thought she was perfectly sane," my friend added. "At least when she first got home."

"Humph. Perfectly sane people don't obsess over mistakes made decades earlier."

"Mistakes? Like breaking up with Ross?" Or what else?

Helen snorted. "Are you kidding me? Back in the day, as I heard it, Violet jumped between beds like a cricket. I guess it was sleeping bags back then. All that bed-hopping must have worn her out, 'cuz old Chet was no prize, at least in the looks department. Knew how to make money, though."

Hmm. Ross's sweet wife wasn't quite as endearing when he wasn't around. "Yes," I agreed, "she had quite a lot of property here in Cottonwood. Guess that made some people angry."

"Yeah. If Violet had a talent, it was for getting on the wrong side of people." She paused and gave me look. "You seem to have a knack for that, too."

Whoa. I'd obviously grilled the poor woman enough. "Hey, I didn't come here for your life story." I chuckled, a totally lame chuckle. "How can we help? I know my alphabet and can stock things. Or dust. Boss me around."

"Me too," RK added.

He and I exchanged a look. This woman was not a fan of Violet's and it didn't look like she'd be joining my fan club soon, either.

Insisting there wasn't much she couldn't handle, Helen set me to work alphabetizing the albums. "If it's obvious something's out of place, go ahead and move it. If you're not sure, ask. I don't want you making more work for me." She assigned Roadkill the task of dusting the higher shelves from a ladder. "Ross made me promise to get lunch for you two." She took our orders for lunch and set off to the deli.

* * *

Ash arrived while Helen was out fetching our lunch. He toted two cameras, a tripod, a folding screen to bounce light where we wanted it, along with some other photographic equipment. "Ross has added a couple of people to the mural since our photographer last came, so I borrowed some of his stuff. Adele? I'm loving her. But Justin Bieber?" He made a face. "I'm sure the boss will be willing to run another feature."

"Even when there's a murder mystery going on in town?" I said, only sneering a little.

"Hey, between you and Willa Doughty, this thing's gonna be a wrap soon. Especially with what I discovered. I think you were right about someone wanting to stop Violet from talking about an incident in her past."

Helen came out of the back room, laden with bags and a couple of bottles of soda. "I didn't know what you liked to drink—." She jerked to a stop. "Is this your photographer?" Her face revealed her displeasure.

"Hi, Ms. Zelinger," Ash said. "Didn't Madrone warn you I was coming?" He gave her one of his signature smiles designed to melt feminine hearts but her expression didn't warm.

"She said someone would help. She didn't tell me who."

"I promise to be as silent as the guys on the mural. The publicity's good for The Whistle Stop."

"I'm sure that's true," she said, obviously making an effort to be hospitable. "I bought extra sandwiches. You three can fight over them. I'll make some fresh coffee." She disappeared into the back.

As we rummaged through the bags, RK said to Ash, "You seem to be ticking off the ladies today."

"Yeah, I'm not one of Helen's favorite people. Did a story on Ross taking on Mateo, giving the recovering addict a new start, and she thought it was a bad idea."

"Mateo didn't mention that to me," I said.

"News flash—brothers don't tell their big sisters everything about their lives."

"Got that. Okay, what did you find out?"

"I took a cue from your theory that the date she blew up in Jerome might have some significance. I started—" He stopped abruptly. "Now where do you want the focus to be?"

I stared at him, trying not to notice his deep blue eyes. Wait. Those deep blue eyes looked right past me. I turned and looked over my shoulder. Helen Zelinger stood silent, gazing at us. Listening?

"I'm thinking we focus on the new additions. But I'd like a shot of that first section. I love all those guys. Johnny and June Cash, Waylon and Willie. My mom and her mom were big Frank Sinatra fans—and why not? The man could sing." I knew I was babbling, but Helen's silent observation creeped me out. "I'm going to try for some with my cell phone, for grins. Sometimes I catch the right angle."

"Okay if I use the ladder?" Ash asked RK.

"Only if someone brings me a cookie. Helen," he called out, "did we leave any cookies?"

"Right here," she said. She turned and walked to the back room, calling over her shoulder, "I might miss the bell with all of you in here working and chattering, so let me know if a customer comes in."

"Easy-peasy." I raised my voice to reach her. Hmm. Helen didn't like having us there. I could understand her aversion to Ash, but moi? And RK? We were there to help. I scurried to the check-out counter where the lunch bags still lay. A smaller bag contained a variety of cookies. I took three, and shared one each with the men.

I returned to alphabetizing and emptying the carton near the "Country" section, but as soon as I could, asked Ash in a low voice, "What did you find? Something to do with that date?"

"I think it's a good direction to begin with, and I can easily search by that date backwards through the years. But I barely started. I knew you were expecting me here. I'm slower than our staff photographer at setting things up, but still, we should finish getting some good shots in an hour or so. Once we're through, I'll head back to the office and conduct a thorough search."

RK, after downing his cookie and ransacking the bag for any bite-sized crumbs, toted the ladder to Ash. "If you don't need my brute strength, I'll do the sorting and stacking for Madrone and she can help you." He shot me a sly grin. He'd seen me staring at Ash when his back was turned. After all, that was his better side.

I flushed. Why the interest in this nosy reporter who'd so far done me no favors? "Go ahead," I said. "Know your alphabet?" The task Helen had assigned me was mindless, an indication of the trust she put in me.

I wanted to protest to RK that I'd been admiring the mural, but that would give Ash a hint about where my eyes had strayed. So I concentrated on the mural and considered the intensity of the artist who painted it. It didn't fit my concept of the casual, cannabis-friendly, pony-tailed ukulele player who at this moment played poker with my brother. Reminding me that none of us is exactly as we appear to the outside world. We're seen through others' filters, and we reveal or conceal parts of ourselves as we choose.

Ash called out questions about where to focus, and I directed him, helping him move the ladder and the bounce boards—as I learned the reflectors were called—to get the best shots. After more than an hour of this, we were both ready for a break.

"Think we have enough?" I asked him. "I'd like to work a little longer on getting LPs in place. I did promise Mateo and Ross I'd help Helen."

Ash descended the ladder one last time. "I deserve a treat." He trotted to the counter, upended the cookie bag, and shot RK a glare. "You hogged all the goodies."

"You'll survive," I said. "I'd like to frame a few of the prints that turn out well—for the Adventure Calls office, for Mateo as a memento of his work here, for my room. Think Ross will be okay with that?"

"I'm sure he would. He's always happy for people to take pics. Maybe ask Helen?"

"Before I leave. But I get the feeling Ross is more generous," I added in an undertone.

He smiled. "Guys are much cooler. But you're right, Helen's a little uptight about things, and Ross is more laid back." He drew close and said, "I need to do more research, but I found some info on forest fires.

I think you were spot on about the fires. Could be something that happened with Ross or Leonard, or even Chet, that would be embarrassing—or worse—if the news came out."

From a few yards away, Helen chirped, "Could one of you big strong young men bring more cartons from the back? I promised Ross I wouldn't lift them again." To me, she added, "I'm perfectly capable, but Ross would never let me forget it if somehow I strained something. The big silly. Once they have the cartons in place, maybe we could all work to put the LPs on the carrels. Holiday shopping season will be on us soon, and I want it to be ready."

We worked for nearly two more hours, Helen stopping to assist the occasional customer. Not many. Paying Violet a higher rent might have proved tricky. But I had no idea how much sales increased during the holidays. If the inventory they'd ordered was an indicator, Ross expected a large rise in traffic and sales.

When Helen and I were within chatting distance, I said, "I gather that a good percentage of your profit comes from the rental and sale of instruments to students. That must be a good income stream."

She looked at me as if I'd farted. "Would be and definitely used to be. But nowadays the serious music students go to specialty, target schools, outside of Cottonwood. And lots of the rest of them get their instruments online, for less than we can possibly charge. "

"I see," I said, without seeing anything.

She frowned. "If you're questioning the big inventory bump, you'll have to ask my husband. He has always been, always will be, an optimist. Says he has high hopes for Christmas this year." She gazed at the mural for a long moment. "One of many reasons I love him."

I looked at the empty cardboard cartons. "We're about done," I said. "And I bet Ross will be home soon," I added, not knowing what else to say.

Her expression darkened. "If he plans to come home at all. He's spent the entire day with your brother. Wish I had Mateo's appeal."

I picked up two of the empty boxes. "These go out back? Mateo's bored and Ross has been kind to him. It's a burden on you, as well, and I really appreciate it."

"I'd do anything for Ross, and right now that means saving

Mateo's job, I guess."

"Love makes us all do strange things," RK said, from behind me.

I jumped into the air and squeaked. "Don't sneak up on me like that!" I scolded.

He wasn't listening, but reading a new text. He closed his eyes and drew in a breath. "Erin got into a fight with her father and quit."

Like her brother Gabe before her. I wasn't sure I ever wanted to encounter the senior Ramsay. "Speaking of doing strange things."

Helen tilted her head. "Is that your sweetie?" she asked RK.

I chuckled. "He's pretty sweet on her. And hoping she feels the same."

RK squinted at me. "How sweet does, 'I'm flying into Phoenix tonight and hope you can pick me up?' sound?"

Ash joined us. "Romantic." He grabbed the empty pastry bag, shook it, and frowned.

"Very sweet," said Helen.

"Sappy," I said. Too much romance makes my skin itch.

They all laughed.

"Seriously," RK said, "it presents a problem. I promised to keep an eye on you."

Ash waggled his eyebrows. "I'll keep my eyes on Madrone. No problem at all." He shot me that puppy dog look. "If you can forgive me for the news article."

"Ahh," Helen said. "I see our local reporter has irked you, too."

"The news article Ash wrote threw me for a loop," I replied. "However, I don't have to forgive him to welcome, if reluctantly, his bodyguard services," I said. "Leah has a spare bedroom. Far be it from me to interfere in the course of true love."

RK shook his head. "Yeah, heaven forbid." I think his statement might have been ironic.

Ash clapped his hands together. "It's a plan, then. I need to stop by the office and my house, but I should be at your place in a couple of hours. Then we can talk. I should have more data by then."

"Can you make it sooner?" RK asked him. "I hate to make Erin wait too long."

Ash smirked. "Afraid she might meet someone smoother than

you?"

"Clean up after yourselves and get on out of here," Helen said before RK could make a comment he'd regret, waving her arms at us. "Don't make the poor girl wait."

"Are you sure we can't help you finish?" I asked.

"Oh, poop. There isn't all that much to do. I'll be fine and I'm sure Ross will come in tomorrow. Surely Mateo can survive without him."

I steeled myself to hide my reaction to the acid in her tone each time she mentioned my brother. Sheeze. He was a good man and Ross liked him. Reason enough for Helen to treat him better. I said nothing. That relationship was Mateo's problem, when he got back to work.

45

All by Myself

RK dropped me off at Leah's cottage, a place I now considered a haven. Since he'd moved his belongings here in his role as bodyguard, it was easy for him to shower and change clothes before heading to the Phoenix airport. Dressed and ready, he lingered in the kitchen, muttering about not feeling comfortable leaving me alone, breaking his promise to my brother. I gave him a big hug and handed him the insulated bag with snacks and water for the long drive south and the return north.

"Are you coming back up tonight? Not that I have a say in it. Do whatever you two decide is best. I'm sorry about saying you were moving too fast with Erin. Sometimes, people click and this must be the time for you two. She is a strong, desirable woman, and by flying to Phoenix she's displaying her commitment to you."

He peeked in the fridge, pulled out two cans of fizzy water and stowed them in the carrier. "Nowhere else to go, except France."

"Not true. She could head to Tucson and stay with Gabe. Or stay in Durango and hang out with other friends. She's putting her trust in you, pal. Now live up to it and get out of here. I'll be fine. Ash will be here soon."

He meandered toward the back door. "Lock this after me and check all the other doors. Don't let anyone else in the house, except maybe Sergeant Doughty." He backed up, hands on hips and stared into my eyes. "Promise me."

I pondered that one. "Ash has to wait on the porch?"

He laughed. "Ash is clean. I checked his alibi for the night Violet was killed and he's in the clear."

"You checked up on him? When?"

"Today at the library. I called Sergeant Doughty, asked her if she'd checked him out and she told me he'd been on assignment in Prescott."

"Comforting, I guess, but why had she checked into Ash's whereabouts? I didn't have him on my suspect list."

"Which is why Doughty's the cop and you're not. Apparently, Violet had tried to get Ash fired when he covered town council meetings and reported on her violent outbursts."

I nodded. "Makes sense. He didn't tell me, but . . ."

"Not sure you and he have had much chance to chat. Maybe tonight. I think he's one of the good guys, despite the story."

I frowned and opened my mouth but RK stopped my protest with a finger to my lips. "He was doing his job. Like we were doing our jobs with Violet. Not everyone's always going to be happy with our work." He hefted the carrier in one hand. "There's enough for an entire platoon here."

"Like you know the size of a platoon."

"Bigger than two, smaller than a thousand."

I waved my hands at him in a "scoot" gesture. "Go on. Don't keep her waiting. And drive carefully."

"Yes, Mom. Speaking of which . . ."

I scrunched my nose. "Yeah, yeah, I'll call mine tonight."

"Sooner's better." He crossed to the door and left.

I immediately felt bereft and alone. What a weenie I'd become. I was a woman who could camp alone in the Sonoran Desert, drive all over the Southwest on my own, and now. . . I shivered. My grandmother would call it a premonition. I chalked it up to nerves and vowed I would *not* start baking, my go-to response to anxiety. In my bedroom, I slouched into an ancient pair of sweats and a long-sleeved sweatshirt. Evenings here cooled down more than in Tucson in the fall and I needed the comfort of soft old clothes.

Instead of baking, I checked all the doors, looked at the clock and hoped

Ash would arrived soon. Would he want dinner? No, Madrone. There are plenty of things to munch on in the fridge. I sat at the counter and pulled out my phone.

Mama answered immediately. "You should have called sooner." No hello, no how are you.

"It's been a little hectic here."

"Not too hectic to let me know my son is in the hospital. Fortunately, they phoned me. I have to find out about my family's disasters from complete strangers. I'm angry with you, Madrone."

"Mateo is fine, getting better fast."

"Sure, sure. I know all this. I spoke with his doctor this evening."

My mouth fell open. "You—"

"I'll be there before noon tomorrow. Gabe and I are leaving Tucson very early. I wanted to drive there by myself tonight but he convinced me to wait for him. I only hope you can manage to stay alive that long."

My mother, who hated to drive, especially at night, had planned to cross the state after dark to reach me and Mateo? I shut my mouth, opened it again. "You and Gabe are coming?"

"Did something happen to your hearing? Your thinking? We're coming. I thought about chartering a plane, but I'd have to get a second mortgage on the house and there was no time. When you love someone, that is what you do. Care for them, do everything you can for them, even when they don't want you to, when they refuse to tell you what is going on. I would have been there sooner if my only daughter had thought to keep me informed."

My pulse soared with the pitch of my mother's angry voice. "But—"

"I can read the paper, you know. I even know how to use the internet and read papers in your area. And my friend Anita's cousin works at the 911 center there in Cottonwood. She filled me in on what's going on, since you have been silent. How can you be *loca* enough to pursue the murderer on your own?"

What to say to this woman who seemed to know more than I myself did? "I'm being careful," I said. "My friend RK, Cliff, is helping me." No need to provide every detail.

"Sure, sure, sure. And that's why my poor little Mateo and his girl are in the hospital. Do you not remember how all the neighbors thought your father was involved in drugs when he looked into the dealers in our neighborhood? You are bound to get into trouble. I thought I could trust you."

Nothing to say, but, "Sorry, Mama."

Her voice softened, went from angry to sorrowful. "I always knew that your father's supposed accident back then was a result of his looking into things that were none of his business. Please, please, be careful, *mija.*"

Her words struck like needles under my nails. She had never voiced that thought before. If I said anything, I'd yell or burst into tears, so I kept quiet. We said our goodbyes and agreed she'd phone me when they got close.

I stomped to the refrigerator and stared inside. Instead of something healthy, I poured the remnants of last night's wine into a glass and rummaged in Leah's stash for chocolate. My mother was furious with me, and Gabe wasn't a happy camper, either. Mateo and his girl were hospitalized due to my snooping, and I was not much closer to finding Violet's killer.

The tiny, persistent, optimist in my brain said, "Not true. You've narrowed the field and Ash is looking into Violet's past and her obsession with fires. The killer is someone who felt they had to stop Violet before her obsession with "coming clean" revealed something about him or her." I needed to let my squirrely brain rest and the answers might appear from where they'd been hiding.

I carried the wine and a bowl filled with miniature bars of chocolate out to Leah's back yard. It was fenced and the gates were locked. I was safe. I forced myself to sip rather than slug my wine. Considered, but rejected as too much work, going for a swim in the pool—a gem surrounded by artfully placed, immense stones. Pondered my suspects.

No. I needed to relax. Swimming might soothe my tense brain enough to think outside the box. I'd poked and probed Violet's past and come up with only a few names. In Jerome that evening, Ross had hushed her when she started wailing about regrets. That day when I overheard him on the phone with Violet, I didn't believe he'd been talking about her relationship with her granddaughter. I still didn't. There was anger, even threat in his tone on that call. And no one would tell me much about the disappearance of the other daughter.

But Ross cared about Mateo. A lot. Enough to make his wife jealous. Until

I'd seen Ross in the hospital, fussing over my brother, I'd almost concluded it was he who'd silenced Violet and threatened me. But no way would he hurt Mateo to keep me off the scent.

Why did people kill? Rage? Yes. Robbery, but not in this case—nothing had been stolen. Money, which gave Violet's family good reason to kill her. But they were off the list—Ven and her husband cherished their daughter and would not harm her. Unless, of course, Wes had not known she was with Mateo. Money, again. Would anyone else profit from Violet's death? Leonard, possibly, but he and his partner had already made their way past Violet's refusal to sell land for their development and looked to be doing well enough, even if more land would have meant more profit.

Jealousy? I chewed on that. Leonard, the long-rejected lover, could have finally snapped. And maybe he and Violet shared secrets from their past that he didn't want out.

Doggone secrets. Maybe people had been more forthcoming with Detective Doughty and she knew all those secrets. I hoped.

Yes. I kept coming back to someone's desire to silence Violet before she confessed the sins of her past. And who would that be, other than Ross or Leonard?

My phone vibrated and I answered the call, figuring it was my mother again. But it was Ven Sturgess. "Wes and I are on the front porch. We need to talk. It's time to bring some secrets out in the open."

I downed my wine in one gulp. "I'll be right there."

I passed through the kitchen to the front door. It was way past time for some honest answers. Did they truly intend to tell me something new tonight? RK would not be happy that I let them in, but I was pretty sure they hadn't conspired to kill Violet, injure their daughter and then, after asking me to investigate, kill me. Where would the logic in that be?

Besides, Ash would be here soon. This wouldn't be dangerous.

46

A Time for Answers

After Ven's statement on the phone, I didn't want to do anything to change their intention, so I escorted the Sturgesses in silence to the kitchen table, the place in my mother's home where we kids always revealed our secrets.

Once they were seated, I offered them water or wine or said I could make coffee.

"Water," Wes said. "I'm about talked out."

"Yes, water would be nice," Ven said.

With waters all around, I sipped mine and waited.

"There have been too many secrets," Ven started.

Wes nodded. "We talked this evening, really talked for the first time in a long time."

Oh, no. I did not want to be their marriage counselor, even if this couple truly needed one.

Wes held his palms out, facing the sky. "We're going to be honest with you. You'll have to decide if you believe what we tell you, but we're going to talk to the police after we talk to you."

Ven gave a lukewarm smile. "Willa wanted us to come straight to her home, but we told her we needed to talk to you first. We'll speak with Kirsten in the morning."

"If I'm not in jail," Wes clarified. At my horrified expression, he added, "No, no, I didn't kill Violet. I couldn't have, even though she treated me like a worthless buffoon."

Ven put her hand out toward him. "You were my husband. I shouldn't have ignored the way she spoke to you, about you."

"Yeah, we agree we've both made mistakes, but we're working to clear things up."

Get to the secrets, the good stuff.

Wes continued, looking toward the back door rather than either of us. "Neither of us killed Violet, and we don't know who did. I imagine that's the main thing you wanted to know."

I opened my mouth to deny I'd harbored such suspicions, but he shook his head. "Here's the thing . . . I have a gambling problem and I got into debt. I made the mistake . . ." he paused and huffed out a breath, "of getting Kirsten involved. It was a bad move, but I knew she'd help her dad out of a jam and I didn't think Vi would ever catch on. You gotta believe me, both of you, I didn't know what she said that night in Jerome until the next day. I was working at the bar. Otherwise, I'd never have let Kirsten even meet with her grandmother. I would have confessed."

"But Mom never made it to the meeting with Kirsten," Ven said, "and, well, I didn't know about it either, until Kirsten phoned to see if Mom was at our place. I'd already gone into work, to do some bookkeeping, and to work on plans for my bistro. The one I'd never told you about," she said with a sad nod to her husband. She stared into my eyes. "Everyone will think I only told Wes because I knew the truth would come out, but when he confessed his gambling pro—"

"I think we're supposed to call it what it is, an addiction," Wes interrupted. "So they tell me at my Gamblers Anonymous meetings."

"Whatever. I couldn't keep lying to him."

Time for me to say something. "Uh, you both realize I already knew about each of these things, that this isn't a big reveal. Also, why would Sergeant Doughty need to know these things?"

Wes crossed his arms and smiled. "Patience, grasshopper. That's where the story begins." He cleared his throat. "Here's where it gets trickier. I didn't know that you overheard Kirsten and Mateo arguing about her borrowing from her grandmother's shop to cover my gambling debts and she certainly didn't want to tell me. All I knew is if you kept nosing around, you'd be bound to find out about my problem. So I left you that note on your door, cut the words out of magazines at the hotel. But I swear that was the only threat I left you. And I don't know who left the dead toad or threw a rock through the window. I couldn't do something like that."

"And he definitely wasn't the one who ran Kirsten and Mateo off the road," Ven said. "Wes has his faults but he loves his daughter fiercely."

"Which explains why those first threats came so close together. They were from two different people."

"It couldn't have been more than two. Surely the person who broke the window and who injured Mateo and Kirsten are the same person. That's why it's important we tell Willa."

"Thing is, it doesn't get me a lot closer to solving Vi's murder. Some things are clearer, but others remain murky." I stared at the table top but found no answers there.

Ven shifted in her chair. "One more thing. Another secret I've kept for way too long, from everyone. Something I'll regret as long as I live." She stood and meandered to the back door, then spun to face us. "I already told Wes, earlier today. But you were curious about my sister Rose, speculating, I think, that she came back into the picture and killed Mom for her inheritance."

Wow. A little harsh, but I had dallied with that theory.

"I didn't know anything more about Rose's disappearance than my folks when she left. All I knew was my beautiful, talented older sister was gone. And that the sounds in our home changed from Mom and Rose shouting at each other, to Mom, weeping, wondering where she'd gone, what had happened.

"When people want to disappear, it isn't that hard, especially back then, before the internet and social media. Rose changed her name and her appearance and moved around a lot, living in communes, doing menial labor of all kinds. But always working on her art. She did all kinds of art."

Ven wiped a few tears from her face. "About five years ago, Rose got in touch with me. She now lives on Long Island, outside New York City and teaches art in a community college. She also sells her art. She wanted to know about the family, but refused to let me tell Mom she was alive and in touch."

An artist? With a name similar to Ross? Could it be possible? I sat, waiting for more.

"It's hard to understand how after all those years, she still didn't want to talk to Mom, but the two of them had been at loggerheads for as long as I remember, even before Rose was a teenager. Their personalities were so similar, you see. Stubborn and inflexible. I kept her informed about our mother, about my family. She knew when Daddy died, had been checking the online news. I tried to convince her to come for a visit and she finally agreed. For Christmas this year, she planned to surprise Mom."

"Rose changed her name to Althea. She was crushed about Mom's death. We're still trying to decide if she should come for the memorial service. She's worried her return would take the limelight from Mom. She had a small gallery opening the night before Mom was killed. It couldn't have been her, and she'd have no reason to hurt Mom. She's a pretty successful artist."

Wes grinned at me. "You're considering when she was born and the possibility that Ross Zelinger might be her father, him being an artist and all. At least, that's what I asked Ven this afternoon. Because, believe it or not, today's the first time I heard that Ven's long-lost sister had been found. Or was never lost."

"I know," Ven said with a shake of her head, "not the recommended way to run a marriage."

I raised an eyebrow. Ven chuckled. "I had the same thought years ago, so I checked into it. Ross returned to Cottonwood, joined the Army, and some six months later Mom came home with her new love, Chet. They got married five months later, and Rose wasn't born until two years after that. Nothing but coincidence about the artistic abilities. But the name? Who knows? Maybe yes, maybe no."

I pondered the information Wes and Ven had shared. "Wes, your note scared me but didn't stop me. I did wonder how that second threat came so quickly, so you've cleared up a part of the mystery. But I'm not much closer to knowing who killed Violet. Any ideas?"

Ven shook her head. "I wish we did, but no. We're off now to tell Willa all this. We came here first, in case they detain Wes. We both wanted to talk with you. I'm hoping the police will find Mom's killer. In a horrible way, this has brought our family closer."

"Sometimes tragedies do that," I said. Or as in my family, people grow farther apart, mourning their losses, keeping their concerns secret, trying to "save" others from pain. How would things have been different if my mother had shared her conviction that Papa's death was a vengeance killing? If I had done the same? We all thought staying quiet eased others' pain. So not true.

I saw the Sturgesses to the front door and locked it behind them.

Alone once more, with even more to consider.

47

Who Wants a Dip?

More facts, yet more secrets to mull in my muddled mind. A swim would do me more good than the white wine I held in my hand, having traded it for my water glass. I sniffed its citrusy aroma, put the glass back for later, and trudged to my bedroom to put on a suit.

I did a shallow dive into the water and swam until the skittering thoughts in my brain slowed into almost mindfulness. I felt the pressure against palms as they stroked downward, savored my almost silent passage up and down the pool, tasted the salinity of the water that touched my lips, relished the bite of cool night air when I breathed.

I jerked to a stop in the middle of a lap and made a beeline for the steps. I snatched up the towel I'd left by the side of the pool. On the phone my mother had said, when you love someone enough, you will do anything for them. Anything, no matter the consequences. She was willing drive at night, to spend money she didn't have to charter a plane to reach her son. Someone else had said she would do anything to help the one she loved.

Helen Zelinger adored her husband and worried that hiring a felon like my brother would bring him shame. She cared immensely about appearances and status in the small town of Cottonwood. And earlier that day she'd said she'd do anything for Ross, at that time meaning save Mateo's job for him.

I dried my legs and wrapped the towel around me before I padded into the kitchen and traded my water glass for one of white wine. Then returned to my new thinking place, a chair on the back porch, overlooking the pool.

If Ash had been successful in tracking down Violet's activities in her youth and found something that would bring shame to Ross Zelinger, we'd have enough to bring my theory to Willa Doughty the next day. She was good friends with Helen and Ross, so we'd need a well-thought-out premise to convince her.

Ross had evaded my questions about Violet and fire, yet at some point had mentioned he'd not have been surprised if Violet had killed herself. They shared a secret, a big secret.

"Where are you, Ash? Move that cute butt."

48

You're All Wet!

Distracted by thoughts of Ash's rear end and other admirable body parts, I lost my focus on sleuthing. I pulled the towel snugger around me. Why didn't Leah have a hot tub? My mind wandered to a scenario of the two of us in a hot tub, sipping from a shared glass of champagne. My pulse quickened.

"You're something else, Madrone. Gabe's coming here tomorrow and you're daydreaming about some slick reporter who tricked a story out of you."

I needed a pet. Then maybe I wouldn't spend so much time chatting with yours truly. Would Mom bring her dog with her? I'd love to see Squash, the Catahoula Leopard Dog we'd discovered on a trip to California. Okay, nearly squished, hence her name. Did Ash have a dog? A cat? I'd ask him once he arrived. Something to talk about that didn't center on death and anger.

I gazed out at Leah's yard in the dusky evening light. Saw a blur of movement in the shrubs. Leah loved Arizona but she still had some Oregonian in her and made an attempt to grow roses. With care, they thrived, but without attention, disaster of many kinds could set in—too hot, too cold, too wet, too dry, bugs or varmints. What I was looking at was a cottontail rabbit munching on rose leaves, a treat for desert bunnies.

I held still, but the bunny noticed me and darted off and disappeared, possibly under the fence, unless it had dug a burrow somewhere in the yard.

A car pulled into Leah's drive, slid to a halt way too close to the garage. There was plenty of parking on the street. Why the driveway?

Was it really Ash or was I being an idiot and assuming it was him because he'd said he'd come?

I looked over but the drive was in shadows. Leah had high fences to keep kids out of her pool, and the gate was locked.

A car door slammed, and then a man hollered. "Woo hoo, Madrone. I'm here. Let me in, weeh-ooh, hoop wee ooh!" He sang that last part, in a bad echo of an old song.

I rose from my lawn chair. "Who is it? What's going on? Are you drunk? Or plain crazy?"

I started for the gate, unsure if I should open it. Not certain it was Ash Coretti. He called out again. "Hey, why's this locked? I'm here to help. Let me in. No, wait! I'll climb over." Yes, that was Ash Coretti, but Ash on drugs or booze. Something was off, very off. Why was he looped when he'd promised to do research?

The hackles rose on my neck. Really. I yearned for Squash beside me. I backed up, putting distance between me and this man I didn't know at all well. He was Mateo's friend, and a distant relative of Sergeant Doughty, but something was definitely wrong.

A huge thump, followed by scrambling, accompanied by oofs, ughs and more "wee-oohs" and the rattle of a wire fence. A few choice curse words, more rattling and another thump. I stepped backward and bumped against one of lawn chairs scattered around the yard.

I inched toward the gate. Ash Coretti clung halfway up the eight-foot-wire fence but then lost his grip and hit the ground. Grunting, he rose, apparently unhurt from the fall.

I trotted to the kitchen and retrieved the padlock key from a hook by the door. Back outside, I unlocked the gate. Ash staggered through it. He looked down at his hands, which were stuffed in his pockets. "Where's my laptop? I have research results."

"You're drunk. How could you have been researching and drinking at the same time?"

"We ace reporters have our ways," he said. "Multi-tashking." He headed toward the pool, but tripped over the lawn chair. He jumped up, brushed himself off, and said, "Where'd that come from? It jumped out at me." His expression held terror. "Keep it away from me," he yelped. He backed away from the chair so that I was between him and it.

I slammed the gate behind me and grabbed the chair back in one hand and Ash's arm in the other. I dragged both to poolside. "What the heck is wrong with you, Ash Coretti? You're acting weird." No, insane. Again, I shivered.

He smiled. "Nothing's wrong. You're beautiful, Madrone. So's the pool." He jumped in, fully clothed. Into the deep end. This was worse than drunk. Was he stoned? I barely knew this man. Maybe this behavior was normal for him.

He surfaced, treading water, and I screeched at him. "Ash, you idiot! Your phone. Your wallet."

"No worries. I can swim, they can swim, we all can swim." He giggled. "Come on in. Water's perfect." He frowned and added, "But these jeans are heavy when they're wet."

The deep end of Leah's pool was over eight feet, so she could do her SCUBA training. The pool lights were on and Ash's legs flailed in the deep water.

I didn't want to jump in after him for fear he'd suddenly panic and force me under. I ran to where the skimmer hung, grabbed it and ran back to the pool. By now Ash looked confused but not yet panicked. "Madrone, why am I swimming in my clothes?"

I struggled to keep my voice and expression calm. "You fell in, but there's no problem. Grab this pole and I'll pull you to the side."

I extended the skimmer toward Ash and he snatched at it, missing the first time as if his vision was blurred.

"Stop waving it around. You'll hit me," he yelled. He dipped beneath the surface. When he came up, his face portrayed terror. He grabbed the pole I extended and jerked. "Give me the pole. I need a weapon. There's something in here. I think it might be a hippo."

"Hang on and I'll pull you in, Ash. I'll keep you safe."

"Not a chance," said a voice behind me. I spun around, dropping the skimmer and then grabbing frantically for it as Ash pulled it toward him. Helen Zelinger stood behind me, holding a handgun. "You're too damn nosy.

Both of you."

I'd guessed right. The murderer stood not five feet away from me. My first response was to try acting dumb. "Helen? What's going on? Did Ash hurt you?"

She snorted out a laugh. "Ash can't hurt anyone but himself. Possibly you, once you join him. This is almost too easy. Lovers drink too much, take a few drugs, and fall in the pool, drowning together. Pitiful."

"Helen," Ash cried. "Did you bring more cookies? I want a cookie."

"I have some with me." She reached into a large satchel hanging from her shoulder and pulled out a plastic bag filled with cookies. She waved the gun at me. "Catch these or I'll shoot our swimming friend." She tossed the bag.

I watched it fall in front of me. "Oops." I squatted to pick it up, moving a few inches closer to Helen and to the lawn chair in front of her.

"Take one out and eat it."

She'd laced the cookies with some kind of hallucinogen. "Are they gluten-free?"

"You're kidding, right?" She pointed the handgun at the pool, where Ash's thrashing was slowing.

"What's in them, Helen?" I said, as I slowly opened the bag.

"Must be the ones with LSD if he thinks he's swimming with hippos," she said. She sneered at me. "My hippie husband has a variety of edibles, some with cannabis, others stronger. I simply shared with the poor boy when he dropped in to ask about Ross's whereabouts the night of the ukulele concert. He looked hungry."

"But it wasn't Ross who killed Violet, was it? It was you. Because she was going to reveal secrets from their past."

She ran her free hand through her hair. "That stupid woman. She caused trouble for him since day one. She had no right to destroy our reputation." She shrugged. "Ross stayed in Jerome to jam with his friends, didn't get home till early the next morning. I decided she'd gone too far. I took her some cookies after I got home from Jerome, suggested we take a stroll, have a chat, woman to woman, about what was bothering her. The cannabis made her a little easier to control, but face it, I'm strong."

"Did you intend to kill her when you went to her home?" I inched nearer the chair.

She smiled, a cold, blank smile. "Who knows? I thought I could convince her to keep her mouth shut. Ross is an important member of this community and I didn't want her to ruin it. But she was one stubborn woman. Starting screeching, so I grabbed her throat to shut her up. When she fought me, kicked me, I grabbed a rock and knocked her out. Guess I'm stronger than Ross thinks." Her careless way of describing the murder made me want to vomit. "Afterward, I scuffed the ground around her, hid my footprints. It wasn't as hard as you'd think. It was her time," she added. "Now it's yours. Eat the cookie."

"No. You'll have to shoot me and then Sergeant Doughty will know you were here."

She pointed the gun at the pool and fired.

Ash screamed, terror mixed with pain. I'd hoped she'd miss from this distance but the woman was full of surprises.

"Start chewing, Madrone," she said. The elegant woman I'd seen earlier had transformed into a red-faced monster.

"You hit Ash. Everything's over. The police will know. Time to give yourself up," I said. I sprang from the crouch, moving diagonally toward the lawn chair. She fired at me.

I ignored the hot fire of pain in my arm and grabbed the chair with both hands. I flung it at her, and it struck her chest. She stumbled backward and tripped over a glass-topped table. She and the table, tangled together, fell backward. She struck her head on a rock, but wobbled to her knees and fired, shaking her head as if to clear it. The shot clanged into something metal but I had no idea what. Not me and not Ash.

I glanced at the pool. Ash clung to the skimmer pole, which he'd somehow dragged to himself. A dark stain blotched the pool water.

I had to reach Ash, fast. I threw my entire body on Helen's back and she fell forward, dropping the handgun. I grabbed her shoulders and hung on. I was younger and stronger and taller, but her strength came from insane rage. She scrambled toward the gun, screaming. I grabbed her arm and twisted it back toward me, yanking, pulling with all my strength until I heard the pop that meant I'd dislocated her shoulder. She bellowed in pain, an almost inhuman screech.

I dragged her by her feet across the pool deck, not caring what further injury I caused her. Her head thumped along the tiles. She hollered and cursed. Her long hair likely saved her from a cracked skull. I stood, grabbed my fallen beach towel and wrapped it around her and the ramada support beam, tucking it in and over itself. She thrashed so much her bounds wouldn't last long, but Ash had less time.

Ash had sunk to pool bottom.
I dove the short distance down to him. I threw my right arm around his torso and nearly gasped in water, so intense was the pain. I switched to my left arm, kicked up from the bottom, surfaced and swam to the side. I rested for a moment, then swam to the shallow end, so I could drag the reporter onto the deck. This time I remembered to use my left arm only, making the rescue awkward.

Once he was out of the water, I took an instant to debate calling for help or administering first aid. With one hand? But the rule was: Call first if you can.

I ran to my phone, pushed the emergency call button, put the phone on speaker, and immediately reached one of Ven's old buddies. He knew who I was and where Leah lived and walked me through the very basic procedures to help Ash.

I turned his head to the side so he wouldn't vomit into his airway. Then I shook him, trying to rouse my poor friend. At the operator's insistence, I ran to the kitchen and grabbed several towels. In the kitchen light, I wrapped a couple of thin cotton towels around my bleeding arm, but not too tight.

I took a few seconds to wrench open the junk drawer and snatched a roll of duct tape from it. I ripped off a length and tied it around the towels on my arm, making an awkward bundle.

I ran back to Ash and tried to discover where he was bleeding, but he was wet and fully clothed, and I couldn't tell.

I decided to start one-armed CPR, which might not work but might be better than nothing. Doing something also staved off the terror and shock. Some.

I hummed, "Ah, ah, ah, ah, stayin' alive, stayin' alive." After I'd kept going for what seemed forever, I risked another glance at Helen, who'd been wriggling and squirming the entire time. My phone hero dispatcher said it would be okay to stop long enough to make sure she wouldn't get away. I ran to Helen, and used the rest of the roll, wrapping it around and around her body so she could barely wiggle.

She alternately cursed me and muttered, "You don't understand."

Nope. I didn't. Nor did I care.

Not until I again knelt beside Ash did the pain begin. Maybe it was because by now the kitchen towel was soaked in blood.

49

You're Alive

I awoke to three beloved faces staring at me. Okay, two beloved and one I'd crushed on.

"What am I going to do with you, *mija?*" Mama clutched my good hand tight enough to hurt. Most days, my mother wouldn't enter the local *panadería* without immaculate make-up and perfectly groomed hair. Today, her eyes were red and swollen and the skin beneath them puffed like a horned toad's throat. I tried but failed to wriggle my fingers free from her grip.

"You never know when to say 'uncle,' do you?" Mateo said. His precious face beside my mother's was also set in a frown. But he was out of his hospital bed. Yay.

Gabe Ramsay's was the only smile in the bunch. "Nice to see you, Madrone. How you feeling?"

"Water," I croaked. Mama released her grip long enough to give me a few sips of the precious fluid through a straw. I smiled through cracked lips. "My mouth feels like the bottom of a bird cage." I coaxed another sip from my mother. "Ash? Did he make it? How is he?"

Mateo managed a tight smile. "He'll be okay. Nothing like a partial drowning to bring you down from a high. Plus a twenty-two to the thigh. He's lucky."

I tried another painful smile through cracked lips. "Lucky? It was no accident. She . . . gave him some cookies with LSD. She shot him. Tried to force me to eat some."

"Plus she shot you, too," Mateo said. As if I needed reminding. "She never liked me all that much, but she never shot me."

Mama glared at him. "No. She ran you over with a stolen car. And your lovely girlfriend." She gaze went from her son and back to me. "It's good they have her locked up or I might kill her. My precious babies." She stroked my hair back from my face. "Your hair is too long and needs washing."

Ah. Mama would get over this.

"RK? Erin?" I said. "Do they know? Are they back from Phoenix?"

Gabe touched my good shoulder. "They're fine. Got in about an hour ago." I had no idea of the time, but who cared? Everyone I loved was nearby and safe. "Full of surprises," Gabe continued. "RK sounds more like a robot than a person."

"But suaver than Roadkill," Mateo said.

"And you need to be pretty dang suave to seduce my sister and convince her to leave Durango." Gabe didn't look thrilled at that surprise, but he'd come around. With luck.

"I forgot I promised to take more Adventure Calls flyers to the Chamber of Commerce. If I still have a job, could you do that for me, boss? You'll like the women who work there."

50

Epilogue

Helen eventually confessed—to killing Violet, and to executing several threats against me, including sideswiping Mateo and Kirsten with a car she'd stolen for the purpose. She swore she'd only meant to nudge them off the road. Oddly, that act seemed less forgivable to me than the murder of Violet Brock. Killing Violet had been to prevent her revealing the secret she and Ross Zelinger had sworn to keep so many decades earlier. When Violet refused to stop her plan to reveal all, Helen erupted and killed her.

The attack on Mateo and Kirsten was only to stop me, she said. However, I think she secretly wanted to get Mateo out of The Whistle Stop, so she could return to being Ross's assistant.

Ross was devastated. When questioned by Sergeant Doughty about the terrible revelation Violet planned to make, he readily revealed it. When he and Violet had been activists in Idaho, they'd had a huge fight one morning and left their campsite without taking their usual care in cleaning up and burying the campfire.

Violet had driven off in their Volkswagen bus and forced Ross to start the long hike to the nearest town. After an hour or so, she'd cooled off and drove back to pick him up. They'd seen the fire, still fairly small, and agreed there was a chance it had started from their campfire. The weather was breezy but there'd been no lightning, the usual cause of fires.

They drove to town and reported the fire, but by then it had grown and a firefighter had died battling it. They swore each other to secrecy about their possible involvement and had kept that secret for more than forty years. Ross had always maintained that the fire might not have started from their campsite, but Violet had, over the years, obsessed about it and about the firefighter's death. Hence her frequent generous contributions to firefighting organizations.

Interviewed in the *Verde Valley Times*—byline, Ash Coretti—Ross said, "I'm ashamed, sure, but it was a mistake, even if the fire began at our campsite. Nowadays if a human is to blame, they might assess them for damages, but back then, they maybe lectured folks for a while. I don't know why Violet assumed such a load of guilt. Even though the death of a firefighter was tragic. My wife's efforts to stop Violet from revealing the secret were far, far worse. What a waste."

I thought that statement might be used by prosecutors against Helen, but Ash was good at extracting pithy quotes. And Ross truly was appalled by his wife's actions. He moved to a tiny rental in Jerome, closed The Whistle Stop, and asked Mateo to manage it when he felt up to it.

Ross had hidden a teenaged image of Rose among the many in his mural, an image that many a tourist puzzled over. Violet and many townspeople were so accustomed to the mural that they rarely scrutinized it.

With no broken bones or deep tissue damage, my arm healed quickly. RK and Erin helped me clean up the backyard before Leah returned. I stocked her freezer with enough breads, cookies, and casseroles to earn her forgiveness.

RK and Erin were still debating her next steps—a move to Arizona, or a return to her mother and sisters in France. Before they made a decision, however, he planned to join her for a visit to Paris. Imagining the flavors of French cooking, I wished I could join them.

Rose came home for the celebration of Violet's life. RK and I were honored to share some good memories from Violet's last trip to Indian Territory and to meet her beloved and not-so-lost daughter.

The End

AUTHOR'S NOTE

Thank you for taking time to read *Murder, Cottonwood Style.* If you enjoyed it, please take one moment more to leave a few words of review on Amazon. Every review means so much!

Should you have the opportunity to visit northern Arizona, stop in Sedona for sure, but don't miss a trip to Old Town Cottonwood and to Jerome. My book may well contain some inaccuracies to support the fiction, but each community has a compelling charm of its own—and some dynamite dining!

About the Author

Kathy McIntosh has loved words since her father quoted limericks and her mother shouted, "Not in front of the girls!"

After some thirty years in Idaho—eight of them five miles up a dirt road—Kathy traded snow shovels and Idaho potatoes for sunscreen and Tucson tamales. She and her husband enjoy the warmth, the cuisine and the exotic flora and fauna of the Sonoran desert. The scorpions? Maybe not so much.

Murder, Cottonwood Style is Kathy's fourth book. The first two—in the Havoc in Hancock series— are set in Idaho. All her novels are mysteries with mirth and a mission. Her Adventure Calls series is about an ecotour company. The first was *Murder, Sonoran Style.* Read an excerpt following this bio.

If you've enjoyed your time in the world of Kathy's words, please place a brief review on Goodreads, Audible, or Amazon, or do it the old-fashioned way, and tell a friend. Your few words help Kathy find readers and readers find laughter and adventure.

Find out more about this award-winning author—for her novels and short stories—at her website, www.KathyMcIntosh.com. For a free short story, sign up for Kathy's Very Occasional Newsletter. In it she'll share news of new releases, fabulous recipes, other great reads and writing tips.

Excerpt from Murder, Sonoran Style

In Book One of Kathy's Adventure Calls series, *Murder, Sonoran Style,* Madrone's boss, Gabe Ramsay, enlists her help to discover who killed a nasty opponent using Gabe's skinning knife. Their first adventure, set in the Sonoran Desert near Tucson. This and all of Kathy's novels are available on Amazon and in local bookstores.

ONE
MISTAKEN SALVATION

Gabe Ramsay put his hand on Kate O'Shea's arm. "He's not worth your anger, Kate. Trust me."

The young woman shook off his hand and ran to the front of the stunned party crowd. "You pompous, self-serving, pretentious braggart," she yelled at the evening's surprise guest. "You know nothing about preserving the environment and even less about quality of life. The world would be better off without you!"

She stomped out of the room and up the stairs to the guest bedrooms. The other party-goers stood silent, appearing shocked yet pleased.

At the back of the room, Gabe stood with his host and new business partner, Tripp Chasen.

"I'd call that a success." Tripp crossed his arms and leaned against the wall.

Gabe stared at him, unsure whether Tripp's words were sarcastic or sincere, less sure how to respond. "A success?"

"Hey, they ate all the food. Nobody threw up or fell asleep during his ridiculous raving. Can't say you were bored, can you?" Tripp smiled. "Not much worse than boring."

Gabe grimaced. What he had believed might be his salvation could become his biggest mistake.

TWO

KEEP YOUR ENEMIES CLOSER

Squatting in the Sonoran desert can be risky. Gabe Ramsay crouched on the ground next to the saltbrush and focused his camera on the collared lizard basking on a flat rock. The calls of the doves and woodpeckers faded into a pleasant background melody, the early morning sun warming his back as it did the lizard's.

Photos like these could illustrate a mini-guide that guests would receive when they registered for a tour. His photos, combined with the knowledge of the guides and Madrone's incredible cooking, would make Adventure Calls Touring soar to number one on the list of eco-touring companies. Eco-tourism was hot and he'd make his new venture the hottest on the market or poke himself in the eye with an agave leaf.

But first they had to make it through the two-day "scavenger hunt," the brainstorm of his new partner. He glanced over to where his battered backpack lay beside the casita door, packed with everything he thought he'd need for the two day adventure. He'd had two special pockets made for it: one for his knife and one for his field microscope. Tripp had laughed and told him the scope was just extra weight, but to an entomologist the scope was perhaps more essential than the skinning knife. Certainly he'd used it more often.

The tiny reptile cocked its head. Was it warning him against getting his hopes up about Adventure Calls? Mocking his optimism?

The crunch of gravel alerted him and he jumped up. He did a quick 360, trying to locate the source of the sound. Couldn't be Madrone. She was busy in the casita.

There. Coming down the hill that led to the road. Everett Poulsen. Every muscle in Gabe's neck and shoulders tightened. Hadn't last night's debacle at Tripp's party been enough? If only he could wipe that smile from the arrogant developer's face.

"Gotcha," Everett crowed. "Can't believe you didn't hear us coming. We weren't exactly stealthy."

"I heard you," Gabe said through clenched teeth. Should have heard the car but he must have been focused on the lizard. Damn. That kind of careless inattention would have gotten him killed in Afghanistan. He looked past Everett but saw no one. "We?"

Everett spun on his expensive hiking-booted foot. "Where the hell'd she go?" he muttered. "Lorraine should be here any minute. Whining witch. She spent the whole trip here nagging me not to come."

Too bad Lorraine hadn't been more persuasive. "What do you want, Everett?"

In his early 40s, Everett Poulsen was losing the battle to keep his youth. His potbelly almost hid a showy turquoise and silver buckle. His brown hair brushed upward from an increasingly high forehead. But his short-sleeved polo—not enough for the chilly desert morning—revealed muscular arms and his scruff of a beard was fashionable instead of sloppy. What a way to ruin a great morning. He breathed in. Stay cool.

"You sent them off already?" Entitlement whined in Everett's tone. He spat on the ground. "Call 'em back. I'm sure you have some clever signal."

"Can't see as how I want to call anyone back. In fact, I'm about to head out myself." He gestured toward his backpack that lay beside the door to the casita.

A woman cursed. "If I fall on my ass, I swear I'll kill you, Everett." Lorraine Poulsen stumbled at an angle down the sandy hillside. "Crap, crap, crap. Why did I even try to stop him?" she muttered. Her shoes—ballet slippers, thought Gabe, who had learned way too much about fashion from his three sisters—were totally inappropriate for the desert. She must have left home in a rush, yet she still sported her Arizona bling—dangling turquoise earrings, a pounded silver band bracelet, and several native American designed rings.

The manners long ingrained by his mother surfaced. He smiled at Lorraine when she made it down the hill. Her light sweater wouldn't keep her warm this morning. "Madrone's in the casita. Bet she'd give you a cup of coffee."

Lorraine headed for the small adobe structure.

"Bring me a cup, too, sweetie, if you would," Everett said to his wife. "Black. Three sugars."

Lorraine kept walking, giving Everett a one finger salute over her head. "Aye, aye, your lordship." Why had Everett's seemingly innocent request warranted that response? Eh, who knew about married couples?

Everett gave a slight frown in his wife's direction and then seemed to dismiss her and refocus his anger on Gabe. "What happened last night was inexcusable. I can tolerate disagreement. I cannot tolerate flat out rudeness. You're making a mistake assuming I'd still want you . . . people traipsing all over my land."

At least he called us people. Gabe had expected radicals, idiots, terrorists, worse. Everett generally spoke in hyperboles. When he wasn't outright lying.

"Something about a written agreement you signed?" Not that the Everett he'd known in school would honor inconvenient promises. "We have the use of the casita and any of your property adjoining BLM lands. We'll leave it as we found it."

Everett curled his lip. "As if I'd trust any of you after last night." His scowl faded and left a pained expression in his eyes. "You may not believe me but I respect this land, too. I could make a hell of a lot more money building ticky-tacky houses shoulder to hip, but Mountain Shadows will be a tribute to nature. Not some sort of desecration."

"Last night you spoke about your commitment to preserving the natural environment. And you welcomed everyone." Everett had droned on and on about his commitment and about his plans. "What changed?"

"What changed was that little spitfire screeching at me after I spoke. I know of ecos like her who import endangered species onto people's property just to stretch out the environmental approval process. I saw how the rest of you grinned when she hollered at me. I should have known this whole thing was a bad idea." He looked into the distance. "Like I said, call them back."

"Like *I* said, no. Much of the land we'll be on is BLM. We have a signed short-term agreement with you to use your casita and to be on your property. This show's already on the road. Give it up, Ev." He used the nickname Everett had hated in high school. With luck it still annoyed him.

"It's Everett. I don't want you, your partner or your ridiculous eco-guides on my land or in my casita. Have your hot little chef start packing up. Or you'll all regret it." Everett stomped toward the casita, where Lorraine stood in the doorway, smirking. "Where's my damn coffee, Lorraine?"

Her face tightened. "Aren't you worried the 'hot little chef' might have poisoned it?" She extended the mug to her husband.

Gabe ambled toward Everett. At 6' 3", he stood a few inches above the other man. Gabe had managed to stay in decent shape, and keep more hair than Everett, a fact which shouldn't please him, but did. "Watch your mouth. And trust me, you're the one who's gonna have regrets. Not me. Maybe Lorraine will, for marrying a total bozo."

Lorraine smiled.

Poulsen sipped his coffee, then thrust the mug back at his wife. "This is cold. I don't drink cold coffee." To Gabe he said, "I see. Interested in the little brown cookie? I'd better warn her. Got some stories about you the little hottie needs to hear."

Gabe pulled Everett around by the shoulder. He breathed in, out, in, but couldn't hold the tether on his temper. "Keep your filthy mouth shut. One of these days someone will shut it for good."

Everett reared back and raised his fists. "Not a wuss like you."

"Exactly like me." Before Everett's fists twitched, before Gabe considered the density of a jawbone as opposed to a gut, Gabe slugged the developer in the jaw. Everett fell backward and slumped to the ground.

Lorraine knelt beside her husband, lifting his head to rest on her thighs. She looked at Gabe. "Big mistake. Everett doesn't forget or forgive."

Made in the USA
Middletown, DE
21 March 2022